The Miracle Tree

The Miracle Tree

A novel

David Tracey

pure wave media edition, 2010
Copyright © 2010 by David Tracey

All events described in this novel are imaginary. Any resemblances to
actual people, except for a newscaster named Peter Jennings, are wholly
coincidental.

ISBN: 978-0-9865055-0-8

Printed and bound in the U.S.A.

pure wave ✦ media

Los Angeles • Tokyo • Vancouver

Life, so I read in the Science Page of the City Herald (back of the Living section every Thursday), is so statistically improbable as to amount to a miracle.

If you can accept that, you open yourself to the prospect of even more astonishing events, convergences of matter and intent that go beyond the ecto-physical limits of any one organism to resonate on a collective level some of us may only ever wish were true.

What I'm about to relate is, like any miracle, a matter of perspective, open to interpretation. I can only describe my own involvement in it and let you decide whether you are indeed looking upon a genuine display of "signs and wonders". . .

Or just a sideshow.

Truth is the silliest thing under the sun. Try to get a living by the Truth — and go to the Soup Societies.

Herman Melville

ONE

I stepped off the bus tired and achy, fuzzy and dull, but happy to be free, relieved to be anywhere that was not a metal tube on wheels. How many hours had I lost in that asphalt monotony? Once the batteries in my Walkman died, I felt like a hostage. I might even have empathized with my seatmate if I hadn't soon tired of his muttered observations on the unfairness of our penal system.

The depot was a one-story wooden building in need of paint, which leaned in a way that would have caught the eye of a public safety official back home. I turned to gaze back at the bus almost with longing. The door swooshed shut, and the bus did a frantic Y-turn and sped away. I watched it grow smaller between fields of corn that marched all the way to the horizon as if in mass escape.

So this is Fraleton, I thought: not exactly bustling. Then I realized I could just as well think these things out loud since there was no one around to overhear.

The town could be taken in with a glance. Behind the depot, bungalows and ranch houses lined rows of streets ending at a green river. The water in the river must have been moving or it would have been a swamp, but you couldn't tell from a distance. Across the river, pastureland stretched out to rounded foothills speckled with isolated trees. Beyond them, blue mountains faded like smoke into the sky.

I was downtown, in the commercial hub, marked by a dozen or so shops on either side of the depot, none of which showed any sign of commercial activity. I eased open the door of the depot, and when the building didn't fall over, stepped inside. A round-shouldered man with wool pants and a poorman's tweed cap shuffled behind a janitor's broom. Intent on following the broom in vague patterns about the floor, doing little in the way of sanitation but at least not making things any dirtier, he didn't see me come in.

I cleared my throat with an obvious "Ahem." The Sisyphus of the Sticks plodded further away. I stepped nearer to try again. Still no response. Was he deaf? Or whatever the correct term is these days. I walked closer to tap him on the shoulder.

He looked first at his shoulder and then further back at me. He had a mustache that could have served a walrus. His cheeks sagged in a way that made it droop further.

I countered with a friendly smile. "Sir," I said brightly, "excuse me, I'm wondering if you can help me."

He continued to stare, so I tried again, this time raising my voice and, in case he was a lip-reader, stretching my mouth around each syllable.

"Do you know... where... I might find a coin locker?"

He took off his cap before answering, like some gesture from an out-of-print etiquette book, his forehead scrunched in contemplation. Eventually he looked at me in earnest, before answering with a shout of his own.

"Why you want to lock coins?" His accent may have been European: "want" sounded like "vant."

"I mean for my luggage," I said at a normal volume. I pointed to my suitcase, an outsized rectangle of leather and brass, wide enough to carry shirts unfolded but only a thin layer of them. It had been my father's, an heirloom of some sort no one else had cared enough to keep. "So I can look around town."

He seemed baffled all over again. Hadn't I just looked around town from the curb?

"Until I can find a place to stay," I added with dawning hopelessness.

He nodded thoughtfully. "You don't know nobody?" he asked.

"No. I guess I don't."

He wiped the back of his neck with the cap, which must have been bad manners somewhere, then sighed. "Hokay. You vant, you stay with my vife and myself. There is a sofa. It becomes a bed."

"Gee, that's, um, kind. But is there no hotel at all?"

"Ah, I see, I see," he said rapidly, his eyes glistening now with the light of comprehension. "You would like the Grady Inn. Yes. Go through the door this-a way. You turn right at the corner. Yes? You come to the big street, you turn right again. There is the Grady Inn."

"Thank you. You're very kind."

"Yes," he admitted, as if it were a flaw.

I followed his directions, which led to Perry's Gas Station and Dry Cleaning Store. Perry didn't come out from under the chassis of a purple Volvo, but he kicked encouragingly in the direction of the inn. "It isn't far," he said, unnecessarily. Nothing would be far away now. Except home. And Shirley. She would probably be pleased to hear I had just considered them the same thing. It also meant my assignment was already paying off.

I'd been sent to cover a tree that was reported to make wishes come true — who knew how that would spin out? — but by measuring achievements this way I could count myself ahead of the game even if I got skunked, which seemed unlikely given my winning streak.

Even scoring the assignment had both surprised and annoyed

people who knew me back home, at least the ones who couldn't believe I got the job in the first place. The whole economy had gone south in 1999, which meant the job prospects too. It had been a bit of a miracle to get on full-time with any newspaper, let alone one as prestigious as the *City Herald*. Friends from j-school who were still mailing résumés to podunk places they had trouble finding on the map knew I'd latched onto something good. One natural reaction was resentment. I never blamed them. I sensed it even in Shirley: somehow my employment had become a source of friction between us.

Shirley is tall and fit and blonde as a straw bale. She's also uncommonly pretty, one of those head-turners who can make guys walk into street poles. In j-school she was known as the cerebral type, the star of our graduating class who landed the previous summer's plum internship with the *Weekly Times*. When it didn't lead to a job offer as expected, it surprised all of us who knew the way she succeeded at everything she tried with relentless drive and grace.

To get by, she took a job serving drinks in one of the financial district bars popular with bond traders. That put us on different work schedules, which meant opportunities withered for the more preferred source of friction between us — sex. Even when we did find ourselves together, in bed, and awake, Shirley was often not in the mood. As one of the country's last pure communist sympathizers, she was easily put out of sorts by a night spent in servitude to capitalist swine.

I knew enough to leave my career accomplishments at the office, but sometimes I couldn't help but talk about it. Lying in bed together the night before I left for Fraleton, I marveled at how much had changed since that morning I'd been chosen to sit in on a meeting of the honchos. It had something to do with a union demand to include rank-and-file reps in key editorial decisions, but I didn't know the details, having given up on union meetings once the

Ultimate intramurals began. Nevertheless I was still pleased when the managing editor asked me to be the first one.

"Who would have thought?" I asked Shirley. "Earl Brododsky. Riding to the top of the *City Herald* tower. Getting into it with the major players."

She put down her book, something on the semiotics of Marxist garden design in Cuba, and shot me one of her what-planet-are-you-from looks. "They chose you because you're just a rook," she said. "Can't you see that? It's their way of telling the union to fuck off."

"I don't know if it's all *that* strong a message."

She rolled her eyes and pulled the blanket up to her chin. She reached for the bedside lamp to end the discussion.

"Wait," I said. "I am a reporter, you know." This was technically true, even though to date my contribution had involved nothing beyond compiling examples of the previous day's more interesting murders, assaults and robberies into the Daily Crime box.

"Right," Shirley said. "You regurgitate police statistics."

"Regurgitate?"

"Where's the reporting in what you do? What have you ever uncovered?"

"Regurgitate. . . .That's quite a word."

"You know what I'm saying."

"Hello, what do you do for a living? Me? I regurgitate."

"Let's go to sleep, Earl. I'm really beat." She hit the light and rolled over to face the wall.

I wasn't sleepy. I stared at the red neon reflection on our ceiling from the Chinese take-out downstairs. Lucky Dragon Lucky Dragon Lucky Dragon. The more I thought about Shirley's comment, the more it irked me.

"Blaaaaaahhhhh," I blurted out at last, mimicking the sound of someone throwing up.

"Earl," she said evenly.

"Whut," I answered with just as much warmth.

She sat up, throwing a handful of hair to the far side of her face. Even when pissed off I couldn't help admiring how the yellow waves caught the glint of neon red. She took in a slow breath, like a diver on a high board.

This is it, I thought, the beginning of the end: we're going in, and under, to emerge at different sides of the pool. I wondered whether I should strike first. Grab what I could before the roof came down — as if it would help. There was never an easy way to break up, even if you wanted to — and I didn't.

"Earl, listen. I'm sorry for what I said. It was mean and uncalled for and yes, the biggest reason I said it was because I'm jealous that you got a job with a real paper and I didn't."

"Aw Shirl," I said, reaching for her shoulder.

"And I wish I could be a better person so I could enjoy your success without also worrying about my own pathetic lack of meaningful employment. Because I do care for you."

I put a palm on her belly, circled a few times and then started south. "Hey precious, you don't have to—"

She flipped back towards the wall with a suddenness that reminded me of a documentary on leopards. "Now shut the fuck up so I can get some sleep."

So she did, but I'd stayed awake, thinking about her and me and the alarm clock I needed to hear if I was to make the early, and only, bus to Fraleton. I did make the bus, and suffered through the long ride, but now I was snoozy. I felt like a sleep-walker on my way to the hotel, startled every time I crossed paths with one of Fraleton's citizens. I met two white-haired women carrying cut flowers and grass in a basket, then a nerdy man in his forties wearing an obviously hand-made cardigan. All three smiled and said hello in a way that left a big opening to chat if I had the tiniest inclination — at least that's how I interpreted the lack of urgency in their pace: it wasn't walking, it was ambling. And why not interrupt it to talk to a complete stranger? I could imagine their curiosity. What brings you *here*? Do you know somebody? Did they die? Are you aware there isn't another bus out of here for twenty-four hours? Are you *mad*?

It may have been inappropriate, but I couldn't help feeling a twinge of pity — the poverty of options when you live in a no-account town in the middle of nowhere. I wondered whether they got cable. How dispiriting it must be to see the same faces year in and year out, the ones you'd run into every day since kindergarten, everyone gradually losing their glow, just marking down the years as they got softer, rounder, slower, duller. I smiled gamely and walked on.

"Need a hand with that thing, son?" called a voice from across the street. I turned to see a man old enough to be my grandfather. He was wearing what looked like slippers. Somebody — a frantic relative, a nurse's aide — was probably looking for him.

"Excuse me?" I said.

He aimed a trembling finger at my suitcase, where the corner was scuffed from being dragged. It had been made before the luggage industry discovered the wheel.

"No, thanks, I'm fine," I told him. "Really."

He seemed to doubt it, but shrugged as if this time he would let it go.

On the next street I spotted Grady's Inn, and stopped on the sidewalk to admire its grandeur: so the little town had something to show off after all. It was a heritage-type home with peaked roofs and dormers and a railed porch that wrapped around three of its sides. It could have been a hundred years old or older, but somehow it seemed new. Maybe it was just the gleam of a recent paint job, a cobalt blue base with vanilla trim that made the structure seem majestic and yet quaint at the same time. It was the kind of house that makes you wonder what's wrong with the people who build houses these days.

The front door was not completely closed. I knocked, got nothing, then tried again. I added a few thumps with my fist, followed by a loud hello. Still no answer, but now the door was fully open so I stepped inside. The front room had been half-converted into an office. The other half, separated by a calico curtain, was still a living room. The TV was on, showing a black and white Western I didn't recognize. A cowboy who looked like Montgomery Clift with a hangover said, "I intend to earn that badge. . . and your respect along with it," before gulping down a drink and swaggering out of a saloon. This was followed by a commercial with a woman angrily scrubbing a toilet.

I tapped a bell on the counter. A ping echoed off the high ceiling and died. After the third ping I went exploring. The doors on the second level were all closed. Each was labeled with a painted ceramic number. The highest was eight, but there may have been more rooms leading off a second spiral staircase at the back of the house. I called out again, this time making it loud enough to cover them all, but no doors opened.

I went to the kitchen, an open and airy space with a blue tile floor and one wall decorated with copper pots and pans. I'd seen the copper look done before, but never with pans that were charred and scratched and looking as if they might actually have been used to cook food. I made a mental note to describe it to Melanie, a friend back at the paper. She was another new hire in my group who'd been assigned to the "Modern Kitchen" section. We assumed it was a joke on the part of Ted Hanover, our managing editor, to put the butchest woman in the building onto the girliest post. Later we realized Hanover lacked the irony for that, or at any rate the courage: he was known to be a toady motivated mainly by a fear of getting fired in one of the editor-in-chief's legendary tirades. The older reporters referred to Hanover behind his back as Bendover.

The real joke came later when Melanie turned out to revel in her new post. She took to it as if she'd been dropped into a hostile environment to conduct agit prop against the patriarchy. She once got a reprimand for adding a subversive message about our society's need for women to hate themselves into a feature on cooking with chocolate, but by then readers were already writing enough fan letters to get her past a minor blip.

I was tempted to open the double doors of the industrial-sized fridge, just to peek, not to steal. I noticed a tray half-filled with brownies wedged on top of a bag of beet greens. With that much food, I reasoned, they wouldn't miss a single brownie. A real thief would have emptied the house of its furniture by then, so I was probably doing them a favor by just being there, protecting the stocks. I was halfway through my second brownie when I saw through a window to the back a rangy, white-haired, hook-nosed man moving slowly along a row of tomato plants. He had the question-mark posture of someone who had bent over a lot of vegetables in his time.

"Hi there, yoo hoo, sir?" I called from the porch, smiling until it struck me that I might still have brownie chunks in my teeth. He turned with a vacant grin that would serve for friend or outsider alike until the rest of him sorted it out. It took a moment for his blue eyes to hit the right focal length to take me in: even then he seemed to be trying to place me.

"I'm a customer," I called. "I mean, I'd like to be. Is this Grady's Inn? Do you have any rooms available?"

"Wonderful," he said in a croaky baritone, perhaps delighted to have the mystery of me solved so effortlessly. "Yes, of course. It is an inn. And I'm Terrance Grady. I most certainly do have a room. You would have to share the facilities, I'm afraid — a loo down the hall. It's clean, though, I can guarantee that."

"Sounds fine. Since the Hilton lost my reservation." I put my best Bob Hope spin on the line, but Grady didn't respond. I chuckled feebly and let it die. Poker-faced, he nodded to indicate that he did recognize the attempt, thank you, but had no intention of encouraging me.

He walked towards me on the porch in a meticulous gait, perhaps fearing a sudden collapse in his house-of-cards skeletal structure. I stepped down to shorten his trip for the greeting. He removed a leather gardening glove to reveal a hand that was mostly bone covered by papery skin. Even so, he had a firm grip, and it actually got tighter as it went on. I finally had to squeeze back hard to keep my own fingers from getting scrunched: no more Hilton cracks for this guy.

"Your room will be Number Five. Upstairs," he said, indicating the way with arched white eyebrows. "The bath is the third door on the left. That's the WC on the right directly across from it. I can help you with your luggage now if you'd prefer to rest up and sign in later."

"That's okay. Are things busy?"

"We're not full."

I resisted the urge to make a crack about the ranking of the town in the global tourism market. He struck me as a man unlikely to find anything funny in it.

"To be honest with you," he added, "we've never been what you might call full occupancy. Well. Least not so long as I've been here."

"How long is that?"

"Fifty-four years," he said with his chest out. "Bought the place the same week I came home from Europe. After the war. I was a pilot." He spread his arms out to form the wings of an airplane.

"Oh. I see." That kind of pilot.

"You're here on business?" he asked.

"You might say that," I answered, straightening my spine. I'd never thought of myself as the type to travel anywhere on business, and only now wondered whether my new Top Man Discount Tailors sports jacket might have been the clue. So this was how it felt to be a real newspaper reporter, out in the world, meeting the people, checking the pulse of the body politic.

"Not too many folks make it to Fraleton for a vacation," he pointed out. He led me back inside, and from behind the lobby counter produced a form, watching as I filled in the address.

"The big city," he noted, then looked past me out the window. His eyelids drooped, perhaps in a reverie of times spent in big cities of the past. I thought of the picture of the soldier kissing the nurse in the street after World War II. Somehow it wouldn't have been Grady:

he would have been holding the lucky guy's coat.

"And how many nights will you be staying?"

"I'm not sure yet. I'm actually a reporter, I'm here to do a story on the tree — the Miracle Tree?"

"Goddamned Filco," he spurted out, adding a scowl that pulled the age spots on his cheeks out of shape. "Pardon my language."

"Who's Filco?"

"Not who — what. It's a company. A corporation, HQ'd in Hubbensberg. Now they want to build their infernal plutonium dump right here in our town — when it's not even our nuclear waste in the first place."

"Whose would it be?"

"How would I know? Whoever's got a nuclear plant, I imagine. It's not from Fraleton, I can guarantee you that."

"You're talking about a radioactive waste treatment facility?"

"That's what I said. A dump."

"And they want to build it on the site where the tree is now?"

"Right again."

I felt my shoulders slump. I carried on, but with a gathering sense of dismay. "And folks here don't like the idea, because, well, who would? So they're angry. And that's why they're against the tree getting cut down."

"Most of us are," Grady said. "Not Dangworth. Or his lackies."

I didn't even try to hide my disappointment. It may have looked like confusion. Grady sighed before going on to explain.

"Dangworth is the mayor. And he's getting his cut, you can bet on that. A pox on that silly bastard. Excuse my language again. Talking about this thing always puts me on the boil."

"Naturally," I said.

So that was it: my miracle, my first shot at landing a real story, possibly a feature, and it comes up a dud before I even get a chance to light the wick. I'd come for a glimpse into the great unknown, only to walk into a garden variety turf war.

At the editorial board meeting that had led me there, all the heavyweights had come, including some I knew by reputation. Hanover was the managing editor, but my first impression was an image of the inevitable winner of a Don Knotts look-alike contest, if they ever held one. Scott Pearson was the sports editor, a guy who should have been branded with the word "crass" on his forehead to warn newcomers. The prematurely grey assistant managing editor was Renee Dubois, rumored to be an intellectual Everest rising above the lowlands of Hanover, and also kind of hot if you liked the librarian-about-to-melt look. Then there was Nigel Kendricks, the foreign editor, who was blonde and handsome and British in an exaggerated, Ascot-wearing way.

But the center of attention was a heavyweight in every respect, Harmon Gallantine. The editor-in-chief had the bulk of an industrial appliance, yet it was not his size but the expanse of his personality that was so compelling. Gallantine had an unseen power, a force of authority that couldn't be diluted even by a fondness for paisley bowties or an odd hair style that left his pink scalp surrounded by a wispy ring of white floating up towards the ceiling. All chairs were angled towards him, and all conversations stopped when he cleared his throat. He nodded, his signal to start the agenda.

Kendricks spoke first, in that excruciating British accent, through clenched teeth, biting down on an imaginary pipe. "I say we go with the Bosnia negotiations. They've just broken down. We're facing the very likely prospect of major repercussions."

"Bosnia," Pearson moaned, as if it were a contagious disease.

"What about the council by-election?" offered Renee, tracing one earpiece from her glasses across her lower lip without seeming to know it. "Clauson has almost closed the gap. The polls have them close to even."

"The vote's not for another two weeks, Renee," Hanover whined. "And we've already got Dirkson's feature in the can for Saturday."

"Exactly," she countered. "That's why I say we go with it now. Build up the interest. A little every day. Then by the election—"

"By the election they're still going to be lucky to see a twenty percent turnout," Kendricks squeezed out around his phantom pipe stem. "If nobody else cares about some bloody by-election that isn't going to change a thing in the council majority, why should we?"

"Damn straight," Pearson chimed, "I know I don't. I can bet you that."

They were arguing about the lead story, the one that would go over the fold on the front page, the day's biggest news item and, if you were a sidewalk customer peering into the box, the thing which just might get that fifty cents out of your pocket. If Bosnia and the by-election were the only contenders, it was going to be a slow news day no matter what they decided.

Gallantine watched the discussion through steepled fingers. He said nothing yet was the biggest part of the process, the grand old chieftain letting the young braves cut up in council. Even his silences were significant: the others kept an eye on him for sign of any reaction that might signal a change in the weather.

"There's always the nurses' strike," Renee said, without conviction.

Pearson muttered, "You can say that again," and no one else took up the cause.

"Or we could go with the building collapse in Seoul," Kendricks offered. "Six dead, scores injured."

"We do have a sizable Korean population," Renee offered.

I wondered whether her support for another section's bid had anything personal to do with Kendricks. With his tennis tan and swept-back hair, I could see how he might have a rakish appeal; some women might even go for that accent. Of course, some women like Marmite too.

"Yes, but has anyone ever seen one of them reading a *Herald*?" Pearson asked.

"It came in five hours ago," Hanover said, again with the whining tone. His family members would have to be loopy to endure that grating pitch every day. "It's already stale."

"All right, people," Gallantine said. "We got zilch. Why fight it? Let's go with Bosnia, put the by-election first-up on the city page and get something new out of Korea for the front left. Didn't I see a Reuters piece about all the buildings collapsing over there? What are they making them with anyway?"

"I think that was airplanes," Kendricks said. "It was a list of crashes. They're dropping like. . . like. . . ." He waved his hand in circles but couldn't think of a word. I wanted to say *crumpets* in a horrid British accent.

"Whatever," Gallantine said, "find something. Let's move on."

The giddy sense of privilege I'd felt when walking in had withered and gone. This was the heart of the city's media empire? The informational vortex? If readers could see the people responsible for our biggest news decisions, they'd cancel their subscriptions. I remembered a line about not watching sausages get made. To think that a lout like Pearson might actually have an impact on the public discourse was more than discouraging. I consoled myself with the fact that it was a slow day, so maybe they were like seagulls fighting over scraps: during a crisis they would rise to the occasion and uphold the nobility of the Fourth Estate.

"We're all set then?" Hanover asked.

Nods came from around the room. Renee smiled, looking more attractive for it. Kendricks didn't seem to notice, probably because Pearson was whispering into his ear with the expression of a naughty boy telling a dirty joke.

"Good," Hanover continued. "Let's wrap up. What've we got?"

Postures eased, Pearson jump-shot a crumpled paper into a wastebasket and someone exhaled with a noisy lip-flutter.

Renee looked up from the running shoes she'd just begun lacing up. "They found a crater in Siberia that might explain why the dinosaurs died," she said as she placed her pumps in a handbag. No one reacted. She shrugged and added, "My six-year-old is gripped with the whole dinosaur thing."

They were talking about "It Happened On Earth" — a daily box containing a single quirky short on the bottom of page three. Surveys invariably found it one of the most popular parts of the paper, but I hadn't realized the bosses took it seriously enough to make it part of their main meeting. Unless this was some kind of reward for staying awake until the end.

Kendricks snapped his fingers as if recalling something good. "I've got a witch doctor in Zambia accused of casting a spell on the visiting squad before a major football match. The thing is, you see, it actually worked: they all got sick to their stomachs."

"And?" Renee asked. "Same thing happens to me whenever I eat a hot dog at Pyle Stadium."

Hanover tilted his head in a gesture of deep thought, or whatever the equivalent would be for him. "Wait. Wasn't there a thing about a guy in Iowa suing his doctor for a botched penile implant? It may have been AP."

"I saw that," Pearson said, "only I thought it was Manitoba. And wasn't it his wife who was suing?"

Everyone laughed.

Kendricks said happily, "On what claim?"

"It wouldn't work — or something," Hanover said. "You sure you want to know?"

"Maybe it worked too well," Pearson suggested. "And now he can't tie his shoes without getting all mixed up."

Groans mixed in with laughter. Pearson, typically, had to drag it further than it needed to go, bending down to mime a man tying his shoe and fumbling badly.

"Who has the copy?" Gallantine asked.

No one spoke. Then Renee pointed beside me to a table covered with stacks of paper that had been torn from the wire machine rolls.

"It's probably there on the right," she said. "Should be near the top."

Leaping up would have made me appear too eager to actually contribute, an admission that I had no business being there. At the same time I didn't want to come off as young and lazy.

"Check," I said as I stood up.

I rifled through a few stories before I found it. The dateline was Akron: that seemed to call for some kind of a snappy remark but I couldn't think of one, and anyway they were waiting. I read through the beginning out loud, humming along with some of the words to let them know where I was skipping.

"An Ohio man. . . bzzz bzzz. . . $15 million claim for damages. . . bzzz. . . says it doesn't feel the way it used to even though, according to the physician, quote, 'medically speaking his apparatus appears to be functioning as expected.'"

"Pshhh, forget it then," Renee said.

"We've still got the witch doctor," Pearson tried.

"There's the UFO convention we didn't use yesterday," Hanover offered. "They're not through yet. Today's the final day."

I was almost back to my chair when Gallantine, with a flick of his finger, motioned for me to look through the pile. I flipped through stories quickly, discounting most for not being absurd enough to make the "It Happened On Earth" grade — until one caught my attention. "Here's something," I said, interrupting some side chatter between Kendricks and Pearson on whether soccer players were wussies. "It might be good."

Gallantine's bushy eyebrows went up. A few heads turned around.

I paused, suddenly aware of the attention. "Or not. I don't know. It's just a thing about a miracle tree."

"Yeah, right," Pearson scoffed. "That's what the guy in Iowa thought."

No one laughed harder than Pearson at the unexpected success of his own joke. When it was quiet again I continued, reading directly from the copy.

> A century-old oak in the remote town of Fraleton is being called "The Miracle Tree" after two construction crews were mysteriously unable to cut it down.

"Send them some power tools," Pearson cut in, but I acted as if I hadn't heard.

> Tony Golito, a foreman for the Ganite Construction Company, said his crew refused to go near the tree after one worker was hospitalized with a broken arm suffered while attempting to cut it down.
> "They're calling it haunted," Golito said. "I've got some tough men working for me but now they're afraid to even go near the thing."

Someone snorted. I looked up to see a few heads nod in what I took for encouragement to continue.

> A second construction company brought in from Hubbensberg was also unsuccessful when their power generator burst into flames shortly before work was to begin. The tree-cutting project was suspended, pending an investigation by local authorities.

I looked up, leaving room for comments. Renee made a how-about-that humph from the back of her throat, but no one else spoke. I kept reading.

> Residents of the town say the tree has long been considered sacred by the native tribes which once inhabited the region.

More silence. "That's it," I concluded.

"Yes, but, what isn't sacred to an Indian?" Hanover asked. "Trees, rocks, birds. The whole world, really."

"It's a bit sketchy," Renee said. "Two little screw-ups, whoopty-do."

"I say we go with the witch doctor," Pearson said. "It was a pretty good game besides. Two to one."

"Sounds workable to me," Hanover said.

Gallantine leaned back in his chair, generating a loud creak. He lowered his hammy arms into two empty slots in the desk clutter. When he looked up, his eyes were on me. "And what do you think?" he asked. I waited for a beat but no one else replied. "Me?"

"Yes, sport. As our reporter representative for the day, you must have an opinion."

"Right, of course." I was still wrestling with the concept of representing any group, reporters included. "I think we should go with the miracle story," I heard myself say.

Pearson chortled unkindly. No one else reacted.

I waited, and when they still didn't say anything, went on. "People are interested in that kind of thing — miracles, otherworldly stuff, the mystical. Whether it's true or not doesn't really matter, if you think about it. Sometimes we need little stories like this just to remind us that there's more going on out there than we think, or know."

"Woo-woo," Pearson said, wiggling his fingers in front of his face.

"No, really," I said. "I had something like that happen to me once. On a lake one time when I was just a kid, in winter."

It was out of my mouth before I knew it. I watched one head after another turn to get a better look. I felt my face flush with hot blood. My ears felt like irons.

"In a manner of speaking," I said inanely. "I mean...not like a miracle miracle, or anything like that. But you know how it goes: stuff happens. Weird stuff. Sometimes."

They just kept staring, as if I might suddenly snap my fingers and produce a dove or a stream of colored scarves — anything that would help explain the real mystery: me, in their presence, talking as if I'd just had a bong hit.

Gallantine cleared his throat and they all turned back to the front. "We'll go with the witch doctor," he announced. "See you tomorrow."

They made for the door like a pack of kids spotting an overturned ice cream truck. I got stuck holding it for Renee, and then everyone else crowding behind her. When I was finally out the door myself, and about to silently close it, Gallantine held up a palm.

"Just a minute, sport," he said.

I leaned back into the room.

"I've got an assignment for you. Go home and pack: you're going to Fraleton."

Six hours later, in the lobby of Grady's creaky inn, the whole story had just fizzled. If the miracle angle was dead, I would have a hard time justifying a feature, or any article at all, on nothing more than a small town property spat.

"We're not just going to give up, though," Grady vowed, his mouth set into a scowl. "We don't care if they are bigger than us — or richer, or anything else. They don't know who they're taking on when they try to mess with the good folks of Fraleton."

I closed my mouth so it wouldn't say a word. Life wasn't supposed to happen like this: you don't get the big call up, stand at the plate, then have the game called on account of rain — or in this case on account of familiarity, or dullness. It was a land dispute in a land nobody cared about, the same thing you might find in any town anywhere. I hardly needed to hear more to know the whole scenario: in this corner, some corporate monolith led by a jowly CEO whose year-end bonus could buy Argentina; in the opposite corner, the usual smattering of lefties and greenies with their holier-than-everything indignation, swearing solidarity with their cause forever, chanting that the people-united-will-never-be-defeated — until the first bulldozer appears, and everyone can go home.

I'd seen it all before — and so had everyone else, which meant it was not news. By the year 1999, not-in-my-backyard-stories meant not-in-my-newspaper-either: they didn't sell, not beyond the few people directly affected. We were about to enter a new millennium, with more dire prospects to spice up the daily reports — the world's computers and civilization along with them were about to crash in a colossal Y2K meltdown, and I was supposed to get people interested in some bush league waste disposal scare?

My disappointment, I knew, was compounded by a secret desire of my own. I'd come this far hoping for a story, but perhaps even more for the prospect of at least a minor miracle. I hadn't admitted, even to Shirley, my dreams of pinning down an authentic otherworldly phenomenon, one that wouldn't fade away in the harsh light of logic. Instead I'd stepped into the reeking pile of an old media cliché. No wonder no one else had bothered to follow up on the story. I could already picture Pearson back at the next *Herald* editorial meeting, laughing out loud at my expense.

Grady fake-coughed to interrupt my gloom. I tried to put on an upbeat expression, but he brought me immediately back down. "And will you be taking your meals here as well?"

"I have a choice?" I immediately hoped it didn't sound as mean as it felt coming out.

"You can try Lon's Red Lotus," he answered, "but the food's greasy." He lowered his voice to a conspiratorial whisper. "Plus you have to eat it with sticks!"

"I see." I nodded.

He broke into a whinny that made his blue eyes swim. The fact that I hadn't gotten his joke may have been the best part of it. "Actually, it's fairly standard Chinese restaurant stuff. The heavenly veg chow mien isn't half bad, if you make him skip the MSG. Otherwise you get a killer headache. Lon adds it on with a trowel."

I felt on the verge of a headache myself. I realized I still hadn't shaken off the bus sloth. "Maybe I'll start out with a meal here and see how things go," I offered, picturing a long, empty dinner table with me at one end and Grady at the other, boil-a-bag stew dribbling down his chin — an image that fitted my expectations for my story.

"Excellent decision," he said. "Yes." He smiled, and opened his mouth again to speak, but his focus seemed to wander and nothing came out. I started backing away towards the stairs. The elderly and their personal weather systems: foggy patches, heavy at times. He snapped back to attention only when my suitcase collided with an audible bump on the first step. I turned in time to see him cringe, but something in my face may have put him off commenting.

I dragged the suitcase and myself up the stairs. My eagerness to start on the story had been a kinetic buzz racing through my veins. Now all I had was a dull hum fed by a corrosive infusion of worry. I still had to pull an article out of this mess. This was my first test, but who knew? It could also be my last. New hires all begin on a three-month probation. This was believed to be no more than a convenient way to get rid of someone truly bad, because they'd lied about their serial killer past — but I could picture management being tempted to use it on an over-reaching rookie who had gotten all the breaks, including an early travel assignment, yet still came home empty.

I wondered what a real reporter would have done. The veterans talked about a guy named Lanny Stoopovich: although gone, he was still their high water mark for the profession, partly because he had refused any promotion that might have turned him into an editor. If I had even half of Stoopovich's smarts, I thought, I might know my next move. Already I felt I was letting Gallantine down.

Anyone who isn't confused doesn't really understand the situation.

Edward R. Murrow

TWO

The sun had sunk low over the corn rows by the time I made it downstairs. I asked Grady for directions to the Miracle Tree. Apparently I couldn't miss it: the biggest thing in Fraleton was also the only thing to see in its single park.

I stopped before the Old General Store. At least they hadn't added an extra "e" to "old." That would have to wait until some yuppie couple escaping the city bought it. I peered in through a front window coated in dust.

The entire inventory could have fit into a display corner of my Food 'n' Such back home. They could call it Country Deelites, and squeeze it between the faux-Euro deli and the Vital Ital Jamaican nutritional supplements. But they would need to leave the pickle barrel behind. Give Food 'n' Such shoppers an open vat of brine with a self-serve fork and they'd fight over the chance to stab themselves into a trauma worthy of litigation.

A woman was slouched behind the cash register, fingering pink curlers in her hair. She looked up from a paperback to check the wall clock. I watched her slide the remainder of a celery stick out of her mouth to mark the page, and wondered why I'd never thought to use chewed food for a bookmark. She brought the book with her along with a big ring of keys towards the door. The book was called *Flames of Abandon.*

I felt like a voyeur until she spotted me through the glass and smiled. I couldn't decipher the meaning. It may have been lascivious, or the effect of an unswallowed portion of celery. The best part was how it made her eyes crinkle, in a pretty way. It took some of the emphasis off her plastic Medusa display.

I tried to smile back but it probably looked forced. Just as well: I looked nothing like the bare-chested firefighter on the cover of her novel. Who knew how far these romance fans let their imaginations run on a slow afternoon?

She jiggled a key into the lock, toying for a moment with the rest of the dangling set before whipping her curlers up to aim two big brown eyes back through the window directly at me.

"Six o'clock, sugar," she called in a loud voice to carry through the glass. "Means closing time. But if you need something quick?"

She curled the tip of her tongue across her top teeth, another suggestive gesture that could instead have been her way of scouring for celery.

"No, no, really," I said, shaking my head and waving my palms. Something quick I'm sure. "Another time." And six or seven beers, maybe. When beauty is but a light switch away.

She winked as she shut the door. Perhaps for ironic effect. I tried to think of a single person back home I knew who winked, for any reason. Her hips, padded at least twenty percent beyond my cut-off point, swayed as she walked back to the register. Just being friendly, I told myself, backing away. Small town romance. I couldn't help but shudder.

I thought instead about the way Shirley walked back home —

always as if late for something. I hoped she was thinking about me too. She would never care to admit anything like dependency, that she needed anyone, even me, but I would know by how she hugged me the moment I stepped back in the doorway whether the thought had crossed her mind. Shirley's body language was like the rest of her, incapable of telling a lie.

I walked on, slowly. I was in no hurry to see the tree. I may even have been reluctant. I contemplated, not for the first time since my frozen lake episode, whether I'd reached my lifetime quota of mystical experiences. Or does having one create the potential for more? Some people can only wonder about the reality of things unexplainable. I had the unshakeable belief I'd seen it, a real phenomenon. I may not have understood how or why, but I was young and ambitious enough to think I would eventually find out.

Despite my personal history, or maybe because of it, I was probably more disappointed than most by the miracle-of-the-week peddlers on TV. One lesson I had learned from trying to explain my story to others was how pointless it was. You can't tell anyone anything about a truth they're not ready to accept. People believe what they already know. If realizing that much made me more cynical than the norm, well, it wasn't a bad approach for a journalist.

I decided it didn't matter whether I got to the tree that afternoon because I already had a head start on the real work. Hanover had said not to bother trying to file anything on my first day. His tone suggested my second might not be any more productive. In fact, he'd seemed uninterested in the whole affair. We were standing in the main newsroom, surrounded by dozens of reporters in cubicles all clicking away at computers, which might have explained his air of distraction.

"This might work best as a wrap-up once you get back," he said, not adding the obvious fact that it also might not. His fishy lips stretched into a downward arc. "Maybe something for the religion page." The frown went yet lower. "If some space opens up."

"Um. . . sure," I said, adding that brief hesitation to show that I would be thrilled to get a bylined story anywhere in the paper, but realized the religion page was a lousy place to have to do it. It was the *Herald*'s informational dungeon, existing only to provide space for the same church ads that had been running since Jesus. Articles to fill out the rest of the page were typically mailed in by doddering ministers with an incomplete grasp of the prose styles favored by print media in the twentieth century. One time we ran a 1,500-word feature that turned out to be a requiem for a dead beagle. Even then no one would have cared if some dog-lover hadn't sent a letter to the editor to complain. The copy desk was known to treat the religion page like a malarial swamp.

Next door to the Old General Store was Croft's Electronics. Also empty of customers. The front window was almost filled with a sun-bleached poster of a satellite dish the size of a jacuzzi. So the little outpost did give you options. Trash novels or global TV. Choose your own escape.

Fraleton Park was three blocks away. I plodded on, walking into a warm scent of freshly-mown turf that hit me like the true smell of summer. The lawn was as flat as a floor all the way to the river. There were no buildings, no benches, no shrubbery, no signs of development. The lone object rising above the horizontal plane was the very thing I'd come to see, standing out in the center of the space like a massive green lightning rod. I made the effort to close my mouth, and realized that "jaw-dropping" was another of those clichés that occasionally reveal their source. The Miracle Tree, at last, in its singular glory.

I stopped to marvel at the distant sight of it. The tree was a spectacle. On size alone it seemed to call for reflection, the way people quietly contemplate a zoo elephant or a beached whale. But it was also remarkable for its beauty. I tried to recall a single plant I had ever seen that was so striking.

The visual wonderment began with the trunk, a massive structure rising out of the earth like a public works project. It was covered in brown-grey chunks of bark that folded over and into each other in no discernable pattern. The lowest branch emerged at about the height of a basketball hoop, and continued horizontally that way for a ridiculously long span. It and the others above went on and on, colonizing the surrounding space as if determined to create a forest of one. Someone standing on the drip line, where the last sausage-shaped pointed leaves shone yellow-green in the angled sunlight, would have to shout to get the attention of someone else on the opposite side of the circumference.

From my first vantage a block from the park, the tree's outline resembled a schoolboy's drawing: a thick tube topped by a giant ball. From closer in I detected the anarchy in the array. The main trunk dominated the lower quarter of the structure, but then it seemed to lose control as six or more higher trunks broke off from the leader in a race to the sky. The branching from there was chaotic. Some limbs spread out radially, but others confounded the design by sprouting thick or thin leads in odd directions, including a few heading right back towards the center.

I went nearer, but slowly to savor the experience. I stopped to stare again when I noticed the tree was festooned. I took it at first for tinsel, then realized they were ornaments of the plant's own making, strings of tiny pale green flowers dangling in yardstick-long ribbons, as if the tree had devised a way to celebrate its own regal stature.

When I got close I tilted my head back to stare up into the layered spread of wood and leaf and flower rising skyward. There were gaps far up at the top where the blue came through. I imagined floating slowly up into the foliage, everything going greener the deeper I got, until the whole world was no more than a three-D wonderland of pulsing chloroplast.

My mind yanked me rudely back to the ground the instant I realized I would need to convey this effect to the readers. Whether the paper opted to use it or not, I had to send in a report, which first meant describing the tree. The size alone ought to translate, I concluded, but how big was it? All that time I spent in j-school, and no one ever taught me how to figure out the dimensions of over-sized objects.

I walked back for perspective. I tried to picture a man standing beside the trunk, then added another man on his shoulders, and so on, in six-foot increments, until I had ten or maybe eleven imaginary men teetering in a human tower, yet they still reached no higher than halfway to the top. I gave up and concluded it was a big tree.

I let myself lapse back into a trance to appreciate the last glints of sunlight on leaves high in the canopy that glowed or dimmed as they twisted in a breeze unfelt at ground level. It was mesmerizing. I stayed that way until the light went out on the last of the chosen leaves.

I must have had other nature-based experiences that made me feel as good, but none that I could recollect. Nature worship wasn't my thing. The street trees in my neighborhood were safe from the possibility that I might ever feel the need for a hug. But this was different. I thought I understood at last why those anti-logging protestors could get so worked up about cutting down trees even though the forests were still thick with them. Here I thought I may have just had an inside look into wonders of the living world. The Miracle Tree might have been similarly convincing people for generations. No wonder the locals wanted to keep it. Unless there really was something to the wish-fulfillment thing.

The sky to the east turned purple and the color drained from the leaves. Only then did I notice a section of lawn on the other side of the trunk where a few hand-lettered signs had been propped up. They had the mark of a grass-roots, no-budget political campaign. They proclaimed their messages loud and clear:

NO TO FILCO.

LEAF US ALONE.

THE MIRACLE TREE LIVES!

HELL NO, WE WON'T GLOW.

Three protesters appeared, picked up signs and began marching like convicts in a circle around the tree. The people, united, would never be defeated, or at this rate, noticed. I knew it was a small town, but *three* people?

The Save-the-Tree campaign appeared to be led by an old-growth hippie wearing tire-tread sandals. Behind him were a tiny, prim-looking older woman in khaki shorts, and a red-faced wino-type who would probably last no longer than the bottle.

I slid my notebook and pen out of my back pocket. I took a deep breath, steadied myself, then walked towards them. Even considering the target, I felt nervous. I compensated by straightening my back and lifting my chin. It was, after all, my first professional venture into the real world of gathering news. I wanted to be relaxed, to feel as natural and familiar as I would asking about the happy hour specials, but I couldn't deny the excitement that surged through my circulatory system.

Before I could open my mouth, the hippie spoke up. "It's a criminal act of corporate aggression against nature and against the decent people of this beautiful community."

"Ooo-kay," I answered, a little miffed at having my command of the situation so easily pre-empted. "Can I get your name?"

He paused, sniffing for the trap, before giving in. "Morning Mist," he said in tone that might have been defiant.

I stopped writing after the first M, assailed by a sudden vision of Pearson reading my copy out loud back in Gallantine's office. Of course he would break up the editors with some caustic observation. Not about the tree but an easier target: me.

"Uh, Morning? Do you have a more. . . conventional name I might use?"

"I gave it up. Eight years ago," he said. "I didn't choose it. Why should I be stuck within the life-confining designs of other people?"

"Because they're your parents?"

He scoffed. "Get out of the box, man. Your mind-set is restricted by the paradigms placed upon you by a commercially-dominated world. Free yourself. Lively up. You have the talent. The resources are all there. You're a child of the new age of information. There is no edge to the end of the universe that you have the capacity to explore. You just need the heart. And also the will."

"Mister Mist," I said, smiling without trying to. "In spite of everything, and for reasons I don't quite understand, I kind of like you. But listen, I really do have to get some quotes. I have a story to write and this doesn't seem to be the way to do it. But maybe I'll see you around."

"Dude," he answered in agreement. He gave me a fisted salute. I wished I'd brought a camera. I'd never seen one outside a rerun of "The Mod Squad."

The woman in the khaki shorts provided me with a more coherent argument against outsider developers who would destroy a local community's environmental integrity along with its legacy of fostering appreciation for spiritual engagement. She seemed to have been through the drill before, slowing at the ends of long sentences so I could get everything down in my notebook. It was all good stuff. She even had a fitting name to go with the quotes: Agnes Weatherby. What more could I have asked for? I was so pleased I wanted to take her home, introduce her around at the next party. Earnest but decent types like Agnes were an endangered species back in the city.

The wino sized me up as an out-of-towner. He pushed a clump of stringy hair off his forehead and asked, in a voice strained through gravel, for a fiver.

"Five bucks?" I asked. "Where I come from they're happy to get a quarter."

He snorted as if a quarter wasn't worth the effort. Given the demographics of Fraleton, he was probably right. A quarter from every inhabitant might still leave you scrambling for lunch.

"I'll tell you what you need to know," the wino offered. "Really."

He could have been using the same shampoo as Neil Young. I looked past him, then behind me, but he was the only protester left on the site. I sighed as I readied my pen on the notebook, then nodded.

"I am pleased to meet your acquaintance and my name is Harold," he said. He didn't bother holding out a hand, perhaps sensing I wouldn't have welcomed a shake. "Harold Whitley. With an E. That's W-H-I-T-L-E-Y. I am an applied physics research engineer."

I must have looked dubious.

"Formerly," he added, with dignity.

"Fine. What can you tell me about the tree, Harold Whitley?" I asked.

"I can tell you why it's called the Miracle Tree."

"That's a start."

"Where's my money?"

"We don't actually pay for stories at the *City Herald*. Not our policy."

I wondered if it had showed, the excitement I'd felt at saying "we" to refer to such a prestigious newspaper. And then whether my next thought wasn't just as obvious: that I was flattering myself.

"It's not for the story," he said, "it's for me. Let's just say the peace of mind engendered by a temporary relief of my financial burden would more effectively enhance my memory."

A wino with flair. Every town had to have at least one. I decided I would give him the money. But I still wanted him to earn it. "Okay. You talk, I find that it's useful information, I give you the money. Deal?"

He needed a moment to think it over. As if any more lucrative prospects were crowding his day planner. "It's called the Miracle Tree because if you make a wish under it, and you're sincere, and you truly deserve it, it'll come true." He nodded as if to confirm the veracity of what he had just said. "It will."

"Uh huh. For that story," I fished in my pocket, "here's your quarter."

I started to leave. Helping a wino was one thing but I wouldn't be taken for a complete dupe. Like Harold, I needed to keep some sense of pride.

He tugged on my sleeve, his face reddening with some insistent emotion I didn't recognize. "Look, don't believe *me*, I don't care. But ask anyone in town," he urged. "Things *happen* because of this tree. Strange things. Nobody knows why. Look at my watch."

He held out a wrist strapped with a yellowed Seiko. The second hand had stopped.

"That darn tree," I said.

"It happens to a lot of them. Compasses too. They go haywire."

"Harold, what's the story with the construction crews?"

"Exactly! They didn't believe it either. And look what happened to them."

"What did happen to them?"

"One guy broke his arm in two places. Snapped like a *twig*. You don't play around with the forces of the physical universe without considering the implications. There are powers here that go deeper than you or me. You know what I mean? Of course not. Because you don't *feel* it. Some do. Some don't. Many are called, but they lose the number. Trust your own body. Believe in things that you know yourself to be true. The rest? Trial and error. What else is there? Science: hypothesis, evidence, confirmation. The truth comes out. It may not however set you free. That part is up to you. The laws of physics apply irregardless, do they not? Energy flows, but *people* choose. You take the next construction team to get this job. Didn't even get close. And *why* is that? People say their so-called power tools shorted out. I call it an electrical coup d'etat, a look into the universe's own gear box, if you will. You understand? It *happens*. Right here. I saw the sparks myself."

He made a shower of imaginary sparks with his fingers, adding a verbal mimicry of the sound of electricity that sprayed spit in my direction. I stepped back. He had taken on the piercing stare of the believer. Cleaned up and toned down, in a white shirt and tie, he could make a great Jehovah's Witness.

He must have read my mind.

"You needn't be so quick to *judge*, mister fancypants babyface reporter. How do you know what's true or not when you just got here? I've lived here all my life. I've *seen* this tree since I was a child. I know what happens when people get close to it. I'm not an idiot."

The last part was debatable, but I didn't want to wind him up again. He seemed not far off from a diatribe on crop circles or cow mutilations. I took my wallet out, twisting my back so he couldn't grab it and run off. I would not have had much trouble catching him, but still, what an unhappy pursuit that suggested. I extracted a five dollar bill. Without a receipt I wouldn't be able to claim it for expenses, but that couldn't be helped now. Playing the nice guy isn't always redeemed. I palmed the bill to him in a handshake so I wouldn't be taken by anyone looking on as an idiot myself. "Don't drink it all in one place," I suggested.

He transferred it to his other hand so he could slide it into his pocket without breaking the shake, a deft move for a man in trousers with suspicious stains.

At least I had a solid start on the locals' side of the story. I would still need to put in the background, as well as something from the developers to counter all the negative stuff. But it wasn't hard to imagine what the other side would say. I could probably say it myself, although I would need the quotation marks to prove I was doing my job. I may have had little hope they would ever run my piece, but at least no one could fault me for delivering incomplete work.

"One more thing," I asked Harold. "Where would I find somebody from Filco?" But he had already turned to go. I'd served my purpose.

"Hubbensberg," answered a beefy man with a bald spot poorly covered by a sideways sweep of chestnut-colored hair. He was hefty already, but looked all the bigger for the red plaid blazer he had unwisely squeezed into. It could have come from the back of a vaudeville juggler. A boxy tape recorder hung on a nylon strap that disappeared into the suety folds of his neck. The machine was marked with the white stenciled letters COWR.

"George Templington," he said, shifting his microphone from one plump hand to the other for a shake. It was, as I had feared, clammy with big-man sweat. "So I'm not the only dog-and-pony dupe here after all," he noted.

"Earl Brododsky," I replied. "From the *City Herald*. Is your station in Fraleton?"

He looked offended. "Here? It would be two tin cans and a piece of string. We're in Hubbensberg. I got sent out to pick up after the same AP piece of doo-doo you must have stepped in. Looks like we're the only two fish wriggling in the net."

"I guess."

"I know why *I* came," George said. "My boss is an asshole. And there's nothing happening in Hubbensberg today anyway. But I can't believe a paper like yours would care. Bullshit on a stick or what?"

"It's not exactly what I was expecting. Who did the AP story?"

"I don't know. Some pudwhacking stringer passing through probably had car trouble and needed something to do while waiting for parts. Beats hitting your own head against the pavement."

He swiveled his fleshy neck to take in greater Fraleton with a sad head-shake, followed by a curl of his upper lip. "Then again."

"I gather you don't go for small towns."

"What's to like? No pro ball, no cul-cha, probably one decent-looking broad in the whole bunch. And she's been locked in the hay barn since she was twelve."

I'd thought the only people who called women broads were characters in '40s detective novels. I tried to picture George in something noir. The bad guy's muscle man? No. He had the brawn and some of the surly demeanor, but lacked the menace. He'd be the first to back down from a fight, not out of fear, but disgust. I made a mental note to tell Shirley there were still people on the planet who talked like George. She liked it when I caught things like that. It helped her believe I was politically diligent.

"People seem friendly enough," I tried. It was weak, I knew, but I didn't want to start feeding my own cynicism with his ample supply. I still had to get my story out.

He hefted his shirt and slapped his belly like a watermelon being tested for ripeness. "I'm just about to go look for something to eat. If you care to join me."

"I've got plans," I said. "But there's a Chinese place around here that's supposed to be excellent."

He grimaced. "Chinee foo! Well, why not? If it's still open in a one-horse heap like this. What time you got?"

I checked my watch, a gift from my father that had belonged to his father before him, but it had stopped. I could never remember to wind it up.

"Some time past 7:04," I said. "If that's any help."

George pretended to answer in irate Cantonese.

"Seven o-crock! Gung now choy fat han baaaaaaaaah!" he said, then slapped his belly again. "Christ I'm hungry. I could eat the whole dog."

Here was something else to report to Shirley. Or maybe to Danny Wong. He was a friend and occasional rival from back at the paper. We'd been in j-school together, where he got honors for exposing a local triad's attempts to muscle in on the lucrative day-care business. We were hired by the *City Herald* at the same time. Danny got off to a crummy start too, being assigned to the obit desk, although he acted as if he liked it. He began showing up to work wearing all black clothes, and would discuss even the slightest topics in the somber tones of a mortician. Sometimes after lunch he would pretend to bless the leftovers before murmuring how he was needed back in "necro-city." Remembering all this was enough to convince me that Danny probably wouldn't make any more of George's questionable ethnic rant than I did. Despite the fact that Danny was, genetically speaking, entitled to be upset. Although on some deeper or perhaps just more elusive level, we both were.

My own position on the paper owed at least something to the fact that I was of Native American heritage. At least as far as anyone knew. I didn't make much of it, what's past is past and all that, but I suppose I did check that box when it came time to fill out the job application. It hadn't come up in the interviews, or at any other time, until I was called up with the rest of the new hires for the welcoming ritual in Gallantine's office on our first week.

Hanover was standing in Gallantine's doorway to welcome us. Me, Danny, Melanie, a tall black woman named Shantella who could have eaten her porridge off any of our heads, and Xavier, a dapper Hispanic guy whose parents were rumored to have been Salvadorean political refugees.

"Well, then! Hello there, troops!" Hanover called out with unnerving vim. "Come in, everybody come in! My goodness. Yes! Here we are. Right?"

We'd all met him during our interviews but he carried on as if we were a group of Japanese investors on a fact-finding tour.

"I'm pleased and proud to welcome you all to the *Herald,*" he gushed, "the finest daily publication this city has known for the past eighty-seven years. I know you'll all do your best to keep our publication number one in the greater metropolitan region for many years to come. So, gosh, welcome aboard and, well, okay, heeeere's the Chief."

Gallantine sighed through his nostrils. It might have been a sign of exasperation at the performance of his right hand man, but might equally have been a reaction to our group. He looked us over one at a time, top to bottom, like a county fair judge eyeing a pen of 4-H steers. It struck me as rude, boss or no boss, but then he chuckled in a way that made his wattles quiver. He leaned forward with a squeak from a chair that must have been custom-made for bulk.

"And the rain was upon the earth, forty days and forty nights," he announced in a voice that reminded me of an old Orson Welles radio clip.

Danny stole a glance at me. I shrugged. The others didn't seem to get it either.

"Is this everyone?" Gallantine said. "I don't think so."

Hanover snapped his fingers. "You're absolutely right, Chief. My gosh. We're missing. . ." He looked stricken. "Hang on."

He opened the door to hurry out, but didn't get far. We heard the crack of his shin colliding with the metal foot-rest of a wheelchair coming in. Gerry Wilkins, driving it, started to apologize, even though it wasn't his fault, but he was as distracted as the rest of us by the sight of Hanover jumping back with an exaggerated jerk. It was as if he'd just been told the wheelchair was radioactive. He landed with an expression that went in a flash from shock through anger and then embarrassment into pain.

Gallantine hog-snorted the start of a laugh, drawing an involuntary yelp of delight from Danny. The rest of us held it in, fortunately, because it stopped as quickly as it had started.

Gallantine eyed the last of the recruits with a satisfied nod. "Good. Now we're about set, right?"

Hanover didn't reply.

"Every year we do this. And every year my heart sinks a little deeper," Gallantine muttered once we were all lined up. He looked questioningly at Hanover. Hanover cleared his throat but said nothing.

"Pop would seethe at the way we do things these days," Gallantine continued in a louder voice. "Filling every slot of the crayon box straight out of journalism school. As if you can learn reporting in a classroom. Some bloodless hack with elbow patches spouting the who what where. When did we lose it? How come we never seem to get anyone with piss and vinegar in their veins anymore? Eh? Someone like Sullivan taking on that entire Third Precinct cop shop?

Or, hell, I don't know, Stoopovich."

Hanover shook his head and puffed out his cheeks in a slow exhale. "Stoopovich," he repeated.

"I know," Gallantine continued, smiling. "The conniving little runt."

His face suddenly clouded. He stared at me over his glasses with an expression I took as annoyance, then realized was confusion. He seemed to be working out just what was wrong with the picture before him. "Your name again, son?" he asked at last.

I tried to make my voice deeper than it really was. "Earl Brododsky," I replied.

"Brod*od*sky?" His white eyebrows went up in surprise then back down in puzzlement. "Hmmm."

Hanover solved the mystery. "You're of Indian heritage, Earl, isn't that right?"

"Yes, well, ahem," I answered, trying to appear stoic. "On my father's side, that is." I wanted to be seen as reluctant to discuss our business with outsiders, a difficult act for someone who looked, well, white as I do. Although I did have an explanation of sorts if needed: my grandmother, a clerk at a remote Hudson's Bay outpost, had once been the scandal of the Northwest Territories for running off with a wealthy Cree trader.

Gallantine stretched out a hand, palm down, fingers slightly bent. Was he doing his impression of the Pope? We stared for an uncomfortable moment until I realized this marked the high point of the ceremony, the welcoming handshake. He didn't stand up for it. It would have been an ordeal for a man of his bulk. I hurried forward and pressed the soft mound. One firm squeeze followed by a quick release. Not too eager, certainly not a clinger, but no wimp either.

Once Gallantine had physically welcomed us all to the firm, he took off his glasses, sighed again and twisted his knuckles into his eyes. Blood vessels had formed a spidery red pattern in his nose. From drink? Old-school editors were supposed to be whiskey-soaked curmudgeons with iron livers. It looked to be true here, as far as appearances went. I wished I could open the bottom drawer of his desk. A bottle and two grimy shot glasses would prove it.

"Look," he said at last. "I don't care where you come from or who you know or anything else about how you got here. You look like a goddamn ad for Benneton but who cares? You're reporters now, and that's what counts. Plus you're working for a damn good paper. Doesn't mean it can't get better. That's your job and that's why we chose you over all the other whiz-bangs who wanted your spots. You're the future of the *Herald*. You're here because we think you can help us improve. So do it. All right? And if you can't? Dig deeper. Give us what you got, but give it straight. There's enough bullshit in the world already without you adding more. Fair enough?"

We looked at each other for the proper response.

It was Melanie who broke the spell. "Yes, sir!" she said with a voice filled to bursting. She looked as if she wanted to salute.

"You got it, Chief," Danny added, offering a thumb-up. Hanover winced, maybe because Danny had assumed a familiarity by using Hanover's term, Chief.

"No adding to the shit," echoed Shantella in a tone that might have sounded like sarcasm in anyone else's office.

Gallantine nodded. "Good. Then go to work," he commanded.

Hanover went to the door. Grimly favoring one leg, he held it open for Gerry with a backwards lean that would have allowed the passage of a backhoe. I was the next one through, getting a coach-like pat on the ass that must have felt as weird to Hanover as it did to me. He didn't repeat it for Melanie right behind me, nor any of the others. Danny was the last one out. As soon as the door closed behind him, it flung open again and Hanover joined us in the corridor. By ordering us to work, Gallantine apparently meant him too.

Hanover stopped on the way to the elevator to talk to Betsy, Gallantine's receptionist. He might have had something important to discuss, but it looked rather as if he did it just to avoid riding down with a crowd of rookies.

Betsy smiled at us over his shoulder. She was said to be the human Rottweiler protecting Gallantine from the daily ilk of urban affairs, an impenetrable force keeping out the unnecessary, the boring and the dangerously disgruntled, but you wouldn't have known by looking at her. She had a warm and doughy face topped by a blue-washed beehive that was then back in style, although in her case perhaps by coincidence. Her ivory-white teeth gleamed in the halogen lights as the elevator doors slid shut.

"So that's what a grand poohbah looks like," Melanie said.

"Bigger than I expected," Danny said. "He's got to weigh. . . how much you figure? Two-ninety? More?"

"Big and full of it," said Shantella.

Melanie looked at her. "What do you mean?"

"I don't care if he is His Eminence. The man's a cracker. You see the way he looked at me?"

"I know. He thinks we're only here because we're minority hires," Xavier said. "Typical."

Danny shrugged. "They have to play catch-up some time. This editorial department is like, what, ninety percent Wonder bread?"

"I was summa cum laude at Yale," said Shantella. "Let him catch up with that."

Back at the tree, George was still eyeing me like I'd just let down the journalists' team with a bonehead play.

"I can't believe you gave that alkie money," he said, peering at me as if genuinely trying to understand.

"Yes, well, actually, he gave me some important background information. And he looked like he could use a little help."

He nodded as if it had been confirmed. I was a sucker.

"Anyway," I said to change the subject, "you get your story?"

"Story. Shit. That AP piece was all bunged up. As usual. If that's an oak tree I'm the Prince of Fucking Wales. Any idiot will tell you it's a sycamore. I don't know how they stay in business."

"You didn't do anything on it then?"

"Phoned it in an hour ago. Historical tree in peril due to zoning dispute blah blah blah. I squeezed out a minute-twenty, but I was stretching. How much can you do with an overgrown hunk of wood in a no-hope place like Fraleton?"

"Why are you still here?"

"If I drive all the way back tonight they'll just assign me to the Parks Commission hearing tomorrow morning. You haven't suffered until you've sat through one of those verbal gas leaks. They can sit there with straight faces talking duck pond contingencies for hours. The mallards themselves would walk out from boredom. This way, if I leave in the morning and let's say I have to stop around lunchtime for the corned beef special at Netty's, it means I get back just in time to miss the traffic round-up. Then I can go home."

It is better to read the weather forecast before we pray for rain.

Mark Twain

THREE

The morning sun through lace curtains made a filigree on the wall when I woke up, paralyzed. Except that parts of me could move. Just not in unison. I couldn't get up. An unseen force from under the bed seemed to be pulling me down. I raised my legs and arms up towards the ceiling and bucked for leverage, but it was hard to lift my head above the horizontal at the same time. At last I gained enough balance to get my shoulders up, too, so I could edge crab-like to the side of the bed and roll off, landing on the floor in a clump.

I wanted to know why the furniture seemed to have a grudge against me. The quilt-covered top seemed normal enough, but from underneath I could see how severely the whole contraption bowed in the middle. Halfway through a rejuvenating stretch I was stopped by a spear of pain in my lower spine. Great: now I had a bad back to add to everything else. Not hard to believe, sleeping in a bed designed for it. If I ran a chiropractic business I would invest in that product. We could call it The Lumbago.

I considered the accommodation alternatives. Having toured the town, I wasn't encouraged. There was the janitor's sofa that becomes a bed. A longer shot might have involved the romance-reader at the cash register. She was pretty, in her own way, and could only improve without the hair curlers. Plus she seemed friendly. Maybe willing as well. Would she beg me to do her on the kitchen Formica to recreate some steamy Harlequin highlight? And then what? Would we watch Geraldo and eat processed cheese slices from each other's fingers? Sip Gallo by the jug while dissecting the epic drama of her weekly bowling league?

No, I concluded, Fraleton was a good place to keep a bed once you found it, even one that should be posted with its own warning sign. For comfort, I would have to wait until I got back to my own bed. Mine and Shirley's. Actually more Shirley's than mine, but only because she'd had more money the week when we broke clear through the frame of our previous one. And that was her fault as much as anyone's — she was on top at the time.

Judging by the meal I'd had the night before, staying at the inn would have another advantage. Grady had made a right show of puttering about the kitchen during the preparation, his pulpit for a discourse on modern nutrition and the lack thereof, thanks to factory farms. But it was easy to see the culinary symphony was really conducted by his wife.

Mrs. Grady was a peach. She looked like the grandmother you would hire for a TV commercial featuring straightforward talk about laxatives. She had a quick full-cheeked smile and a stretch of white hair that tied up neatly into a bun, but she was not the doily type this description might suggest. At one point when Grady got so flustered describing an election result that he dropped his watch into a mixing bowl, she fished it out and concluded his argument for him by describing the winners as "suck-holes."

Dinner was thick yet tender slabs of roast beef, sided by Yorkshire pudding and steamed broccoli heads that tasted better than any plant I'd ever swallowed, perhaps because, as Grady pointed out from the head of the table, mere minutes before they had been bursting with life in the back yard. Organically, of course: no multinational war-derived petro-chemical poisons would foul his domain. The world may have been hurtling towards ecological ruin, but he'd created a sanctuary. He practically shook with pride in describing how nature obviously agreed with him, as proven by all the nattering birds we could hear out the window just then, while his neighbor's medicated lawns appeared barren.

He tapped my elbow to herald an important announcement. "For fertilizer? I use my own blend of compost, fortified with free-range poultry droppings."

"Thanks for sharing that," I said. Even the image of chicken shit on a plate couldn't spoil the repast, and I let myself be talked into seconds of everything. We were in the middle of raspberry pie and vanilla ice cream, the berries coming from the back yard, naturally, when George Templington walked in. He cast a jaundiced eye on our Norman Rockwell dessert scene and asked, with a grim expression clouding his blanched face, for the key to number seven.

"You all right?" I asked. His forehead was shiny.

He closed his eyes and rubbed his belly with his fist. "Got any Pepto-Bismol?" he asked Grady. "I think that chop suey is trying to tell me something."

Grady gave me a knowing glance before getting up. Mrs. Grady said there was still some dessert left, but George let out a gutteral bark that obviously meant no.

"I actually like Lon's," she told me in a conspiratorial whisper. "But it does take getting used to."

Grady returned carrying a jar filled with floating leaves.

George looked unimpressed. "The hell is that?" he asked, wavering. But Grady made him sit and drink the entire liquid contents before letting him have the key.

Next morning, George seemed happy enough: his skin tone was back to blotchy pink. I found him sunk into the living room sofa watching a perky female newscaster with blonde hair varnished into the shape of a Bronze Age war helmet. She was interviewing a man who had written a book about mushrooms as they fried a basketful of chanterelles. George eyed the screen hungrily and even made a slurping noise.

"You're in no hurry to leave," I pointed out.

He scoffed. "I called the station manager. He had a story lined up for me about the new hippo at Hubbensberg Zoo. Luckily it got canceled."

"That's a shame."

"A hippopotamus with a bladder infection." He shuddered. "Can you picture it? Torrents of reeking piss is what we're talking about."

"So what are you still doing here? You going to file another story?"

He shrugged his shoulders and rolled his eyes.

Mrs. Grady announced breakfast. At the table were two places set with identical plates of scrambled eggs and ham and home-made hash browns.

George didn't hesitate out of politeness or to say something pleasant about the food or the presentation. He sat, lowered his head and started his fork in elliptical motion from plate to mouth.

"A complete recovery?" I asked, still tucking my napkin into my shirt collar.

He answered through a mouthful of biscuit. "That weird tea must have done the trick. I slept like a baby. I had a dream that I was a chef trying to get the world record for the biggest steak and kidney pie — and I don't even like steak and kidney pie. At least I think I don't."

We finished breakfast to the end of a TV episode of the Beverly Hillbillies show, followed immediately by another. I sopped up the last of my eggs with a biscuit. Another winning meal. When I started for the stairs to get my notebook, George feigned surprise.

"Wait, you can't leave! I think this is the one where Ellie May goes swimming."

On the lawn outside the inn, heading towards the park, the sun had just finished its first assignment of the day, collecting dew. The sky was an oddly luminous blue. That might have been normal, but I'd long grown accustomed to seeing everything through a gauzy urban haze. Here the air seemed scoured clean. All the colors were brighter. From an open window I heard a man sing a shower song, "That's Life," in a fairly good imitation of Frank Sinatra. The scent of pancakes came to me on a warm breeze.

Fraleton Park was busier than it had been the previous afternoon. Maybe the locals were morning people. A dozen or so chatted in clusters just beyond the shade of the Miracle Tree. Five of them carried signs in their sluggish circle around the trunk. They were still being led by Morning Mist, but his enthusiasm wasn't catching on. He tried to enlist everyone in a chant but got nothing more than murmurs to his call of, "One Two Three Four, We Don't Want Your Stinkin' Plutonium."

Not far off were some nonparticipants watching with the dull stares of the chronically bored. They might well have been waiting for something they didn't honestly expect to happen. A familiar condition, perhaps, when you live in a town with the population of a single apartment tower back in the city.

Agnes Weatherby appeared wearing a spotless gardening apron, walking towards the tree at a healthy clip. Her white running shoes made a contrast in the luminescent grass. Something about her gait, or the angle of her jaw, suggested a retired schoolteacher, the kind who may have been sweet and dainty but still knew how to rap a knuckle if you'd forgotten to mind your manners. Those she passed nodded or offered quick hellos while stepping out of her way.

Morning Mist halted his circle of zombie impressionists with a raised hand, an imperious gesture he may have picked up in a cavalry movie. He stepped forward with raised arms to hug Agnes, but stopped at the last step to turn it into a palm-together bow.

She nodded without breaking stride.

Morning Mist steered his comrades away for a break. They sat themselves in a semi-circle, faces tilted towards the sun, as he rooted through a purple daypack for their rations: a bunch of carrots and a plastic baggy filled with what looked like seeds. Fuel for the revolution, or for any hamsters the rebels might find on the way.

Agnes stopped beside the trunk of the tree. She stared at it without speaking, then reached out to touch the bark. Her fingers traced a pattern across the surface, perhaps letters. At last she brought her hands together in a gesture of prayer, lowering her head at the same time. Her lips were moving but no sound emerged.

I sensed an event, a journalistic moment, the actual news about to blossom. It struck me as a blessing. The air seemed charged now with more than the freshness of a small town's summer morning. Even the tree seemed more alive, the green of its leaves more striking against the crisp blue of the open sky. There was something going on here, I knew, because I could feel it. I whipped out my notebook, eager to capture the scene.

She stayed in the same fervent pose long past the time it would take me to make a simple request of a tree. Even a big request. I thought of wishes that might need some explaining, a sauna date with Uma Thurman in a Tunisian resort or the winning lottery numbers. Maybe her plea was a real challenge. World peace and all its corollaries. A cure for childhood leukemia. Or not. Who knew what desires burned under that multi-pocketed apron? She could haven been wishing for a new seventeen-year-old body, or one more shot at some awkward missed opportunities of youth.

I wondered if I should start my wish list with something small, then work up. A big, warm, happy hug from Shirley as soon as I walked through the door. She was just then starting her second full day without me. What would she wish for?

We hadn't been apart this long since the summer vacation after our senior year at high school. She took a month off to help Cuban mothers raise their awareness of something, perhaps their own health. Or perhaps not – the Cuban mothers in the pictures she brought back looked happier than our own. Whichever it was, Shirley came back admitting to some disillusion, which was rare for her. First, their medical clinics were better than ours, and free besides. That much was fine, of course, the triumph of a superior social system and all, but it didn't leave much for the foreign cadres to do when it came to promoting public health. Second, after three weeks of living with a typical family and eating the same rice and black beans every night, she said she was ready to kill for a cheeseburger.

She'd explained it to me on the way back from the airport. It was a late afternoon and she hadn't eaten a thing since morning and we were both starving and a MacDonalds was right there. I described the all-beef patty delights, trying to get her to cave in, just once, but Shirley was the type who would gnaw her own limb before stepping under the evil golden arches. We ended up eating later at a locally-owned diner where it wasn't until dessert that she stopped chewing long enough to remind me that eighty-seven cents of every dollar I'd wanted to spend on the corporate clown would have left the community.

Now, standing under the tree, I watched Agnes with growing admiration. Like Shirley, she would not let up. She was a marathoner who had turned from running to praying. I sat on the grass to wait her out, still believing she held some key to my story. She may have had resolve, but I had decades on her. Not only was I young and active, but I had nowhere else to go: I couldn't lose this one.

Morning Mist may have deduced what I was after. He left his crew to approach me with both palms held up like someone blocking a photographer. "You already talked to her once," he said in a deliberately soothing tone, the guru-in-training again. "You got your quotes. I wouldn't push it if I were you." A single alfalfa sprout dangled from his beard.

"Wouldn't push what?"

"I wouldn't bother Mrs. Weatherby with any intrusive media questions."

I wondered how much of the day he could get through with the food still there on his face. It might be a test of his social circle: if everybody saw it, but no one told him, what would it say about his friends?

"I guess that ought to be my job to decide what's intrusive," I said.

"Yeah, well, calling it your job don't make it right," he drawled, a line I thought I recognized from *Cool Hand Luke.* Someone like Paul Newman might be able to get away with carrying part of his lunch in his facial hair, but not Morning Mist. Gaffes like that would define him. The sprout was still green; by noon it would have begun to wilt. I might chart its progress as the day went on: at sunset it would be brown and dry and hard to pick out from the rest of his beard, and then who would ever know? More of them might have been nesting in there already.

"Thank you for your advice, Mister Manners," I said. "But yes, I have talked to her, so I know she's a good interview subject."

"On her terms."

"Whatever that means."

"When she chooses. She may have times when she's not feeling up to it. You have no right to intrude."

"Again with the etiquette lessons."

"She lost her husband," he said flatly. "Last week."

"Oh." I swallowed. "That's terrible."

"Yes. Well — he was smoking two packs a day."

"Damn. Lung cancer?"

"Car accident — but that doesn't matter. She's a lovely woman and I wouldn't want to see her upset. I'm sure you wouldn't either."

"No, I understand," I said quickly. "Thanks for letting me know."

I shook his hand to show him I meant it. I forgot to tell him about the alfalfa sprout. I was too absorbed in the image of Agnes collapsing into great grieving sobs on my neck because I'd asked the wrong question. Then what? Do you keep standing there with your notebook open like a smoking gun while people turn and stare? Do you slink away backwards while muttering empty apologies? Or plow ahead with some rapid covering questions and hope the fact of one's own creepiness gets quickly forgotten?

I tried to read the expression on Agnes' face. She had faintly Oriental features, which may have explained why she seemed to be smiling vaguely the way one does at a pleasing view or an old family photograph.

"Did you talk to the flackmeisters at Filco?" Morning asked.

"Not yet. I will though."

"They're weasels. Hard to pin down. Then when you do, watch your fingers. They don't bark before they bite."

"Running dogs," I said, thinking of Shirley's take on any business that could not fit into a two-car garage.

He tilted his head to size me up. He seemed on the verge of telling me something: he opened his mouth but closed it again, firmly. Finally he said, "You need work."

"Got a job, thanks."

"Personal work. You're like this bundle of negative energy swirling in and feeding on itself. I'd go for a polarity massage first thing, big time, if I were you."

"If is right."

"Om and shanti and homage to the light within you," he said.

"Ooo-kay."

"You might try at least once in your life to be where you are. You know what I mean? To really feel it. Stand in the moment. Let go of distractions. Realize the answer isn't somewhere else. It's right here. Groundtruthing. Tap into the energy of the living universe. It's moving all the time and it's flowing right now, right through you. But if you're not open, how would you even know?"

He didn't wait for an answer. He pressed his palms together and walked away. Whatever.

Agnes lowered her hands, reached out to touch the trunk again and then looked up into the swaying and shimmering branches and leaves. She swayed a little herself, her head back and her arms out, like a girl staring up at clouds on a perfect summer day.

When she turned to go, I didn't try to stop her. I watched her walk slowly across the grass. At the parking lot she continued past the cars towards the bus depot. Without knowing why, I started to follow. I kept a distance to stay undetected. My first ever attempt to trail a source, although admittedly not much of a challenge: even wearing sneakers, Agnes was not about to race away out of my sight. And if I wanted to, I thought, I could trail everyone in Fraleton. Where could they go?

Agnes stopped in Perry's driveway. He came out, wiping his hands on a rag but still keeping them at his sides as he leaned in to plant a kiss on her cheek. They didn't appear to have much to discuss. He shuffled in place and looked over her shoulder, then said something to her feet. She took off again.

I watched her round a corner and walk into an eggplant-colored bungalow. Suddenly I felt exposed, like the stalker I supposed I was. I kept walking with a casual gait, not looking at her house as I passed, trying to appear as if I somehow belonged on a street I'd never seen before. Three houses later the street came to a dead end that backed onto an empty lot. I had a choice: I could continue walking into the empty space, where I had no conceivable business unless I faked a sudden interest in soil science, or I could stop and look about in puzzlement so that anyone watching from behind a curtain would realize I was new in town and simply lost.

I tried the second option in a forced pantomime, knowing even at the time it was ridiculous: I'm a bad actor. Finally I gave up, lowered my head and hurried back the way I'd come. The curtains were still closed on the windows of the yellow house.

I stopped at Buffy's Doughnuts and Video store. The window was painted with a rough drawing of a man holding an éclair in one hand and a Top Gun tape in the other. The model for his body looked like Homer Simpson but the face resembled Sally Field. Peering in the window, I could see a single customer perched on a counter stool. He wore blue jeans and a backwards collar, a combination I found appealing: it could work for any number of articles. The tough-talking clergyman. The street-wise preacher with mud on his work boots. I quickly jotted down the details, leaving out the disappointing fact that he wore penny loafers.

I caught the eye of the doughnut-slinger behind the counter. He was wearing a hair net and had several days of chin stubble; his apron was too stained to reveal the original color. He glared at me as if I owed him money. I would need to see proof before believing his name really was Buffy.

I walked in knowing I should make a good impression on my interview subject, so I assumed the demeanor of a doughnut shop regular. I smiled and nodded a friendly hello, but the proprietor continued to stare out the window. The minister didn't look up from his newspaper. "Hi," I announced in a voice meant to take in both. "I'm Earl Brododsky, I'm a newspaper reporter with the *City Herald*, and I wonder if I might ask you a few quick questions."

The preacher looked up with a benevolent gaze, then nodded, a touch of amusement curling the corners of his lips. It might have been my youth, or maybe he was just easily amused. He patted the neighboring stool. "You're most welcome to ask anything you please. My name is James Kennedy," he said in the mellifluous baritone they must teach at preacher school. "But most folks call me Jimmy."

The counterman still seemed miserable. I cleared my throat and asked for a grande cappuccino with skim milk and extra nutmeg if he had it, but just a dash of cinnamon if he didn't. That produced a raised left eyebrow. I tried for a plain espresso, got a definite scowl, then settled for a black coffee — as long as it was fresh. When even that didn't work to animate him I also asked for a maple cruller. This wasn't enough to bring sunshine into his day, but he did turn around to fill the order. I watched him with newfound admiration. I wanted to tell him his customer service skills were lost on Fraleton: he belonged in the city where people crowded into places with staff showing that kind of attitude.

"I'm curious to hear what you think about this Miracle Tree business, Father," I said, forcing myself to pronounce the title. His fading red hair and freckled cheeks made him look nothing like a parent of mine, and I felt awkward using a word I wouldn't have applied even to my own dad. But I once went to a Catholic school so I understood how feeling awkward was all part of the religion.

"Miracles," he said, gazing up at the ceiling as if it alone blocked our view of the infinite where the answer might be written. He let the thought drift.

"Well, yes, if that's the proper word," I said.

He nodded thoughtfully and murmured, "Indeed."

In the gap that followed I began to wonder if he was testing me. Perhaps, before offering anything like an answer, he needed to know I was worthy.

"Actually," I began, pushing down a brief reminiscence of the confessional with an unseen shudder, "it's not just for the newspaper story. I'm interested, myself."

He nodded again, but didn't speak.

"Partly because of something that happened to me, when I was nine years old."

He didn't say anything to stop me, so I went on.

"It was in winter and I was skating home on Preston Lake, after playing hockey. I guess I played a little later than usual because it was nearly dark. I got kind of scared because the ice on the south end of the lake where I lived was never the thickest. I was just thinking maybe I should skate back and walk home the long way around the lake when I heard a crack. Before I knew it, I felt my feet starting to fall through. I tried to skate faster to get away but everything broke all at once and I dropped completely under. I didn't even feel the cold. I guess that's how surprised I was. I yelled for help but there was no answer."

He slowly stirred his coffee, then lowered the spoon even more slowly to the counter.

"I was yelling and crying and trying to climb out all at the same time when a big chunk of ice broke off in my hands and I dunked completely under again. Only this time I had to kick hard just to keep my head up. I tried to yell louder for help but my lips must have been too cold because I couldn't get them to make any words. The last thing I remember was feeling tired, like my body was so heavy I could hardly keep holding onto the ice, and then something pulled me up by the shoulders and out of the water. It was a man with a long overcoat and a hat, like you see in those old movies? I couldn't see his face with that hat, not in the dark, but he carried me to the shore and then all the way to my yard and right up the porch. The whole time he didn't say a word and neither did I. Just outside my door he said, 'Scoot in. Your mother has some hot soup that'll warm you up.' Inside I realized I hadn't even said thank you. So I turned back — and here's the really strange part — he wasn't there. He was completely gone." I snapped my fingers. "As in, disappeared."

I glanced at the preacher, feeling even more exposed than when I'd began. He pursed his lips, stroked his chin, then suddenly snapped his fingers to mark a revelation. "He fell through the ice himself on the way back?"

My blank stare made him grin. "Very sorry," he said. "I must beg you to excuse my attempt at levity. I sometimes suspect the deepest truths are buried under layers of solemnity. I meant no disrespect, to your or your experience. It certainly has significance for you. Please go on."

"Well, so, later that night I wondered about it, and I've been wondering ever since. How could the guy pull me up like that without falling in himself? He must have been heavier than me. And how did he know where I lived? Even what we were having for dinner? And then how could he just disappear like that?"

"Interesting," he said. "Hmm. Just like that, you say."

"I still don't know who or what he was. I never got a good look at his face. I only remember the aftershave or whatever it was he was wearing. It was something tangy, like citrus, or maybe a tropical flower. Something I've never been able to forget, even though I don't think I've ever smelled it since then. The next morning my mom went out to trace his tracks so she could find him and say thank you, but it snowed that night." I shrugged to say: end of story.

"Hmm," was all he had to offer.

I felt embarrassed having put myself in that position, expecting answers from a guy in a bean and grease joint. He didn't seem to mind gaps in the conversation, no matter how lengthy. Unless he was just drowsy. He continued to look thoughtfully at his empty mug.

I cleared my throat. "Apart from that," I said, "I would still like to hear your opinion on the belief some people seem to have in the tree."

"Hokum," he said, sitting up straighter on his stool. "Not the devil's work, necessarily. I won't go so far. Some are quick to subscribe anything potentially otherworldly that may not be clearly understood at initial investigation to be the work of the cloven-hoofed one, but I cannot count myself among them. Perhaps mysterious phenomena have occurred; perhaps they haven't. On whom shall we call to be the judge? This is one question. What is mysterious in this day and age? In any day and age, for that matter. One must learn to decide for oneself what events are central to the important questions, and what is mere chatter. Now, if you ask for my personal opinion? I suspect it's a lot of malarkey. Miracle — my foot. It's a tree. C'mon."

I got all that down, my pen scribbling furiously, though I suspected it would read back as demented as it sounded aloud. I prompted him again. "People talk about how some construction company workers got hurt just trying to cut it down."

"I've heard that," he said. "And maybe that's just how it happened. Or maybe the fellow who hurt his arm fell out of bed the night before and now he's hoping to have it covered by workman's compensation. Or maybe he slipped on a banana peel that came from his own lunch box. There are dozens of perfectly plausible explanations. I don't know, I'm not saying I do. You realize — I wasn't there."

"Right. So you don't accept the story that the tree somehow caused the accident? That there's more to it than meets the eye? That for lack of a better word it really can inspire miracles of some sort?"

"Ah, now: this is the crux — miracles. This is a subject with which we in the church do have some experience. Throughout the ages, in fact. One thing we have learned is that it won't do to simply discount as nonsense those things which cannot be explained with everyday logic. I dare say the Bible wouldn't hold up long under such vigorous critical appraisal, although, if it came down to that, I wouldn't care to be quoted stating as such."

Could the man not mouth a normal sentence? I considered shifting to the point of the story, the nuclear waste dump, but if I was going to work in a line or two about the miracle business it seemed a good idea to wrench out a comment from a local priest. If I could just get him to say it. "So you believe that it is at least possible the tree might actually help people's wishes come true?"

"Not exactly, that is, I mean to say, not in so many words."

This was like fencing. And I was tired of jabbing at air. "Fine, *Father*. What words would—"

"Nor am I denying it. It could very well happen just as you say. Until I receive an edict from my superiors in the Vatican informing me otherwise, officially speaking, you understand, I'm sure I don't know."

I put my pen down and stared at the wall. Why couldn't he just say that up front and leave me to my coffee?

"But if miracles do happen under that tree," he concluded, pointing with his doughnut for emphasis, "I would say it's because the good Lord has been watering it for some time."

I wrote that one down, partly to be polite but also because I thought it might actually fit into the story somewhere if I needed more quotes. God the gardener: it had a certain ring. Keep the holy rollers happy anyway. I congratulated myself on getting at least something out of the man after all the qualifying mumbo-jumbo, and left him to go back to the tree.

Back out in the park, the numbers had swelled. There were enough now to play two simultaneous games of baseball. Not that they looked up to it: most were in the same lethargic postures as before, bovinely watching, although different people were now doing it. Maybe they were idling in shifts.

The unmoving object of their attention this time was not the tree but a microphone stand set up nearby, with a wire running from it to an amp that fed two black speakers the size of broom closets. Thin Lizzy might have appreciated a system like that, but what was it doing in Fraleton?

George stood at the back of the gathering, fists shoved into his pockets, unhappy as ever. I asked him what was going on.

"Press conference," he smirked. "Good thing you showed up. For a while I thought I was going to be the only one. Wait, here he comes now."

A wide-shouldered man with coppery skin walked slowly to the microphone. Conversations stopped, and people turned to watch. With his aura of gravitas he might have had a similar effect no matter where he went, but here, especially, angled against the backdrop of the distant purple hills, he was a magnet. It helped that he was a tall man, and made taller by a pair of reptilian cowboy boots, the heels of which tilted him forward into a rakish angle. On the back of his denim jacket, visible between two coal-black braids of hair, was the Indian chief insignia of the Chicago Black Hawks.

"His name is Sun Deer," George whispered, "but his friends call him Walks With Load in Pants."

Sun Deer raised the microphone up to reach his mouth, then stood with his eyes closed, perhaps in prayer. When he opened them and glowered at the crowd he seemed less spiritual than stern. I thought of my grandfather, or the mystery person said to be my grandfather. Some of our relatives insisted the whole story about grandma running off with a Cree customer was just an old family joke that had only taken on a veneer of truth when some of the slower descendants couldn't see the humor. Others swore it was all fact. Until it came time to fill out a scholarship application form in college, I hadn't really given it much thought.

Sun Deer spoke in a segmented cadence, either to lend a dignified air to his words, or to give me time to write them all down. He had a knack for starting the next phrase at the precise moment I looked up from writing the end of the last one.

"We wish to proclaim—" he began, then snapped his head back to stop a feedback screech that had listeners covering their ears. When he leaned forward again it was with the caution of a deer sniffing an unfamiliar shrub. Sneaking up on the mike seemed to work: the speakers continued to issue powerful static clicks, but no feedback.

"We wish to proclaim. . . to the representatives of the international media. . . and to the world. . . that the Miracle Tree. . . shall live. . . forever."

He paused to gauge the effect of this on the crowd, such as it was. Realizing they were under scrutiny, a few people applauded.

Sun Deer pointed a finger at the sky and held it aloft as he continued: "The Miracle Tree was made. . . by the great Creator of us all. . . and put here in this place. . . for a higher purpose. . . which is why. . . we feel ourselves. . . compelled by the righteous examples. . . passed on to us. . . by our revered elders. . . to denounce entirely. . . the maliciously-conceived plan. . . of certain politicians. . .working in collusion. . . no, that's col-lu-sion. . . with multinational corporate interests. . . who share no regard. . . for the wishes. . . either of the local community. . . nor much less. . . for the ancestral peoples. . . who consider this land. . . a sacred home. . . to callously destroy. . . this sacred symbol. . . of our shared heritage."

Phew. I was certain more than once that he'd lost it, but he actually did wrap the conglomerate into something resembling a sentence. The onlookers applauded again, perhaps more at the grammatical feat than at any information it might have contained.

Sun Deer turned in profile, looking up towards the leaves in a meaningful way, until the final bit of clapping, by Agnes Weatherby, died down.

"So I stand here. . . before you. . . ladies and gentlemen of the press. . . to proclaim. . . that we will defend. . . the Miracle Tree. . . with our blood. . . with our sweat. . . and if necessary. . . with our very lives."

The applause this time was spirited. George checked his sound levels. It sounded to me like good radio material.

"Long live the Miracle Tree!" Sun Deer said.

"Long live the Miracle Tree," the crowd echoed, a little self-consciously and out of sync, like alkies at a mission feed. George winced. Morning Mist raised his fist in a gesture of triumph while lowering his head. He looked like the black American runners on the Olympic podium in Mexico City, except that he seemed to be elated rather than angry.

Sun Deer frowned. His expression remained adamantine as he continued, with a heavy tone of admonishment in the first two words: "I sa-id. . . Long live the Miracle Tree!"

"Long live the Miracle Tree!" came the vigorous response.

"Thank you," Sun Deer said. "My people shall not be moved."

He folded his arms across his chest and stood as if he'd spoken literally: to judge by his posture, his feet could have been bolted to the ground.

"Mister uh Deer," George said, not bothering to raise his hand.

Sun Deer seemed to contemplate for a moment whether answering questions might upset the stoic image he'd managed to create. But it was a press conference after all. He lowered his arms and leaned carefully back towards the microphone.

"Yes?"

"Where exactly are your people?"

His arms went back up across his chest. "We are everywhere," he said, and added, "No more questions."

The crowd oohed in appreciation of how deftly the meddlesome media had been put in its place. When it became clear that Sun Deer was finished, people began to drift away. He remained behind the mike, immobile, and formidably disapproving. I decided to ask my questions later, when neither the onlookers nor George would be around to hear. My encounter with Father Kennedy had left me a little skittish.

George was hunched over his tape recorder, swearing at it in a vicious whisper. He stabbed at buttons, got nothing, then held the box up over his head to give it a hard shake.

"What's the matter?" I asked.

"Cheap Jap crap. It's all fucked." He jabbed the play button again. A glossy brown tangle of tape began to spew out. George tried to make it stop, frantically working his pudgy fingers over every control possible, but without success. Finally he stopped trying. He set the machine down on the grass and stepped back, a crooked grin skewing the lower half of his face. He paused, as if to admire the still blossoming tape display, then jogged forward, lowered his head and kicked the machine hard. He could have been trying for a field goal. It would explain the steel-toed boots, if he did this kind of thing often. The machine flew a considerable distance, then skimmed a few more yards along on the grass before coming to a stop, a long ribbon of glossy brown marking the trail of useless tape.

So much for George's dispatch. I could no longer avoid mine:

it was time to check in with the paper. Past time, in fact, but I'd been reluctant to hear any bad news, such as Hanover realizing I had nothing to offer and ordering me back to the city at once. I envisioned myself slinking home empty-handed, abject, stooped in failure, and later, following Gallantine's pink finger as it pointed me to the janitor's room, where I belonged, with the jeers from Pearson and the rest echoing in the stairwell behind me.

I called from the doily-covered phone in Grady's living room.

"Where exactly are you?" Hanover asked.

"Fraleton." There was an uncomfortable pause. "You know, out past Hubbensberg?"

Another pause. Was he even listening? Did he have any idea what I was talking about? Maybe he didn't even know who I was. "I'm working on that tree story that Mister Gallantine—"

"Oh. Of course, Bardensky," he said. "Good. Okay. So. What have you got?"

"Oh, it's a real important story," I replied, following the reporter's code to sell even the slimmest of assignments as the Second Coming of newsworthiness. "This thing is big. There's this corporation, from out of town? And it's trying to build a nuclear waste processing plant. Right here in Fraleton! Which is deadly and everything, and — well, so they claim, anyway, of course, because the locals, naturally, are outraged, and they have just begun—"

"What about the miracles? Isn't that why you were sent? Something about a tree with mystical powers, attacking construction crews and what-not. Does it hold up? We haven't had a good weeping Mary statue in this country for years. They always seem to pop up in the oddest places. Eastern Europe. Why is that? Think of it: if you were the Madonna, planning your big re-visit, would you choose Romania?"

"No, sir, of course not. You're absolutely right. And yes, I have definitely been looking into the so-called miracle aspects. It's just that—"

"Noooo, why?" he moaned as if I'd just eaten his lunch. Then, "I said eighteen-point. Eight...teen...point. Are you hard of hearing or can't you count?"

He was talking to someone else about a headline. The discussion went on for some time, shifting at one point into a whine that sounded like a police siren. He must have been waving the arm that held the phone.

"Well?" he suddenly snapped back into the receiver, as if I'd been the one keeping him waiting.

"It's all checking out, Mister Hanover," I heard myself say. "Just as you thought. People are reporting a lot of strange things happening around the tree. Very mysterious. Miracles, who can judge, I don't suppose we need to go that far, but there's a whole history behind it. Native Americans and everything. It's always been considered a sacred spot for some tribes, so right now they're organizing a major protest campaign. It could become something really important. We all know how Wounded Knee started with just a tiny incident."

Actually I had no idea how Wounded Knee started, and remembered with sudden alarm something about a shooting, but I reasoned Hanover wouldn't know or care enough to check. The idea now was to keep throwing them fast and hard so he couldn't come up with a good reason to kill the assignment.

"Who knows how big this thing could get?" I continued. "The crowds have doubled just since I got here. There's definitely something powerful going on. You can almost feel it when you get near the tree. At least that's what people are saying. It practically destroys perfectly good watches, for one thing, and—"

"Watches?" he said in a tone that worried me. I didn't leave him the space to think it through.

"The church, Mister Hanover. Organized religion is totally mystified. I talked to a clergyman, the local priest, and he said himself it was impossible to explain. There's definitely something out of the ordinary going on. I'd say it's got a lot behind it, this story, more like a complex tale of a small town caught in the grip of a larger, who knows, maybe even miracle, something they're definitely struggling to understand. Really."

"Hmm," he said. "Well. I don't know. Hmm. Oh, hell, all right. Something might pan out. Give me three hundred words. No more than three hundred fifty anyway. We might be able to work it into the back of the national section — if nothing else breaks in the meantime. Can you do it tonight?"

Three hundred and fifty words was not much: an oversized blurb, an obituary for a minor celebrity, but it was better than nothing or its nearest equivalent — the religion page.

"Without a doubt, Mister Hanover, sir. You can count on me."

Why do you think they call them newspaper 'stories'?
John Otto Cardeau

FOUR

Sitting in my room at Grady's, with my laptop open on the bed, I contemplated the prospect of my byline over an article in the *City Herald*. It made my chest thump and my fingers tingle: pure energy ran through me like an electrical current. Imagine Earl Brododsky, the first Brododsky ever to get his name in the *Herald* for something other than marriage or death. Better than being in the news, this was actually making the news — or reporting the news, to put it more accurately, but really, what's the difference anymore? I considered it somewhat of a miracle, thanks to the tree or whatever, just to be on the brink of such a privilege. All that was left now was to write the story.

As if it were ever that easy. I hunched lower over the rolltop desk up in my room, staring at the grey screen of my laptop, stupefied by my own unworthiness. Where to begin? And even if I could, where to take it from there?

Maybe I'd just talked my way into enough rope. I envied Danny with his obits, even Melanie and her subversive cooking tips. They knew where they stood: they were moving up — slowly, perhaps, but at least they could see the way ahead and were pointed in the right direction — while I had just climbed way above my comfort level. Now I feared I was about to discover the hard way down.

I told myself nervous energy was still just energy, which meant it could be channeled. The thing was to focus: all that mattered now was the story. Nail that, and I was gold. But just what was it? What really was happening here? It had to be something different, I understood that much: I could hardly call it news if it wasn't new. The paper hadn't sent me all that distance to talk up some skimpy property spat. So who was I to go against the grain? The AP piece had already mentioned mysterious circumstances surrounding a tree with a certain history of them. The base was already set: these were the givens. Nobody could fault me for fleshing that part of the tale out, in a thoroughly professional manner, of course. My newspaper assumed a certain dignified approach which I would obviously need to uphold. Balance, that would be a good idea.

I hurried down to Grady's living room to call Hubbensberg for a quote from whatever P.R. gasbag had been hired to lie for Filco. I didn't want to do it, and felt a tinge of resentment at even having to, but it did seem fair to include a line or two to sum up their side of the dispute.

"Filco-Incorporated-can-I-put-you-on-hold," a woman asked in a minimum wage drone. She didn't bother to make it sound like an option.

"Actually—" I began, but there was a click followed by a syrupy rendering of Vivaldi's Four Seasons. If the interlude was meant to be soothing, it didn't work. By the time the woman came back, I'd been through most of summer and was not looking forward to autumn.

"Filco-Incorporated-how-may-I-direct-your-call," she mouthed with no more enthusiasm than before.

"Hello. May I please speak to your media relations liaison? My name is Earl Brododsky and I'm a reporter. From the *City Herald*?

And I—"

"Just a mo—" she said, cutting herself off with another click. More Vivaldi. So this was how winter sounded to an orchestra. How nice. Could we get a few more violins in here?

At last the music cut off, there was another series of clicks, then the sound of my call going through with a ring tone. It was answered by a taped message that said my call was important, and might be monitored. Now would I please listen to all of the following seven options before choosing one? But I didn't want any of them. I settled unhappily on number seven, to return to the switchboard.

A different taped message came on. My call was still important. This time I had three options, none of which were attractive.

"A human!" I yelled into the mouthpiece. "I want to talk to a living, breathing human!" I could hear my own labored breathing in the space that followed. I was mechanically scolded for not making a proper choice and ordered to listen to the three options again. On it went, like a mechanical taunt. I was a lab rat in a telecommunications maze, bumping into walls at every turn. If this were a psych study there would have been white-coated researchers watching me with stopwatches. How long would it take for that throbbing vein in his temple to explode?

I was given another list of options that at least included the choice of returning again to the switchboard, which I did, only to hear a hiss followed by a click and then a hang-up buzz. I forced myself to inhale a long, slow, calming breath. Reporters do not give up. Even if it was tempting to ponder the route of the Unabomber, a guy who probably had had one too many calls like this. But not me: I was now a bona fide journalist — I would learn to eat this kind of obstacle for breakfast.

I called back. More Vivaldi and more buttons at last got me the direct line to Margaret Lionel who was, according to her message machine, the public relations director in charge of media inquiries. An option on her system led me to the person to contact if she were temporarily unavailable. Only he was temporarily unavailable too. His machine advised anyone needing immediate assistance to try Margaret Lionel. Then it hung up on me too.

I called back and got to the switchboard, which started into another recording of options. I punched every button I could, with vigor.

"If my calls are so fucking important to everyone," I seethed out loud, "why won't you cheap bastards shell out another eight dollars an hour or whatever it would cost to pay some fat-assed gum-cracking tech school dropout to at least pick—"

"Hello?" a female voice interrupted.

I started to hang up — but she was, at least, a person. Maybe she hadn't heard me.

"Yes," I said, in a voice deeper than my own. "I'm a reporter and I'm calling for someone — anyone — who can give me a quick comment over the phone."

"Of course. You want Margaret Lionel. Hold on while—"

"Wait! Don't do it!"

"Excuse me?" she said. I detected a trace of interest in her voice. She may have been enjoying herself for the first time that week.

"Margaret isn't in," I explained quickly. "If you switch me to her number I'll just get lost in the message maze again. I need a person, someone who's in, someone who can talk. I'm working on a deadline here."

"Jill Ferise?" she offered, sounding dubious.

"Yes. Perfect. Jill Ferise. If she's there."

Jill was there, to my immediate relief, and she was polite, even pleasant. She said she wanted to help, but she didn't feel right commenting on trees when her own department, maintenance, was more directly involved in cleaning and such. Perhaps I wanted the number for grounds and gardening?

"No, I don't think that'll be necessary," I said, keeping my voice calm. "Just tell me one thing, if you don't mind. Jill, what do you think about nuclear—"

The phone clicked and I was back to Margaret Lionel's answering machine.

"Listen," I said after the beep. "I'm a reporter. All right? I just need a simple, easy answer to a few—"

A woman's voice interrupted — an actual woman, saying hello and apologizing for the delay and wondering what help she could offer.

"Margaret Lionel, is that you?" I blurted as if she were an old girlfriend at a high school reunion.

"Ms. Lionel isn't in at present," the woman said. "May I ask who's calling?"

"Earl Brododsky. From the *City Herald*?"

"Mmm-hmm."

"I'd just like to ask Ms. Lionel, or if she's not in, anyone in a position of some authority — you for instance — a couple of questions for an article I'm working on about the tree situation in Fraleton."

"I expect you would."

I recognized her voice. "Sorry?"

"Precisely what kind of questions were you hoping to ask?"

It was the switchboard woman. Her interest had taken on a malicious edge.

"What kind of questions? What does that mean? They're questions. Sentences that end in a rising cadence indicating the desire to receive an answer."

"Mmm-hmm."

"So?"

"So."

"I'm still waiting to hear what kind. You just told me 'questions.' There are many kinds."

"What are you talking about?"

"Leading questions. Self-serving questions. Innocent questions. You see where I'm going with this?"

"I just want to ask about the tree controversy in Fraleton. I have to get a comment from someone at Filco for the story I'm writing. You can understand that much, can't you?"

"Ah. A snide question."

"Look. What's your name?"

"A threatening question! Very good. You see my point?"

I groaned. "Please," I said. "I just want to talk to someone about the thing in Fraleton. Can we call a truce and both get on with our days and just maybe get some work done here?"

There was a pause. She sighed. "Okay, the Fraleton thing. I know exactly who you should talk to."

There was a longer pause. I said, to encourage her, "Thank you."

"But I can't connect you."

"Why not?"

"I would have to lean all the way over to the left side of my desk to hit the button. And that isn't easy when you're a fat-assed, gum-cracking. . . what was it?"

"Tech school dropout," I started to say but she hung up too fast. I decided it was not a good time to call back.

Back upstairs in my room, with an oversized mug of Mrs. Grady's Ecuadorian shade-grown coffee, I still had the gumption to do my story, but now it had a nervy, stomach-jumbling edge. My hands were practically shaking. Not only did I lack a Filco quote, but even if I did have something useable, I was in no condition to organize it into a coherent piece. I knew I had to bear down and marshal my thoughts, or accept the fact that my first honest effort for the *Herald* would not get a drop of ink. I told myself to break the task down into its basic components. Starting with the answers to a few key questions.

Why was I here? What was holding me back from simply writing the damn thing up? How did other journalists, guys like Stoopovich, handle writer's block? What was Shirley doing? Who could believe in miracles anymore when they're on the shopping channel? Was Grady a cool old guy or a crank? How did his wife know her Ecuadorian coffee growers were better off than any others? What did they put in those beans that made my legs jitter like pistons? And how would I finish the article if I never got started?

None of it was any help. I couldn't slow down and sort out the thoughts pinging around my skull to come up with an opening line.

Two hours later, with no answers to any of my questions, I decided I needed fresh air. I went back downstairs and out to the back yard. A lecture on nematodes and natural pest management might provide the impetus I needed to get back to the computer and stay there.

There was no sign of Grady in the garden. I knew he wouldn't mind my unlatching the gate separating his vegetable plots from the rest of the yard, so I stepped inside for a stroll. He would have been delighted to know I even took an interest. So much so, I reasoned, he would have encouraged me to sample one of his carrots. I had just nudged the fattest one out of the soil and was wiping it clean when the ground beneath me darkened. That struck me as odd, but not nearly as odd as what struck me next, with force. It felt like a boot. It was, in fact, a running shoe, actually two running shoes, with a person attached, falling onto my head from out of a clear sky.

My last stunned thought as I toppled, seeing the ground rush up to meet my face, was, "Great, now I'm being stomped by God."

The first word I heard, when I came to, lying face down, was, "Drat."

I lifted my head out of some cabbage to suck in a breath that was more of a wheeze. My chest felt tight, my lungs were squeezed. Someone was standing on top of me.

I rolled to the side towards a row of beets to get free, which confounded my attacker's progress enough to make him fall into a sitting position, on my stomach. He made more noises that were hard to decipher, sighing and clucking like a school librarian, as he tried to get upright. I wasn't willing to wait so I jerked my shoulders the way pro wrestlers do to avoid a pin. It didn't launch him off me after all: so much for the physics of wrestling on TV.

"Oh my goodness," he said in a reedy voice. "Just a moment. Please." He scrambled to get up again, forcing out what air I'd managed to eke into my lungs, but at least it gave him the opportunity to plant both feet on the ground. He stood up at last.

Beside each of my ears was a hightop running shoe. The socks inside didn't match. I looked up into a hockey-helmeted middle-aged face with an expression of utter concern clouded by woe. That, or he was about to be sick. He reached down with a hand to help me up, but I wasn't ready to be perpendicular. Instead I stared at what he held in his other hand — a rope connected to three lemon-colored balloons, each as big as a compact car.

His concern turned into something more like despair at my feeble response. He muttered something that sounded like, "Oh dear me." He brought his hand up to hold his head, and only then appeared to realize it was covered by the scuffed white helmet. He fumbled with the chin strap, unsuccessfully, with only one free hand. All the while his I'm-a-bad-puppy eyes blinked rapidly at me through the steel-framed and thick-lensed glasses of a classic nerd. He even had a classic nerd's name, introducing himself as Wilbur. "With a u," he said, drawing the letter in the air. "Wilbur Callahan, and I am so sorry." He certainly looked it. I thought he was going to cry. "Shall I call a doctor? Are you badly hurt? This is all my fault, you know."

I did know, but why dwell. "Nah," I growled magnanimously, propping myself up on an elbow to pick a chunk of cabbage out of my ear. My teeth were still intact. Nothing on my face felt broken. I gingerly moved each of my limbs: all in working order. Except for the sore spots on my head, I seemed to be fine. "I'll live. Don't call the doctor."

He smiled widely enough to show me his gums. Though obviously a reaction to my condition, this display of happiness still seemed inappropriate. I was, after all, recumbent in a pile of cabbage and chicken shit.

"Actually, do call the doctor," I suggested, "and ask him bring a strait jacket for you. What the hell were you doing?"

He giggled. "Oh I'm happy you're not hurt and you're even able to pull my leg," he said. He tied the balloon line to Grady's gate and squeezed his head out of the hockey helmet. His brush cut was misshapen with sweat.

I let him help me up. He made a show of brushing the dirt off my shirt and pants, smearing it deeper into the fabric — now I would smell like chicken shit too. I pushed his hands away. He thought I was being polite, so he kept brushing. I pushed away again, more firmly, but he was like a dog with a bone when it came to brushing my clothes, so we ended up playing a silly back-and-forth slap game for a moment until I blurted, "Will you *please* keep your hands off me you stupid moronic *geek!*"

He stepped back in alarm, then stared down at his high-tops. Perfect. First he'd stomped me in an aerial assault, and now I'd hurt his feelings.

"I am really, really, so terribly. . . sorry," he began again. His entire body drooped under the burden of his guilt. I'd never seen a man so earnest with contrition: the Japanese could learn apologizing from this guy. He opened his mouth but, perhaps because words alone would never do, nothing emerged.

"Listen, forget it," I said. "I'm sorry I was rude. I shouldn't have called you a. . . whatever. It was a spur of the moment thing; I was still a bit rattled. It's not every day that I get. . . what did I just get?"

"I was testing my flight balloons," he said shyly. We both looked up. They floated above our heads like oversized stage-prop full moons.

"You can fly with these things?"

"Oh yes!" he said. "Throughout modern history, balloons have been recognized as one of the purest forms of transportation available. It's physics at its most elemental. And most beautiful, I should say. The wind is an incredible energy source! Visionaries as far back as Da Vinci have longed to tap into its potential for travel. With a little planning and a fairly rudimentary knowledge of meteorology, the wind can take you anywhere. All one need do is get up in it."

"I think you have to stay up in it too."

He smiled in a way that took a few years off his face. I might have misjudged him as middle-aged. "You're right. I'm still working out the optimal dimensions. I was doing fine until I lost a balloon when I got too close to a power line. That made the descent somewhat less gradual than I had expected."

"Luckily you had a mound of human flesh to break your fall."

"Yes. Oh no! You are such a kidder. I was actually planning to come down in the park, but I overshot it. I'm really, really—"

"Forget it, Wilbur."

"Is there something I can do to make it up? You'll send me a cleaner's bill for that shirt, I insist. Or let me buy you a new one. The trousers too. What's your size?"

The idea that Wilbur, in his brown corduroy slacks scrunched at the waist, might select my wardrobe was enough to make me laugh out loud. He laughed a little too, although warily.

"Don't worry about these rags. They're practically a week old." I could get them cleaned, and if not, Tip Top Tailors would have another half-off sale — half off the already doubled price, but who cared now that I had a job. Which reminded me.

"Well," I said, touching a few shirt buttons and shooting my cuffs in the gestures of a man with places to go.

"Before you leave, may I ask you one favor?" Wilbur said. He was looking down again. "I know it's not my place but. . ."

I let him suffer a moment in silence. For a full-on wimp, he had nerve.

"I don't know. But you can ask whatever you want."

"Could you please not mention any of this to my family? They don't understand. They think it's dangerous. I've tried to explain, but, well, it's difficult. If you don't feel it yourself, I don't suppose you'll ever quite get it, will you?"

I believed I'd felt enough of Wilbur and his scheme to know it as well as I needed to. "No problem," I said. "My lips are sealed." Swollen shut, more accurately: I could still taste the cabbage.

Wilbur gripped my hand with a nervous energy that shook my torso. "Thank you, thank you, thank you," he sputtered, his voice cracking with emotion. He slid the helmet back onto his head to free his hands and gather the balloons. He pushed his thick glasses up his nose and offered a final apologetic grin before walking away.

"Say, Wilbur," I called out after him. "Wait. Have you got any comment about that tree?"

But the helmet must have covered his ears. He kept walking without turning around, the balloons drifting over his head like quote spaces in a living cartoon.

I went back up to my room determined to sit at the computer until I'd finished. I probably had enough material to pound out three or four three-hundred-and-fifty-word stories, once things got started. But, perhaps driven by a newcomer's overreaching sense of duty, I still wanted more. I went back down to Grady's living room phone to track down the injured construction workers.

After a familiar series of re-routing escapades through various departments at Hubbensberg General Hospital, I finally got through to the injured man's room — except that it was occupied by a woman recovering from a liver operation. She was eager all the same to talk to the press: apparently things were not going well with her recovery.

"Awfully sorry to hear that," I said, interrupting a litany of complaints. "Maybe you could have a friend bring sandwiches. But right now, would you by any chance know where the patient who had the room before you might have gone?"

She snorted in indignation before calling me a certain body part and slamming down the phone. I couldn't blame her: if I were in the hospital and hurting, I probably wouldn't put up with me either.

Eventually I did reach the construction worker, after getting his home number from the company by pretending to be a cousin. He spelled out his name, Blaine Geary, through the haze of the five or six beers he mentioned drinking "to keep the painkillers honest."

Geary swore the tree was haunted. "It wouldn't let me near it. Frickin' incredible. I tried. I mean, I had the contract, I was game, but what are you going to do?"

"What happened?"

"I've been working a chainsaw for, like, eighteen years, right?" he said. "So excuse me but I know a little bit about what I'm doing. I used to log every summer out on Bailey's Point, before they turned it into a goddamn parking lot. But I never had a saw act up like this. I swear, it started bucking like a hungry whore. Every time I brought it near the trunk, it got all snakey on me. Almost like it was in someone else's control. Moving and swaying and doing all kinds of shit. Like with magnets, you know? When you try to bring the two of them together but you just can't get them to touch? Finally I said, to hell with this, I'm going to cut the fucker down no matter if it kills me. Excuse my language, but that is what I said. Pretty much. And that's when I slammed my wrist so hard I sprained it."

"Sprained?"

"Yeah. Pretty bad too." There was a gulping sound.

"I thought your arm was broken."

"So did I, at first, but then they did X-rays."

"Everybody thinks you got a broken arm. You know that don't you?"

"Well it sure felt broken."

"And that you were in the hospital for it."

"I *was* in the hospital for it. That's where they got the X-ray apparatus." He negotiated the last word with drunken precision.

"Blaine?"

"Not overnight, if that's what you mean."

"What time did all this happen anyway? Was it in the afternoon?"

"Yeah, around three, three thirty. Why?"

"Kind of close to quitting time."

"Yeah. I guess."

"Did you happen to have a beer or anything before you started working on the tree?"

"Hey, I can handle my alcohol."

"I'm sure of that, no doubt. But how many did you have? Do you remember?"

"Two. I don't know. Maybe three. No more than usual."

"You can handle that much no problem."

"Fuckin' A."

Fuckin' AA, I thought. "Listen, Blaine. Do me a favor? If anyone else asks, like a reporter? Don't mention the beer. They might not understand."

"Yeah, you're probably right."

"And about that sprain? You might just as well stick with a broken arm. It's easier to explain, medically speaking."

"It does feel pretty bad."

"What happened with the other construction company anyway? Did they really have some kind of weird electrical problems?"

"Beats me. I was on my way to the hospital."

Back in my room I opened the laptop lid yet again, with even less anticipation but perhaps more determination. This time I would not fail. I would earn my feed for real. No excuses now. Crank up the word machine. Earl Brododsky is in the building. Writing it up. Getting it down. Speaking truth to power. I put my fingers to the keys, properly lined everything up, then lifted them ever so slightly to begin. . . but nothing came to me. The cursor blinked like a summons. What was my opening? The first sentence was everything, the only chance I might get to hook the average reader, but what was it?

Herman Melville must have had moments like this: look how many words it took him to cover a story about a cranky guy and a whale. Whereas in my case I had severe space restrictions. And yet there were facts and rumors, background, science, religion, historical context, personalities, an overview — far too much going on to capture in some tiny block of text on a single page of newsprint. It was impossible. I willed myself to start anyway, to push the boat away from the dock to see where it went. All I lacked was the first simple string of words to open the floodgate. Yet still I came up with nothing.

Then I realized my problem. I needed a real working atmosphere. I was, after all, a city boy: I thrived on commotion. To function, I needed to recreate the bustle of the newsroom, where everyone was on deadline and we all fed on the collective angst. I went back down to the living room carrying my laptop in two hands with the lid still open.

The TV was tuned to a documentary on power lines which may or may not cause cancer. Either way it looked sad. One shot after another of hospital beds with hairless kids, intercut with dark clouds and the power lines, all backed by cello solos from some funeral compilation CD. I switched to an afternoon talk show with a studio audience leaping from their seats to shout unsupportive remarks at a mixed-aged couple who sat nodding and smiling before giving back just as good as they got.

That was more like it: conflict. It meant I could write. "Residents of this small town east of Hubbensberg have long believed..." I began, and the rest poured out like blood from an Irish boxer.

> FRALETON – Residents in this small town east of Hubbensberg have long believed their famous "Miracle Tree" has mysterious powers. Now Blaine Geary has the crushed arm to prove it.
>
> "It was amazing," Geary explained after failing in an attempt to remove the majestic specimen for a controversial development project. "I tried everything, but the tree wouldn't let me near it."
>
> Geary, a self-employed contractor with decades of experience falling trees, described the event as "bizarre." He said his chainsaw "bucked like a hungry horse" whenever he brought it near the tree.

The volatile gyrations thrust him against the trunk, leading to injuries requiring hospital care. He is now in stable condition and recovering at home.

"I know how to cut down a tree," Geary explained. "But this was different. It was almost like my saw was being controlled by someone else — someone or some thing."

A second construction team was also unable to complete the routine task. Witnesses have reported the crew being forced back from the tree by strange electrical emissions which also caused odd showers of sparks.

Plans to remove the tree have been temporarily halted. This has given the citizens of Fraleton time to rally around their treasured vegetation.

Supporters maintain its powers run deeper than a simple small town rumor. They attribute little understood yet powerful forces to the tree, including the ability to make watches and electrical equipment in its presence go awry.

Most significantly, townspeople insist, the Miracle Tree can make wishes come true.

Standing yesterday underneath the towering plant, a Fraleton senior with her head bowed and hands pressed together in prayer seemed to crystallize the aspirations of those who turn to the tree for assistance in trying times. Onlookers watched the woman from a respectful distance as she murmured her request in a voice as gentle as the breezes stirring the sun-dappled leaves.

Throughout its history, this remarkable sycamore has been the focus of many such expressions of hope. Students are said to stop here on their way to important exams. Business people precede the signing of major contracts with a joint visit to the tree. Patients have sought cures, and young lovers each other under its sprawling branches.

Fraleton residents explain that if a seeker is sincere, and the request is worthy, it will indeed come true.

How this visually spectacular specimen developed such an aura of wish fulfillment is yet another of its mysteries. Native Americans are said to have revered and protected the tree for generations.

Charismatic Indian activist Sun Deer is leading the campaign among his people to save the Miracle Tree. He speaks nobly of its role in "nurturing all pure-hearted seekers, from time immemorial, to this day, in the quest for fulfillment."

Now, however, that day may be about to end.

The Miracle Tree's supposed powers may not be enough to protect it from modern development. The tree stands in the way of an outside corporation's plans to construct a nuclear waste facility on the site.

Outraged at the idea of their icon of sincere yearning being replaced by a dangerous stockpile of plutonium, Fraleton residents say they intend to stop the project. Yet they admit they lack the resources to challenge a corporation as powerful as the secretive Filco Incorporated.

Officials at Filco headquarters in Hubbensberg did not reply to repeated requests for comment.

That was it. I'd nailed it. The tree, the town, the challenge, all in a little over five hundred words. It was more than Hanover had ordered, which worried me, but not too much. They could always shorten it, just a little. But even Hanover ought to recognize a sharp piece of insightful reporting, so he might as easily decide to run the whole thing.

I read it back again, and felt even more encouraged. I'd managed not only to keep the miracle angle alive, I may have even have improved it. The original AP piece had made the whole thing sound like a joke on the local hayseeds, but I'd been able to nudge it back where it belonged, into the territory of a genuine mystery, if not an outright wonder, with Native overtones as a bonus.

Without going out on a limb myself, of course: I never called it magic, I simply reported what other people had said — with a few minor adjustments, for clarity and all. There's no harm in offering a little help with the quotes to shape them into what people really meant to say. The facts were all there, and that's what counts in serious journalism.

I read it over once more, still liked it, then connected my laptop to Grady's phone jack. Slurpy static led to a beep signaling a successful connection. I emailed the story to Hanover, copying it to the national editor as backup in case Hanover had been run over by a truck or something. I wondered if it might even reach the desk of Harmon Gallantine himself. Did he ever pre-check copy or did he wait until everything ran to yell at the editor responsible? I pictured him reading my email while nodding those ruddy cheeks, maybe even smiling, then congratulating himself on having had the foresight to spot an uncommon talent when the rest of the world saw nothing of the kind.

I disconnected the modem and sat unmoving in the delicious silence that followed. Then I bounded from the sofa in an actual jump for joy. I shadow-boxed the lamp stand, making an Ali shuffle of pure giddy energy. I was brimful of it and wanted to share, even if only over the phone. I called Shirley.

She wasn't home. That was strange, since it wasn't a work night. I tried her bar, the Rising Expectation. I knew I wasn't supposed to call her there, but under the circumstances I thought I could get away with it. No luck, though: Shirley wasn't there either.

"Oh. Do you know where she is?" I tried.

"Is this Barry?" the woman asked.

"Who's Barry?"

There was a pause. "I don't know where she is," she said. "I'm sorry."

I hung up, but immediately wished I'd stayed on to ask a few more questions. You're sorry? Oh really? For what? I tried not to read anything more into the word than the fact that Shirley wasn't available to take my call. I could easily put Barry out my mind. It was a stupid name anyway.

Later that evening the downstairs area at Grady's was crowded. George was joining us for dinner. So was Sun Deer, who, it turned out, was staying at the inn as well. They sat together on the living room sofa, absorbed in a hockey game on TV.

"Slice the fucker up like a spring ham!" blurted George, but he covered it up by lowering his head and murmuring "Shit. . . I mean, 'scuse me," in the general direction of Mrs. Grady. She grinned and went on cooking. Grady was busy almost to the point of distraction, ostentatiously helping her choose spices or lecturing us on the perils of salt as he set the table.

They both seemed to lose a little of their gentle air of leisure amid the cooking rush, but a little stress may have helped to enhance their results. The meal was first-rate: swordfish steaks topped with roasted garlic and soy-ginger sauce along with acorn squash that was grown, Grady would have us know, in the usual pile of animal droppings not twenty paces from where we sat. Dessert was another achievement. Mr. and Mrs. Grady walked in side by side bearing a homemade rhubarb pie and a jar of their own four-berry jam. When we'd all been served our slices, and were waiting for Mrs. Grady to sit down before taking the first bite, Sun Deer stood and placed his hand on his heart, then waited until we all fell silent.

"I wonder, friends, if I can take just a brief moment from your meal to ask you to join me in offering a word of gratitude." He didn't bother with the I-Have-a-Dream cadence. Murmurs of assent went all around. "We offer our thanks to the Great Creator, to the spirit in each of us, and to the daily miracle which is the ebb and flow of all precious life. We offer thanks for this bounty of the land, the fish, the potatoes, the excellent squash, and especially the pie, and indeed for all the food we harvest and consume with respect and reverence in the timeless cycle of life taking and replenishing life."

Grady was smiling as proudly as if the Great Creator line had referred to him personally. His wife seemed bemused, but not entirely convinced. Sun Deer went on.

"Moreover, we offer our gratitude to Mrs. Grady, Evylyn, the keeper of the hearth, for putting it all together with efficiency, with grace, and above all, with love."

Everyone applauded. Mrs. Grady blushed and reached for her husband's hand. Even George Templington softened enough to smile and murmur, "Awwwwww."

Just before midnight I called Shirley again.

She still wasn't home. Shirley was not the type to stay out late — unless my absence had inspired a lifestyle change. Maybe a change of heart too, stunning as that would be. Although they say a breakup almost never comes as a surprise, at least when you look back: there are always clues. Could the facts that we argued a lot and had sex a little be two big ones?

Despite the evidence, I doubted it. Shirley and I knew what we were getting in the relationship with each other. We'd been together since we took the same pre-calculus class in high school. To me this meant our union had a strong mathematical foundation, even if it remained a puzzle to the rest of the school. If Shirley represented the top of the popularity chart, I would have been written in at the bottom, with an arrow explaining the unseen distance between us as if I were Guam or some other territory that had to be included even though it was a nuisance.

They didn't know that her interest in me began the day she saw, in the local free weekly, a historic picture of my grandfather taken in Nicaragua when he was with Augusto Sandino, spiritual father of the Sandinistas. Shirley was a big fan. She stopped me after class the same day and just like that, we started helping each other with our math homework. We were a team: she would work out some confounding integral while I helped with tea or bagels or neck massages. The massages were mostly just that, real massages, but one time I ended up crawling under the desk in a dim corner of the library. She was wearing black tights but not for long. She made a pretense of pushing me away but I explained in a whisper that I'd read how the stimulating effects of oral sex could reach directly to the brain to help in problem-solving. She called me a liar and more, but I didn't care. I was seventeen and damn glad to be there.

Later we developed a kind of intimacy and trust that came automatically. We became so much a part of each other's lives it was almost self-interest to grant some space. We both recognized that one plus one equaled three: me, her, us. We were as solid as the Pythagorean theorem. Ups and downs in the relationship come as no surprise. I didn't even get along with myself half the time, so it was only normal to expect snags. The core, our relationship, was intact. What's more, my stock was almost certainly about to rise once the article came out and I was elevated to the ranks of the bylined correspondents of the world.

Some bond-jockey named Barry is going to change that? Bah. That night I went to sleep without a worry.

The pure and simple truth is rarely pure and never simple.

Oscar Wilde

FIVE

I woke up in the dark in the fetal position. Even in sleep I had been bending my spine to try to counter the effect of the bed's evil infrastructure. It didn't work: my skeleton ached from the abuse.

Noise from the front porch must have woken me. The random sounds of people coming and going filtered into my open window, but they were hard to make out. At one point a man's voice said something in a gruffly questioning tone. Grady answered, but his mumbling diction was hard to make out under the best conditions. I thought I heard him insist, "I'm all bull and you have to race the blacks." It took me a moment to realize he said he was all full and the person had to face the facts.

Later, when I made it downstairs, Mrs. Grady was alone at the kitchen table, smiling to herself as if the late-night fuss outside had had nothing to do with her house. She looked up from a bowl of waffle batter to bid me a good morning. From her apron pocket she produced a note.

"He called twice," she said. "I didn't tell him you were still asleep or I'm sure he would have tried to make me wake you. He was rather abrupt."

The message was from Gallantine. I was to call "immediately upon receiving this message if not sooner." The grandfather clock in the living room read nine twenty. Gallantine never arrived at the paper before ten. It seemed unlikely for His Eminence to go in early just to fire a scrub, so maybe it was something worse. A zillion dollar lawsuit from the legal hyenas at Filco, for example.

It would be against the paper, of course, but they might have named me as well. I had no assets to protect, my financial position being perpetually delayed bankruptcy, but the scandal would be enough to drive me out of the profession: no paper would hire a proven economic disaster. I pictured myself in the unemployment line or some hungover re-training seminar, drinking Styrofoam cup coffee with the captain of the Exxon Valdez.

I heard the operator ask Betsy whether she would accept my collect call.

"From Earl Brododsky?" she replied. "Any time."

So she knew who I was. That could be either good or very bad. "Um, I have a message to call Mister Gallantine?" I began.

"Of course. How are you, dear?" Betsy answered. Now I was a dear?

"I'm fine, just great," I said, hoping to convince myself with my own words.

"I'll put you right through. He's been waiting."

"Yes, I'm sor—"

"Earl!" Gallantine's voice boomed out loud enough to startle me. I'd gone from "sport" to my first name.

"Mister Gallantine?" I ventured.

"Bang-up job, young man. First rate. I knew I was doing the right thing when I hired you."

"You did?"

"Keep it up. We want more. Give us whatever you're working on. But make it longer this time."

"Longer? Wow. Okay. How many words?"

"Don't worry about the length. We'll make it fit. That was a damn fine piece of work you filed last night. You're a credit to this newspaper. And to your people."

I tried to imagine any one of the people I knew not being surprised by that sentence. He hung up without saying good-bye.

I put the phone down in a stupor. It was almost too good to be true. Immediately I suspected it couldn't be. He hadn't mentioned the topic of the article. Maybe he had my name confused with someone else's brilliant work. I called the newspaper back, but the switchboard was busy, for three calls in a row. That was strange for a publication with nearly a million weekday customers to consider, many of whom called to complain about the smallest things. Subscribers with their morning editions lying in puddles would be all the more vexed. On the fourth try I got through, then transferred to the obit desk.

"The tree man speaks!" Danny said. "Ride that pony, cowboy, aaaaall the way home. You are *on*, buddy."

"No."

"People have been calling in since the early edition. They moved your story up to the front page for the two-star. It's been manic. That tree is gold. Can you bring me a leaf? Better yet, make it a box of them. I know a place we can get them laminated and labeled. Real professional job. They'll look slick. Packaging is product, you understand."

"I don't think it's a good idea to strip the tree right now, do you?"

"Yeah, I suppose you're right. Lucky bastard. Wish I could be there. The obits are starting to drag me down, man. Celebs just aren't dying off the way they used to; they're getting all the best care. I've had, like, nothing, for a week and a half — some soap opera star from the '50s I'd never even heard of. Big deal."

"Hang in there," I said, seeing George walk through the front door wearing headphones that made him look like a giant bloated version of Mickey Mouse. "Things will pick up. I have to run."

George hit the stop button on a new recorder dangling at his hip. "Earl," he said briskly, "we're on. The thing is taking off. As in, rocket launch. It's gone from zero to red-hot in no time. And it's just beginning. There's no telling — this could become the O.J. trial of the botanical world."

"No," I said, this time with the notion that I was about to wake up, find myself still in bed and realize the last twenty minutes had been a dream.

"People are driving here from all over just to see your damn tree."

"No."

"I was an hour out of town when I noticed the road getting busier in the other direction. It's like the Exodus or the Okies leaving the Dust Bowl or something. Only I guess they're all coming instead of going."

"That's a pilgrimage," I said.

"Right. They're massing around the tree right now."

"No."

He pressed a button and pointed to his headphones while speaking along with the playback: *It's a tremendous sensation. You can feel the energy coming right off the branches and flowing into your skin. I told my wife, that's Jeanette here, I says, Jeanie-girl, I haven't felt this excited since THACKA-THACKA-THACKA—*

"Aw fuck me, he gets screwed by a helicopter. But I can still use the first part."

"But George, how? Why? I don't get it."

He shook his head. "You can never know for sure. Our station would have picked up your piece on the wire late last night. Probably went national the same way. And now people are suddenly into it because. . . people are suddenly into it. These things take on a life of their own. It's like a growth, or a cancer, you can never predict it. It's been the only topic on our call-in lines since the Early Birder at five thirty. We just bumped the entire hour of "Ask Doctor Digby" right off the schedule. We're going blanket coverage. It's getting a massive reaction, calls like you wouldn't believe."

I felt dizzy. The synapses in my brain seemed to be firing all at once but none on their normal circuits. I was excited to the point of being stupid, but also scared: if the story really was spreading that quickly, somebody would get tangled up in it before long. And it would probably be me.

"What are people saying?"

"It's a miracle, baby."

"No. I didn't write that. Not exactly."

George snorted for a laugh, then saw I hadn't meant it as a joke. He lifted his wide shoulders.

"Whatever." He tapped his headphones and turned to go.

I grabbed his elbow. "Wait, George, help me. What am I supposed to do now?"

He shrugged again. "Beast gets hungry, you gotta feed the beast." He gestured to his tape recorder. "I need to cut some more sound. Now they're asking for hourlies. You believe that? Hourlies."

"No," was all I could say but George wasn't listening. He pulled his heavy body along the handrail up the stairs to his room.

I needed Shirley. She would understand, she would help me — nobody was better at perspective. I called her at home but she wasn't in. Again. Even at this time of the morning. Unless she'd come home late and then left early. Or she was still lying in some Barry's swanky apartment, sipping champagne in bed while he tried to impress her with an omelet.

I didn't have time to think it through. I had work to do. It was enough to tell myself Shirley wasn't the type to fool around on the sly. Honesty was like a fetish for her. If she were going to have an affair, she'd let me know. And besides — Barry? It was the name of a fruit.

Or was that a shrub? Either way. I gulped down one of Mrs. Grady's waffles, slid another without syrup into my jacket pocket and hurried off to the park.

I heard it before I saw it, a low metallic hum. It turned into a buzz which grew in volume the closer I got. I imagined walking towards the massive beehive of a bad sci-fi film. In front of the Old General Store the sound began to shift from a drone into individual voices with distinct shouts and squeals.

I saw the park and stopped. It was crawling. The people were teeming in numbers so large I couldn't guess how to count them. It was as if a huge carnival had set up in the night, then removed the rides and booths to leave only the customers behind. The word "multitudes" came to me. If they had been locusts, Fraleton could have qualified as a disaster site.

The parking lot told some of the story. People arriving during the night had packed in wherever they could. Mini-vans, sport utility vehicles, compact cars and pickup trucks, all wedged into random blotches of colored metal. The only sense of order came from the RV owners who had turned a far corner of the lawn beside the river into their own trailer park. Side-mounted awnings shaded people in lawn chairs while they watched children squeal and splash in inflatable pools. The rest of the site by comparison looked like a refuge camp.

I pushed my way in through the chaos. The crowd was thickest near the tree, some circling it in a Mecca-like trudge. Many of the slow walkers had the glassy-eyed stare of believers, or groupies. As if drawn by some gravitational force, they seemed compelled to travel towards but never quite to the tree, spinning instead in perpetual orbit around it. In every direction I could see people bowing and murmuring with their palms together, much as Agnes Weatherby had been doing the day before. Were they copying her posture from my article? And if so, was I supposed to feel proud or guilty?

Whenever I stopped, people streamed past me to get closer to the tree, some eyeing their watches as carefully as Geiger counters.

They squealed in pleasure if the readings seemed off. I'd mentioned that phenomenon in my story without giving it much thought: here people were using it as an acid test.

"I told you!" a pudgy man in overalls called to his wife, his face shifting from amazement to joy and then admonishment. "Look at that. Stopped cold! And you thought it was all crap."

His wife glanced down at the watch thrust under her nose and turned away.

I needed distance, some way to get a big picture look at the thing, but whenever I stopped the human tide nudged me back towards the tree. It was beginning to bug me, the relentless bumping with hardly a word of apology. I was about to say as much, but I knew I couldn't. Anger would never work on a crowd this big — and besides, why were they here in the first place? This was my story, which meant it was my crowd: I had summoned it into being. I had called these rootless seekers away from communing with the "Wheel of Fortune" or whatever happened to be on TV. Something was happening here, something important, that the world wanted to know about, and I was the one to tell them. An event, even a tree falling in the forest, doesn't really happen until someone hears about it, preferably from an expert with sharp analytical skills and a keen outlook for the public interest. I wasn't entirely confident in my own ability to pull it off, but I felt I might grow into the role of the walking, talking conduit to history. Go pro or go home, I told myself. I could do this: Stoopovich would have nothing on me.

I pulled my notebook out of my back pocket, uncapped my pen, and began looking for people to interview to help me get a handle on the scene before it lurched completely out of control. I wriggled through the human flow until I came to an open patch of grass. This would give me room to size up my targets.

It seemed sensible to start with an easy example, so I chose someone even younger than I was. I nodded to get the attention of a teenage girl with a nose ring and crimson-dyed hair. She was standing on her tiptoes for a better view of the distant tree. I gestured to my notebook, and when she didn't balk, walked over to her.

"So," I said, flipping to an open page. "Tell me, what do you think of all this?"

"Ho-lee! Are you a real reporter?" she asked. Her voice had a Courtney Love hoarseness that seemed affected.

I had to think for a moment before answering, "Absolutely."

She turned to face me square, lifting a fallen spike of hair like a stray flame off her forehead. She seemed to grow older instantly by adopting a serious, furrowed-brow expression. Then she cleared her throat and settled her shoulders. It struck me as odd behavior, even for a teenage girl, until I realized what was happening: she was shifting into TV mode. It was a form of modern yoga, this preparing oneself for the camera. She must have assumed there was a distant lens somewhere zooming in on her. Or maybe she didn't care: this was now the way you were supposed to present yourself for any media moment. You needed to look the part to be believed — only then could you display your capacity for concentration and deep reflection, and affect the distant gaze of one able to snap out pronunciamentos. But just as quickly she let it all drop with a shake of her arms, and two or three rapid stretches of her jaw from side to side.

"Okay okay, tell me the question again?" she said hurriedly, as if she were an actress who had finally located her motivation.

"I just asked what you think of all this."

"It's a. . . a. . . um. . . shit! Okay just a sec, let me start again. Okay. Ready? Okay." She laughed like someone deranged before composing herself with a slap, then went on. "I think it's a wonderful thing in our present era to find people who can still believe in and recognize the true value of—"

Suddenly her motor seized up. The veins in her neck bulged. She swallowed once, hard. Her stricken face suggested the realization that her one chance at fame had just come and gone. Still she managed to gather herself for a brave finish. "Something that, after all is said and done, is not some big, expensive techno-thingy put out by some mega-corporation, but just an honest-to-god regular tree and all. Y'know?"

She glanced at me from the corners of her eyes. What network had she been listening to? The Disney Channel perhaps. That wasn't a sound bite, it was a gnaw.

"Okay okay," she said, waving her hands frantically in front of her face to wipe the statement from memory. "Sorry. I'm not usually this hyper. I'm like, whoa. Let me do another one. I can do it better, I swear."

"I think we got everything we need. Thanks for your time." I closed the notebook and turned to go.

"The kids of today. . ." I heard her call out behind me. "Wait! Where are you going? The youth of today need a symbol of. . . a leadership that, or could be, of. . . leaders who. . . or those who could be the ones that lead. . . shit!"

I walked faster, but felt a tug on my sleeve. She may not have been articulate but no one would beat her on determination. I spun around with a glare that I hoped would daunt her, only to see instead a man unwisely displaying his physique in a purple muscle shirt. He had the heavy florid face and worn leonine expression of a barroom philosopher. He tapped one of his sagging breasts.

"I can give you whatever quote you need, young man," he said in a deep voice, rich with pulpit mysteries. "My name is Tom Griendly, that's a friend with a g and an l-y, no e. Tell me, what angle are you working here?"

I hadn't considered it. Did I have an angle? Did everybody else but me? "Hmm," was all I could produce. To cover up, I accompanied it with some sagacious head-nodding.

"All right, you're still fishing. I appreciate that, not a problem. This will work no matter where you take it. Check it out. The Miracle Tree has been discovered at the very time we need it most. Now if only our cynical and self-serving politicians could stop worrying so much about their. . . excuse me? Aren't you writing this down?"

I thought my closed notebook would be enough to answer that question. He went on all the same.

"Some may ask of the Miracle Tree for personal gain, even untold riches, but I say. . . look, really, why aren't you writing this down? This is gold, baby."

"I really should. . . ah," I began, unable to complete the sentence. Suggest a therapist, I wanted to say. Instead I smiled, or tried to, and shrugged as I walked away. Interviewing was never like this for school assignments. We asked and answered each other's questions like people do every day, all over the planet, using normal patterns of human communication. But this was different: these people had yet to show they belonged on our planet. Or maybe this was typical of a crowd caught up in a miracle frenzy. I'd seen pictures of Lourdes, though. Mystery and salvation didn't automatically lead to abandon. They lined up. Although to be fair, the folks making the trip to Lourdes knew what to expect. Here, perhaps, everything was too new and unknown for anything like normal behavior or social decorum. There were no known limits yet, so a certain excitability was understandable. Replace nuggets with fulfilled wishes and you had the Fraleton version of the gold rush coming to town.

I wondered if I might learn from other reporters working the horde. The TV people were the easiest to spot because their careers depended on it. They had expensive clothes and perfect teeth and the flawless features of a successful line of clones. The print reporters by comparison looked like a downtrodden race who could have scampered up from underground caverns. Apparently without company perks that ran to gym memberships and personal trainers, they dressed with an almost defiant slovenliness.

Sometimes the hunting paths of the tribes crossed, and then it was something to stand back and watch as the two journalistic institutions clashed over a single interview subject. In one case the prey was a woman in a canary-colored muu-muu. She collapsed, although slowly, to her knees, from where she began trembling violently in shimmies that moved from her orange permed hair down to her running shoes, but not so forcefully that she couldn't lift a palm to the sky to testify.

A chunky print reporter in Dockers noticed the scene and rushed over. He was joined almost at once by a svelte TV woman in a pin-striped suit. They bent down on either side to address the woman like willing acolytes, beginning a contest to see who could ask the most questions in the shortest amount of time.

"Where are you from?" fired the TV woman. "Why are you here?"

The print guy sneered, perhaps at her lack of overview, and leaned in closer.

"Readers would like to know what this is all about," he tried. "Can I have your name and occupation?"

"How has the Miracle Tree affected your life?" countered the TV woman.

"Your thoughts on what may be one of the last, great, unexplained mysteries of the twentieth century," edged the print man.

"Or that of your loved ones, including any ailing relatives?"

"Can you tell us an episode that struck you as particularly interesting or remarkable once you arrived?"

"What did you feel?"

"Who did you see?"

"When did you realize you were in the presence of a force so powerful it could change your world view?"

"Where will all this lead?"

"Why is it important for you to be here right now?"

The witness, hand still raised but now at a limp angle, had stopped shaking to watch her inquisitors, swiveling her head at each verbal volley like a spectator at a tennis match. Sensing a choice about to be made, they rushed the net, doubling and tripling their questions.

"What exactly does the Miracle Tree mean to you, in your own words?" tried the print man, kneeling for a more intimate approach that must have stained the knees of his khakis. "What have you heard about the tree so far, and how do you feel about what you heard, now that you've seen it? Can you tell us what's going through your mind?"

The TV woman smoothed her skirt to squat, carefully, wary of unseen camera angles. "Have you personally experienced any miracles or hints of miracles after your moment with the tree? What is a miracle after all in this age of supercomputers and rocket probes to Mars? If Jesus Himself came back today, would you or any of your—"

"*Jay-zus*, praise the Lord the holy redeemer ever*last*ing!" the woman bellowed, startling them both into silence. She tilted her face to stare in earnest at the empty sky as if Jay-zus himself might just then be orbiting by.

Instead of the deity it was a helicopter, descending with a hacking tumult that momentarily drew the crowd's attention away from the tree. A TV cameraman leaned out the open doorway for the perfect shot of the throng. But people didn't appreciate the aerial intrusion, especially those who had, a moment earlier, been wearing hats. First one, then several more, and then scores of hands went up with only the middle fingers raised, surely ruining the shot for any respectable network news show.

The helicopter lifted and spun and flew away, inspiring a round of applause and cheers for the impromptu accomplishment. Two cameramen from rival TV stations stopped body-checking each other to exchange a high-five. They followed it by pivoting to stand, back to back, like duelists holding Beta-cams instead of pistols.

Just beyond the arm's reach of one stood an attractive blonde readying herself for a live report. Her topped-up hairstyle had miraculously suffered no damage from the helicopter's wash. Behind the lens her partner switched on a light. In the brilliant glare her expression shifted to the smile of a patient kindergarten teacher. She began speaking in a truncated rhythm as if the listeners were non-native English speakers. "And that (pause) may be one reason (longer pause) why they're here. No. Again-in-three. Three. Two. One. And that (pause) may be the biggest reason (longer pause) they're here. For News-on-the-Go, I'm Kimberly Price. Jerome?"

Her cameraman held up the okay sign with his free hand, then switched the floodlight off. The other cameraman flicked his light on, illuminating a handsome male model type whose smile emerged at the same time. He kept the genial expression going as he read off a TelePrompTer mounted below the lens. His gosh-and-golly delivery sounded natural, rather than something read from a script, although the contrived attempt at charm was blatant. "Thanks, Gene," he started. "Fraleton is a small and some might say sleepy town. A place where families know each other, folks get along, and no one locks their doors at night. But today, it is pandemonium. Hundreds, if not thousands, of people are pouring in here every hour from all over the country. . . for this. They're calling it. . . the Miracle Tree."

His face drooped. The cameraman rolled his head on his neck and checked his watch. The reporter's lips counted off a silent one-two-three-four-five-six-seven. The gleaming smile reappeared.

"This tree has been the focal point of Fraleton's spiritual life for generations. Native Americans have long considered it sacred. Biologists will tell you it's a sycamore. But to everyone else, it's known simply as. . . the Miracle Tree. Why miracle? Heh heh heh. Well, the good people of Fraleton will tell you. . . if you have a wish. . . and if you really mean it. . . it will come true. Don't believe it? Now that's fine, of course. That's your prerogative. But if you're going to step on the toes of Mother Nature. . . be prepared to get just a little bit squished. That may be exactly what happened here yesterday when a development company sent a construction crew to cut down the Miracle Tree. Oh, don't worry — they didn't succeed. In fact, a veteran lumberjack hired to do the job, using a fully operational and quite powerful chainsaw, came out of the attempt not only having failed, but with his right arm broken in two places. So, for now, the Miracle Tree stands. Proud. Tall. Secure. More visitors continue to come here in droves for what they believe could be their last chance to have their fondest, deepest and most heartfelt desires turned miraculously into reality. The questions is: for how long? The mayor of Fraleton says the construction project will go ahead. . . as planned. For Spotwatch News, I'm Dirk Mallory."

He kept nodding with a knowing grin at the camera. "Yes, that's right," he said after a moment. "I'm informed that Native American activists are organizing what could be a *significant* mass protest." Then: "Ha ha ha. Let's hope you get it, too, Bill. Ha ha ha. Now back to you, Sarah." His smile was tucked away in Props before the floodlight element stopped glowing.

I wove determinedly through the crowds to get closer to the tree. Morning Mist and Agnes, looking besieged, were standing with their backs to the trunk. They pleaded with people to back up, to stop hurting the tree, but hands kept raking at the bark, one even ripping off a chunk for a souvenir that several other hands instantly tried to grab. Danny may have been onto something with his shrink-wrapped leaf plan. Luckily the lowest branches were high enough to be above greedy fingers, but how long before people thought of ladders?

I pitied Morning Mist, and imagined in his clenched jaw I could see the inward dilemma he must have been suffering over the whole issue of nonviolence. He and Agnes employed a pantomime of gestures. Dismay (palms on temples), incredulity (outstretched arms), outrage (shaking fists). None worked: the two were no more effective than evangelists in a Saturday night tavern. They could not hope to convince the individual to step back when the group mentality urged everyone forward. Tear gas, I thought, that might have broken the collective spell, or a pack of snarling dogs.

"If you please!" Agnes railed in a wavering voice swallowed by incoherent shouts from the crowd.

Morning Mist was handed a wooden stake. For one uneasy

moment I thought he might jab the pointed end towards someone's heart as a ghastly example of his resolve. Instead he stuck it into the ground and wrapped a rope around the top to begin marking a safety zone around the tree. Before he could straighten up, though, the stake was trampled. "Ouch!" he moaned in an aggrieved whine while flicking his fingers. "That really hurts, you know."

A loudspeaker crackled, hummed and issued an electronic squelch that continued for several excruciating seconds.

"Hello," came the voice of Sun Deer in the silence that followed. He spoke in a deliberately calming tone. Heads turned to find him. He was standing a short distance from the tree, holding the microphone down at his side with his head bowed, as if he might not speak again unless people behaved.

A pulse of excitement passed through the crowd as more people spotted him and pointed for others to look as well. Some could be heard asking who he was in the reverent whispers reserved for celebrity sightings.

"I think he was married to Jane Fonda, or maybe it was Elizabeth Taylor."

"Wasn't he in *Dances With Wolves*?"

"It's that Indian guy with the shows on public TV."

"I said: Hello," Sun Deer continued, this time sternly. "And stop this shoving nonsense at once. Have you come here, to this sacred site, with no manners at all?"

The crowd, for the first time, slackened. The constant push from the back towards the tree stopped. Those around me, freed from the struggle to stay upright, seemed to share a sense of relief.

"Now then. I will say it one. . . more. . . time. Hel-lo."

"Hello," a few people replied, raggedly, like a sullen class of fifth graders.

"We shall pray," Sun Deer announced.

A number of people put their palms together and closed their eyes. He began singing in what must have been a native dialect. It went on longer than I expected it would. One by one the people in praying postures dropped their arms. By the time he was finished, everyone had their eyes open.

"Thank you, Great Spirit," Sun Deer said. He turned slowly to gaze out over the crowd a section at a time. "We all know why we have come here today," he said at last.

A long pause ensued, followed by a few sporadic murmurs of assent. I wondered if someone would have the courage to demand clarification. But perhaps they knew, the only way to challenge a celebrity is with another, bigger, celebrity.

"We stand humbled in the shadow of this precious gift from the Creator," Sun Deer continued. A few people in the crowd responded with, "Amen."

"And we gather, in reverence, to treat the Miracle Tree with the respect it has earned over the course of many, many generations. Do I speak the truth?" He finished the sentence with a challenging edge to his voice.

"Yes," a few voices answered. Others nodded, more or less in agreement. Most just looked confused.

"I ask you now, those nearest the tree, to step back. There is no need to grasp at the gifts of the Miracle Tree. They are given to those in a state of sincerity — never to the greedy. You know this. I ask you then, step back so our monitors can place a protective rope around the tree. That's right. Back. Yes. Everyone. Together. You there, in the blue jumper, yes *you*. Step back, young fellow. Give room for others to move. Step back, all of us. Ours is a shared movement. We are here for the same reason. Let's move together now."

The crowd began to shuffle. Once it became clear there was a combined effort, they took up the cause with the earnest expressions of lowlanders building an emergency dike.

"Back it up for the Miracle Tree!" bellowed a bearded man with the Biblical fierceness of Charleton Heston in *The Ten Commandments*.

"Back!. . . Back!. . . Back!" The chant was quickly picked up by most of the crowd.

This time Agnes held the stake while Morning Mist pounded it through the turf with a rock. Volunteers rushed in to wrest the remaining stakes and rope from their hands to complete the job.

Soon the barrier was strung, marking a protective space three feet wide around the tree. A self-congratulatory cheer swept through the crowd. Strangers hugged or shook hands or high-fived.

Another chant, more exuberant than the last, started and rapidly grew into a roar. "Save the Tree! Save the Tree!"

Sun Deer launched into another native song, this time with enough volume of his own to forgo amplification. The crowd immediately halted their own exercise to listen.

He ended it just as abruptly, held his arms akimbo, then walked through the delighted crowd, accepting thanks and pats on the back but no handshakes. He got as far as the rope and then, in a move that surprised everyone, stepped over it. Inside the barrier he turned around and sat, cross-legged, directly under the tree.

The crowd needed a moment to digest that. A few heads tilted in wonder. One man muttered, "Now wait just a second, here."

"Bastard wants it for himself," another voice added. "I'm not being racist here, but I swear, you give 'em an inch."

"Typical," whined another.

But no one else spoke up in time to steer the thought into a shared complaint, and the opportunity was lost. The crowd resumed its self-interested buzz. Just one person inside, and an Indian at that, who seemed to know something, and might even be somebody? They could handle that.

The rope barrier was established, with Sun Deer alone inside, staring above the many faces out to the horizon.

Belief in anything is simply a way of labeling the mystery.

Chogyam Trungpa

SIX

I still needed quotes. Sun Deer seemed a likely prospect, although not just then while he sat like a boulder with issues. I walked back towards the parking lot through a stream of more arrivals. The newcomers were obvious by the urgency with which they strode to reach the tree, as if it might vanish or lose its powers before they had a chance for an encounter. I wondered how much my article could have contributed to the collective sense of concern for its immediate future. If there indeed was a connection, hadn't I done a good thing? Wasn't this all about saving the tree?

George sat on the bumper of a BMW with his thick arms wrapped across his chest. He saw me and slowly shook his head. "Sun Deer," he said. "He's something else. Last night I asked him where he learned to chant like that. I thought he was going to say from his great grandfather the warrior chief or some such. You know what he told me? He got the whole idea from a "Bonanza" episode."

"He might have been putting you on," I pointed out.

George mulled it over. He nodded. "And I might be Pocahontas," he said.

An orange van marked RADIO CREP bounced towards us across the lawn through an area no other driver had deigned to go, either because they weren't from the media or they weren't driving popsicle-colored vehicles. It jumped the curb back into the parking lot and jerked to a halt, occupying a spot that would block at least four cars from pulling out. George swore under his breath.

The driver hopped out holding a tape recorder just like George's. He was a big-boned kid with cropped hair and sideburns bleached platinum blonde. George took a hard sideways look and hawked a ball of phlegm onto the asphalt.

"Hey ya, George!" the young guy said, waving. He jogged to us with the happy expression of a puppy.

"Fuck off, creep," George answered.

The youth didn't flinch. He clipped a plastic tag onto his shirt that identified him as a reporter from station CREP. "Aw George, you old veteran newshound you," the boy said. He gave him a playful punch on the shoulder which George ignored.

The boy turned to me. "William T. Curren," he announced, extending the same hand that had punched George. He had an athletic grip that matched the linebacker physique. I pressed back pretty hard myself and he smiled even more, like we could be playmates. I introduced myself.

"Earl! Earl the Pearl! You da man! All the way from the big bad city." He leaned back to better take in the impressive sight of me. "You know, I gotta tell you. That was a real good story, Bud. I felt it here." He punched his own chest.

George scratched his nuts. "Shee-it," he muttered.

"Let me introduce you guys to my friend," William said, sticking his head through the open van window to look into the back. "Kendricks! Hey Kendricks man! Get up! We're here, dude!"

That's a coincidence, I thought, I know a Kendricks too, then the van's back door opened with a loud creak to reveal the astonishing sight of our paper's foreign editor, looking as if he'd just trekked through a desert. His hair was a mess, he had a three-day start on a beard and his clothes appeared to have been slept in. He barely resembled the upper crust honcho I remembered from the editorial meeting.

"Bloody hell," he said in that heavy British accent. It was apparently his form of greeting because nothing more followed. He stood a little precariously. Was he drunk as well?

"Kendricks," William told us, "is originally from England so it's not his fault. He just talks that way. Anyway, dude, this is George Templington, the radio man extraordinaire from COWR. And this is Earl, Earl Brododsky."

"Actually, we've—" I started to say, but Kendricks interrupted me.

"Yes, yes of course, the chap who wrote the *Herald* piece," he said. He fixed me with a look as he lurched to shake my hand. "Stupendous work. My accolades. Really."

I didn't know what to say so I just kicked my instep and tried to appear modest.

Kendricks quickly filled the gap by explaining he was sure the Miracle Tree could be turned into lucrative fodder for the tabloids back "across the Pond." Or, if they wouldn't bite on all the "transcendental guff," he might try selling it to one of the more established dailies as an expose of the "sort of wacked-out religious aberrations one finds more and more these days in the colonies."

"Right," I said, unsure what he was getting at, or why he was even there, acting like a freelancer. Kendricks already had a job, he had an entire section of the paper to manage — what was he doing in Fraleton? Maybe he'd been sent to check up on me. But any number of lower-ranked staffers could have done that. It must have been to take over my assignment. I hadn't realized the story could be that important not just to readers but to the paper's own Brahmins.

George chuckled. "Every religion is an aberration to somebody. Can you imagine the missionaries trying to get through that first Q and A? Excuse me? Why we eat the Jesus? I thought we loved him. Oh we still do? Why we drink his blood? Do we not have much guava juice?"

Kendricks seemed to regain some composure. He swept a wild lock of hair back from his forehead. "Bloody serious," he said. "Readers love nothing better than to see the most devout notions of others get disparaged. Makes them feel that much closer to god. Their own god."

"I picked him up on the highway in," William said with an apologetic shrug. "He was hitching."

"My auto's on the fritz," Kendricks explained, "but I'm already planning on a new one if this works out as I expect it should. Either way it plays, it's all going to be gravy, my friends. Money in the bank. And I'll tell you what."

He leaned closer to me as if to whisper, but still spoke loud enough for everyone to hear. I smelled his breath and leaned back. "We play our cards right, we can have the next Shroud of Turin right here. I can feel it already. And I just woke up. Ha! You see it? We're onto a gold mine. We could call it, 'The Tree of Wishes That Do Come True.' What do you lot say?"

When neither George nor I answered he went on anyway. "You're right, what am I thinking? The Miracle Tree is miles better. The Shroud of Turin. The Miracle Tree. They both have that ring."

George said he needed to go. William trailed behind him, asking questions, earning a scowl from George over his shoulder.

"Mister Kendricks?" I asked as soon as they'd left. "What's going on?"

"Thanks, my good fellow," he said, "for not letting on. Much obliged, I'm sure." He seemed more like the Kendricks I'd remembered, the one with the stiff-necked style that made every vocal delivery seem arch.

"I guess I'm all done here, then," I said, glumly.

He looked puzzled. "You? Done? On the contrary, old boy. Word's out. This is your baby. From the Chief himself, you see. He wouldn't let any of us talk him into sending a team. Said it might only wreck the mood."

"But you're here."

"Yes, well," he said, embarrassed. "Not officially, as it turns out. In point of fact, I've taken the time off. Vacation days and all that. They think I'm in Bermuda. I'd be grateful if you didn't mention it back at the paper."

"Sure. I mean, of course not. But, why *are* you here?"

He flushed again, this time completing the awkward effect by staring at the ground and chuckling uncomfortably. "Right, well, ahem, I really have kept some of my contacts at papers back in the home country, as it were. Naturally they've taken an interest."

But that wasn't it. He was still looking at the ground. "Which might well be the approach to take, for starters, to see if it does indeed lead to a book project. That, you see, being the main reason I'm here."

Except that it wasn't. He clearly wasn't finished. Finally he looked up at me. He seemed to drop a little of the façade of Thurston Howell. "Plus, there's the off chance — isn't there? — that this thing could turn out to be, well, you know. True." His eyes had the earnest appeal of an eight-year-old sizing up a department store Santa.

Now we were both embarrassed. He broke it off by claiming to be late for an interview — an unlikely prospect giving the fact that he'd just shown up, but a welcome one.

"Oh, of course," I said. "Busy busy busy." We promised each other to stay in touch. I hurried back into the crowd, fighting an unexpected urge to get away from people, or at least the people who called themselves journalists. The ones like me, I thought, with a cringing sense of self-doubt. Look at Kendricks, spending his whole adult life in professional pursuit of the truth, yet still having to cook up a ruse just to come on his own to Fraleton. And when he finally does allow a glimmer of honesty in admitting he's as drawn as I am to the deep, what do we both do but immediately shut down and run from the idea?

I turned for refuge to my work. I stopped before a team of researchers, a dozen or more men and women in white lab coats. After all the mumbo-jumbo, some of it mine, it struck me as a good time for some veracity as seen through hard science. I tapped one of the experts on the shoulder to draw his attention away from a metal box with two rows of dials crowding the top.

"I'm a reporter," I said. "Can I ask you something? Have you found anything significant here?"

"Mais oui," he replied, and called over another member of the team. This one had the pointy white beard of a true authority. He introduced himself with a long French name I wrote down too fast for his liking, having missed one or two of the little squiggly things they use over some of their letters. I wrote them in just as he asked, rather than tell him our papers had more important details to worry about than French squiggles. With that settled, he was free to express enthusiasm at what he called a "discovery of ma-zheur scientific impor-tance."

"I'm listening," I said, ready to write.

"You air no scien-teest, but per-aps you 'ave 'aird of ze norss and ze souss poles?"

I looked up from my notebook, having written nothing. Do they teach condescension in French elementary schools? I gave him my best slack-jawed "duh" look for a response.

"Bon. I 'ave ze proof, right 'ere, of a new gravitational force. I call it, ze Mee-del Pole."

"Congratulations."

He looked dismayed. "Or, if you pre-fair, ze Central Pole. It is easier to comprehend, non?"

"Clear as glass," I said. "Merci."

He combined a shrug with a dismissive pout — the French will never beat us at the rebuff — and spun on his heels as if I weren't even there.

"Don't mind him," said another man in a similar white lab coat a few steps away. I assumed he was from the same team, but he handed me a card that identified him as Lars Svenson, from the Stockholm League of Advanced Phytogeny Studies.

"So you're the associate director," I noted.

"Well," he replied. When he didn't elaborate, I wondered if he was at a loss for the right words to go on. It would have given me a lift to finally meet a Scandinavian abroad who couldn't speak English better than I did.

"Good," I said. "Then maybe you can tell me something about your work here with the Miracle Tree — or would you prefer I talk with you later together with a translator?"

"As you like. I am here now, together with six of my colleagues. We are working quite hard on a report for our institute, and for the wider world of arboricultural aficionados, naturally. It will be ready soon. In the meantime, I would be happy to discuss any preliminary results you may find interesting."

"Maybe just sum it up for me. What have you learned?"

"Well, we find it to be a healthy, even robust, extremely large and strikingly attractive example of its kind, *Pterocarya fraxinifolia*, in the Juglandaceae family, of course, and by our estimate to be at least two hundred and forty years old."

"In other words, a sycamore."

"Oh no, not at all."

"But I thought. . . that's what I was told. They've been calling it that." I didn't explain that I had been calling it that too, ever since George had pegged it for me.

"Which is why using common names to identify vegetative species is discouraged within the scientific community. What most people refer to as a sycamore, or plane tree, is a completely different thing. A simple glance at their leaf structures is sufficient to realize this. "

"What's the regular name for this one?"

"Caucasian wingnut."

"Lars, you must be joking." I wondered if that sentence was heard much in general Scandinavian conversation.

He was serious. "It is a member of the same family as the walnut — you see the resemblance in the pinnately compound leaves. The nutlets of this one are winged, thus the name. It's closely related to the Chinese wingnut and also the Japanese wingnut. Native habitats vary. This species is found naturally from the Caucasus to northern Iran."

"You're saying it's not even from around here?"

"Non-native," he said. "Introduced to North America in 1782, or so we had believed. This could mark an even earlier arrival. Which is, of course, tremendously exciting."

"It's a foreigner."

He did a minor hem-hem laugh, probably to be polite, then went back into scholar mode. "A great many of the vegetative species you find around you today are non-native. Trees are like people — they like to travel. If they find a place that fits, they like to stay. If they succeed, and breed more trees, we refer to them 'naturalized.' But yes, I suppose you could call them foreigners."

I wondered how to work the science angle into my next story without pointing out my own earlier mistake. A tree that could change species in just one night — talk about a miracle. But I wasn't comfortable with my chances of pulling that one off, and it was almost with relief that I slipped away from Lars and found my next interview subject back in the more fertile field of spirituality. Standing before a sandwich board advertising their group were three members of the Heaven's Gate cult, the same one that had made all the papers for the wacky mass suicide.

"Hey!" I said with genuine interest. "I've heard of you guys. Congratulations on even being here. I thought your whole membership put on new track suits and running shoes and took off to reach that spaceship behind the comet."

"Some of us never made it to headquarters that day," explained one of the trio with a forlorn expression clouding an already long face. "We had engine trouble outside San Clemente. We called ahead but they said they wouldn't wait."

"I guessed that worked out okay. For you three, at least."

"We're still miffed. It's a comet. It's not like it's going anywhere we don't know. Give me a break."

It was only then I noticed they were wearing matching track suits and new running shoes. "You guys aren't planning any more big trips soon, are you?" I asked. "To space?"

"It takes at least six people to operate the craft," said the third member. He raised his eyebrows in an invitation while appraising me for size. Maybe they had a new track suit that would fit me.

"Tempting," I said. "But I have a job to do."

Lon Chin was standing nearby watching our exchange. He grinned while twirling a finger around his temple.

The sad-faced member saw him. "They say that about every new religion," he pointed out.

I acknowledged Lon with a nod and walked on, arriving at a small campfire where a young man with a flourishing mustache and a shaved head stood wrapped in a colorful blanket.

"It's Love Isreal," explained a teenaged girl who may have been his assistant or perhaps a disciple. "I can ask, if you want to request an interview."

"Don't really need to get into the political thing right now," I said. "Things are complicated enough."

The blanketed guy got it with a snap of his fingers. "No, no. Love Is Real. I'm not against anything. I'm for every one."

I still hadn't written a word.

"And I'm here to support the tree and all those who recognize it as a symbol of higher growth."

"Nice try," I said, meaning it. "But I really should—"

"Okay, okay," he said, "you win. My real name is Lamar, Doug Lamar. Use it if you like, I don't really care. You have no idea how hard it is to start a cult these days."

"Tell me about it," I said, looking back at the glum Heaven's Gate crew.

He took it literally. "Everybody thinks, big deal, there's nothing to it, you head to the Greyhound station and pick up some hungry disciples, you make a proclamation or two about the next life and, bang, you're the new Messiah. It ain't that simple. Maybe it was at one time, but not any more. This is practically the twenty-first century. I'm not saying a lot of people aren't dumb — look at pro wrestling — but you still need a special appeal to get any followers worthy of the name these days. I mean real followers, the kind who will surrender everything to you in the name of the cause. I don't have it yet, I admit, but hey, I'm only nineteen. Give me time."

"Stay away from the ones who promise spaceships. That's my advice."

"Actually, my role model is Jim Jones."

"Nooo," I said. "Not the suicide guy. What's with you people and knocking yourselves off? When did dying become such a great career move in spiritual circles?"

"I'm not necessarily saying that particular aspect of his mission was all for the good. It's not my place to pass judgment. The important thing is, he had what, nine hundred-plus people willing to go with him into the jungle? That's some serious numbers there, bro. That's world class charisma right there."

I pointed out that Jones's legacy was measured in corpses, including his own.

Doug dismissed that fact with a flick of his hand. "Hey. You gotta go someday. You may as well do it while you're on top. Who wants to be an old cult leader anyway?"

"Moses?"

"Point taken. Moses had clout, you have to give him that. Great numbers. And that Red Sea trick? Nobody's even trying to match that kind of stuff these days. Sometimes I think we're all rank amateurs when it comes to our cults, even the big boys. Can you imagine what Moses could do today? Say with a website? A simple satellite hookup and a global feed? Hoo!"

I walked on, moving further away from the tree, and the madness. Back on the street, I turned for a distant look. An Australian TV reporter had been caught sneaking under the rope to climb the trunk with a machete in his teeth. The outraged crowd got him by the ankles and yanked him down. He was able to clear some space with the weapon, but it was soon wrestled out of his hands. The mob chased him to the edge of town, rumbling past me. A laughing teenager wielded the machete with wild swipes that swished nearly to his heels.

I needed to get further away from the pack, to get more distance from the confused swirls of human energy still streaming into the park. A gathering uneasiness in my gut told me something was wrong in Fraleton, and I was a big part of it. Was it my fault the spinny crowd had chosen this park for their playground? Maybe it was. I went for a contemplative walk around town.

Twelve minutes later I was back. Fraleton lacked the dimensions for a restorative stroll. The short break did nothing to improve my mood — I had thought getting a little time away from the tree might give me some insight, but I didn't even come close. In the parking lot I leaned against a motor home the size of an African village while I rubbed my temples.

"You look like you could use some of this, sugar," a sympathetic voice said. A female voice. I opened my eyes to see the romance novel reader from the Old General Store. She held out a Ding Dong, the wrapper opened but the chocolate goodie inside still smooth and unbroken.

"Thanks, but I don't think so." She had probably never heard of hi-carb energy bars.

"Oh g'wan," she insisted, pushing it closer. "As if a few calories are going to hurt a string bean like you."

I accepted it with a reluctant thank you. To be polite, I took a bite.

"Whoa," I said without having to fake it. It brought back a taste memory from childhood — and I thought I'd outgrown a grade school love of sugar and cocoa fat steeped in chemicals.

"Told ya," she said, then took a sip through a straw from a can of diet cola.

"How come you're not working?" I asked.

"Needed a breather. So I came here to check out the scene. We've been swamped. This morning they bought up a month's stock of potato chips in like twenty minutes. Wish I had known. We could have stocked ahead." The edge in her voice sounded like blame.

"Yeah. Well. Who knew?" I said.

She chuckled. "I thought you did."

"Why me?"

"That's what people in town are asking. You don't look the type, to tell the truth."

"What type?"

"Now that depends on who's doing the talking. Some people take you straight, as a reporter, just like you say, from the big city. And some think you're more likely to be an organizer from Greenpeace or something, here to stir up all manner of trouble."

She said the word "trouble" with a sly expression. Was it a flirting gesture? I wasn't sure until she parted her lips a little wider than necessary to grip the straw, finding it at last after a probe of her pink tongue. She smiled around the straw while taking in a silent gulp. From the neck up, she had a sassy, small-town, devil-doll appeal. She could have had a decent part in any Burt Reynolds car movie. Below that she was a wreck, dressed like a housecleaner. An oversized sweatshirt and ripped-knee jeans hid her body like a loose blanket. But from her face I could see she wasn't as old as I'd first thought. Thirty-three, or maybe a little more. So she had decade or so on me — that was acceptable. Maybe even better, to go by what I'd read about peak sexual performance in females. If biology really did turn young males into root-hounds at seventeen, yet made girls wait another two decades to feel the heat, no wonder the genders were so out of synch.

I found myself leaning towards her, almost involuntarily. My body seemed to have ideas of its own. "Now do I look like I could cause anyone any trouble?" I said with a smile.

"Then there's Oris Kendall," she went on, "who says you might just be an outside infiltrator sent as some kind of vanguard from hell to destroy the very moral foundation of our town."

"What?"

"But nobody's listened to Oris for thirty years. He ran for mayor once. He got eight votes? His family has twelve people in it."

I finished the last of the Ding Dong. One good slurp of her drink would make the perfect chaser. Could I ask her? It might be a test. She could always take out the straw to keep things formal. "And what do you say?" I tried instead.

"Well, now," she answered, smiling and sucking on the straw again. There was a gurgling sound, then a whoosh of air. So much for my share.

"My daddy says you seemed a right fine young gentleman. I guess I haven't seen any reason yet to disagree with him."

"That's kind enough, I suppose. Did I meet your father?"

"He says you did. His name's Wilbur?" She looked away. In a quieter voice she added, "He has balloons."

The resemblance hit me only then: the sharp nose in profile. It worked better for her, a pleasing little counterpoint in the visual frame of her head, something your eye would notice after lingering on that mass of teased-up hair.

"Wilbur. Of course. I liked him." I didn't even have to fake it. "He was very. . . how should I put it? Apologetic."

"I know. He's a bit geeky. But good geeky. Everyone likes him. That's not his problem. It's that damn fool idea he has to fly with those giant balloons. He's going to end up frying himself on a high-power wire somewhere, I just know it."

"A man's gotta do what a man's gotta do," was the best I could come up with.

Her face didn't bother to hide its disappointment — in me. Suddenly I felt bad, for both of us. I opened my mouth to try to make up for it, but nothing came out.

"Someone's got to make him stop," she said. "I thought maybe it could be you. There goes that plan."

"I really shouldn't take sides," I reasoned. "Journalists' code." As if it could ever be that easy. And even if it were, whose side would I be on?

She hook-shot the can into a garbage bin. "Whatever," she said, looking down the street where a middle-aged couple beside a loaded station wagon stared back at us. They had new-in-town smiles. The man raised a video camera to his face to film us, two locals in their natural habitat. The woman hissed something to him and then looked quickly away with the falsely occupied expression people adopt when their dog hunches up for a public shit. He whipped the camera down and they disappeared quickly back into the crowd.

"Guess I'd best get back," she said. "The public wants me." A hint of the smile returned.

"I'm Earl," I said, offering my hand.

She eyed it for a moment. Did she really have to decide? What were her options? Keep her hands to herself and spit on the ground instead?

She took my hand and lifted it for a single mock-hearty pump. "Nice to meet ya, Earl. I'm Trish. It's actually Latricia with a C-I-A but nobody calls me that anymore."

The seductive undertone flickered and went out, gone like a flash of breast on a cable TV show. She was just being friendly now. Maybe she had been all along. I conceded the possibility that the longer I stayed apart from Shirley, the greater my imaginative juices might flow.

"Trish, tell me one thing. What do you think about the Miracle Tree? Is it for real?"

She laughed. It was a pretty laugh, as unrehearsed as a songbird's trill. It made her eyes sparkle and her mouth open wide to reveal two perfect rows of gleaming white teeth. "You know what," she said, "some folks say it makes them feel, how shall I put it, frisky."

"Oh. Well now. Does it make you feel frisky?"

I liked her innocent brashness. I decided it didn't matter she dressed like someone ten pounds overweight and determined not to reveal where. Or that she was over thirty, in a backwater town, working a register and reading schlock on the side. It didn't sound like a happy fate for anyone, but she had the air of a survivor. I thought I might like her, even if the attraction was just a glandular thing brought on by the absence of Shirley and a life on the road.

She laughed again. The songbird was back. "Sugar, I was born this way." The trickling sound of her laughter faded as she sauntered back towards the store.

After we parted, I felt good. Maybe it was the stroll along the edge of the park beside the river, or the encounter with Trish, or the three refills of Buffy's coffee-flavored sludge I fired down to revitalize. It could also have been just being near the tree. Whatever the cause, I felt positive. Better than good. I vibrated on a higher plane of energy and motion, like an enhanced version of myself, or an Olympian runner whose endorphins were just kicking in. I was keen to plunge back into reporting.

I started at the parking lot edge of the crowd, picking off quotes from people at the fringes like a savvy hunter, choosing targets who would go down easily without disturbing the others in the thick of it. Then I waded in to talk to them too. People must have sensed I was getting somewhere, because they wanted part of it. They fed off my confidence. They answered whatever questions I had, even the lame ones, with enthusiasm, and seemed eager to offer more. Opinions, insights, anecdotes, analyses. Anything I might be able to use, they were eager to give.

More than a few offered the impression of wanting to hang around, or even become friends, but I showed no inclination to stop. I wrote while I walked, always moving forward, a shark after prey, sniffing the water for facts. When I did pause before someone, I asked my questions in a late-for-something cadence, and would bother writing down answers only when someone hit a solid, quip-sized winner.

This must have helped make them feel a part of things, jacked into the media grid. I was the conduit to their fifteen minutes of fame, an all-access pass beyond the velvet rope into the VIP section of the information age. I had only to chuckle or raise an eyebrow in interest for them to feel they could rise above the TV addicts and radio call-in regulars and celebrity magazine gleaners who merely consumed the news. Through me, they could reach the source — they could immerse, and become the news.

Back at Grady's that evening, I took my laptop down to the living room, but it wasn't the right atmosphere for work. George, Sun Deer, Mrs. Grady and an elderly man I took for a neighbor were playing poker at a table covered with matchsticks and cards. They laughed and jeered and accused each other of cheating, which may have been the point of the game. I saw they were drinking a clear liquid out of Mason jars. Mrs. Grady pointed to an empty chair and raised her eyebrows in invitation. I said I'd love to join them, without meaning it, and gestured to the laptop under my arm with a shrug. I hit the stairs at a run.

"Knock one out of the park, my boy," George called out behind me. "I need something good for my first piece in the morning."

The neighbor made some comment about first pieces in the morning that was followed by a cannonade of lewd laughter. I shut my door.

I did precisely what Gallantine advised, taking whatever space I needed to tell the story.

It turned out I needed 3,065 words — practically a tome. It wasn't writing, it was gushing. But how else to fit it all in? I read it over, and couldn't find any fat to cut out without interrupting the narrative flow or leaving some important story development behind.

I started with a detached view of the once bucolic town and contrasted it with the present multitudes, offering an almost epic sense of the occasion with a description of the cornfields outside town and the highway leading through them now lined on either side with parked cars. From there I brought the reader down to earth with some close-up looks at a few key visitors: Vanessa Sturn, a plucky nine-year-old girl with some kidney condition, and Lieutenant Colonel Lawrence Garson, an eighty-seven-year-old war veteran who arrived in a wheelchair but *walked* away from his encounter with the tree. I chewed up a lot of column inches detailing Garson's incredible story, which really belonged in a TV "Movie of the Week." It was such an amazing tale of perseverance, from the muddy trenches of Germany to the sunlit grass of Fraleton, told largely by his wife since Garson tended to nod off mid-sentence. The TV movie people wouldn't need to bother with technicalities such as the fact he actually used the wheelchair more as a resting place than a necessity since he could, strictly speaking, walk even before he reached the tree.

As good as all the color stuff got, I was mostly proud of how I managed to weave in the politics of the piece, making it a combination of flash and fact. Or near fact — I didn't have the time to chase down every detail. Readers now knew the important stuff, namely that Filco planned a nuclear waste storage facility on the site, and was furthermore refusing to even admit it.

Since it was the company's decision to play hardball, not mine, I had no qualms about printing some of the other rumors I'd picked up in my forays, such as the potentially inflammatory suggestion that Filco was just then drawing up plans to send a kind of SWAT team armed with silencer chainsaws to cut down the tree — or, failing that, a backup squad of horticultural commandoes to poison it.

To counter all the gloom and doom, I added a more hopeful message from Sun Deer about sincerity being a crucial factor in making wishes. That opened the door for me to add a point about the many Native Americans planning to rally around the tree, something I hadn't exactly seen but felt a rare sense of kinship in reporting all the same. I was still less than convinced they actually existed, but felt nonetheless that I might be speaking for my people, even if by proxy.

An article more than three thousand words in length would be a huge spread for the *Herald*, or for any newspaper in a time of diminishing attention spans. Like most publications, we were going the MacPaper route of shorter copy and flashier layouts. Color was the thing: color photos, color ads, color graphs bigger than the stories they were supposed to augment. The model seemed to be the comic strip pages, although the stories themselves weren't getting any funnier.

My first article had caught fire, but could I expect to draw lightning down twice? I put a lot into the piece, offering Biblical crowds and wartime minefields and kidney failures gone right. I ended it with Sun Dance and a quote I neglected to mention was actually made in reference to Mrs. Grady's cooking but was too good to leave out. It captured the scene, and wasn't that the whole point?

Once done and delivered, it was hard to think about what I'd written without some worry. No wonder I had trouble falling sleep. I had no Shirley to cuddle up to, and my bed sagged underneath me like a question mark.

It doesn't matter how you live or what you did wrong.
As long as you're on TV, people will respect you.

Bart Simpson

SEVEN

It was too late to even think about it, but I thought about it. Then I did it — I got up and called Shirley.

No answer.

Two nights in a row? Didn't she have to come home sometime? To change underwear, at least? Or was she going completely without by now? Romping from one room to another in some garish Barry love palace, naked as a forest nymph?

Despite the prospects, I still had trouble working it up into a serious worry. Shirley and I were too tight to dissolve over some sudden interloper. We knew we were the future, even if we didn't know what exactly that meant. We'd never discussed anything like marriage, that vestige of a property-based patriarchy, but we sometimes riffed wistfully on kids. We both liked the idea of a big, happy family, maybe because neither of us had had one growing up. By the age of ten, both of our fathers were out of the family portraits for good.

A midnight snack — that was what I needed, food to soothe the soul and calm the nerves. I needed to take my mind off my mind and get my stomach back in charge of physical affairs. Something zappable from the convenience store was my standard comfort food back home, but the snack options in Fraleton took on a new dimension with a fridge of leftovers à la Grady.

I looked up from a forage with nothing but a small bowl of cherries and a jug of juice to see Mrs. Grady, dressed in a bathrobe and carrying a book. She looked at me over half-moon granny glasses.

"Earl, my dear," she said.

I was a dear. How nice. Over my bogus protests she warmed a plate of things assembled from the fridge, freezer and pantry. It was, as ever, a culinary accomplishment: half a Cornish game hen stuffed with wild rice along with saffroned cauliflower. She fussed over me while I ate, trying to add more selections to my plate. I gave up coaxing her back to her book, something by or about Spinoza.

"Philosophy, Mrs. G.?" I asked.

"It's a hobby I picked up a few years ago," she smiled. "I don't always understand it, but that's rather the point, don't you suppose? It's like going to the gym for my brain. Something to do as I get older."

"I'm sure," I said, although I wasn't.

"All noble things are as difficult as they are rare," she quoted. "Isn't that something? I just got it from this book."

I allowed that it was, or could be, something, without understanding it or feeling the need to. I asked instead what she thought about the Miracle Tree.

"Oh, well, I don't know. . . " she replied, seemingly reluctant. She eyed me for a moment. When I didn't say anything, she continued, "People say all kinds of things, don't they?"

"Do you believe them?"

She laughed a little. "I've been telling people what to think since the first march I joined when I was just a girl back in, oh, whenever it was. But what to believe? That's something altogether different, isn't it? I believe in things I know to be true from my own experience. That much is easy enough. Then there are the areas where we'll likely never know. So how to decide? Is it enough to reduce it all to percentages and practicality? Then it becomes almost a numbers game. And I'm not sure I trust numbers."

"Have you ever wished for anything under the Miracle Tree?"

She laughed openly this time. "Oh, yes. All of us girls did. I remember one summer night when I was back visiting from college. I stood under the Miracle Tree and put my hands together and wished so hard to have this handsome boy I had a crush on at the time ask me out. It sounds silly now, I know, but I remember standing there next to the tree like it meant the whole world to get it right."

"Gee, that's great. What happened?"

"He asked me out."

"Hey, that's cool."

"And now he's upstairs in bed."

"Yes? Mister Grady."

She smiled.

"That's very cool," I said, and meant it.

"He proposed to me later, at that same spot. You think he's the stubborn type now, you should have seen him then. He kneeled down in the grass, which sounds sweet, and I suppose it was, but then he told me that if those bastards who'd started the war couldn't stop him there was no way my parents or anyone else could either. And may the tree itself fall over and strike him dead if he were ever to lie or falter in his vow to respect and cherish and love me so long as he lived."

"Wow."

"Oh he was quite the romantic," she said, beaming.

I thought about Shirley and me. Were we romantic? Last Valentine's Day I gave her a pricey sports bra. She gave me a leather-bound copy of *The Communist Manifesto*. It seemed like a fair exchange.

"That's really something," I said. Then, "For all time?"

I wondered why the eternity part of it always stuck in my mind

— and also why the word "romance" conjured up those afternoon tea-time dances at the mall where old people in polyester shuffled to a Guy Lombardo-like band.

"We bought this house the following month. We've been here ever since."

"It's quite a house," I offered, forking in the last bite of poultry.

"We've been very fortunate here," she said. Before I could stop her, she took my plate to the sink to wash it. She came back with a slice of apple pie under a wedge of cheddar cheese. I didn't even try to resist.

"I just hope we can stay this way," she said once she had sat back down.

"Why wouldn't you?"

"I've been in enough battles to know being right doesn't mean you get to win. Now they're talking about how much they can make this thing grow. Once the door's open and the tax base gets going they're looking at factories and condos and who knows what else. There's even supposed to be a plan for an airport. An airport!"

I shrugged to say, "What a shame." But the airport idea didn't seem so bad — the drive out had felt geologic, and it could only help in creating a more efficient distribution system for goods. Trish's shop had a selection of chocolate bars so paltry it would make a Muscovite feel at home.

After the pie I felt ready for bed, and said so. Mrs. Grady offered to make me an Ovaltine. It sounded like something from Ozzie and Harriet. I declined, insisting that she'd already done too much, but she said she was making one for herself anyway to help her finish the chapter she was on. I took mine upstairs with me. She smiled and said good-night without looking up from her book.

My eyes were drooping as I reached the top of the stairs, but I wasn't confident about getting a good night's sleep. If I could still walk upright it could only have meant my sponge of a bed was not through rearranging my physique. I almost stepped on George's toes before I saw him. He was sitting on the top step, knees beside his ears, wearing big, floppy, striped pajamas that could have doubled as a circus tent.

"What are you doing up?" I whispered. "If you're looking for eats, Mrs. Grady's got some more apple pie. It actually goes good with the cheese."

"Had two slices after dinner," he replied in a low voice. "I thought about walking it off but this was as far as I got. So I'm just taking in some air. My roommate's working late. I came out to give him a little space."

"I thought you had your own room."

"I did. But there's nothing left in town and this guy was desperate and Grady had an extra cot."

The thought that it could be Grady's only extra cot was disturbing. I might never get off that bed. But I managed to look impressed: George the Samaritan.

"All right, so I'm a chump," he said. "What the hell. All I'm doing is sleeping there anyway."

"Except that you're not, at the moment."

"Yeah. Damn. I guess you're right."

Downstairs the kitchen light switched off. Mrs. Grady's slippered feet shuffled away and up the back stairs to the master bedroom. Maybe Spinoza finally wore her down — or maybe the Ovaltine suddenly made her more interested in the fighter pilot in her bed.

"You married, George?"

"Yep." He didn't elaborate.

"Good for you," I said, without meaning it.

"Three times."

I was sorry I'd asked, but he didn't mind.

"For the third one my buddy refused to be best man. Said he wouldn't sign on to a bon voyage party for the Titanic. But I don't know. We're still shacked up. It's not so bad. Never say never. You file yet?"

"A couple of hours ago."

"You don't sound too thrilled. Yesterday you were like a virgin who finally rode the skin boat to tuna town. Now you're jaded already?"

"I think I might have blown it. I just went on and on with it this time. I don't know. I'm afraid they're going to hate it. It's way too long for one thing."

"So they'll cut some. No big thing."

"I guess."

"I got my first two morning reports all taped out already. I'll send them in soon as I get up. They'll think I'm humping it on an early shift and be impressed. Not that they shouldn't be anyway."

"Hit them homers, George."

"Out of the park, bro."

I went back to my room and entered the maw of the bed. I still couldn't sleep — and even when I could, I kept waking to the sound of distant traffic increasing in volume as it approached Fraleton. It was that and the disturbing fragments of dreams. One scene in particular was so vivid it seemed real: Gallantine's fist pounding on the pages that contained my article.

The noises below my window took on an annoying pattern. The sound of a car stopping, the door opening, sometimes voices. Then footsteps on gravel, footsteps on the porch, watch that third step it's got a. . . creeeeeeak, then the heavy brass knocker rapping, as if they hoped to drive the whole thing through the wood. At three in the morning, no less — some people have no respect for other people's schedules. They wouldn't dare be that rude at home, I almost felt like leaning out the window to point out.

Grady got up time and again to confirm the No Vacancy sign on the lawn really meant what it said.

"But, I'm just, I mean, everything else is taken," I heard a raspy female voice plead. This one made me sit up straight: I was sure I recognized it. "I'm a reporter and I've got to stay somewhere tonight so I can do my assignment tomorrow. It's really important. I don't care where I sleep, I don't need a bed — the floor or anywhere will be fine. Really. Please?"

I did recognize the voice: it was Lindy Rondelle. She had been in the same j-school class as Shirley and Danny and I. Practically every guy in the class had a thing for her. I'd even half-considered making a move myself, one drunken night, sprawled on a couch at a party, but Lindy had a boyfriend, and of course I had Shirley, and someone put on a Billy Joel tape and that was that.

I ran down the stairs before Grady could send her away. Lindy looked at me as if she were caught in a current and I was the lifeguard.

"Earl B.!" she beamed, flashing her best feature. She started to put her arms up for a hug but just as quickly put them back down, perhaps not wanting to make a show of it. Grady seemed confused.

"I know her," I explained. "She's a good friend, Mister Grady. She can share my room." I added, innocently, "If you have any extra cots."

Lindy's face lit up in delight, but Grady needed time to absorb the idea. He scratched the back of his neck and stared out at the darkened lawn. Maybe he was still half asleep. Or maybe he had some innate elderly objection to the concept of mixed-sex rooming. Lindy watched him with diminishing hope. She chewed her lower lip and looked back to her Nissan: it would be a rough night for anyone trying to get some sleep in there.

Suddenly Grady grinned. The mind lag must have finally caught up. What we had told him had just completed the last connection of nerve-endings and now made sense. "You're in, missy," he announced, jerking his thumb upstairs.

I didn't help Lindy carry her suitcase. She didn't seem to expect me to. Grady looked as if he felt he should offer, but would defer to my judgment. He shrugged and shook his head a little sadly, perhaps a comment on youth and manners these days, and slouched back to his bedroom.

"You're looking good, Earl," Lindy said when we were upstairs, in the room, with the door closed. "And ripping up on the story. I couldn't believe they ran your picture with the piece in yesterday's three-star. Was that from your high school yearbook or what? You looked like Donny Osmond."

"Lindy, you're looking. . ." What was the word? Stunning? Desirable? Imprisoned by that tight white T-shirt and those almost epidermal jeans? ". . . good yourself," I managed. "What are you doing here?"

She held her fingers out in a V for Victory sign. "Check this out. The *Weekly Times.*"

"No way. They aren't hiring."

"I know. But I got them to give me a freelance assignment. And if they like what they get. . ."

Grady knocked, waited for an answer, then staggered into the room under a metal and canvas army cot.

"I can sleep on that," I said at once.

"No, you don't," Lindy insisted. "It's your room. I'll be fine."

"No, seriously."

We wrestled with it while Grady, still unsure whether he could safely let go, was pulled and tugged between us. There was no way I was going to lose this one. My back was begging for an alternative. I yanked the cot free, quickly unfolded the legs and flopped down on the canvas. "No problem at all," I said.

Grady shrugged again and left. "Sleep well," he mumbled and closed the door quietly behind him.

Lindy hefted her suitcase onto the bed. "We have a lot to catch up on. We should do it in the morning," she suggested, maybe for my sake.

"You must be exhausted from the drive," I offered.

"You sure about the bed?"

"Don't bother thanking me," I replied. She smiled. Angels could take smiling tips from Lindy Rondelle. She had a pair of dimples that would look good in any art museum.

"Okay, I won't."

"You're welcome."

"I know." She started to yawn, but swallowed it in a way that made her nostrils flare. She took a few things out of the suitcase. Women's apparel, some of it probably intimate. I told myself not to look.

"It's a long drive," I pointed out, brilliantly.

She nodded, then sleepily started to pound her own shoulder with a fist.

"Don't let me keep you up," I said.

This time she yawned in full. "Boy oh boy," she said through it. I caught the yawn and joined in.

She sat down on the edge of the bed, facing away from me, to take off her boots and socks. I pretended to find the ceiling tiles interesting. Next would be her jeans, a thin layer of denim that looked grafted onto her legs. This was a moment I could not miss and still face myself in the morning mirror. I had to watch.

She lay back, bent her legs, and arched her pelvis up to peel them off. So that's how it's done. I gulped, then immediately hoped she hadn't heard.

Lindy Rondelle liked peach-colored high-thigh panties with a bit of frill around the waistband. Well well well. Who would have known? I felt privileged, like I'd just been let in on a secret. I was now a huge step ahead of all the other guys in j-school who might wake up from a nap at ninety in some old folks home and only wonder.

If only that were enough. If only my body hadn't immediately wanted more, to be let in on more secrets, maybe even share a few. Lindy left the panties on along with the T-shirt. Fair enough: no man could expect more, under the circumstances. But the show wasn't over yet.

She was lying on the bed on top of the blankets, and still had to get under them. The prim way, the boring way, would have been to get off the bed, untuck the whole thing, and slide back in. She did not exercise that option. Instead she raised her legs up to tug the blanket out from underneath her partially elevated butt. This created a brief V of flesh in two graduated columns that rose up in glory to the ceiling. I almost wished I hadn't seen it. I groaned inwardly, and then hoped I hadn't made a sound.

She lowered her legs and slid backwards into the bed. It wondered if it still had any warmth left from my stay. She pulled the covers up to her neck and turned towards the wall. "G'night," she said, as if to a pet, then clicked off the bedstand lamp.

Good night? Night, yes, obviously, but good? Let's ponder that. Perhaps we could. . . ah. . . expand on the idea?

It was too quiet. The in-coming traffic must have hit a lull. I could hear Lindy breathing. It was faint, but noticeable all the same.

"I'll be fine," I said. "This cot's practically big enough for an adult." It got me a chuckle at least. But I wasn't fine. Partly because the army engineers had not considered the human shape when designing their cots, but more because I'd forgotten it was impossible to sleep in the same room as a beautiful woman unless you were sleeping *with* her. This was a law of nature, and I was breaking it, I knew that. She might have too, if she opened her eyes and looked over to where my anatomy was playing its own game of pup tent with the blanket.

Instead I heard the long, deep, rhythmic breathing of Lindy Rondelle asleep. I sat up to watch her in the pale glow of moonlight coming in from the window. Her mouth was open just a crack, enough to reveal the glistening tip of her tongue, a sight which would not help me get drowsy anytime soon, but one I couldn't help staring at. I imagined the things that tongue might do. I wanted her to stir and turn. I wanted her to wake up and discuss the possibilities. I wanted. . . her.

All of me did, but especially my work unit — it was a dog straining at the leash for a nearby steak. I considered jerking it into submission, but I was afraid of getting caught. Then what? Not an easy one to explain away. Who me? What am I doing? Uh, isometrics? Instead

I stared at the ceiling. When that didn't help, I sat up again to watch.

Lindy's head had lolled to one side. She had round cheeks that I remembered would glow red in winter whenever she came into class from the cold. The best thing about her was currently not on display: her smile, the quick way it crafted the dimples that turned her face into pure joy. Her eyebrows were thicker than necessary and her light brown hair was nothing you'd want to keep a lock of, but when it came to dimples Lindy was unmatched. Fortunately for all of us, they were displayed often. She was the type to smile first and ask questions later.

Later, finally, I did fall asleep, only to be woken up by the sound of Lindy thrashing for balance as she tried to sit up in the posture-ponderous bed.

"This thing. . . sucks!" she hissed to herself.

"I know," I answered in a whisper. "I should have warned you. Say, you know what might work?"

I didn't know just what might work myself, but I was happy to let my mouth sound it out before my brain could think of the good reasons not to. Lindy must have gathered what I was onto by the tone of my voice.

"How's Shirley doing?" she asked politely.

"Great," I answered, rolling onto my stomach. "I'll tell her you said hello."

When I woke up in the morning, more tired than I had been before going to bed, Lindy was gone. George was already out too. Sun Deer was alone at the table finishing a bowl of porridge with fresh plums and maple syrup.

"Morning Mister Deer," I said on my way to the fridge. For some reason I couldn't help feeling a little intimidated — something about him always unsettled me.

"Good morning," he replied. He looked at me with what could have been a frown. "You didn't sleep well?"

"Like a baby," I said. "Up every hour, thrashing and crying."

I squeezed two grapefruits for juice and looked into the pot of porridge on the stove. "Good breakfast?" I asked.

"Nothing but the best."

I filled my bowl and took it to the table. "If you don't mind the company," I said before sitting down. With anyone else I wouldn't have bothered to ask.

"You're most welcome, Little Brother," Sun Deer said. Once I'd settled and had a few spoonfuls, he spoke again. "I understand it was your article that turned the spark into a fire on this campaign."

Was he accusing or thanking me? It was always hard to tell with Sun Deer. Those stern expressions could go either way. "I guess," I said. "I don't know."

"That's what I was wondering. Just what do you know?"

It was a good question. I had to think it over. "Not much," I admitted. Maybe honesty would work with Sun Deer. "Just what I'm told."

Was it a hint of a smile that touched his lips or a last bit of porridge he was working down? "George Templington thinks the aboriginal involvement in this issue is spurious," he continued. "What about you?"

I took in a heaping spoonful of porridge and pointed to my mouth to gain time while I gummed and swallowed. I didn't want to admit I couldn't remember what spurious meant. Was it something like hasty? "George is pretty set in his ways," I offered. "But deep down? He's not such a bad guy."

Sun Deer seemed to accept the dodge. Before he could ask more, I changed the topic.

"You know, I'm actually part Indian myself."

He didn't extend his arms to clasp me to his chest as a blood relative. He didn't launch into a traditional chant to celebrate the fact of our unity in the greater cause of cultural self-determination. He grunted, a tiny little, "Hmm."

"On my father's side. Apparently it was my grandfather," I offered.

He nodded slightly. I could see no encouragement to go on, but I did anyway, mostly for a lack of anything else to say. "He was a Cree. As I understand it."

Did he doubt me? Could he sense I was no more native than John Wayne? His expression gave nothing away.

"So I guess that kind of makes us related. In a way," I said.

He looked briefly askance as if I'd just announced I was pregnant with his child. An instant later his face was blank again. This time I was pretty sure I detected a smile.

"Maybe so, Little Brother," he said. "Maybe so."

He seemed unwilling to pursue the topic, so I didn't disturb him when he turned back to a file folder full of documents he'd been marking with a highlighter. I ate quickly and left.

The park looked like a scene from a '70s movie about a natural disaster, the part where the evacuees flee by the thousands — except here they were all coming *to* something. People were packed in all directions radiating out from the tree. Only when you got to the edge of the crowd, a good distance further from the tree than the day before, was there any space to walk easily around without bumping into people.

I spotted Kendricks talking with a bare-chested man in purple drawstring pants. He had his notebook out but wasn't writing. The man said something that Kendricks replied to with an aggressive laugh. The man looked at him stonily. Kendricks shrugged and moved on. He approached a girl in a gauzy headkerchief, beads and Indian-print regalia. Maybe he had a thing for hippie-chicks. Maybe he used to be a hippie himself. With his longish hair, a beard and a headband would have completed the part. It was odd that I hadn't seen that at all back in the city.

The girl didn't respond to whatever he asked, unless her answer was meant to be transmitted via interpretive dance. She broke into a head-bobbing, snakey-armed, cosmic-child sway even though there was no music playing. It was strange enough, but Kendricks was game. He matched her for a few moves, which made her smile, before he moved on. I didn't bother stopping him to say hello. Maybe he was finding his element, or whatever he had come for. He seemed to be doing all right without any input from me. He disappeared into the thicker part of the crowd. What could I do but keep plugging away myself?

The healing parts in my story had apparently hit a chord, to judge by the many more visitors today on crutches or in wheelchairs. One patch of grass was covered by wheeled hospital beds parked in a tight formation, some with IV drip bags dangling over the patients' heads. It looked like a field trip for a casualty ward.

I headed back to the street to find a pay phone to call the paper. I got a hold of Danny on the obituary desk.

"The tree man checks in!" Danny said. "You're my hero. Did I ever tell you that? Despite the fact that I now also hate your guts. And that nobody, but nobody, of any significance at all, has died lately. You ever hear of Jerome Parsificks?"

"Who?"

"Exactly. That's what thousands of readers are going to ask tomorrow when they see it's the number one obit of the day. Turns out he used to write plays or something. 'Who cares?' is the real question. I'm now engaged on a quest to discover the least possible achievement you need to rate an extended obit — the LPA, you might say. So far Jerome Parsificks is right up there. But he could get edged out by the person who coined the use of 'and/or.'"

"Danny, did they run my story this morning?"

"Did they run it? You didn't hear? They practically crowned it. They made like it was the biggest thing in on-the-scene storytelling since Homer. Starting on the front page, column side. Starting, I said — with a dog-ear promo on the masthead besides. Using that dorky picture of you, by the way. You look like one of those singing geeks, the Osmonds? Speaking of celebrities who ought to be landing in my section. Give me a light plane and an overconfident has-been and

I'm a happy man. Anyway, then it ran onto a page six continuation, but you were the only thing on the page, except for an ad for washing machines. Then page seven, same story, only the ad was from the diamond industry telling me how much of my salary I need to spend to escape a lifetime of chiseler guilt. Then onto page fourteen, then twenty-two, and finally the back page, entire top half including some wire pics. How many words did you write?"

"No shit? They went with the whole thing?"

"It's you and Tolstoy, my friend. At least that was Pearson's take — he called it *War and Peace and Fraleton*. But you know Pearson."

"Unfortunately. Tell me the truth, was it really bad? I didn't expect them to run it whole hog, I was just getting it down like Gallantine said. I thought the copy desk might bail me out."

"Word is you're on some special Gallantine gig so they're probably afraid to touch it. So what's it really like there? Any home-town Bettys worth checking out?"

"I'll tell you soon as I get the chance, Danny. I should get back to work."

"Oh sure, of course, the star reporter, does he have time to talk to a lowly scrub in the necro-dregs of the paper? Nooo."

"People are waiting to use the phone. Honest."

The last part was true. Three of them had formed a line that began a few uncomfortable inches from my face, though they looked everywhere but at me. Each one had a freshly shaved head, although apparently by coincidence. They didn't seem to be together.

I left the phone booth to mingle back in with the crowd where shaved heads now seemed to be general. Was this a new thing or had I just not noticed earlier? Now that I looked, they gleamed everywhere, popping out of the haired masses like dandelions infesting a lawn. Men, women, old people, teens, it didn't seem to matter. They could have all just stepped out of a huge chemo convention.

But they weren't the only visibly striking people there. Maybe you couldn't have a Miracle Tree without attracting the furthest of the fringe element, the ones who went to Stonehenge for a Druidic epiphany without realizing the Druids had only found it fifteen hundred years after the fact. This was one attraction where the whole space could be considered left field.

One muscular fifty-ish man in a loin cloth had a group of twenty or so followers facing him for a breathing-and-chanting exercise. "*Expel* the negativity," he said, adding an exaggerated whoosh that doubled him over. He rose up slowly on the inhale and said, "*Invite* the prosperity." The group followed him as best they could. A few at the front wore loincloths like his. If that was their idea of prosperity, they were practically there.

A woman's voice behind me called out, "Hello Mayor, so good to see you."

I turned to see a jowly, grey-faced man in a grey suit shaking hands with anyone who would let him. "Mayor Dangworth?" I interrupted.

"A pleasure," he said, his pink, piggy eyes fixed on me in practiced bonhomie. He worked his mouth into the smile of the career politician while pumping my arm as if searching for oil.

"Earl Brododsky of the *City Herald*," I announced, and he let my hand drop.

"So you're the one."

"I just write what I'm told, sir," I said.

"Who told you Filco was building a nuclear waste dump? It isn't true."

"Not true?"

I hadn't considered the possibility. My mind reeled back to where I'd heard it in the first place. Was it from Grady? I pictured him as I had seen him last, at one in the morning, wearing tiger-stripe pajamas, looking somewhat unsure of just where he was.

"It is definitely not."

"True, false," I said, trying to buy time. "There are so many interpretations. As you of all people know." What did that mean? I was practically babbling.

Dangworth looked at me in disbelief. I saw it in his eyes. Could I really be the same person who was writing for the *Herald*?

"You're distorting the whole thing!" he blurted. "No one wants to hurt this town. We love Fraleton! We want to see it prosper."

"*Invite* the prosperity?" I said, drawing a blank look. I couldn't think of anything to follow this with. After an icy pause, he answered.

"Well, yes, that's the idea." Maybe I was capable of reason after all. You just had to talk slower to me, as if to a difficult child or a foreigner. "With the kind of investment dollars this project will bring in, we think the town of Fraleton will virtually blossom."

"Glow is more like it."

Maybe I wasn't so reasonable. He wiped his forehead and snorted in a gesture of disgust at my stupidity. "You have no idea what you're talking about."

People were watching us. Why hadn't I noticed them before? We were the center of a growing circle of curious faces. "And how much will your cut be, may I ask, *Mayor* Dangworth?" I put a little snap into his title to suggest the prospect of a recall, then wondered whether the Fraleton civic system even allowed for them.

He narrowed his eyes. "My cut? Of what?"

"Your pay. Your fee. The loot. The old back-door delivery of ill-gotten goods." I saw interest grow in the eyes of the bystanders. They were scrutinizing Dangworth, and not liking what they saw. I pressed on.

"Just what do you, sir, stand to gain by turning Fraleton into a nuclear dump? Hmm? A site unfit for human visitation by anyone not wearing a lead suit?"

"You silly bugger when I get—" he began, then dropped the hands that had reached instinctively for my throat. He continued in a calmer tone the crowd could hear. "It's not going to be a nuclear dump. It's a bio-tech facility. And you'd hardly even know it's here. It would be almost entirely underground — we've got a beautiful network down there already, built as air raid shelters in the 1950s. It's under the park here right now and no one's even using it. This is about science and innovation, which my administration encourages. With the climactic properties of our region, and the atmospheric pressure conditions found in the subterraneous strata of our hydrated-silicate rich soil, we're ideally positioned to create a unique, very hi-tech, and most of all, clean genome research and production facility. And that," he concluded with a broad smile, extending a palm to include the crowd in his future scenario, "means jobs."

Hydrated silicates? It could have been a bluff. I wished I could remember something, anything, from my high school Earth Sciences class beyond the fact that the teacher wore clip-on ties. "Obviously," I countered. "But that's hardly the point. What about the tree?"

It was a gamble — a top-spin forehand aiming for the far corner when I should have been happy just getting a lob back over the net. But it worked.

Dangworth flinched. "Ahem. We are of course sensitive to the desires of those in the community. . . um. . . those who have developed a fondness for the. . . ah. . . plant subject, or object, the tree, as it were, in question."

I had him. I knew I had him. I started to smile myself. "Ahem?" was all I said. The crowd sensed it too. They pressed in closer, jostling, no one wanting to miss an opportunity to see an elected official squirm.

"We have a contingency plan that is expressly designed to keep the tree's best. . . and future. . . interests in mind. Forever."

He was flailing now. If you squinted your eyes, the way his hair receded on both sides would make his forehead look as if it were sprouting horns.

I didn't say a word. I merely raised my eyebrow, or tried to, in my best Peter Jennings inquisitive impression.

He swallowed audibly. "The tree would be moved," he said at last, punctuating it with a grim smile.

The crowd wasn't sure it liked that at all. But it wasn't sure, period.

People looked to me to determine how they should respond.

I shook my head at the sadness of a town burdened with a devil incarnate for a mayor. "I'm no horticulturist, Mayor Dungworth," I began, trying to help him now, even though I deliberately mispronounced the first syllable of his name. I spoke slowly so he could follow the simple logic of my point and perhaps redeem himself. "But how do you go about moving a tree that's more than two hundred years old without killing it?"

"Yeah," someone said.

"*Move* the tree?" asked someone else incredulously.

"Kill is a loaded word," Dangworth said at once. "We would preserve it, in perpetuity, with a special sealant. Scientists have this all worked out already."

He turned from me to address the crowd again — the politician, back in his element. He raised his right arm to point at the sky, as if the Lord above should strike him dead if he were to utter anything but the gospel truth. I wondered whether God believed in a tight bombing pattern. Wouldn't a lightning strike cut a fairly big swath?

"This way, we need never have to worry about our precious tree growing old, becoming sick, and, yes. . . dying. Which all trees, bar none, will some day experience. This way, my way, the Miracle Tree truly will live forever."

He did it, he turned back the tide. The wily creep. People were divided again, which was exactly what he had wanted. Nobody had even considered the prospect that a tree, like everything else alive, would eventually die. And the idea of eternal life could have struck a chord in the more pious members of the immediate gathering. The murmuring got louder. All I could do was keep shaking my head, dragging out the poor-Mayor-of-Bedrock routine past its sell-by date. Clearly I was stuck.

Of all people, who should come to my rescue but Harold. He looked as if he hadn't spent much time grooming since our last meeting. Nor had he spent my five dollars on a clean T-shirt. But his voice at least carried conviction.

"A plastic tree," he pointed out, "is not alive."

"A *plastic* tree?" a woman shrieked. "Oh my. Heavens no!"

"Not plastic!" a man said. "Is he serious?"

The sentiment spread like brushfire. You could have substituted the word "toxic" for plastic in any of the conversations erupting around us.

Dangworth whipped his head back to see who had started it. He spotted Harold and winced. "I never said—" he began but people were not listening: they were still trying to digest the concept of a plastic tree.

"Like a goddamn hunk of vinyl," commented a beefy-armed man in a John Deere cap. "Our Miracle Tree."

"Who wants to replace the tree with plastic?" a newcomer at the back of the gathering wanted to know.

"The mayor," several voices answered, uttering the title with contempt.

"Mayor of what?"

"He wants to redo the thing in plastic? Is the man mad?"

"But that would kill it!"

"Why does a speed bump like this need a mayor anyway?"

Dangworth was on his tiptoes now, trying to peer over the heads of the mob. He could have been looking for his security crew — or a getaway car. "Now, now," he said with a mirthless chuckle. "The good people of Fraleton don't consider our little municipality a speed bump for anybody or anything, and furthermore—"

"Long live the Miracle Tree!" a woman shouted in a voice cracking with emotion. Dangworth stared open-jawed as if he knew her, and was therefore all the more dismayed to find his own neighbor playing Judas.

"Let's put *him* in plastic!" the John Deere supporter suggested.

"Ha! See how he likes it!"

"Saran Wrap," someone announced. "We need ten, no twelve

rolls. Jumbo size."

Fists thrust forward clenching bills to fund the project. Harold assigned himself the task of collecting the money. That seemed a bad idea to me, but nobody else appeared to mind.

Dangworth could consider himself lucky the crowd was turning in a direction away from his neck. Still, he wouldn't take the chance. He may have been a small town mayor elected on a groundswell vote of dozens but he knew a few things about working a crowd. "Damn right," he proclaimed in a loud voice, "a collection is just what we need." He reached into his vest pocket for his wallet.

The crowd didn't get it. "Yeah, but. . ." one man said.

Dangworth looked into the wallet and then slapped his forehead.

"Shucks. I was afraid of that," he said in a tone of lament. "You folks just hang on right here. I'll go look into the official funding."

He slid past people like an eel swimming through pylons, patting the backs of two or three, shaking the unwilling hand of a man towards the rear, and was gone.

I got back to find Grady's living room empty. The TV was on with the sound muted, George Foreman grinning over a tray of grease. I sat on the couch to work out my next story. It would have to focus on the looming nuclear threat to Fraleton: that seemed the only way to head Dangworth off before he could steer the public perception his way. A little speculation on the mayor could go a long way. He seemed an ideal bad guy to make the story good. I might even interpolate what could have happened if the angry mob had caught him. A man wrapped in his own plastic contradictions? It was too good a scene to leave out just because it may not have happened. At least to the point where it "was widely rumored to have occurred." In a different mood I might have let the wrapping go up all the way, but I felt generous enough to stop just before it reached Dangworth's air supply.

The simmering outrage of the citizenry provided a good backdrop for the story overall, so I decided to stick with it for as long as I could keep spinning things out. The idea was to go on hammering

Dangworth on radiation, nuclear waste, birth defects and more. Use his own denials against him. Who were people going to believe, a major metropolitan newspaper or some tin-pot town mayor?

But then, for the first time since I'd arrived, the issue of credulity made me pause. It wasn't only what the people believed, I had to admit. What I thought mattered too, if not for the paper, and the reading public it served, then for myself, and my own soul. Just what was the tree to me?

On one level, a big hunk of wood and leaves I hadn't even heard of a week earlier — but there was more. Did I honestly believe there could be something to all the miracle stuff? If the answer was no, it meant I had to pull the plug. Which would be difficult now: the parade had already left the parking lot and I was, after all, the leader. The fallout from a debunking would come down hard on the town, but more on me for having gotten everyone riled up.

On the other hand, if I could work a way out of this mess with something like my integrity still intact, I might be seen as a guy who refused to let a mob of misguided hopes and dreams stomp all over common sense. That way I could still be true to the kid who had been pulled out of the frozen lake, someone who'd touched a mystery but didn't let it make him touched, or soft in the head. That way I might even save my career.

But a career as what? Another journo-hack pooh-poohing anything beyond the obvious? Who was I to say whether or not magic really happened? Maybe there are unseen forces affecting our lives in profound ways we can only occasionally capture in glimpses through the fog of so-called science. And maybe they're all we have to connect us to some deeper level of reality that we won't fully understand for decades or even centuries. I was the boy who had been saved by somebody or something unworldly: it shouldn't matter whether I'd worked it all out in my own head. It wasn't my place to snatch the prospect of unseen forces out of anyone else's hands. So hang the reputation. I may not have understood the Miracle Tree, and I definitely had my doubts about the whole wish-fulfilling thing, but I was certain about one thing: it deserved to live. If I could help, and my reports coincidently landed me on the side of the people standing up against a corporate villain, so be it. I would write on.

I wrote faster than I usually do, but still managed to keep to my outline, which included some more nuclear waste warnings but also went heavy on the miracles. I whipped through the Dangworth episode in a blaze. The end came a little more slowly as my mental batteries started to run low and I found myself fishing for quotes to spruce up into zingers. Still, by the conclusion, I was happy with it.

I fell back against the sofa in a satisfied slump, and watched an infomercial for the "Bun-Buddy" — a concave box that looked like a bigger version of a toddler's potty, but was actually a weight-loss device. Guest speakers with firm muscles packed into bright Spandex proudly showed before-shots of their flabby, spreading hams.

I took my laptop up to the room to read the article back. Different room, different ions, sometimes a whole new mood — you never knew how you might react to your own story once you've had a little time away from it. It still read fine. I had the ball.

Lindy came in just as I was about to go back downstairs to email the story in. She looked flushed from the hunt. "Holy smokes, what a freakin' mess!" Even exhausted, her blouse clinging in curious places to her sticky torso, she managed to exude a fresh-soap spunkiness some girls would never know.

"I know. I was in the park most of the morning."

"No, I mean Filco. I just got back."

"You went to Filco? That's impossible. It's out in Hubbensberg."

"I hitched a ride with one of the TV helicopters. The pilot was a good ol' boy. We were buzzing cows and everything."

"No kidding? What happened?"

"We didn't hit any of them."

"I mean at Filco."

"Well Mister General Public, if you'll kindly pick up a copy of the

Weekly Times the day after tomorrow you'll find out, along with the rest of the nation. Can you believe it? Earl, this is so cool!"

"I'd rather hear it first here."

She sat on the edge of the bed and rubbed her neck. The convoluted bed frame apparently affected different people in different ways. I considered the innocuous massage move, a simple start that could lead anywhere, but I was too disturbed to follow through with it.

"You'll steal it," she said happily.

"Lindy, c'mon. It's me you're talking to." I tried to look hurt. It wasn't that hard, since I was already feeling dreadful.

"I'm kidding," she said. "So. After a lot of wrangling, we finally got into the new CEO's office. The jefe. And it turns out — you're not going to believe this — it's Toshihiko Takahashi!"

I thought about pretending I knew who Toshihiko Takahashi might be. "That name sounds familiar," I said instead.

"Right. The samurai businessman who's in the news all the time. The new captain of industry, the tiger of fast finance — with controversial ties to some supposedly shady elements. He bought Filco. Like, totally. Paid cash, if that's even possible for however many gazillion bucks it was. I forget exactly but it's in my notes. On paper it was done as a consortium deal but he told me that it was really all him. It just happened — it hasn't even been officially announced yet." She raised two fingers into a V and smiled. "Until now."

"Anyway."

"Anyway. We did lunch."

"Really? And what did he say?"

"He said my dimples would look lovely reflected in the moonlight on Lake Washisushi or some place like that."

"He came on to you?"

"Is that so surprising?"

"No. Yes. How old is he anyway?"

"Probably fifty, maybe not — it's hard to tell. He's the virulent type. He had samurai swords all over the walls. You could imagine him in a black belt smashing bricks with his bare hands."

I could have, but I didn't want to. I wanted to know what she had on the story. I wanted to know if I was in big trouble. "Anyway," I said, a little more pressingly.

"The point is, we did an interview. That makes it a scoop — he didn't even let the TV guys in. Can you imagine? After I just got here? He's been unavailable ever since some unscrupulous business rival started those awful rumors that he was involved with the yakuza. You know, Japanese gangsters?"

"That's all terribly interesting, but I don't see what it has to do with a nuclear waste processing facility."

"Neither does he."

"Filco is going to put a nuke dump where the tree is."

"That's just it — they're not. Filco has got nothing to do with nuclear waste. Toshi said he wouldn't know a nuclear fuel rod if it turned up in his golf bag."

"What are they building then?"

"Some bio-tech thing. They want to do genetic research and development stuff. Genomes."

"Genomes?" I echoed feebly. This was bad. It meant Dangworth's story could hold up — and he could bury me with it.

"That's right. Very advanced hi-tech stuff. You know the Japanese. And all very clean. He's big on cleanliness."

"How about that?" I said. I tried to look only vaguely interested. Inside, my mind was taking a pounding. I could get scorched by the *Weekly Times*. People read it — the *Times* has a reputation for authority. I never understood why: every few months it ran a cover feature on something like talking pets, but it was still a journalistic force, certainly big enough to ruin a scrub like me for bungling a story. And the person holding the key to everything was sitting here on my bed, rubbing her own creamy neck.

I pounced with both hands out. "Let me get that," I said. "You'll never be able to write."

She jumped at the first touch, but I held on. It's hard to resist someone, anyone, kneading a sore muscle.

"You're so tense," I said, working a little further down her back. I tried to picture just how having sex with Lindy would get her on my side regarding the story. My thought processes refused to travel any further than the sex part — living proof that when it comes down to a contest between your wiener and your brain, bet on the one that can change shape. All the same, I pushed her gently on the shoulder to suggest she lie flat on the bed. "Can't get a decent grip at an angle like this," I explained.

This time I slid my hands inside her shirt and pressed down on her shoulders with enough force to make the mattress sink almost to the floor. I held on for balance, but didn't stop kneading. Lindy let out a long, deep, satisfied sigh. You could even call it a moan.

I got a rolling rhythm going with my hands. Deep pressure from the base of the palms: the wave comes in. Light fingertip circles on the skin: the wave goes out. It was feeling good, for both of us, but I stopped abruptly when I reached her bra. I let out a tiny "tsk" of frustration, as if it were the lone glitch ruining the entire experience. My suddenly limp fingers were meant to send the message: how can an artist work with such an obstacle?

"Let me get that," she offered, starting to sit up.

"Nah, I can do it," I said, without a hint of seduction, knowing fully well that once I had it off, I was as good as in. I unhooked the clasps, and had just pulled the last loop of the bra past her extended fingers, when the sound of the door opening made me turn around.

It was Shirley.

According to quantum mechanics, space is filled with virtual particles and anti-particles that are constantly materializing in pairs and separating and coming together again and annihilating each other.

Stephen Hawking

EIGHT

Why hello, Lindy," Shirley said. She nodded in a way that didn't seem unfriendly. Then she turned to me. "Why hello, scumbag."

"Shirl. This isn't what it looks like," I said, untangling Lindy's bra from my fingers.

"He was just giving me a massage," Lindy said.

"He can give you the whole. . . " she fluttered her fingers while searching for the right word. "Whatever." She spun and walked out, closing the door softly, not giving in to the satisfaction of a slam. I felt a little put out. After all we'd been through? We rated at least a slam.

Lindy sat up. She snatched back her bra and put it on with a rapid contortion of arm-twisting maneuvers. I didn't offer to help.

Shirley's footsteps sounded like Godzilla fleeing down a staircase. That was more like it, and a formidable exit for an ex-dancer who could walk on a pie crust without breaking through.

I felt stuck in place. I knew I had to go after her but what would I say? Or do? Make a scene of it? Come clean? With what, exactly? I bolted for the door, knowing she would not be in the mood for a discussion of widely accepted massage techniques. But I couldn't just let her leave. If I didn't at least make the attempt, she might hold it against me for years.

"Look, um. . . later," I said to Lindy.

She didn't bother answering. She was already bent over her laptop, working out the story that would send me back to the farm team for a dismal career in the minor leagues. Nice job, Brododsky. From page one by-liner to class-ad proofer in one bleak day.

Out on the lawn I caught Shirley by the elbow. She had her car keys out. Would she really turn around and drive all that way back after coming so far?

"Shirl," I said in a conciliatory tone.

She shrugged off my hand with a snap of her arm. Yes, she would. Of course Shirley would not think twice about something like personal comfort when it came to doing the right thing. She was a slave to her own convictions: even when they were impractical, when seeing them through might cause a shit-storm of unseen proportions, it had to happen. Right was right in Shirley's world, and there was no way around it.

At the same time, I knew it also meant she occasionally looked for confirmation that her position was correct. When your political beliefs carry that much personal weight, you can't afford mistakes. This was one more thing that helped make our relationship a bedrock, even when we weren't getting along. We, the two of us, were the emotional constant in an ever-changing world of political uncertainty. Which meant I was the port to come home to. Honesty, loyalty, dependability — they all came to Shirley as easily as sympathy for a lost kitten. But tolerance? I had to worry about that one. It was not what anyone would call her strong point. When it came to forgetting a perceived transgression, Shirley was like the Hezbollah.

"Shirley, c'mon," I tried. She was fumbling to fit the key in the Beetle door. "Don't go."

She stopped for a second, tilting her head, perhaps thinking of the perfect answer. She didn't have one. Not a verbal one anyway. She opened the door.

"Shirl. You have to at least look at me while we do this," I said. "Otherwise it isn't fair."

I'd said the magic word. She happened to be interested at the moment in my definition of "fair." She closed the door and leaned back against it. She was tall enough that even when bent at an angle she still towered over the roof. Her arms went up across her chest.

"Fair," she mused. Then: "Hmm. Fair?"

"Okay, I know, I get it. You're angry. What exactly do you want? An apology for something I didn't even do?"

"Five more minutes would have taken care of that."

"I think the point here is not what might have happened, it's—"

"Thoughts carry the same karmic weight as actions, Earl. Who was it told me that?"

I smiled. Then immediately stopped when I saw her reaction. She bore into me with a look that made me lean back.

"So?" she insisted. "Where do you think that puts you?"

I was stuck for an answer. She had me. Shirley would always have me. That was part of our deal. When all else fails, try honesty. It had always worked between us. At least up to then.

"You're right," I said. I raised my hands in contrition. "Who knows what could have happened next? Maybe nothing. I was ready for it, though, I admit it. Hey, I was horny. You weren't around." I tried to make the last sentence sound accusatory.

She didn't take it that way. "What's Lindy doing here anyway?"

"She didn't have a room and everything in town is all booked up and I knew this place had cots and we're all friends after all, right? So when she showed up and it was already late there was no—"

"No. What's she doing here for work?"

"She got a freelance gig."

"For?"

"The *Weekly Times*."

"No shit? Good for Lindy."

"Yeah, well, maybe. But bad, very bad, for Earl. She's up there right now writing a story that's going to bury me."

She perked up at that. Finally a development that struck her as promising. I told her about Lindy's visit to Filco, how it did not quite resemble the company I'd been writing about, how my nuclear waste angle could have been off the mark, and how once the confusion was cleared up I would properly be the object of well-deserved ridicule no matter where I went in the journalism world. If I managed to go anywhere beyond some *Dog Walker Gazette*.

"Aw Early, you mean your meteoric rise to the top of our craft is stopping just when I show up to be your assistant?"

"My assistant? That doesn't sound right."

"I know. I actually came to see if I could help with some volunteer organizing for the native campaign. But I also wanted to get out of town — I needed a break, some country air."

"Uh huh." Shirley was not the outdoorsy type either. She considered bugs all the proof we needed that people belonged in cities.

"All right," she conceded. "Maybe I missed you."

"Hey. That's my gi — my woman." I moved closer to take her in my arms and lean with her against the warm steel of the Beetle.

But she pushed me back. "I did say 'maybe.' Horn dog."

I laughed, even though it wasn't funny. "Speaking of which, precious," I said, achingly close but not about to disturb the truce by touching her again. "When's the last time we had our nice time, you know, just you and me?"

She didn't answer.

"Hey!" I tried. "Did you notice how many stars you can see out here? Check it out."

I thought I'd done well in not bringing up Shirley's late-night absences from home. I still had something in reserve in case things got worse.

"The stars? You're walking the plank here, do you not see that? One more step and sploosh, you're in the water, and yet all you can think about is getting laid."

"No, that wasn't what—"

"You're such a boy."

"Well. When it comes right down—"

"And it says more about me that I've stayed with you this long — because I can't admit to myself that I ought to have outgrown you years ago."

"Shirl, c'mon, this isn't—"

"No, don't even say it. You'll just turn it into a joke."

I put a hand to my chest. It might have been a gesture of sincerity, but I used it to buy time. The next words I spoke could be crucial. I already had the looming sense of this conversation as the type of exchange you look back on as a turning point. But from what to what? "Shirley. I swear. You've always been the only one for me."

"Stop. Don't even say it. It wouldn't help. Believe me. You're on the shit list. I'm just trying to think of some reason why it shouldn't be permanent. We need to talk."

I willed myself to nod in agreement. A conversation our about relationship. To discuss our feelings. When I knew mine already. They were straining against my jeans.

"Yes. Of course. Let's talk. About us. Right. Okay."

"Not that, you tool. Your story. You file yet? For tomorrow?"

"I was just about to send it in when I ran into Lindy. She's writing her piece right now. The one that's going to kill me."

One eyebrow went back up. I would have preferred a furrow of concern. I explained how Lindy's scoop would trump the story that had brought so many people out to Fraleton.

Shirley was not the type to stretch a journalistic rule. She had the stiffest ethical backbone of anyone I'd ever known — but her notion of proper editorial practices was based on a somewhat different model than we'd learned in school. She was motivated by a higher cause: her mission was to serve a greater ideal than some myth of journalistic objectivity that could never be achieved anyway given a corporate-dominated capitalist mainstream media. You had to go after the truth, not just the simple facts. The capital T Truth. I hoped she could see the higher political implications involved here and get me out of the hot water.

"So Toshi Takahashi bought Filco?" she mused. "I'll be damned."

"You and a lot of other decent, hard-working folks," I pointed out with an indignation that she ignored. "Listen, Shirl," I continued. "Lindy's story is going to paint Filco as a misunderstood organization headed by an unjustly accused Japanese gentleman of high finance who simply wants to bring good to the community."

I shouldn't have laid it on so thick. She shot me a dubious look.

But she was still thinking. "Everybody knows Filco is run like a gulag for its workers," she said, "and Takahashi is a corporate criminal. It makes sense they would come together. Good on Lindy for getting it first."

"Good on her. Not on me," I said.

"Not much you can do about that. It's hers."

"Naturally."

"Then there's the bio-tech thing."

"Not nearly as threatening as a toxic nuke dump," I lamented.

"True — but who's to say just what they're building? These companies are famous for calling it one thing and then when it gets to the approval stage, admitting it's something else. I wouldn't be a bit surprised to hear the waste dump stuff is part of the whole plan."

"Exactly. Proof, schmoof. When it comes to a company like Filco, I mean."

But Shirley was already ahead of me, figuring out the angles. "Lindy has such potential," she said, pinching her lower lip between her fingers.

I might have agreed, picturing our cute j-school colleague on the bed, her legs angled up to the heavens, but I kept my estimate of her potential to myself.

"I'd hate to see her take a wrong step now. Even if it is a giant step. She's really here for the *Weekly Times*?"

"Stringing. It's a spec piece."

"Hmm."

It was always a treat to watch Shirley think. She would tug on an ear lobe, smooth out an eyebrow, trace the line of her lips with the tip of a finger. Sometimes, nearing a solution, but not quite there, she would dig her curled fingers into a mound of hair and whip it all around for an air shampoo. That's what happened now.

"I got it," she said at last. "At least I think I do. As far as we're concerned, Filco can eat it. Right?"

"You bet," I said crisply. It was best to keep comments supportive and short whenever Shirley was churning towards a solution.

"They deserve to eat shit no matter how it ends up getting served to them. Even if it has to be through you and what would seem to be your psychotic imagination. By some miracle, it's worked up to now. You're ahead of the game, so you may as well keep on hitting homers. Fuck Filco, and fuck Takahashi in particular — he's the major creep who buys companies and ships the jobs off to places like Saipan where they get kids to work in factories run like prison shops."

"He's a thug," I said.

"Probably that too. It's the standard line anyway: suspected of close ties to organized criminal elements blah blah blah. Maybe he is, or maybe it's racist pandering. He is foreign and rich after all. We'll have to watch for that once his role in this is out there — you wouldn't want to feed into any anti-Asian stereotyping."

"Of course not." I made a mental note to delete the line in my draft about samurai swords and the common torture fetishes of Oriental sadists.

"Either way, he's a corporate scum of the worst stripe," Shirley continued. "So what difference does it make in the long run?"

"No difference at all," I said. This was just like old times, working out a math assignment. I felt a surge of confidence with Shirley back on my side.

"Filco has been bleeding people dry for decades, only now with Takahashi running the show and plenty of financing muscle they're going to be doing it a lot faster."

"Another capitalist greedhead planting his boot on the necks of the people," I ventured with what I believed was an appropriate degree of venom.

"Watch it, Early," she warned, adding a suspicious sideways glance. She knew I was with her on most political counts. I just didn't treat them with the same measure of outrage that she did.

"So. We've got two things to do. Keep you in the game, and stuff it up Filco with their own slam dunk."

"Exactly." Shirley hated sports, those spectacles to distract the masses, but liked the metaphors and appropriated them to occasionally baffling effect.

I looked up to the single lit window where Lindy was working, typing out my downfall. Shirley sensed what I was thinking. "So you got beat on Takahashi's buyout. Tough testicles. You've still got your own story. I say stick with it. Gallantine has gone too far to pull back now."

"But our stories don't exactly match."

"Who says they have to?"

I had to hide my disappointment. That was the best Shirley could do? A gamble like that? My career on the table and she turns cavalier? This was too important to leave to some magazine editor to decide. If Lindy's people at the *Weekly Times* went big with her piece, mine would have to back off. And once that happened, I would have lost it — the story wouldn't be mine any more. They probably wouldn't even let me stay. It would be like getting sent down to the minor leagues: a lot of players never get a second call-up.

We walked back into the house together. I thought about taking her hand on the pretense of leading a guided tour of the place, but didn't want to press my luck. We walked up the stairs in silence and stopped outside the door. It was my room, but I knocked anyway.

From inside Lindy said, "Come." Hunched over her laptop, she typed a few words quickly, hit the save command and stood up. She eyed us warily. The dimples were primed — you could sense them under the surface, crocuses about to push up through the snow, but she needed to know first that we were all right.

Shirley broke the ice. "You're looking awesome, girlfriend."

It was not only true, but apparently the right thing to say. Lindy grinned. Full watt dimples. "You too," she said.

They met for a hug. So far, so good. I wasn't about to clutter anything up by trying to make it a three-way grope.

"I heard about your *Weekly Times* gig," Shirley said. "Way to go."

Lindy tilted her head to one shoulder. "I don't know. It's totally on spec. They probably won't even take it."

"Your stuff is sharp, girl. They'll have to."

"Thanks! But writing's like pulling teeth for me. I wish I could be like you. You're the natural."

"No, you're the best, you always were."

"Excuse me," I interrupted. "If I can edge a word into the sisterhood support committee. I'm going to go downstairs to finish up." I hefted my laptop under my arm.

"Great," Lindy said, looking at her own computer, then at Shirley, then at the bed, then back at me. "When I'm done here I'll just go."

"No way," Shirley said. "You're here. You're staying."

"Of course," I insisted, but not too forcefully. Emily Post herself would have been in a pickle here.

"I don't want to be in anyone's way. . ." Lindy offered.

"No problem," I said. "Really. We can work it out. And you don't have to worry about being stuck around any excess couple energy between us. For one thing, Shirley's still a tad miffed at me for massaging you, although not all over, I might add, and for another thing, I'm going to sleep on the floor."

"No, I couldn't let you do that."

"You certainly could," Shirley said. "He's lucky we even let him stay in the room."

Lindy laughed. The dimples came out like headlights. "I'm cool with whatever you guys want to do," Lindy said. "I'm just anxious to get my story filed. Then I don't much care what happens."

Half an hour later, I was in the living room reworking my story when Sun Deer walked in. "Late night?" I said in a low voice. One side of his face was illuminated by the glow of the TV screen showing a Stallone movie set in a prison. The rest of the house was dark. There were no signs that anyone else was up.

"As usual. Meetings. Work." He plopped himself onto the couch with a gesture of collapse. He rubbed his face, then picked up the remote control. He raised his eyebrows towards me to ask permission.

"Feel free," I said. "I'm not really paying attention. I just like the ambiance."

He kept the sound muted while zapping through the channels. He stopped at a documentary on the life of Foster Brooks and eased the volume up.

I wrote up everything I knew, and a lot more I didn't know, but could easily imagine, about Toshihiko Takahashi, based largely on a long late night call to Danny. He'd spent a year as an exchange student in Osaka. He said he hadn't liked it because, big surprise, it was crowded, but he came back with an obsessive interest in yakuza movies — he had boxes of them on video. No one had ever showed an interest until my phone call. He was happy to fill me in. It made for some lively details in the story, but I still felt a little self-conscious using it. I'd gotten the Takahashi thing straight from Lindy. I wondered if I should wait two days for her piece to come out before mentioning him — but by then I might lose the whole thing. It wasn't just me, it was the town's future that was at stake. She would see it that way too, eventually. Besides, it wasn't as if I was stealing; more like borrowing, a little ahead of time. What was forty-eight hours between friends?

Shirley came downstairs, nodded to Sun Deer and started reading over my shoulder.

"Hey," I protested. "C'mon." I covered up the screen with my hands. "You know the rules."

"Early, be cool. Just the lead."

"You ever let me read one of your stories before it was done?"

"Don't be such a baby. Scroll up. At least give me a couple of paras." So I did, after ensuring they had no mention of Takahashi.

"Not bad," she said, approvingly.

"Is it better than Lindy's opening?"

"Lindy can write. You know that. You still going with the nuke dump stuff?"

"In a way."

"Lindy's got something solid going with those genomes. They might even use something like that on the cover. The Geekly loves science stories. You sure your nuke angle is strong enough to hold up?"

"How can anyone be sure of anything?"

"Oh no," she said. "I recognize that tone."

"Hey. It's not like I just made it up. Don't be silly. What do you take me for?"

She eyed me like I was a garage sale toaster. Very suspicious. But it was a good question. What did she take me for?

"Earl Antonius Brododsky," she warned.

"It was on the original wire service piece. Remember?" I reasoned.

"Was it?" There was a pause. "Okay. And you followed up on it," she continued.

"Naturally. Well. As best as one could. Under the circumstances."

"Then there's no prob. Nobody would expect you to have to handle the plutonium yourself. So you go with what you got."

"I'm holding the ball."

"And you should keep running with it."

"Good one!"

"I just hope you know what you're doing."

She patted me on the head like a good pupil. She smiled for the first time since I'd seen her that night. I reached for her hand but she pulled it away. Instead, she took it over to Sun Deer and offered it to him to shake while introducing herself.

He slid over to make space for her on the sofa. They talked in low voices. When Foster Brooks stumbled several times on the word "purpose" Shirley laughed out loud, and Sun Deer's lips rose slowly up into the biggest smile I'd seen on him yet.

I was relieved that Shirley hadn't pressed to read more of my story. She might have accused me of laying things on. Although I'm not the one who first calculated the lethal effects of nuclear waste would last 350,000 years. Or maybe it was 250,000. I couldn't remember, but I didn't see any point in cutting the potential dangers short. It was already an established fact. Who's going to quibble when it's obviously a long time?

Some of the rest may have relied on what could be called extrapolation, but I made sure to include those catch-all reporter cop-outs like "reputed" when calling new Filco CEO Toshi Takahashi a "yakuza strongman" and "rumored" to describe Mayor Dangworth as "heavily influenced by well-heeled developers." I couldn't resist adding my own observation that Dangworth was "unable to hide a nervous tic when confronted with troubling questions," but that was more for color than anything. You have to give the reader some encouragement to keep plodding on.

I did feel a bit out of my league with the yakuza stuff, but didn't let that stop me. Danny had been a great help. I even used his quote, attributing it to a specialist in the sociology of Japanese crime. He'd explained they were "hardly the chivalrous outlaws portrayed in films. The real-life yakuza is more of a thick-skulled hood in white enamel shoes."

In a minor aside, I had a man near the park quickly reduced to ashes in a case of spontaneous combustion. I'd always had a soft spot for astonishing stories of human torches. When else would I ever get the chance to write one?

Lindy waited for me in the living room while I emailed my story. Then it was her turn to plug into the phone jack. "Wish me luck," she said, crossing her fingers. When her connection was announced with a static hiss, it sounded like a death knell, for my career in reporting.

"Luck," I said, trying to keep any trace of worry out of my voice. She finished and we hit the staircase together, just as I had earlier with Shirley. Obviously we would not be walking up hand in hand, so I did the polite thing, motioning for Lindy to go first. When that gave me a close-up view of her ass moving all the way up, I wondered if I had gotten the etiquette mixed up.

Shirley was lying on the bed reading a magazine article about some outrage in Eritrea. She got up at once.

Lindy started to pack her laptop and gather her things. "I can just scrunch over in the corner," she offered. "You won't even know I'm here."

"No way," Shirley said. "You take the bed."

"I couldn't."

I'll second that, I thought. No one could.

"You have to," Shirley said. "I can do the cot. Earl's fine on the floor."

Later, when Lindy was in the shower, I sat up from my floor space and fired a question I hadn't planned on asking but for some reason did anyway. "Hey Shirl," I said, as if bemused. "Who's Barry?"

I timed the response. It was an instant too long.

"Barry who?" came her flat answer.

"Barry who," I cajoled. "Do you know someone named Barry or not?"

Another second passed. A second is a long time for some answers.

"Oh, do you mean Barry Fleming? He's just a customer. Why?"

"No reason."

"You asked me. There's a reason."

Lindy came back, ending the discussion. She smelled like a combination of chemicals and herbal extracts. She was still buzzing from writing her story: I recognized the glow, the shining eyes, the rapid speech. "Thanks a mil, you guys," she said. "I can't believe I just sent my first ever real story in to a place like the *Weekly Times*! That's so cool! And thanks a lot for letting me stay here. I'll look for somewhere else tomorrow. I don't want to be in the way."

"You don't have to do that," Shirley said. "We don't mind."

Didn't we? I couldn't be sure. That night I learned it is also impossible to sleep in the same room with two beautiful women if you weren't sleeping with at least one of them. Lindy and Shirley shifted from a conversation in soft murmured sentences I couldn't decipher to giggling whispers, followed by first one and then both lost to the slow, steady breathing of the peacefully asleep. I heard their limbs sliding across the sheets and their soft exhalations and their nocturnal murmurs as a summons to my manhood. I just couldn't figure out how to work the math.

Later in the dark I heard Shirley came back from the bathroom.

"How's that cot, Shirl?" I whispered. Maybe I could convince them that the most comfortable solution to the bad bed frame would be to have two people balance out the sagging bedsprings. It could be a squeeze, but so be it. Two people would, under the circumstances, probably have to be the girls — and once they were in bed together, who knew? Maybe the concept of a squeeze would be suggestive. The rest would be self-explanatory. Shirley once said she wouldn't mind experimenting with another girl, all together, if I really wanted to.

I did, naturally, but at the time lacked the foresight to say so. Now, if ever, we seemed to have the ideal chance. If we were on a fishing trip, and Lindy was a giant bass, it would be the equivalent of the fish jumping into the boat.

"The cot's a cot," she whispered back. "How's the floor?"

"Hard," I said.

"I'll bet." She turned to her side, away from me, and drew the covers up over her ears. Lindy hadn't moved at all.

I still couldn't sleep. I was like a harem pool cleaner, unable to focus. I gave up trying. I decided fresh night air might be settling. I headed, naturally, as if on a migration, straight to the Miracle Tree.

I spotted Kendricks in the flickering light of a bonfire. He was sitting with a group of NuVooduns — white kids, mostly, all with dreadlocks and matching cream-colored robes. I'd seen them earlier but hadn't stuck around, having taken them for posers. I wasn't interested in their latest affinity, borrowed from a long line of dubious reggae trends that included space dub and competitive toasting, although this time it borrowed not from Jamaican culture but the darker recesses of Haitian occult drumming. Most of the tribe were playing hand drums while a few made a fuss over a long and shiny machete, pouring rum onto the blade and waving their fingers at the dripping runoff.

Kendricks eagerly waved me over to sit beside him. "Bloody hell," he said, which sounded right, under the circumstances, although for him it was a common term. There will always be an England.

"What now?" I asked.

He lifted his shoulders for an answer, but didn't take his eyes off the ceremony. "Some sort of sacrifice, I expect," he said. He made his eyes go wide. "Big medicine."

Those of the NuVooduns who were not pounding out the demented rhythm or staring at the machete were dancing — if that's the proper word. It looked more like a charade of the spirit possessed. The dancers held their arms straight out in front, palms down, while trudging in place to the droning beat. I recognized it and had to bite my tongue to keep from laughing out loud: they were doing the zombie stomp from an old Peanuts cartoon.

The music got louder. Kendricks said something I couldn't hear. I shouted back but he mimed a deaf person with one hand cupped behind an ear. I pitied the people trying to sleep, then realized I was among them. It took some effort to keep a blink from stopping on the down stroke and staying there. Or perhaps I was being drummed into a spirit trance myself — my brain felt gummier with each new round of drumming, which now sounded more like a dirge. That wasn't an entirely pleasant thought, but I didn't let it stop the sound from lulling me into a near-slumber.

"Super," Kendricks said, drawing me back to attention. I could hear him clearly now, even though the drummers were still active. "Couldn't have asked for better," he went on, as if answering a question I had no recollection asking. "Plenty of interest in a book deal either way. Freaks of colonial in-breeding on the one hand. Astonishing tales of the supernatural on the other."

I felt like asking about the third hand, his own take. But that might have opened up his own questions of me. At that stage, trying to decipher the real story, or my own level of commitment to it, seemed a burden too heavy to ever lift off the ground.

One of the dancing NuVoodun girls spun in tight circles long past the point I would get dizzy, then unrolled the top half of her robe down to her waist. She was not wearing a bra. The white patches of her breasts glowed red in the firelight. I realized she was dancing dervish-like around an object someone had placed on the ground. I saw between her spinning ankles that it was a cauliflower.

Kendricks was visibly impressed. His head jerked in synch with the main beat while his wide, fire-reflecting eyes seemed to radiate in appreciation of the grandeur of the spectacle, although he could have just been admiring her tits.

The dancer raised the cauliflower slowly up and over her head as the drumming sped up. Her body resonated with the new urgency of the beat, no longer swaying, now closer to vibrating, as if it were her very blood being driven by the music. She closed her eyes and let her jaw drop in an expression that might have been bliss. Kendricks gulped, transfixed. She rocked with a gyration that started from her pelvis and spread in shimmering waves up and down the length of her body. She turned the cauliflower in slow circles above her head, a calm eye in the center of her eerie personal storm.

One of the men approached with the machete and, from one knee, offered it up to her. An oversized knife was not the first thing I would have thought to hand someone in her condition, but what do I know about pseudo-Voodoo rites?

She wanted the machete, but with her eyes closed she had to grope down his arm until she reached it. Now she had a cauliflower in one hand and the machete in the other — but what she did next was not what we were expecting. She suddenly leapt — or maybe flew — a good five yards to close the space between us. Kendricks and I were no longer on the fringe of the scene: we were the scene. All eyes were on us.

The drumming shifted into a throbbing cadence that seemed less like music than a summons to some malevolent region of the soul. The priestess swung her machete with unathletic flourishes as she continued to spin, each circle coming ever closer to us. I was just thinking about escape routes when I felt a whoosh. The blade passed nearly under our chins.

"Goddamn!" I blurted out, sensing the bare skin on my throat as a potential target. I had never felt more exposed.

"Brilliant!" Kendricks said. "This is what I'm talking about!"

"Decapitation?"

"The true spiritual warrior is unafraid to walk through the valley of his own fears," he said.

"That doesn't even make sense," I started to say, but was cut off when she spun nearer again, this time swinging the blade over our heads. It wasn't as close as the lower swing, but I wasn't about to wait for the third attempt to average out the distances. "That does it," I announced. I started to get up. "These people are insane."

A hand on my shoulders eased me back down. The rest of the NuVooduns had crowded around us. We were hedged in as if at the center of a rugby scrum.

"What the hell?" I said, trying to sound too tough to intimidate, but it came out more like a croak. A scared croak. I turned to see who had touched me but the cool steel of the machete across my cheek drew my eyes back to the front. She wiped the flat side of the blade across the skin of my forehead. It didn't hurt, but also did nothing to soften my opinion of her concern for safety.

"Listen," I said, angrily. "You can take your—"

She stopped me by leaping with feline quickness into my lap. She extended a foot on either side to straddle me, as close as she could get without being behind me, yet seeming not to register I was even there as she continued writhing to the incessant beat. The machete twirled and gleamed in the firelight, sometimes an inch from my nose, sometimes out of sight behind my back. I felt her warm breath on my forehead. Her nipples bounced in front of my eyes.

"Yes!" I heard Kendricks exclaim in a voice riding somewhere above the music. "I say. You bring a camera?"

Her eyelids started to flicker and then only the whites showed underneath. It would have made a ghastly picture.

"Miss," I pleaded. "If only we could talk, I'm sure whatever it is that has you so riled up could easily be worked out."

She let out a shriek in reply. It was not the sound you might think a young woman in a performance piece would produce. This was no theatrical scream — it was the howl of a panther caught in a trap.

The drummers responded with various murmurs of encouragement. "Yasssss, mon," a voice behind me said.

Now I seemed to feel the drums rather than hear them. They rumbled in my chest. It was as if I were the instrument.

She opened her mouth, breathing harder. She smelled like sweat and fear. Or was that coming from me? I was suddenly aware that it was very hot. Her body pressing me down to the earth had a warm heft.

"Okay, I take back my comment about your group being insane," I offered. "Now maybe we could all just settle down a tad here and get our bearings."

Her panting took on a more manic edge. Everything was escalating. The pace could not possibly hold. We were moving very rapidly towards something.

"Uh-uh-uh-uh uhhhhh." Her grunts came out faster, an urgent longing for release. For the first time, incredibly, despite all the evidence, I wondered about the sexual aspect of the whole thing. To my own private horror, I felt the first stirring of a boner.

No. Not that, I thought — please. If all it took was one teeny comment to get her this emotional, what might a major faux pas of the flesh do? I willed myself to think of something, anything, except the weight of her body squirming on my groin. Shirley. Lindy. Shirley and Lindy. This wasn't helping.

"Hooona hooona hoooooooo-nahhhhh," the people around us began to chant.

"Kendricks," I hissed. "They've lost it. They're going to kill us. You got to get her off me."

But he was lost in a trance of his own. He bounced like a cross-legged yogi trying to fly. Failing that, he switched to whipping his arms in elaborate geometric patterns above his head — his version of the dance. He looked like an agitated chimpanzee.

"Uh-uh-uh-uh-uh-uh-uh-uh uhhhhh uhhhhh," she moaned, higher now, the rhythm quickening as she went on, the drums racing in turn to match her. The machete snaked in front of my eyes. I caught the emblem on the handle: L.L. Bean. What? Were they kidding?

Her lower jaw went slack, opening her mouth wide — so wide I could see a fair way in and down. Was that her esophagus? From out of it came what might have been a silent scream, but was not silent for long. When the actual sound emerged it was a ghoulish cry. I sat there, barely an inch from the source, and felt myself consumed. My ears didn't hurt like they should have, perhaps because I was too close. The shock waves must have started somewhere beyond me. As it was, my head felt enveloped, a rock jutting up in a rushing river of scream.

The cauliflower appeared in mid-air just above my head. I'd forgotten all about the vegetable's role in this. She must have just tossed it up. When it reached its apogee, she aimed a mighty two-handed swing, a home-run effort. But she missed — the cauliflower fell, untouched, onto my head, bounced once and rolled down my chest to wedge into the narrow space between our bellies.

She raised the machete for another swipe, but I knocked the cauliflower away. I jumped up, knocking her off, and spun around. I took off at a run, not bothering to look back.

Behind me I heard another, shorter scream from the women, followed by the thwit of steel slicing through something wet. I could only hope it wasn't Kendricks's head.

I ran all the way back to Grady's. Before pulling my body up the stairs for a well-earned sleep, I decided to call the copy desk to confirm the email transmission had gone through.

The night editor told me Hanover was still in the office, which was one surprise, and also that he wanted to talk to me, which was another. Hanover usually left much earlier, unless there were some breaking story to follow through. I hadn't thought my piece would be enough to keep him around. I cursed myself for being so stupid as to bait my own trap like that with a phone call.

"Bororsky," he said, demonstrating an improvement on pronouncing my name with each day. "Hang on. Something in your copy doesn't fly right."

I gulped. That sentence encompassed so many possibilities there was no way to begin assembling anything like a defense. All I could say was, "Oh, really?" I tried to make it sound like genuine surprise, while still remaining casual, as if we were about to discuss some arcane grammatical point about a dangling participle rather than the crux of my piece, that the possibility of miracles was in peril because Filco was a nuke-infested plague run by a dangerous foreign criminal.

"Are you certain the person you describe went up like. . . wait a minute." I heard a rustle of paper while he searched for the line he wanted. "Like a marshmallow placed too close to the campfire?"

He was referring to the throw-away vignette I'd dropped in about the guy who spontaneously combusted.

"Yes, sir. Just like that. *Whump.*" It was too late to back down now.

"Not like a Roman candle?"

"No — definitely a marshmallow."

"And you didn't get a name?"

"He was hardly in a condition to answer questions."

"From the police. Or family, friends. Whomever."

"He seemed to have come alone. I think I put that in the story."

"Yes, so I read," he said, drawing out the sentence to convey suspicion. If that was his biggest complaint, I wasn't about to panic. I had described the victim being reduced to a small mound of ashes: he wasn't about to get up and contradict my version of the event. Not to mention the fact that it hadn't happened anyway, although I did hear during my interview rounds of a child burning his fingers with a misplaced lighter, which inspired the idea. In any case, with all the human commotion going on in that park, it could just as easily have happened without the benefit of a news professional being on hand to get a description. And anyway, it wasn't as if it changed any of the important facts of the story about Filco and Takahashi. But for some reason Hanover couldn't let that one tiny part of it go.

"I thought this tree was supposed to fulfill wishes," he said, this time in a clear challenge.

"Yes, well, that is what people have always said. And now this. You never know, I guess."

"Indeed. Perhaps it was a suicide. Maybe he wished for it and his wish came true?"

I didn't care for his insinuating tone, but I felt compelled, perhaps by a lingering sense of professional pride, to defend my version of the story.

"No, that's not it. He actually came to Fraleton to give away his kidney. At the cost of his own life. It was an act of self-sacrifice."

"A kidney?"

"As a donation. To his brother. Because his brother is terminally ill — or would be. Without the kidney."

"But he could have done it anyway. People donate kidneys and live all the time. We only need one. We've got two."

I whapped my own forehead. I was always getting the function of kidneys and livers mixed up. "Naturally," I said. "But he had two brothers. And they were both sick. You know how these things run in families? Apparently he'd given up one of his kidneys already."

Hanover let out a long, loud sigh that said he was unconvinced. I felt like registering my own exasperation. Barney Fife gets into a snit and I'm supposed to care? After all the tangled twists my stories had been through up to then, why couldn't he just take the immolation scene as one more in a series of extraordinary events? Yet here he was, stuck on that spontaneous combustion thing like a junior D.A. prosecuting his first recalcitrant killer.

"That's some rather interesting information about these amazing medical complications. And yet it doesn't appear anywhere in your copy. In fact, you state, just a moment—"

"I know, I *know*. I said that the man was a complete mystery to all around him. Which was true, at the time I wrote it, but I've since learned, from an eyewitness, who was standing right there, and has the singed eyebrows to prove it, a few more facts about his case. I just got through interviewing her. That's why I called in, even though it's late. I thought I'd better check whether you wanted to add her comments to the story.

"Go on," he said, flatly.

I pretended to read from something I'd already written, rustling a flyer for a workshop I'd picked up that afternoon on alien language lessons. "Amanda Filkenheiserfort," I said, stopping to spell out the imaginary name to give me time to think, "a homemaker visiting the Miracle Tree site with her three children, said the man appeared agitated moments before the incident. 'I asked him if he was all right,' she said. 'He said no. His kidney was aching, and his poor sick brother was desperate.'"

Hanover didn't sound as if he was taking any of this down. All he said was, "Mm-hmm."

"Ficklehhouse. . . ah. . . fort went on to say—"

"Wait. What was her name?"

I had no idea. I held the phone out at arm's length and made the pshhhhhh sound of electronic turbulence. "Sir?" I called from a distance. "Mister Hanover? Can you hear me?"

"Hello? Hello? Broderksky? What do you—"

"Sir? Are you there? We seem to be pshhhhhh."

"Listen, I want—" he shouted.

And people in Hell want ice water, I thought, as I hung up.

I waited ten minutes, then called the copy desk, gave them the correct spelling of Finkleheimer and called it a night.

In a time of universal deceit, telling the truth becomes a revolutionary act.

George Orwell

NINE

Shirley and Lindy were up and brushed and dressed before the morning sun had a chance to choose its colors. I recalled seeing them walk out the door hand in hand before my head fell back to the floor with a clunk.

When I woke up again I felt like a shipwreck. First sponge and now wood: somewhere in Fraleton was a bed that was just right. I hoped I might find it, like Goldilocks, before the end of the story.

I splashed water on my face, considered and rejected a shave, then went downstairs. Shirley and Lindy were washing dishes, which didn't seem funny to me but they were sharing some private joke that had them both laughing to themselves.

George looked up from his plate at me. His face went to them, then back at me, displaying a combination of admiration and envy. I sat beside him with my elbows on the table to prop up my head. He whispered, "No wonder. Two babes in your room? Chee-rist. I'm switching to print."

"It's not like you think," I said unhappily.

It was my turn to be surprised when George's door upstairs opened to reveal William from the rival station CREP. He bounded into the kitchen, offering the girls a quick wave and us a sleepy grin.

"Had to keep an eye on the fucker," George muttered. When I didn't say anything, he added, "Care to trade?"

"Hey, you," I lobbed with casual esprit to Shirley when she turned in our direction to check the coffee percolator. I adopted an expression that said: just trying to be friendly. She nodded, the least possible acknowledgment of my presence without being rude. A night to sleep on it and I was still not out of the woods.

Lindy smiled. That was better — dimples on parade.

"And how did you fine ladies sleep?" I asked, but before any answers could come the phone rang. Mrs. Grady called for Lindy.

"Uh oh," I mouthed to Shirley. She looked away.

"But," we could hear Lindy sputter in a helpless voice, "of course that's—" and "it goes without say—" and "but don't—"

The conversation ended with, "Well. . . I guess." Lindy came back looking wounded. At least she wasn't angry, not yet anyway. That would probably come sometime after denial.

"They killed it," she said. She might have meant "my entire family" from the look on her face, but instead added, "My story."

"Bucketheads," I announced. "What do you expect from the *Weak Times*?"

"It's owned by the same conglomerate that forces baby formula on Third World women," Shirley pointed out.

"Did they happen to say why?" I asked. As if I didn't know. If snakes could talk, they would probably sound like me right about then.

"Something about not being fresh. What fresh? I don't get it. I had a scoop on Filco. Direct from the boss himself. The new boss. It was good, damn it all. It was stuff that other people didn't have."

"Editors," I said sourly. I should have just hissed to clarify things.

"They don't want to be challenged, and they sure don't want to be challenging," Shirley tried.

Lindy nodded in slow agreement.

"It's a class thing for the ownership," Shirley continued. "All they really want is confirmation of their role near the top of the socio-economic ladder. It's not your fault, girl."

Lindy still looked as if she'd just seen her first Santa Claus in the back of a squad car. It was hard to witness as her eyes welled up and threatened to spill.

"So place it somewhere else," I said. "You can do better than them." We all knew this was an inane attempt at consolation: the *Weekly Times* was the best-selling news magazine in the country.

"They did say I could stay on," she reasoned. "They'll look at anything I want to send in for next week, if it's still happening. That's pretty good, right? Getting the *Times* to read your stuff and everything. Right?"

Shirley and I nodded with enthusiasm.

"You'll do it for sure, girlfriend," Shirley said. "They're just scared of the story right now because it's offbeat. They don't do offbeat, they never have, unless it's cute. But if things go on for another week the way they are now? They'll have to do something. Everyone else is. They won't be able to miss the boat."

"That's true, I guess," Lindy said in a distracted voice. She must have been thinking what we were — if the *Weekly Times* was serious about doing a Miracle Tree story a week later, they'd send their own team.

Lindy put on a brave-girl smile and turned to me. "Did your article go through all right?"

"I don't know. I haven't checked. To tell you the truth, I've been afraid to."

Lindy looked at the clock. It was just after nine. "Oh man, are you kidding? The Internet version's been out for hours and you haven't even looked? I'm getting my computer."

She ran up the stairs. I started to run myself, for the front door, and was two steps in that direction when a hand on my collar yanked me back.

"No you don't," Shirley scolded. "You are not going to leave me here to handle this alone."

"Shirl my world! A few hours ago you could barely stand to look at me and now we're inseparable again?"

I leaned down to nuzzle her neck and, if that went well, cop a breast at an angle neither George or William would be able to detect. She bent back with a dexterity that could win a limbo contest. I bent further forward to try to stay with her, but it didn't work. I lost balance first and staggered forward against the stove. I pretended to scorch my palms on the burners, screaming in silence. She didn't laugh; she didn't even smile. Her expression summed it up: don't start.

Lindy came back down the stairs, each step thudding in my ears like the knocking of imminent doom. She took her laptop into the living room and unrolled the modem cable to plug in. William put down his crumpled issue of *Surfer* magazine to help.

I slithered quickly to the door, and out, without hissing good-bye.

Five minutes later I spotted Trish in the Old General Store, ringing up a visitor's groceries — a dozen boxes of Ritz Crackers and four jars of dill pickles. The customer looked as thrilled as a refugee to be getting even that much: the shelves were bare. When Trish saw me, she smiled and winked and crooked her index finger to invite me in.

At the same moment I heard Shirley's footsteps approach from behind. "Earl," she said darkly. I turned around and braced myself for Hurricane Shirley. "You stole her stuff about Takahashi." It wasn't a question. The index finger aimed at me was damning.

I shrugged, proving to myself at least that I wasn't all snake. I had shoulders. "Yes, well, actually," I said, but I had nothing to add to this brilliant opening in my self-defense. Daniel Webster it wasn't. I gestured at the notebook in my hand, then in the direction of the park. Busy, busy, I tried to say with a weak smile.

But Shirley stood riveted in action mode, legs apart, torso straight, as if we had squared off center-ring. In old movies, the women tended to slap their men at times like this, although it never seemed to leave a mark or hurt very much. Shirley liked to point out how ridiculous that part was — especially when a stick or a club would make the point so much more convincingly.

"I had to do it," I offered. "It was the only way to get in the game."

"No. It was not. You were in the game already. You didn't get there by ratting out your friends."

"I didn't rat out anyone. I borrowed something that was going to be common knowledge anyway in a couple of days."

"The Takahashi part was hers. She got to Filco first. She earned it."

"I had to. Don't you see? If I didn't, Lindy could have knocked me right off the story. And that wouldn't have been good for anyone. Filco would have gotten the upper hand."

"Not if you had enough to keep your side of the story going. Like you said you had."

Arguing with Shirley was always a bad idea. She had this annoying habit of being right, while I tended to grow increasingly desperate, until I buried myself with my own outlandish logic. Nevertheless I plowed on. "It was all for the story. The readers come first. I did what I had to do. I'm sure you'll see it that way too, once you have a chance to think about it. But right now I have to run. Really. Got an interview. Deadlines. You know how it is."

"I know you can go fuck yourself. Or whatever. I don't really care." She spun and left.

"Shirl, wait," I said. "Don't go like that." As if there were a better way.

My plan to disappear into the crowd was interrupted before I even reached the park. A producer from ABC TV tracked me down, and 12 minutes later I was on the air, live, with their number one newscaster.

"Standing beside me is Earl Brododsky, the dynamic young *City Herald* reporter who came to Fraleton on his first major assignment with that paper. And by all accounts, did he ever land a *whopper.*"

Peter Jennings spoke in the authoritative tone of a likable professor. He looked good, thanks in some degree to the layers of goopy makeup which had turned him into a caramelized version of the face I knew from TV.

I tried to look professional myself, like a colleague, but I could feel my own face harboring a scowl. I shifted instead to an air of breezy competence, but couldn't shake the feeling that I more closely resembled a corrupt politician about to be grilled by investigative reporters holding the evidence of my crimes — Nixon on a platter. I settled on a grim-lipped middle-distance gaze that I could only hope would not suggest the inner turmoil of a madman. But it was all pointless: I couldn't relax. There was no way to ignore the massive camera box looming two feet from my face, its red lamp glowing like a distress beacon.

I wondered if my obvious discomfort could be contributing to Jennings's air of mild bemusement. He seemed so effortless in portraying himself, the media prince. Easy for you, I thought. You talk into a glass-eyed machine every night for a living. At every break he had three people with brushes and tweezers and sprays and jars fussing over his face as if it were an archeological treasure just pulled up from the depths of the Aegean. I was relegated to a shaky intern in overalls who patted my cheeks with a puff ball, getting powder into my eyes, while muttering to himself about "the shine."

"The Miracle Tree has been *here,*" Jennings said, eyeing the camera like a friend, pausing and inflecting, his eyebrows telling half the story, "at this *bucolic* location for generations. Fraleton locals have for *many* years known this as the place to *ask* for things. Things they wanted, things they needed. Things they *may* not have been able to ask for anywhere else. But it wasn't until Earl *Brododsky* brought the Miracle Tree to outside *attention* that anything like *this* has happened."

He pivoted from the camera towards me. I unclenched my teeth. "Peter?" I pleaded in a cracked voice. I saw with a flood of relief that the red lamp was off.

"Quick!" yelled the assistant director. "Does he need water?"

"He needs something," a voice behind me contributed.

Three staffers rushed forward with plastic bottles. I chose the biggest one, and was about to take a gulp, when the assistant director began gesturing like a man waving for help from a rapidly sinking raft. The bottle was snatched from my hand just as it reached my lips.

"Five! Four! Three!" the assistant director called out while showing us the appropriate number of fingers.

"Ready," I squeaked, feeling anything but.

All this time Jennings had been reading from a clipboard that a squatting staff member was holding near his belt. He looked up genially at "Three!" The countdown continued with the fingers only. Peace sign. One-love. The red lamp came on. A glint of interest reappeared in Jennings's eyes.

"Earl, it's been an *extraordinary* experience for you here in Fraleton, hasn't it?"

"You can say that again, Peter." I wished he would. It would give me time to think. Instead I added a thin, "heh heh," to show that I could be genial and relaxed too. The assistant director's mouth dropped open. I may have looked mental.

"It must be *difficult* to express to your readers just *what* is going on in this once-peaceful park. We are standing amid a *swirl* of desperate hopes and conflicting emotions, all played out in an increasingly *chaotic* milieu. Yet *you've* been able to convey a sense of the magic in the air here with your in-depth and heartfelt articles."

"Thank you, Peter. You don't do so badly yourself. Heh heh."

The cameraman opened his free eye to check on the assistant

director, who covered his own mouth with the back of his hand. The horror.

"In your *latest* report, in this morning's edition of the paper, you allege a *conspiracy* of sorts between local politicians and controversial Japanese financier Toshihiko Takahashi."

I did? I tried to remember whether I'd actually used the word "conspiracy." Now I was going to come across as the Oliver Stone of newspaper reporting. Fortunately Jennings moved on.

"Information which hasn't been *confirmed*, or indeed *reported*, anywhere else," he said, one eyebrow now raised. What a voice. It didn't matter what words he used, the intonation alone was enough to brand me. He may as well have just asked how I celebrated after evicting a widow.

"Sorry, Peter," I said, "but I can't reveal my sources. You understand that, I'm sure." Nixon again — this was how he must have felt, stonewalling the nosy bastards. I remembered a line in defense of bullfighting, supposedly not as cruel as it looks because the bull always thinks it's winning.

Jennings' left eyebrow arched higher. I'd always wished I could do that. I realized now was not a good time to try. He flicked out his tongue tip to wet his lips. I'd thrown him, but not for long.

"Understandable," he said. "But you *can* tell us how you feel about the three *million* dollar lawsuit filed against you and the *City Herald* this morning in Hubbensberg Superior Court by lawyers on behalf of Mister Takahashi."

"Three million," I repeated dully. Then: "*Dollars*?" I felt sweat beads emerge on my forehead. One began to trickle: my makeup intern looked aghast. All the time that my career had been slipping under the waves on national television he hadn't shown any interest, but now that I was about to drag his job down too he got all concerned.

"Indeed," Jennings went on. "For defamation of character, *libel*, slander, misrepresentation of a well-documented business plan and *wanton* disregard of known facts."

The red lamp glowed like a lie detector signal alert. I was caught and squirming — I couldn't think of a single word to say to support my case. Instead I was afraid to open my mouth for what anguished sounds might come out.

Jennings turned on the whimsical tone again. "I take it we might be fair in saying you feel somewhat *surprised* at the allegations and—"

"Elated, Peter. That's how I feel. Elated, to be able to stand with the people of this fair town and say—" I cleared my throat. Say what? Even those on the fringes of the TV crew stopped their mike-and-headset conversations to hear this.

Jennings raised his eyebrow again. The assistant director looked ready to cry.

"To say. . . enough!" I blurted out in a spasm of verbal relief at finding the word. "Enough of the lies. Enough of the deceit. Enough of the treachery of Mister Takahama and his thick-necked thugs who are determined to poison the good land of this small, once-pristine town, now and, of course, for all those many generations to come."

A smattering of applause and a few shouts could be heard from the back of the crowd. The assistant director waved from his lifeboat for the rescuers to stop and the crowd noises immediately ended. These people took TV directions well.

Jennings was unruffled. He knew how to get back in control. "It should be pointed out that it was Mister Taka*hashi* who claimed that—"

"Or Toshi, as he's known to his cronies," I interrupted. "But the real question here is not whether a wealthy high-stakes speculator of dubious financial means and questionable business ethics can drag low-paid reporters, the voices of the people, after all, Peter, and the first line of soldiers in our ongoing struggle to preserve and protect our right to free speech and a free press, ah, can drag them into court." Where was I going with this stuff? It was too late to wonder. The train of thought had left the station.

"Obviously, he can," I went on, keeping my lips moving. "Where it is hoped and expected that our justice system will deal with this cynical attempt to muzzle our nation's free and democratic media with all the contempt it deserves. No, Peter, the real question is whether the notorious Taka, ah, gentleman is not already poisoning the people. Although so far, according to reports I've received, the lasting damage resulting from radioactive leaks out of the Hubbensberg plant run by Filco has been confined, largely, to house pets."

"These *allegations* are—"

"Radioactivity, if I may, Peter, that is estimated to last an extremely long, long time. Now, is this the kind of thing the good people of Fraleton would choose for their own once-gentle town?"

"No friggin' way!" came a thin voice from the crowd.

I spotted Wilbur, looking smaller without his balloons. He raised a fist in my direction, a solidarity sign, then quickly put it down in embarrassment. Someone clapped him on the back and he grinned. I felt touched. Trish was standing beside him. She was smiling too. Or maybe it was a smirk. Or she could have had something caught in her teeth again. I didn't have the time to find out.

"Fuck Filco!" someone else shouted, but the assistant director must not have caught it. He was focused on his viewfinder. He seemed to be pleased, for the first time since we'd begun. At least he was animated beyond his earlier frozen-in-the-headlights stance. He twirled his fingers in a "keep-rolling" gesture.

Jennings, to his credit, wasn't put out by my interruptions. In front of the camera we were still on his court, where we both knew he could have skewered me at any time. For the first time he looked at me, actually at me rather than through me. He even smiled. "This has turned into a *remarkable* chat," he said, bemused again, still as comfortable as if we were in his living room. "Not at all what we had expected, but perhaps appropriate for a most unusual locale. Earl, we have time for one more question."

"Absolutely, Peter."

"Do *you* believe in the Miracle Tree?"

A cooling breeze brushed against my cheek. My head no longer felt like a broiler about to burst. It was my turn to grin. I took the luxury of pausing. Each second was probably worth thousands of dollars to the network's programmers, but what did I care? I felt, for the first time, in my element. I realized that I knew TV. How could I not? I'd spent enough hours in its thrall. Nothing else in my life, not even Shirley, had earned such long hours of mute devotion. I knew that where I stood, in hyper-TV-time, a moment of emptiness could speak volumes.

I shifted my gaze away from Jennings, away from the insistent red light, away from the desperately twirling hands of the assistant director. I stared past the immediate crowd altogether and into the distance where the tree stood. He hadn't asked *what* I believed about the tree. He asked *whether* I believed in it. I tried to gather any shred of conviction I might have had running through my brain, or heart, anything I might use to convince not only millions of viewers but also myself. I gestured to the tree with an outstretched arm, then noticed my wristwatch. It had stopped again, only this time I definitely had remembered to wind it. Maybe there was something to those unexplained phenomena after all.

"*Absolutely,*" I said at last.

The red lamp went off, the TV lights were cut and Jennings reached across to shake my hand.

"Interesting," he noted, which could have meant anything. I took it as a compliment. "Good luck," he added with that same near-grin of barely contained amusement he'd had from the start. I thought he was sincere.

"Same to you," I replied, although clearly I was the one who would need it.

The immediate crowd, at least, seemed to be on my side. They pressed in on me as if I'd just kicked the field goal that had won the big game.

A few people shook pieces of paper in my face, a gesture I didn't understand until a voice said, "Can you make it out to my daughter? She would have come ask herself, but for the palsy."

I signed and accepted thanks from others as I walked on, hoping to spot Shirley. If only she could see me like this, being appreciated, some of the sentiment might rub off. Even though I knew it was unlikely. Not as things stood, anyway. But maybe with better material, I told myself, I might still steer this thing in a favorable direction. For now I was on the tiger's back, and the only way out was to ride it. I readied my notebook and strode back into the media maelstrom.

To make the best use of my limited time, I decided to enhance my note-taking procedure. I often found myself baffled later by my own written impressions of an event, unable to decipher the scrawls that could have been inked by a distressed ape. Now I willed myself to watch things, think about them for a moment, then write consciously, not in scrambled word fragments but in sentences or even paragraphs. I thought I might then transpose entire sections of these random observations into my article, creating on-the-scene snapshots of real life, thereby shortening the writing process enough to make beating the deadline a snap.

"Can this remarkable tree truly change lives?" I now wrote. "Science cannot provide the answer — yet continues to ask the question, only now in a Babel of languages as research teams from around the globe pour in to study the phenomenon."

Could people pour in anywhere? I would have to fix the worst language offences later. Better now to just get it all down, collect facts, record quotes, share rumors — keep feeding the beast. But while I was still riding it? Can you do both at the same time? Another mystery, and one that I could shelve with all the others for closer examination another day. I carried on, still determined but back now with an annoyingly familiar sense of internal confusion.

Next to one section of the river was an area that had been commandeered by the God's Hogs biker club, a Hell's Angels offshoot whose beer-swelled members were fond of stripping naked and frolicking in the muddy water. They did this regardless of, or perhaps because of, the presence nearby of families, many of whom who lined up to stare critically at the scene when they could as easily have looked away. I had decided I would refuse to interview anyone naked, unless they were beautiful, so I walked in the opposite direction.

I saw Harold Whitley standing in an odd position, for him — he was perfectly erect. He held a hand over his heart, and, with his chin raised, seemed to be acting out the role of someone declaring a solemn promise. I moved closer to hear his final lines.

"And so, from this day forward," he announced in a firm voice, "I shall drink no more forever."

I couldn't help but smile: alkies and their taste for drama. I looked for the bottle in his back pocket. Forever must seem an even longer concept when you're dying for a drink.

A man with the rubbery features of a born clown saw me taking notes and sidled over. He held out a hand and introduced himself as Zelbar the One. I made a crack about needing a numbering system to sort out all the Zelbars, but it didn't register. I asked him if he believed in the Miracle Tree and if so, what he thought about the government's failure to protect it.

"The government, if you please, is irrelevant. It's a throwback, a legacy of an outdated attempt at social manipulation while civilization as we know it, why, we're no match for the common beehive, or just look at ants. They're eons beyond us in communal development, social engineering, the simple elegance of a civic-minded spirit working as one. But we as a species are surely evolving. Just take a look around you. Right here and now. This has become a place of planetary significance."

"Didn't they say that about Woodstock?" a skeptical woman's voice wanted to know. "Where'd they all go?"

Zelbar the One didn't take the bait. He gazed at the sea of people spreading out from the lone tree. He rubbed a palm over his shaved head bristle and nodded appreciatively.

"This site is now Ground Central for the spiritual forces actively involved in positive change," he continued. "You ask whether we believe in the Miracle Tree — whether the tree, or any tree, can make wishes come true. But that is not the point. We're here — and here is all that counts. Collectively, we have the ability to alter life in ways the mainstream society, as represented by print media scribes, gnats on the rhino hide of history, cannot hope to understand. You will never be clear on this until you can free yourself from the tyranny of your so-called logic. I can't do it for you. Who can? You. Only you. You are the master of your own destiny. Go in peace. Shine with love. Over and out."

I went, not in peace. The tree was difficult to get near with new arrivals forming an ever tighter crowd around it. Someone had had the foresight to erect a huge TV screen to provide close-up views for those on the fringes. An ad on the bottom of the monitor claimed it as the Largest Freestanding Mobile Hi-Definition Outdoor Screen in the World, and thanked a Japanese electronic firm for the installation.

Interesting as it was to see in a glance not only the tree but its digital version, you couldn't stare at the screen for long without feeling disoriented. That may have explained why whoever had set up the screen had programmed it to switch from close-ups of leaves and branches to distant shots of the tree looming above its worshipers like a pylon sticking up out of the sea. Occasionally the screen would offer an aerial view of the entire park, now all but filled to its distant edges with more people than a Hindu dance video, even though no aircraft could be seen. Were they using spy satellites? Finally the monitor medley would be completed by a hand-held medium shot taken from somewhere in the crowd and showing the view most of the people there actually saw: the tree or perhaps just parts of it glimpsed through a multitude of heads, limbs, tent poles and hand-made signs.

A number of visitors unable or unwilling to squirm through the human tide to get near the tree itself had turned the screen into a surrogate object of their veneration. The space in front of the structure was decorated with flower garlands, stalks of burning herbs and mini-posters of Cantopop singing stars sponsored by the same Japanese electronics firm. Oddly, the screen was almost more enticing than the tree itself — you never knew when it was going to cut to a different shot, and the tension this created was compelling. Even better, it would sometimes cut away altogether from the medley of silent tree scenes to offer a live news feed from one of the networks covering the site.

The first segment I saw was from German TV with the reporter, a glum woman wearing a trench coat, scurrying about the site to point at people and make guttural comments that sounded like criticism. But then I've never understood German.

It was an improvement when the screen switched to an extended clip from a program called "I Say," which appeared to be an Australian talk show featuring a roundtable of intellectuals debating a single theme. The topic, written in low-budget or perhaps ironic black marker on white poster board, was: Resolved: The Miracle Tree in Spite of the Intrinsically Empty Discourse Represents a Paradoxical Shift in Meta-Conscious Paradigms of Postmodern Rationality.

Arguing for the Yes side was a ruddy-faced man in blazer whose ID caption said Roland Binginswooly. "A more astute observer might well have gleaned the point long ago," he said in a nasal twang while jabbing the stem of an unlit pipe nearly into the face of his scowling opponent. "Yet my learned colleague here lumbers under the burden of a lacunal intellect born of the unfortunate restrictions in genetic variability caused, one suspects, by an over-familiarization amongst the primary familial units, together with some doubtlessly well-conceived but ill-rendered traumas to the cranial area during childhood. The Miracle Tree is, I repeat, for the benefit of him and any individuals from the lower-ranked intelligence levels who may be watching and having a similar struggle maintaining focus, a metaphor. Right? A metaphor for life. And, yes, for death. Now, when I say this, do I mean to posit a natural demise, the end of one's allotted time in our earthly realm? Obviously not. For my point is rather—"

"Rather protruding so grotesquely from the top of your skull as to make wearing a hat an exercise in futility, one should expect," said the opponent, a smiling man with steel spectacles and a receding hairline. He had a heavy Aussie twang too.

The Fraleton crowd applauded together with the Sydney studio audience. Everyone wanted the fight to at least be a fight. "Now whack the sucker one," a young man in slacks as wide as they were tall shouted at the screen.

"Jab him, jab him," came a call from the hospital-bed-ridden quarter of the field. "You soften him up for a few rounds first and then, blammo comes the money punch."

"If you insist," the second debate participant continued, "on referring to the slathering attentions of a cerebrally suspect local population onto some hyperextended epigealic stump as anything but a modern tragedy of spiritual dimensions so vast that all attempts to explain it as reasonable — let alone sane — taint not only those amassing around the tree right now like flies to a steaming pile of ordure but—"

"Ordure?" came a plaintiff question from another seat at the table. This was not enough to stem the verbal tide.

"But equally, one might say, an increasingly befuddled global public because — and this goes straight to the issue — my esteemed colleague here has proven himself once again to be a living, wheezing paragon of that untold legion of self-indulged sexual abuse victims who consider—"

"Hey," a thick voice interrupted from the park crowd. "Wait a minute. Does he mean us?"

"Slather this," said another.

"Change it! Change it! Change it!" the crowd began to chant, sparsely at first but soon with a crescendo that drowned out the audio feed. The screen shifted to an early episode of "Cheers," drawing a burst of applause that died almost as quickly amid individual calls for more footage of the tree and no re-runs. The screen shifted back to its original in-park series of wordless tree shots, and the crowd was mollified enough to quiet down.

One of the camera pans took in the figure of Sun Deer, still stoic in his We Shall Not Be Moved sitting position. I couldn't help noticing his lack of colleagues, however. Hadn't I written something about them coming in droves? If they had, they were sure blending in well. The fact that there was no Indian demonstrations of note had me feeling doubly self-conscious: I thought I'd helped call them forth. And they were my people after all, so I felt I should have been among them, if only I could find a few.

I turned my back on the TV to concentrate on the notes. I still needed a big catch, something to raise the stakes on the Filco threat I'd introduced earlier. Something new. I couldn't just let the danger posed by that corporation wreck the town for the lame reason that I hadn't been able to root out the entire depths of its intents. But the problem with reporting incredible events, I was learning, is how hard it is to keep topping yourself. I'd already mentioned how residents in Hubbensberg were growing increasingly alarmed at the strange behavior of pets that had been exposed to radiation. I hoped I wouldn't have to start sacrificing cats and dogs just to keep the ship afloat.

"It's too late anyway," I heard from the TV speakers. I turned to watch a stand-up interview in which a TV reporter faked a look of sympathy while a Hubbensberg resident held up an empty leash and continued a lament. "Prince is gone. He'd been acting weird, no lie. He dug up half my rose garden yesterday, and last night he wouldn't stop barking at every car that passed down the road."

"My cat," sobbed an elderly woman in the next cut, this one without an interviewer in the shot. "She used to eat whatever I ate. Broiled salmon or veal and mashed potatoes, it didn't matter. But for the last few days, nothing at all. She won't even look at it. I want to know what Filco is putting into the air and I want to know now. My Fluffy is sick and if she dies, someone is going to be extremely sorry. That's all I can say."

A handsome studio announcer came on, backed by an alarming graphic of a puppy suddenly stamped by a thudding radioactivity symbol. "Filco officials continue to insist they have no knowledge of any radioactive elements released from their properties," the announcer said. He added a delicious pause before saying, "Authorities are appealing for calm." I couldn't help but feel proud.

The next shot had a city health official explaining in an exasperated tone, "Yes, Filco had a plant here, once. It made small-motor consumer items. But that was years ago. There was nothing remotely radioactive about it."

The camera pulled back to show the same stand-up reporter from before. He asked in an aggressive tone when the inspector had last actually inspected the site. The official blurted something about toasters and production schedules, but the real story was told in the knowing expressions shared by the reporter and studio announcer. The news then showed a montage of recap shots: worried Hubbensberg residents keeping their dogs indoors; shoppers lining up to enter a hardware store; shelves where the last rolls of duct tape were being snatched up; children being fitted for painters' masks.

Abandoning the giant screen, I headed for Buffy's in search of sustenance. Morning Mist walked out holding a grease-bottomed bag of doughnuts. The day before I had considered myself lucky to find the dregs of a pot of coffee after Buffy swore there was no food. Maybe he kept a private stock for people he liked.

"My main dude," Morning said. He flashed me a power salute followed by a peace sign. I looked at the grease and didn't much feel like shaking hands, so that was just as well. He offered to split a cream puff, but I let it go. We sat on the grass together.

"Killer story in this morning's paper. You're on the ball, buddy. Who would have thought you were so sharp to look at you? Even we didn't know Filco was that bad."

"Looks can be deceiving," I said, thinking that one good example sat in front of me. Morning Mist looked and talked like Tiny Tim, but if you took the time to listen, he sometimes made sense. Harold saw us from the parking lot and started the trek over. He was not a strong walker.

"Harold is one brilliant man," Morning commented as we watched him lurch into the back of a mime offering flyers for past-life regression sessions. The mime dropped to his hands and knees, which scattered the flyers, but got up just as quickly using a pretend hand-pulley — now that was control.

"Brilliant is one word for it," I said, neutrally.

"Seriously. He's got a brain like a, like a, I don't know, a whip?" Morning's own brain at the moment seemed stuck.

"Don't you mean a sharp tack?" I offered.

"I was going to say computer, but no, that's just a tool. Harold's genius is more creative. He used to be a grand master in chess, did you know that? Ranked third in the Western Hemisphere at one time. You have to know how to use your noggin to get that far."

Harold reached us in a huff and immediately held up a hand to forestall any conversation while he regained his breath. "Fellows," he said at last with his hands on his hips.

"Harold," I said. "How did it go with the mayor yesterday?"

"The scoundrel. He got away. We've still got the wrap, though. We can wait for him. He can't hide forever."

A thin redneck type with a chained wallet and a ZZ Top T-shirt spotted me and did a double-take. He opened a cooler to pull out a sweating tin of beer, popping the top before holding it out to me.

"Thanks," I said, "but no thanks."

He shrugged and showed it to Morning Mist.

"No liquid depressants of an alcoholic nature for the sacred temple of my body, my friend."

Harold was the only one left. Bingo, I thought. But no. He held up a restraining palm to turn the drink down — the free drink.

The redneck shrugged, unaware of the miracle he'd just witnessed. He affixed the tin to his lips for a long slug before walking on.

"Harold," I said. "I thought you were kidding earlier. What gives? A new leaf?"

"I made a wish," he said, motioning to the tree.

His next sentence was drowned out by the music of half a dozen strolling Peruvians in ponchos playing wooden flutes and tiny guitars. When they stopped, an audience gathered that soon grew into the hundreds. The players were good, as polished as any Peruvian group in any public market anywhere in the world. But I had to wonder: are there no musicians at all left in Peru?

"You actually wished for no free alcohol?" I shouted over the song about the condor.

"I want to rule my destiny," Harold shouted back, dignified again. "The Miracle Tree can only help."

"Good luck."

"Luck isn't the half of it," Morning said, drawing a belly-shaking laugh out of Harold. The grand master of humor he was not; neither of them were. It wasn't much of a joke, yet they acted as if it were hilarious.

"Would you mind terribly if I asked you to excuse us?" Harold asked me. He was prepared to let me go without even a touch for money? Maybe he really was up to something. "We have important business matters to discuss," he explained.

"Business," I answered. "Of course." Mr. Ford meet Mr. Rockefeller. They walked away with their heads leaning together, talking so no one else could hear.

Further on Father Kennedy was delivering a sermon to a contingent of believers that must have been far larger than anything he'd been used to in Fraleton. It sprawled beyond the grass into the parking lot where some of the listeners in the back stood on the hoods of cars. He may have been made nervous by the numbers. Twice he stumbled over the name Moses, calling him "Mose."

I saw Lindy talking to a man in a peach-colored bikini-type bathing suit. He was trying to show her how to do a yoga posture. Even though she was obviously reluctant to get down on all fours, he kept at it, tugging at her arm as part of the harangue. A rescue attempt seemed the only decent thing to do.

"Hi-ya, Lindy," I said, from just beyond left-hook distance in case she came out swinging. "Excuse me for interrupting, sir — good extension, by the way — but I need to talk to my colleague here for a minute. A work matter." She let me steer her away by the arm at a fast clip.

"Oh, it's you!" the yoga teacher called from behind us. "I saw how you gave Peter Jennings the gears. Spanking good job. You're a credit to your profession."

"A credit to your profession," Lindy echoed. She had a strange look in her eyes. It was impossible to imagine Lindy hurting someone, but she appeared willing to try.

"Listen, about your story." I cleared my throat. "And, ah, my story."

"What's the difference?" she blurted angrily. Then, "Like you even care." Exhaling loudly, she leaned back against a Mayan miniature pyramid made out of cardboard but solid enough to prop her up. Her arms were crossed at the chest, her legs crossed at the ankles, and her toe tapped an impatient rhythm into the lawn.

"Now Lindy, that's going a bit far, don't you think? I didn't really take anything that wasn't already public information. Or, well, about to be."

"C'mon Earl!" she exploded. "You didn't even know who Toshi was until I told you. Eight hours later you've got some bogus version of his life history in your article and mine is dead in the water?"

"Your piece should've run. They blew that one. You should blame the *Geeky Times*, not me."

"It would have run, if you hadn't made such a big splash about all that radioactive waste bullshit. And it's not even true! You know it isn't."

"That's where you're wrong. I don't know. There are all kinds of things I don't know."

"I heard that," she said. The grass under her tapping foot was flattened. "You know what? I don't mind an honest rivalry. Maybe it's part of the job, even if I didn't understand that much and was only trusting you as a friend when I told you what I had. But what I can't take is being scammed like that. Especially by someone I used to care for. When you knew I needed the leg up. And you were already there."

She unfolded herself and, with a final hair toss of dismissal, stalked away.

"Wait," I called after her. "Used to?"

She stopped with her head bowed. She spun to face me. Maybe I had some pull left after all. Maybe with a bit of charm, not to mention some celebrity points from the session with my compadre Peter Jennings, I might just win her back to my side.

"Earl, I'm going to say this just once, clearly. Go. . . fuck. . . yourself."

Or maybe not.

I walked in aimless patterns around the periphery of the park, hoping to avoid people, until one stopped me to ask in a foreign accent if I would hold a tent peg while he pounded it in. The circus had come to town. The real circus this time. Or as close as "El Grande Top" can come to the real thing. They were not about to challenge the Ringling Brothers franchise any time soon. For a start, they were two rings short of a three-ring operation. It was a Mexican outfit that could be carried, animals and all, in two semitrailers with Tecate license plates. The staff shared a passenger van, according to the tent-installer, who explained he was also the animal trainer and ticket seller and chief of security — the last role impressing me the most since he was also a midget. "Most years on the summer tour we drive straight through Fraleton at three in the morning," he said, "but a crowd is a crowd, no?"

Their dreary attractions were already attracting a horde. The Miracle Tree wasn't going anywhere; who couldn't use a break from earnest wish-seeking? The line-up for The Wolf Boy booth must have had two hundred people in it. I'd never been a circus fan, and had no interest in hairy children, but when I saw Wilbur and Trish head into the arcade tent I decided to follow.

"Hi Trish, hi Wilbur, how are you guys?" I asked.

"Earl, we thought you did a bang-up job with that TV newscaster," Wilbur said. "I never watch him anyway. I'm a Dan Rather man."

"Thanks. I guess."

"Do you think they're really going ahead with that secret plan to cut down the tree in the early morning?" Wilbur asked. He looked dubious himself.

"It all depends," I reasoned. "Probably not with these crowds, in their present mood. But if people slack off? Who knows?"

Trish chuckled. "I used to think you knew, sugar."

"Used to?" I said for the second time in minutes.

"That was priceless stuff about radioactive pets in Hubbensberg. You were joking, right?"

I wished I had been, and that everyone else could have taken it as harmlessly as Trish seemed to.

"And all that nuclear waste hokum?" she added.

"You never know what an international concern like Filco might pull next," I pointed out.

"Oh honey, you are priceless. Keep it up and you might land a job with this circus."

Wilbur was eager to interrupt. "Filco swept six hundred jobs right off the table when they pulled out of Hubbensberg last year. Cousin Al was one of them."

"I know, Daddy, but he was assembling hedge trimmers. There

wasn't anything nuclear about it."

"How's the flying project going?" I asked to change the subject.

"Fine. Very good. Excellent."

Trish glared at me in admonishment.

"I've come up with a more stable seating arrangement that should carry a person comfortably in flight for eight, ten hours, easily."

"Daddy, it's a lawn chair."

"Now Princess."

"Daddy-kins," Trish said. "Don't you have to get to work?" She looked at her watch and then tapped it. "Damn. Out again." She turned to me. "You got the time, sugar?"

"I don't. My watch isn't working so well."

"Same here," said Wilbur. "I thought mine fixed itself earlier today, but now it's off again. Probably is time to go. Bye-bye, sweetness. Good-bye, son."

We watched him weave out through a line of people waiting to play Pacman, the feature game in the arcade. Maybe in Tecate it was still a hit. It was Pacman fever all over again in Fraleton. Trish hooked her elbow in mine for a stroll about the arcade. She stopped to trace her fingers across the glass surface of a Playboy pinball game.

That drew a fierce look from the man playing it, a forty-year-old in a baseball jersey. "No touching a pinball machine when someone's playing," he hissed, not taking his eyes off the metal ball. He banged the side of the box with a loud slap. The machine protested with a flurry of beeps and bells. We walked on.

"Say, aren't you shacked up with two young city ladies already?" she asked, a bit coquettishly, as if I'd just asked her out. "Sounds fabulous."

Fabulous? Sure, if you didn't know the whole story. "Who told you?" I asked.

"Fraleton may be a zoo right now but we're still a small town. Word gets around."

"I guess I am — or maybe was. I'm not sure. I think they may be a little mad at me."

"Oooh," Trish said, lifting her eyebrows in appreciation. "Casanova gets in a lover's quarrel with not one but two alluring conquests."

"It's nothing like that."

"Um hmm," she said. Meaning, perhaps, she wouldn't mind if it were, because she liked it that way. She stopped at a shoulder-high box with two upright metal pegs shaped to accept gripped fingers. The chipped paint display showed a customer holding onto the grips while his eyes bulged and his hair stood straight up.

"Electrobuzz!" Trish said. "I used to love this one!" She read off the instruction panel. "Test yourself! Are you a Dull Spark or a Master of Molecular Stimulation? Place ten cents in coin slot. Grip both handles. Hang on for as long as you dare!"

I was uncomfortable just standing near it. "That thing looks dangerous. It must have been outlawed in this country years ago."

"Don't be a fraidy-cat. It's a blast. You hang on and the current keeps getting stronger, and stronger, and stronger—" her mouth and eyes opened wide — "until you think you can hardly take it any more."

"Look at the notches on the side. That's how many people it's killed."

"Come on, tiger. I'll bet you're a master and you don't even know it."

"I really don't think so."

"You must have a dime, you dress like a big spender."

"Fresh out," I said, not bothering to check.

She slipped her hand into my front pocket. I squirmed at the first touch but I let her. Maybe it was just something they did in Fraleton. I willed myself to play it cool and not get aroused — which is the quickest way known to spring a stiff one. Luckily she immediately pulled her hand out, holding a dime.

"Got one!" she said in triumph. She held it poised at the metal slit, pulled it back, then slid it closer again.

"You ready? Come on, big boy. Grab on."

"You do it," I said, feeling more like a big baby, and ridiculous at the same time.

"We have to do it together."

She pushed the dime into the machine, grabbed hold of one metal peg with her left hand, then quickly put my right hand on the other. She brought our empty hands together.

I watched the machine, not her. A single dim light bulb came on. It was painted yellow. I felt a buzz in my palm and pulled my hand away. "Ow," I complained.

Trish shook her head. "The main thing is you can't let go because that's when it hurts."

"Hurts?"

"Grab on, sugar, it's getting good."

I wrapped my fist back around the grip. It was warm. I felt the vibrations again. They were more obvious now, oscillating in waves that traveled up and down the peg. Trish was enthralled. The light bulb grew marginally brighter. Waves of energy in the peg began moving too quickly to track. The peg itself seemed to be a single shimmering stick of electricity.

"Whoa, daddy," Trish said, breathing harder. "Feel that?"

The current ebbed from my fingers to my wrists. I did feel it. It was traveling inside me. But just where? And how? Was it going through my bones? Through the veins? It was shimmering faster now. I heard a low hum. The light bulb glowed brighter. "Wow," I managed to say. The current seeped still further into me, now up my arm, warming it as far as my armpit, pushing on, inches at a time until it reached my torso, then entered my heart, and burst into a muted explosion of warmth in all directions.

"Oh. . . my. . . gawd," Trish said.

The light bulb glared through places where the paint had come off. It almost hurt my eyes. The current swam to my opposite arm and down to my legs. I turned to face Trish. Her hair started to rise, slowly at first, like a cobra coming out of a basket, until it was eventually all up, pointed at the ceiling and waving like tall grass in a breeze. The electricity flowing between our fingers felt like a warm, surging glow that had become a part of our flesh.

I had just forced my quivering lips to say, "This is. . .amazing," when a jolt snapped my head back. Now I was vibrating on some new cycle I'd never experienced before. My cells themselves seemed to be humming. A gob of drool formed on my lower lip. I tried to suck it up but couldn't. I was a jellified mass, with no authority over my body. But instead of being scary it was oddly liberating — I could have been flying, or dreaming, or floating. The drool spilled out of my mouth and onto my chest, but I didn't care.

Trish had her eyes closed and her mouth open. Out of it came a low feral moan.

I tried to match her, but issued something closer to a peep. Was that the smell of metal burning? I sensed my lips trying to form the question, but I wasn't able to corral my thoughts enough to work it out. I felt adrift on the current, a part of it rather than anything simply going through me. I was a wave, a tiny part of a big electric sea.

The light bulb, impossibly, grew brighter. I heard it emit a crackle of static, then an electronic fzzzt and it shattered. The shock hit my fingers first with a rude jerk, then shot through the rest of me, leaving a sear of pain behind. Trish bucked without taking her hand off the grip, reminding me of a bull rider with his fingers stuck in the rope after a bad dismount. When her shock met mine we were both catapulted backwards, landing in the sawdust in a tangle. Smoke clouded out from the back of the machine.

We slowly sat upright and turned to look at each other. I clenched my fingers into a fist and opened them. They still moved and they still had feeling. I used them to press the flesh of my elbow, my chest, my face. I was all there.

Trish shook her head and felt her jaw with her fingers. She brushed back her nest of hair. She patted her cheeks with both palms and let out a loud shaky whoosh of air. Then she smiled at me.

"Got any more dimes?" she asked.

Shirley wasn't in when I made it back to Grady's. Neither was Lindy. That suited me, for the moment anyway. I had another article to write, an even longer one. The public need to know was voracious.

The metaphor of the hungry beast came back to me. It was a dragon of my own creation, now one with a gaping jaw I had to keep feeding words into even as the creature kept swelling with the persistence of a bathtub-sponge dinosaur. If I ever stopped pitching, the teeth would come after me. Not bad, for a metaphor — too bad I couldn't use it in the article. Then again: the Loch Ness Monster. Whoever started that one must be laughing in the grave by now. Except that no one laughs in their grave. I told myself to get a grip on the metaphors before I concocted something truly embarrassing.

In the backyard Grady was puttering as usual. He pointed out the slime trails marking the assault of slugs on his precious broccoli starts. "They want war, I'll give them bloody Armageddon," he vowed, shaking a bony fist at the ground. "By the way you've got a message. You are to call a Mister Gallantine."

"Oh. Did he sound upset? Or angry?"

"It was from his secretary. She sounded like a dish. Called me sweetheart. She asked me how you were, how you really were. I told her that judging by your appetite you were in tip-top shape."

I went back inside. "Oh, Earl," he called. "She also said to tell you it was urgent."

So this was how my run was going to end: I'd been caught at last. The clincher must have been the three million dollars Toshi was after in his lawsuit. At my present salary, pro-rated for standard raises over time and compound interest, my grandchildren might collectively rob enough banks to pay it off.

I held the phone in my lap but didn't dial. The TV showed a video tribute to Tupac. He mentioned something about getting shot and then laughed with gleaming white teeth. I picked up the phone and got through to the paper, but at the last second changed my mind and asked first for Danny. If there were some bombshell about to drop I thought it might help to know about it first. But the only news he had was about Shantella and Gerry, who were now an office item.

"Apparently they have been for a while, but it was all a secret," Danny said with glee. "It still would be, if Melanie and Xavier hadn't walked in on them late one night going at it in the supplies closet. I didn't even know his wheelchair would fit in there, let alone. . . you know."

"Good for him. For them. I guess."

"You know what they say."

"I don't, but I'm sure you do."

"I always figured she'd land someone like an NBA guard. Maybe it's true opposites attract."

"You sure you didn't hear anything about me? No shouting or swearing coming down from Gallantine's floor?"

"You still da man," Danny said. "Far as I know. But if you are getting canned. . . can I have your desk lamp?"

I told myself it was better to get fired sooner rather than later. The first thing Gallantine had told me — the only thing, come to think of it — was to not write any bullshit, and here I'd been heaping it on by the shovel-load. My only consolation was the fact that I would get my thrashing over the phone instead of at the office where it might turn into a scene.

I clicked the TV sound onto mute, watching Tupac and his posse swagger through a set crammed with gyrating women in bike shorts, then dialed into the office.

Betty sounded slightly testy. Maybe losing three million dollars will do that to you. "He's been waiting," she pointed out before making the connection.

"Mister Gallantine?" I asked in a voice that sounded feeble to my own ears. "You wanted to talk to me?"

"Earl? Is that you, son?" It was his mentor voice — and I was still a son. I was tempted to call him "Pops" but I couldn't get my lips around it. "Harmy" also came to mind, but it would have been even harder.

"Yes, um, sir?"

"Capital work on that yakuza hooligan. It's a treat to see a criminal like that get his due. We need more of that kind of thing — a paper with some bite, fighting for the average Joe and all that."

"Yes, sir, you're welcome." He hadn't said thank you, but it sounded close enough.

"The readers are loving every word of your reports, my boy. You and your little tree have driven up circulation seven percent. That's all the proof I need right there." I'd never heard him this happy. Next I'd be invited over for Sunday pot roasts.

"As you say, sir." Maybe he hadn't seen the Jennings interview. Maybe the lawyers hadn't gotten the word to him yet.

"Listen, I just wanted to tell you — I've got your name on my list. It's a little early to talk promotions officially, you understand. There are a few procedures we have to follow so the rest of that rabble doesn't get jealous. But you ought to know that I'm watching you."

"That's very encouraging to hear. And Mister Gallantine?"

"Son?"

"Did you happen to see a news segment, a little interview, something I did on TV, with Peter Jennings?"

"Hoo boy, did I ever? It was a treasure. He's probably on his way back to cover the Moose Jaw Mufflickers hockey team for the rest of his career." He laughed at his own joke with a low-throated rumble. I could picture the neck wattles in motion.

"Yes, sir, ha ha ha. But he did mention something about some kind of a lawsuit? Did you hear anything more about that?"

"Pshaw. We get sued every day. Why do you think I keep a legal team? There's always some puffball of a politician or an ego-gorged celebrity trying to get our goat. We won't be cowed. Just like you said in your interview. You can't muzzle the press, goddammit, not in this country. My word, you were good — it was like a commercial for the paper. Only, you might have mentioned the name more. *City Herald* this, *City Herald* that, we at the *City Herald* say whatever. Keep it going. Repetition, repetition, repetition. It sells. That's what the bean-counters in marketing tell me, anyway."

"I'll keep that in mind next time."

"Oh hell, don't listen to me. Why am I talking business? You're doing great work, Earl. I'm pleased to know I chose the right man for the job. Did you file yet?"

"Not quite. I'm just polishing, I mean, fixing, or cleaning, a few things up. I hope it's not too long."

"Go with it any way you want: you're in the driver's seat. Don't think about the space, we'll work with whatever you can send. And keep a sharp eye out for more of that unexplainable phenomena stuff — a little woo-woo never hurts in an otherwise respectable outfit. Gets those tabloid peckers off their own game."

The dream was always running ahead of me. To catch up, to live for a moment in unison with it, that was the miracle.

Anais Nin

TEN

I sank into the couch in the Gradys' living room feeling like I'd been rode hard and put away wet. I was spent from writing my story — my longest yet. It also took the most out of me. By the time I typed the last period to end the final sentence, I couldn't muster the energy to read it all back before sending it in. Let them earn their keep back at the paper: it isn't called an editorial department for nothing.

The thought of climbing all the way up the stairs so Shirley and I could begin a conversation about our feelings struck me as exhausting. I curled into the cushions to recharge while staring half-lidded in the direction of the TV, which was showing a monster truck event in some brightly lit indoor arena. Sun Deer and George walked in, sat down and silently watched with me. I didn't care, but they bet twenty dollars on whether a pickup with tires the size of small homes could jump over twelve school buses. Soar, crash, what difference did it make? I just felt tired — very, very tired. There, I'd just discussed my feelings. Now could I please get some sleep?

The pickup landed nose first on the eleventh bus, driving the announcer into hysterics, wailing about the loss of humanity, until the driver crawled out and stood atop the twisted wreckage to wave at the cheering crowd.

Sun Deer handed George a twenty and they left to go upstairs, but not before asking whether I was okay. They seemed genuinely interested, showing a level of concern I found touching. I muttered that I was beat and about to head up myself, then stayed to watch the next program, a documentary on the history of the Osmond family. The adult Donny sat on a stool before a studio audience while a video clip from his childhood played over his shoulder. Either way, he didn't look like me.

I believed nutrients would help spur my slumping muscles to carry me as far up as the second floor, so I trudged to the kitchen. In the fridge I found two slices of homemade pizza and some plastic wrap holding dried mushrooms. I had to marvel — what a couple those Gradys were, as solid and timeless as the ages themselves. Their bond was brilliantly represented by this otherwise simple snack: here I could see no less than the ancient division of labor borne out in their modern day teamwork. Grady forages, bringing in roots and leaves and fungi; his wife prepares, doing up a homemade pizza, and the result is a culinary statement on the enduring alchemy of love. Even if the mushrooms were a bit rubbery after I zapped everything in the microwave, the sentiment came through in the taste.

I sat at the kitchen table dully chewing while eyeing the door of my room upstairs. I could see from the bottom crack that the light was still on, so I wouldn't be able to simply slip in and get some sleep.

I began the trek up, without having thought of an opening line. I needed something to cut through the inevitable tide of abuse. Then, having gained the upper hand, I would want to steer the conversation quickly into some productive direction. We might, for instance, all agree on the benefit of a good night's sleep, and maybe in the morning we would all find ourselves better able to discuss the situation as reasonable and well-rested human beings.

The sound of laughter from inside the room came as a surprise, but it was a good sign: how angry could they be? I flattened one ear against the door.

"Remember Naugles?" Shirley said, and they traded snoring noises before erupting into shrieks of delight. Naugles was a j-school professor famous for his tedious lectures. The only interesting moment in his class would come when more than one late-arriver appeared at the same time and vied for the last empty seat in the back where they could avoid having to feign front-row interest for two hours.

Shirley said something I couldn't make out, which was followed by a giggle from Lindy, then matched by the same from Shirley — a laugh I had never heard her use before. This was indeed good, even better than I could have hoped for. My girl. My girl and me. One happy potential family. I put an amiable grin onto my face, knocked once just to be polite and strode in.

Merriment left the room like a thief. I stopped in midstride at the sight of them staring at me. They were on the bed, together, on their stomachs, their feet dangling and bumping in the air behind them. Two male friends might have divided the same room space by sitting in chairs at its opposing corners; here they were practically mud wrestling on the bed. But then girls are like that.

"Hey," I said, sizing up the slender gap between them. I could have just squeezed in, if we were on good terms — which we were not, to judge by the Arctic cast to Shirley's expression. Lindy blushed and looked down at the blanket between her forearms.

Neither seemed about to say anything, so I went first. "Boy, am I ever tired."

No luck with that one. The ice was thickening. "Did you see the park tonight? It's a jungle out there," I ventured.

Lindy turned to look out the window. It was too dark outside to see a thing. Shirley continued to aim visual daggers at the few parts of my body yet to be mentally pierced.

"And not real homey in here either," I added.

Not even a rumor of a smile. I was bombing. "Look," I said, dropping the forced pleasantness with a sigh. "I'm totally wiped. Okay? I really need to get some sleep."

They were visibly unimpressed with my honesty or my needs.

"But," I continued, "I realize we have some issues here that may need to be addressed. So. Let's talk." When they still hadn't budged, I added, with an inner shudder, "About our feelings. And all that. If you'd like."

"No," Shirley said. "Let's not."

"Okay," I agree, eyeing my floor space as if it were an oasis.

"We think you should go," Shirley added.

"We?" The word had always meant her and me. "What's with the we? I don't remember anybody asking for my vote."

Lindy still hadn't turned away from her fascination with the window.

"We?" I said again.

Shirley's expression softened. She never could stay mad for long, not at a person. Her enduring grievances were reserved for institutions. "Lindy and I have had a long talk," she said. Then she looked out the black window too.

"And?" I encouraged, knowing that I didn't want to hear the rest, that this was a car wreck I shouldn't slow down to see, but would, almost as if I had no choice.

"Good-bye, Earl, and good luck," Shirley said, summing us up with the clipped and bland conclusion Naugles preferred. I'd gotten rid of my old grade school dickies, the ones my grandmother sent me at Christmas, with more formality than that. The injustice of it hit me like a slap — it was too much. Shirley could talk this way? About us? Our responsibility to each other as a couple, whatever stage we might have then been in, called for better treatment than this. Not to mention the fact they were banishing me from my own room. I might have gotten somewhere on that one, with Grady's help, but it didn't seem a good time to score points on procedure. I should take the high road now, I concluded, since it would put me in better standing when we met again in the morning to work it all out. I pivoted and left without saying a word.

The living room was dark except for the TV, which I must have forgotten to turn off. It showed a women's roller derby match. I watched in a stupor as a buxom skater pushed another from behind into a metal advertising sign. The victim hit the sign with a clatter and fell hard, then lay writhing in pain with the spinning wheels of her skates splayed above her while the others whizzed past. I knew how she felt.

I headed to the kitchen for more provisions — not to eat immediately, I wasn't hungry, but stocking up seemed a worthy idea, given my uncertain future. I grabbed the last pizza slice I hadn't eaten earlier, added the rest of the mushrooms and folded it onto itself with a wrap of plastic to slip into my shirt pocket — the closest thing to comfort food I might find for a spell.

This time when I closed the fridge I saw taped to the door a folded paper with my name penned on the front. The message inside, in Mrs. Grady's handwriting, said I was to call Harmon Gallantine. It added the word "urgent." As usual.

I hadn't heard the phone ring — and Mrs. Grady wouldn't likely be up this late. Had I been so oblivious I missed the note completely the first time around? If so, Gallantine might have been waiting for hours. Then again, the telephone number wasn't for the *Herald* office: maybe it was for his home. Or his private club? And now I had the number? I would have to start calling him "Harmy" if this kept up.

It was too late to make a personal call, but I went to the phone anyway. If it really was urgent, someone might pick up. And if not, the message machine would at least record the time of my diligence.

Despite everything, I almost hoped he would answer. I needed a pep talk.

Two rings and his answering machine clicked on. "You've reached the residence of the Gallantines," announced a female voice that may have been his wife's. "We can't get to the phone right now, but if you'll leave your name and number and the time you called, we'll get back to you as soon as we can. Thank you for your call and have a wonderful day. And oh yes — if this is Earl Brododsky? Apparently you're fired." Click.

I stood motionless, still holding the phone. I wasn't sure how to react. I'd never been fired by a machine. On the scale of things, it would have to hurt less than the thought of Shirley dumping me. But since both unexpected blows still struck me as unreasonable, and thus only temporary misunderstandings that could all get sorted out in the clear light of day, I decided not to get angry or weepy or sucky or anything else. Nor to dwell on the prospect that they may not have been unreasonable or misunderstandings after all. Instead I sat down at the kitchen table in the dark. It was my turn to stare out a blackened window.

I couldn't stop my mind from bouncing back and forth between the two rejections. An uppercut followed by a hook. But why now? Why all of a sudden and all at once? Had Gallantine heard how I'd snaked Lindy's work on Filco before she could get it out? That seemed unlikely. And even if he had, he might as easily have been inclined to praise me for keeping the *Herald* ahead. Or maybe he'd had someone check into my allegation that Takahashi had honed his business skills while leading a death squad through the jungles of Burma. But that didn't seem right either: it wasn't entirely my allegation, I just changed the country and job description, and anyway I'd been careful to attribute it to others.

Blocked from any logical route to follow towards a satisfying explanation, my thoughts would swerve to the Shirley conundrum, and then I would feel the ache of solitude threatening to seep into somewhere it might fester. I felt myself perched on the edge of a great looming regret. Soon I would be — or was now — what Danny used to call a "clearly non-coupled guy." You could look for me in the bars but I might also be in the gym or the supermarket — yet another horny male, out baying for some on the street.

A clunk from the front porch startled me back to the present. I tilted my ear to hear better. There it went again, this time sounding like a footstep — but not a footstep with the pace of a late-night room-seeker. This was the cautious sound of someone trying not to be heard.

"*Bakayaro,*" a hoarse voice hissed from beyond the door. It was followed by the sound of a splat and then a grunted, "*Ii-teah!*"

I crept to the living room window to peer through the curtains. Two beefy Asian men were bent over the doorknob, studying it as if checking for microbes. The shiny fabric of their suits stretched against the muscles of their backs and arms. One had the oversized neck of a professional football player. The other nearest the door straightened up and turned towards the porch light, lending the oversized lapels of his suit a maroon sheen. His shaven head revealed a bullet-shaped skull. The other had a dour, fleshy face under cropped and permed hair. He wore white enamel shoes and a double-breasted suit in an outlandish shade of green. I thought of Danny's depiction of the Japanese yakuza dress code as "Al Capone meets pan-Asian pimp." He had said it approvingly.

The permed one was apparently the boss. The other looked to him for approval before reaching for the doorknob. He then stretched out his hand with the exaggerated caution of a man hoping to pet a snarling dog, while my heart went into overdrive. The lamp glow distinctly showed his pinkie, or what was left of it. It ended at the knuckle — a sure sign of a Japanese gangster, according to Danny.

His four and a half fingers worked well enough to turn the knob, very slowly, but even so it issued a loud metallic click. His partner cuffed the back of his head. This launched another round of hissed invectives back and forth that had to have been louder than any door noises they had tried to avoid.

I exhaled in a slow measure and told myself to think. For the moment, at least, they were still outside: that gave me time. But time for what? To even the sides with some kind of weapon. The TV? It was big enough to issue a blow that even the no-neck might feel, but wasn't exactly wieldy. I spotted the phone, but the macramé cover would detract from its potential as a visual deterrent. There was the kitchen with any number of lethal utensils, but the thought of a butcher's knife seemed, even in the circumstances, extreme. I might end up losing my own pinkie in a tussle.

A better tactic came to me in a rush: surprise. I walked quickly to the door and whipped it open. As it was still in the grip of the finger-deficient one, I ended up yanking him clear into the entranceway where he shuffled madly to keep his own feet balanced under him on the polished wood floor. He failed, collapsing into an erratic pile of muscle-stuffed maroon suit.

His superior rushed in, not to grab me but to aim three quick kicks of reproof at the man's legs. The thicker one bounded upright to avoid more punishment and they squared off, each holding a hand cupped protectively over his own nuts while bobbing for an opening kick. These were not the kind of people I wanted to fight.

"Gentlemen," I interrupted in a soft voice, gesturing to the many doors upstairs. "Has no one taught you how to knock?"

"Yes yes, knock yes, I see, ha ha ha ha ha," said the one with the perm. Even in a whisper he spoke with the barking rhythm of a madman. "We so sorry. We thinking, maybe everybody sleeping."

"You right," I answered. "I was just about to go to bed myself."

"Ah yes yes yes, of course," he continued. "Ver' late." His partner bent stiffly to rub his own shin with a forlorn expression, then muttered something that was ignored. "We have request. We are looking for za man whose name is called Aah-doo."

"Aah-doo?"

"No, no," the bald one interrupted. He licked his lips in preparation. "Uuh-ru."

"Uuh-ru?"

"Uuh-lu. Lu. Lu. Or ru. Uuh-ru. Yes."

I raised my arms, palms up, in an international gesture of hopelessness. "I don't understand. This is difficult. What exactly do you want?"

They traded looks of exasperation. "Please to wait," the permed one said. "We show you." He rummaged through a tiny black pouch dangling from a strap around one wrist. It looked like a girlie purse, the kind of thing you might put a Hello Kitty sticker on if you were eleven years old and female and not a thug. He withdrew and carefully unfolded a piece of paper. On it were tight rows of Japanese characters that made no sense to me, but included two words in Western script that did: Earl Brododsky. Apparently my name did not translate smoothly into spoken Japanese.

"Oh," I said, "you mean Aah-ru."

The nodded their heads with vigor.

"He's not here."

"Not here?" the bald one grunted. His grouper lips curled even further down.

"No."

The permed one stepped back out to check the address above the doorway. He frowned, then said something in Japanese that produced a similar frown in his partner. They began a whispered discussion which sounded less like words than the staccato bursts of throat-clearing you might hear from two congested patients furious at finding themselves confined to a TB ward.

Up came the purse again. For such a tiny thing it was quite handy. The paper he produced this time, and again carefully unfolded, then held at an angle to catch the light angling in from the porch, showed on one side the name and address of Grady's Inn, which they checked once more against the brass number over the door. The flip side, facing me, had my picture, the one taken from the paper. In that light, I had to admit, I did look a little like Donny Osmond.

The bald one muttered unhappily at the paper, scratched the back of his bull neck and tilted his head while sucking air in through his teeth with a slurpy hiss. He looked at me as if for clarification.

I shrugged. The mysteries of life, I tried to suggest with a smile. Almost absently he flipped the paper over, surprised to find something on the other side. They stared at the picture with their mouths open. Now where had they seen that face before?

"*Nan jya?*" the bald one exclaimed, looking from the picture up to me and back again.

"*Yappari!*" the other exclaimed.

I heard, over my shoulder, as I raced out the back door, the sound of enamel shoes clacking on hardwood. Their grunts were either orders to me to stop or the involuntary noises of large men suddenly having to exert themselves. Either way, it was urgent enough to drive me out faster. As if my brain had any reasoning to do in the matter. It was my body in control now, and it had one immediate, overwhelming urge — to run.

Run, run, run.

I raced through Grady's vegetable patch out to the lane and then into the next street to head for the park. No sense meeting the pair alone in some corn field. If Toshi's yakuza henchmen hoped to get me, they would have to find me first, in a crowd of thousands. And if they did? I wouldn't give in to the thought. Not then. Better just to run.

Seeing the park was like spotting a rescue plane. The expanse of humanity, the people, my protectors — even though most of them were then sleeping. I scurried into the thick of the masses, stepping around or over dozens of lumpy-shaped oblongs in sleeping bags and blankets, until I came to a place where a few people stood talking in late-night hushed conversations.

I mingled with them, grateful for the smoke from a few hibachis brewing teas of pungent roots and bark. It was a reprieve to stop running and move at a walking pace. I gave in to the luxury of not checking behind me for a full ten seconds, telling myself I no longer needed to, but then did again anyway.

No yakuza, no predators, no harm in sight, just a misty blue night light from a billion stars showing the vast spread of believers on the ground dwarfed by the silhouette of the Miracle Tree. A quarter moon hung low enough to leave a golden ribbon on the river.

I realized I had recovered my normal breathing rhythm, then slowed it further to relax, and listen. I heard soft conversations referencing Nostradamus, the occasional smack or snuffle of a snorer, but nothing resembling the grim rendition of my own name in enraged Japanese. An elation somewhat like giddiness swept through me: so this is how it felt to test danger and live. What a high — no wonder some soldiers miss the war. I tingled all over.

I'd lost my girl and my job and yet I felt grand. Tired as well, but it was more of a good tired now, the serene exhaustion of the safe and warm. I decided to lie down right on the spot, unwind my weary limbs and shut my eyes to put an end to the close of a horrible day. I was almost there, another three seconds would have been enough, but then I heard a muffled shriek. I recognized the voice — it was Trish.

I leaped up to stare in the direction of the sound. When it came to me again I took off running. She was in distress, so much so that she was unable to make out the words to ask for help. I got angry at the depths to which these goons would descend to make their case. Evil bastards — no wonder they were notorious. Here I had taken them for lummoxes who could be confounded by a single doorknob, yet they'd figured out I'd been friendly enough with Trish to use her as a lure.

The closer I got the more insistent her pleas became. They now took on the frantic rhythm of panic. I briefly considered waking others in the crowd for help, but there was no time to explain. I had to hurry, that much was clear — she was practically gasping out her final breaths.

I saw her through a flap in the tent put up by the Mexican circus. She seemed taller than I'd remembered, a lot taller, but it was clearly Trish, in profile, although it wasn't so clear now she was being tortured. Actually she seemed tired too — her head lolled and her eyelids flickered. She may have been just about to lose it.

I wanted to shout, to say something to let her know I was coming and would be there as soon as I could negotiate the space between us, but I also didn't want to give up the element of surprise. I hurdled over sleeping bodies, understanding that once I'd saved her, and we both got away, she would probably want to take me in. So be it: I would get my bed at last. With her in it? I marveled at the capacity of the male mind to leap, even amid the direst circumstances, to the ultimate conclusion of sex. Although that wasn't at all what this was about, I reminded myself: I was on a mission of mercy. I needed to help Trish, whose pleas were now coming out only in short breathless yips.

I made it to the tent and circled around to the back where I knew a wooden door had been built into the frame. It was marked with a sign reading No Entry and something in Spanish. I burst through, my hands up and out in something like a kung fu position, ready for combat, or to do whatever it would take to throw off the criminals and get Trish out of there alive.

I saw then why she had seemed so tall. She wasn't standing but kneeling, on all fours, on top of a pinball machine, her dress flipped up and around her shoulders. Behind her, moving with closed eyes and clenched-teeth abandon, was the midget. Trish slowly turned back to look over a shoulder at her mate, then to the side where her eyes met mine — or would have met mine, if they hadn't looked right through me. She smiled, but it wasn't at me.

I dropped my hands, and backed silently out the door. I remembered a guy I once met from the Bible Belt who assured me small town girls could be had because they were always hungry for it. "They're like cats," he'd said. "You know they're doing it, you just never catch 'em at it."

Only now I had — for all the good it did me. I had gone in one instant from charging knight to cringing voyeur. All my misguided courage poured out of me, and for good reason — I knew from the way the hairs on the back of my neck stood up that I was scared all over again. If the yakuza were not in the circus tent, they could be anywhere, including nearby and heading for me. I looked everywhere, until I saw them, at the edge of the park. They were indeed coming closer.

Run, run, run.

My feet started moving too swiftly to sense the ground beneath them. Yet the yakuza pair kept up.

"Aah-ru," I heard the permed one call. "Aah-ru."

The other seemed to be threatening me, or swearing something in vicious Japanese — either way it was ghoulish. I thought if I could just get some open space in front of me I might lose them over a distance. They didn't seem like the jogging types — unless they kept themselves in shape for just this purpose. Chasing might have been part of their job description.

A second wind must have kicked in, because all at once I felt strong. I got into a rhythm that worked in dodging through the maze of sleeping pilgrims. I no longer felt restrained by the prospect of stepping on someone. I continued at a brisk clip for some time, certain there was no way two thick oafs in ridiculous suits could possibly match me.

Yet I could still hear the wheezing and grunting directly behind me. "Aah-ru. . . Aaaaaaah-ru. Stop-pu."

I got scared all over again. This time I veered towards the river. I didn't know why — my legs had taken over. My heart raced blood through every passage, flushing the capillaries with extra fuel. My body seemed to have commanded some kind of last stand response:

it was pulling the goalie.

I reached the river bank, but there my predicament made even less sense. What had I expected? To swim to freedom? To hope that the yakuza, like some animal predators, might be stopped by a fear of water?

I cut right to race through Camp Hog so I could circle around the main crowd to reach the upper edge of the parking lot. Just what I would do there was a question I couldn't answer; it was too many moves ahead on the chessboard. The immediate point was to get space between me and the hoods.

The first glop sound came to me as a shock. I looked down at my right foot to see it half-buried in a shrinking hole that oozed itself back closed. I managed to pull my foot out, with effort, but only by applying downward pressure with the other leg that left that foot snared instead. I pushed forward that way for a few anguished dinosaurian steps. The top half of my body was still in race mode, torso forward, arms pumping, but my legs felt as if they were surrounded by wet concrete.

I turned back to look for my pursuers. They may have been in the crowd, but not where I could locate them. Maybe I'd lost them at last. That glimmer of hope gave me a resurgence of energy I felt I might use to finish the task of getting away. I grabbed my right thigh and heaved up to free my foot for good. It came out slick and glistening with riverbed mud.

This time I leapt further away from the mud towards the water, hoping to get out of the muck, but my other foot still sank into ooze. I repeated the move twice more until I was on solid footing, now in waist-high water. If I could just wade a short distance upstream, where the water went right up to a soft grassy section of the riverbank, I could climb out and get away.

It worked as planned until my right foot hit a slick stone and swept back in an arc that pitched me face forwards into the water. When I came up, I was surprised to discover my feet could no longer touch bottom. I was also moving — somehow that slip had managed to slide me into the current. The river had always looked placid on the surface, but I knew now that underneath it carried an unexpectedly strong pull.

Just as well, I thought: at least I was moving. Upstream, downstream, I didn't care. I let myself go limp. For once, nature was working with me: I could let myself get carried gently to safety by the water. Then my dangling feet bumped something on the bottom — a snag, maybe, a piece of driftwood sticking out of the river bed, no problem, really, until I hit another and this time my foot didn't come up when I tugged. The shoelace may have been tangled. I pushed down with the other leg to break free, but that turned out to be a bad idea when it got stuck too.

Now as I tried to resist I could sense the power of the water. It was pulling me not along but down, trying to drag me beneath the eerily still surface. Then I went completely under. I stretched my neck to get my head above the water, but managed only to poke my nostrils into clear air for a quick snort before being submerged.

Panic swarmed me. I thrashed like a pronged fish, but this only snared my feet deeper into the trap. I could get my head out of the water with contorted effort for brief gasps, but no more. When I tried to scream for help, it came out in bubbles.

Then something clamped onto my elbow. My first thought was some kind of predator fish, but it turned out to be a hand, with a strong grip, followed by another that clenched my opposite shoulder. My arms went up over my head with a jerk that lifted me clear out of my shoes. One of the hands holding me let go momentarily to tilt my head back so I would float. I coughed and sputtered between breaths as my entire bronchial system fought for air.

That's when the scent came to me. It left me so stunned I went limp. I knew then I would be all right, and gave myself up to the rescue. I let the arms push me from behind towards the bank, and then towards a grassy spot where I could pull myself out of the water onto land. There the scent came back to me more powerfully — a tangy aroma combining a mixture of things, which triggered a flood of memories that transported me back to my childhood and the skating accident on the frozen lake.

I wiped my eyes and whipped my head around before the rescuer might get away. I saw him kneeling beside me. It was definitely him, incredibly him: the tall, dark man who had saved me before. He wasn't wearing an overcoat, and he had on a baseball cap rather than a Fedora. I realized I couldn't claim to recognize the face — but I knew. It could have been in the same way I recognized the scent, or maybe that had nothing to do with it. But I knew.

When he bent down to look closer at me, water slid off the brim of his cap.

"It's you," I said in a voice tinged with awe. "It's really you, isn't it?"

"Of course," he said in a deep voice. He placed a hand on my forehead to help me lie back down on the grass. "You should take it easy."

I grabbed his arm. "Don't go. Are you going to go?"

"I *was* just passing through."

"No. You have to tell me. Who are you? What are you?"

"Earl." He said my name almost sadly.

"See? I knew it was you. I always believed in you, you know. Even when I was too embarrassed to tell anyone. I knew you were real, I just didn't know how. Does this mean you're my guardian angel or am I way off base?"

"Your *what*?" His hand went from my neck back to my forehead. He was feeling for a fever.

"You rescued me. Again. I can hardly believe it once, let alone twice. How did you do it? I mean, that first time. I've always wanted to ask."

I saw the tops of his wide shoulders lift. He leaned back on one arm.

"It wasn't that deep. Maybe for you, but you were just a kid."

"But. . . but. . . okay. I guess. Still, how did you know? How did you even find me?"

"It was dark. You know how your mother worried — she sent me out to look for you."

"You knew my mother?"

"Earl," he said in the same heavy voice as before. When had my name turned into a lament? "We should have talked about this a long time ago."

"You're right," I agreed, then added, "talked about what, exactly?"

"I had to be — how shall I put this — discreet. See, you knew your mother and your father weren't getting along, right?"

"They weren't?"

He sighed. "There must be an easier way to do this."

"Do what? What are you talking about?"

He let out a long breath. "Right. Okay. Here it is, then. Earl, I'm your father."

"No you're not. You don't look anything like him. I've still got the pictures."

"Your real father."

"My real father was a musician. He left us."

"I'm telling the truth."

"Mom never said anything about this."

"It was difficult. She was married at the time."

I felt my own head for the fever. "Who the hell are you really and why are you telling me this?"

"I'm someone who cared about your mother very much — from before you were born. We never meant it to come to this. Meaning you. But, what can I say? Things happen."

"That's it? That's your excuse? Things happen? No — people make them happen."

He shrugged again. "I always meant to tell you. After your mother and I separated, we kind of lost touch, but I never stopped thinking about you. Then when I saw you on TV the other night, I knew I had to come here. I can't believe how lucky it was to find you. Is that amazing or what?"

"A miracle," I said dully.

"Exactly! I never watch the news on that channel."

I sat up on the grass, brushing off his attempt to help with a flick of my hand. "You've pulled me enough," I said. "My arm's going to hurt for a week." I tried to chuckle in a cruel way.

"I know," he said. "I'm sorry. I'm sorry about it all. Not about you, though. Remember, this doesn't mean your father — the other one, not me, the one that brought you up — it doesn't mean he loved you any less or that he wouldn't have wanted—"

"He didn't care. He sent me a postcard once for my birthday. He didn't even get the month right."

I spat on the grass and looked closer at him. His features were hard to make out against the backlight of the distant floodlights, but I guessed he was handsome, or at least used to be.

"Oh, wait," I said. "He didn't care. Now I get it. No wonder."

"It was not my idea for your parents to break up."

"And yet you were apparently pretty thick in it."

"Hey, I was just trying to help."

I coughed up more river water. "Sounds like something I would say."

He made the brief sound of what could have been a chuckle and stood up.

"Listen, Earl, I said I was just passing through, which is true, but really it's more pressing than that. I've got people waiting for me. I really do have to go."

The wet shirt clung to his shoulders. It wasn't a bad physique, genetically speaking.

"Wait. Really? Can't you stay? There's so much I want to know."

"Me too. We'll talk all about it later. I promise."

I wasn't sure if I believed him — or whether it mattered. Talking wouldn't change things.

"Want to know something really funny?" I asked.

He looked towards the crowd, maybe to where someone really was waiting, then back at me. He didn't say anything.

"The only reason I'm here is because of my so-called heritage. Can you believe that? I got the job because they think I'm part Indian — Native Indian. And you know what's really weird? I always went along with it, but I think I must have known all that time there was something wrong with the whole story about grandma and the Cree customer. Blood is what counts, I guess — you can't fake that. You are who you are."

"Yeah, well. . . I guess. I never thought of it that way. Although I'm half Mohawk myself."

"No way. Really?"

"According to my mother. But I wouldn't put much into it — she never had anything good to say about my old man."

He held out a hand. I shook it, then we both must have realized how awkward that was because we immediately turned it into a hug. He squeezed me hard enough to press the scent into my clothes.

"What is that smell anyway? I've never been able to forget it."

"Benjamin's Bay Rum," he said. "Great for after a shower. You used to be able to buy it everywhere. Now I have to get it sent on special order from Jamaica." He ruffled my hair and then smoothed some of the mess back from my forehead. "I'll bring you some next time. Son."

I watched him walk away until he was one of the crowd. Even then I stayed rooted to the spot, staring at the throng, that incredible collection of people that now included my own family, my pa, my blood. I might have stayed that way longer, replaying everything we'd just said, if I hadn't had my field of vision suddenly blocked by the rapidly growing figures of the two yakuza henchmen rushing towards me. How had I managed to forget about them?

I looked in every direction, saw nowhere to run, cursed and

then leaped back into the river, this time keeping my bare feet clear of the bottom so I could swim to the other side. The current, I remembered too late, was stronger than it looked, and because they were downstream, it would inevitably pull me back towards them. They figured it out before I did — they stood at the edge of the water to wait the way bears stand in streams with their mouths open for salmon to leap in.

I tried to swim upstream but the current was too powerful. It was clear that I could only delay but not avoid the inevitable: I was headed straight for them. I tried to smile. The gradual pace of my approach had given them enough time to remove their belts and tie them together. Maybe I'd pegged them unfairly as palookas. It took at least some intelligence to turn an everyday object into a lifeline — unless they just wanted a longer weapon with which to thrash me.

I fumbled with my own belt, made, unfortunately, of meshed cotton with a tin buckle. Once it was off the swirling water dragged my pants down to my ankles. I kicked to try to inch them back up, but it only worked to twist them around my legs. The question now became whether I might drown myself before the yakuza had a chance to kill me. I had to let go of the belt to rescue myself by tugging the pants off my feet and letting them go.

The gangster with the perm held the twin-belt behind him like a fisherman, pausing to gauge the flow of the river before casting in my direction. The buckle landed with a plop a few feet from my head: they were fishing for me. I tried again to swim against the current, but with no more success.

"Take behru-toh!" the bald one shouted between cupped hands. His partner added encouragement with eight or nine rapid nods of the head and a wide smile that revealed a Fort Knox of dental work.

I had no choice: the current would lead me anyway into an eddy just beyond where they stood. There they wouldn't have had to get their ankles wet to give me a thrashing. When the next cast landed an inch from my ear I grabbed hold. Like a game trout, however, I wouldn't just give up — I tugged and wrenched.

"Whoa-whoaaaaah," the bald one said, spreading his feet wider for balance. I pulled more, leading the permed one to get a grip on their end too. Together they began hauling me in. I held on tight, with both of them grunting and straining backwards, making them work for every inch until we were so close I could almost touch their hands. Then I let my end go slack.

They stumbled backwards in a scramble to stay upright — but they didn't let go, just as I'd hoped. I felt with my bare feet for a rock to brace against, waited until they had a purchase, then pulled as hard as I could. This time they fell forward into the water. I climbed up and over their backs onto dry land.

Run, run, run.

This time I headed straight for the Miracle Tree — people would be my best disguise. I got as far as Agnes, who was with a group of ladies of a similar age. Up so late? With a posse? It didn't make sense. Then over my shoulder I saw the sky to the east taking on light. Most of the ladies held binoculars, all aimed at a spot high up in the canopy of the tree. I tapped Agnes on the shoulder.

"Mrs. Weatherby, am I ever glad to see you," I said in a hushed voice.

When she turned around, I saw that I'd been mistaken. It wasn't Agnes at all, but an elderly woman leading a birdwatching brigade. She shrank back, holding the binoculars in front of her like a shield. To judge by her expression I could have been an axe murderer.

"Ma'am, very sorry, honest mistake."

"Oh my," one of the ladies announced, and they all turned in unison. I watched ten pairs of binoculars swivel from the tree to me as if I were a rare ptarmigan. Only then did I understand why they looked so scandalized. One after another pair of binoculars would aim first at my face, and then move lower, and stay there. I realized I was standing, in public, in my underwear.

I spread my fingers in a feeble attempt to cover the sight of the dodgiest, greyest Y-fronts I owned. Why I had chosen that of all days to wear the frayed ones? I knew I should have retired those shorts when the first rip appeared in the cloth, as Shirley had advised; meanwhile the holes had spread. The front looked less like underwear than a suggestion of the fact, the sagging elastic band holding a few stringy patches of cloth.

There was nothing to do, no way to explain. I spun and fled, feeling the backs of my ears flush hot. I tried to dangle one hand behind me to cover the sight but it probably just compounded the effect. The explosive tittering of ladies behind me sounded like an excited flock of starlings.

Run, run, run.

My legs wobbled but still I ran. Shame would fuel me all the way to the horizon. I crossed the gathering of space campers, then stopped and doubled back. They weren't early risers, which was one thing in my favor. So was the fact that one had washed and hung out his clothes to dry on a line strung between two lawn chairs.

It was a jumpsuit I selected, somewhat large for my size but I didn't care — it was cover. I all but jumped into it, and told myself it wasn't stealing, exactly. Better to call it borrowing — I would be glad to give it back when I was done, provided I could find the owner, which was unlikely. In my defense, I reasoned that the owner obviously had something else to wear, or he wouldn't have put this in the wash. So it could be seen as a way of evening things out, giving him a chance to help which he might well have leaped at if asked. Or he might even conclude the missing suit had been taken by aliens that had descended to study earthling wear, turning him into the hero of his next convention.

It was a huge relief to be re-clothed. It hardly mattered that the jumpsuit had once been fire-engine red and was now mostly faded to pink, or that it had enough pockets to carry a week's worth of groceries. Each pocket also came with its own zipper, so that every step I took now produced a jingle — which may have been why, as I ran on, I found I still drew stares, although it could as well have been because I never looked good in red. Or pink.

It didn't matter: I was no longer bare-assed, and I was away from the yakuza. They would probably come later, I knew, but there would be time for that. Now I had something more pressing to deal with: the need for sleep has also chased me, and caught me, and tackled me for a loss. My body craved nothing more.

Except perhaps a last snack before going under. I patted the pocket of my shirt. The plastic wrapping had kept the mushroom pizza slice from going completely soggy. I opened my mouth for the first gummy bite, when the realization struck me like a bell.

These mushrooms aren't mushrooms, I thought — they're 'shrooms! Magic mushrooms! No wonder they'd been stored separately in the fridge. What were the Gradys, anyway, but a couple of old hippies? They knew their fungi all right. They were probably collectors, perhaps even dealers. Who knew? The point was, I was tripping! It was the psilocybin talking, not two angry yakuza!

The more I thought of it, the more the beauty of this logic charmed me. Those poor simple wayward mugs. They'd probably come all this way and gotten lost and had just been looking for directions. I'd blown everything out of proportion when I bolted like that. I would have to apologize if I ever ran into them again. But only after I had a chance to come down — starting with a nap. My brain was already slipping in and out of hypnagogia. Flushed with this newfound relief, I knew it would be a delight to slip into a delicious sleep as the last of the hallucinogen's effects faded away.

I found an empty space amid the flowers and incense at the bottom of the giant TV screen. The sound had been muted, I supposed to permit sleeping. Sitting that close, the screen rose above me like a building made of pixels. I curled into a ball with my back against the base, watching the rainbow glow of colors shift on the skin of my palms. A documentary about undersea volcanoes made my hands go from a shimmering blue to brilliant orange. When I shut my eyes the colors were still there. I didn't mind — sleep was within my reach. It would all be better, very soon. My eyes were closed and my body was horizontal. What could stop me now?

A blast of pure noise, for one thing. The speakers emitted a shock of static that tore into my eardrums. No wonder no one else had chosen that spot to sleep. Next came a female voice. "Notice that separation in the pelvic area," it boomed with enough decibels to be considered an aural assault. "Can you feel it? Come on!"

I stretched my neck to look up at the screen. It showed a fit blonde woman in leotards on a beach with palm trees. She led four other people in leotards, one of them a man with a trimmed beard, through aerobic exercises. They were kneeling on all fours and kicking their right legs back in unison. I wondered about Trish: she might do well with something like this, as a daily thing.

I absently unwrapped the slice of pizza and was about to take a bite when I remembered the contents. I hurriedly wrapped it back up and put it down on the grass.

"If you're not going to eat it?" inquired a tanned guy in a Quicksilver T-shirt and Sri Lankan sarong. He eyed it hungrily. "Haven't had a bite since breakfast."

"It's not what you think," I said.

"I think it's a slice of pizza," he countered.

"It is, but it isn't. Those aren't mushrooms."

He leaned closer to sniff. "Not a problem. I love smoked oysters."

"You've got it all wrong. They're actually magic mushrooms. You know, 'shrooms? They're practically psychotic. Very elusive. I mean they start out creeper but then when you don't even know it, kazam — you're in a whole other universe. Trust me."

"Dude, I work in a deli. I eat smoked oysters all the time. If you're just going to throw it away anyway, why can't I have it?"

"Yes, yes, yes and yesssss!" the TV woman boomed. Not a single person I could see had joined in, although many were now standing and watching. Among them, staring with the same sullen, too-early-in-the-morning-to-be-up stares, were the two yakuza.

"Oysters?" I asked glumly. I looked closer: he was right. I gave it to him.

"Thanks," he said, eyeing me warily but trusting the pizza.

"Damn," I had time to mutter before slipping away behind the screen and taking off again, at a run. The motion must have alerted them. When I finally let myself turn around, at the motorhome section of the park, they were right behind me. The bald one had lost one of the arms of his suit jacket, which may have been why he looked even angrier than before.

Run, run, run.

This time I ran clear out of the park, past the Old General Store, past Buffy's. I cut through Perry's driveway, gaining a little distance when they briefly stopped to look for me in the opposite direction, then I took a right down Maple Street.

It wasn't hard to guess which house belonged to Wilbur. On the front lawn were his yellow balloons tethered to a lawn chair, the whole display set up on a raised wooden platform. Beside it was a sandwich board that read:

GET THE GIFT OF FLIGHT. INQUIRIES INSIDE.

I ran as far as the balloons, thinking I might hide behind them. They were floating a few feet over the chair like a private weather system. A single carabiner held the whole contraption down. One flick of the aluminum catch and the chair would lift off.

It suddenly came to me: would lift off and carry me away. I knew even as I sat in the webbed lawn chair that it might not be a brilliant idea. Who knew how high the thing went, or which way the winds would take me? But I had no time to worry about weather. Who cared, so long as I ended up somewhere else? Moreover, I was tired, too tired, tired of everything — especially running. That alone was enough for me to reach out for the carabiner and unhook the line. I looked down in amazement as my feet lifted up off the platform.

The yakuza reached me when I was just above head height. They made two or three leaping grabs for my feet, but jumping was not their strong suit. All I had to do was lift my legs for them to miss. Soon I was ten feet over their heads, and then twenty. I was slowly floating up and away.

"So long, suckas," I yelled down. It wasn't my nature to taunt, and I had never used the term "suckas" in my life. But that's how giddy I felt.

At about thirty feet, the street patterns below began to make sense — I could see the town and how small it really was amid the sea of corn. I could also see the tree standing out in the park like a giant mushroom being swarmed by ants. Drifting in the breeze, I realized, was a wonderful way to move. No wonder Wilbur got so excited. Anybody could buy a plane ticket — this felt more like flying for real. This was what we had aspired to ever since Icarus.

A backyard terrier saw me and did a double-take. Then, with what looked like delight, it barked. I could have been the mailman of his dreams, drifting down from the sky like manna. More dogs heard it and joined in, until it seemed as if every canine in town was part of the chorus. I laughed as I drifted on and up, the sounds below diminishing the higher I got.

I was rapt. The breeze wafted through my hair and under my bare feet, and I adored it. I wasn't in the wind, I was part of it — the gift of flight indeed. This worked, this definitely worked. How about that Wilbur? Who knew? The man was a genius, or maybe I should call him an artist.

Or maybe a lunatic, I thought next, when I considered that the miracle of flight had to end somehow. There had to be some kind of landing, if that wasn't too optimistic a word. The highway below now looked like a grey ribbon winding through the green and brown quilt of farms. No wonder Wilbur had worn a helmet. Then again, what could a plastic cap do for you once you started into a death plunge? I gripped the arm rests, and told myself to stop looking down.

Far below I heard a car honk. A single white sedan on the highway was tracking me. I could make out an arm stretched out of the driver's window to wave, using big flaps to gesture: down, come down, this way, the ground is here. Gee, thanks for the tip, driver — as if I controlled the wind.

Then again, neither did Wilbur, and he was a smart guy. He would have figured some way to deal with the issue of not wanting to float away forever. I dismissed the thought of the only landing of his I had seen, which had been on top of my head. Besides, even that one hadn't been fatal, so maybe there was some room for optimism.

I felt all over the chair for a switch, or a lever, or something, anything that might indicate some kind of control. Under the seat I touched duct tape wrapped around a cigar box. It was attached with a plastic clip that was easy to unlatch. I slid the box out and placed it carefully in my lap. I pulled off an elastic holding the box closed and then, closing my eyes and willing, with the closest thing I know to prayer, for something good to be inside, raised the lid.

Inside was a pistol. Gun metal grey. An automatic.

Wilbur? The flying bandit? The world's wackiest bank robber? With the world's slowest getaway plan? Then I saw next to the pistol a small box of ammunition: air pellets. Now it made sense — and it explained his emergency descents: you pop the balloons holding you up and gravity takes you back down. So maybe he wasn't a genius after all, and maybe this was why balloon chair travel had never caught on.

Nevertheless, I took aim at the lowest balloon, held my breath and fired. Nothing. I had forgotten to load the gun. At my next attempt, the trigger wouldn't budge, because the safety was on. On the third try I got a shot off but it missed. So that's why they sell ammunition by the box.

My next shot hit the target, producing a surprisingly tiny phhht. A slightly louder hiss followed, and then the chair began to sink. It was a gentle descent, the long idyllic arc of a soap bubble wafting back down to the lawn on a summer day.

"Wilbur you wondergeek!" I cried out with genuine joy. The chair began to rock gently as I got lower, and I helped it, imagining myself in a giant playground swing that just happened to be up in the air.

Then came a BANG that was alarming. The tiny pellet hole had ripped wide open — now it was an ugly, flapping gash. The chair dropped at a rate that made my stomach leap. The geometric array of land below rapidly took on the individual aspects of property lots. There was the white line of the highway again, there was the rescue car, there was the corn field I was about to crash into.

I couldn't slow down, I couldn't steer, I couldn't do anything except clench every muscle I had while waiting for the impact. I had enough time and sense to realize my descent was fast but not that fast, and at least it wasn't accelerating. This was not a terror dive. At that speed, who knew, I might even make it, in some fashion. With enough corn to cushion my fall and a quick roll out of the chair at just the right moment, I might—

The ground raced up at me before I could complete the thought. I lifted my feet, held tightly to the arm rests and shut my eyes. I landed in something less than a crash: more of a skid. I must have been dropping at an angle. I was dragged a short way on top of the corn, until the chair got stuck on a stalk and tilted forward with a jerk which threw me out. The tight pattern of the corn stalks absorbed most of the impact of the fall, and I found myself sprawled over eight or nine plants which bent under me like a green leafy mattress.

I didn't feel bad. In fact, quite the opposite — the fear was gone. I was alive, maybe never more so. True, I was still tired, sleep-depraved, unshaven, barefoot, mud-grungy and wearing bizarre clothes — but I was definitely alive. The more I thought about it, the happier I got. My girlfriend had split. My job was gone. My career was a shambles. Bad guys wanted to hurt me. But none of that could dull the elation buzzing through me. I was alive — and I even knew how to fly. I wondered where I might pick up some balloons of my own.

If this joy seemed out of proportion, I quickly had an answer for it — and it made me, impossibly, even happier. I realized with a jolt of insight what had been happening all along. "Of course!" I said, shouting it triumphantly to the sky. "What a dope I've been! When it was so obvious! And I thought it was 'shrooms. Ha!"

I laughed loud and long, in a way I'd never heard myself laugh before. But then I'd never been in a state like this before. "Getting chased by monsters?" I yelled out in triumph. "So you run as fast as you can but you don't get anywhere? Because your feet feel like they're stuck in what? Mud! Yes! And then, oh yes! You suddenly find yourself in public in your underwear? How embarrassing would *that* be?"

I laughed again, slapping my own face in a celebration of utter silliness. "It never happened! You big dummy! None of it happened! Because it was all a dream! A lucid dream!"

I heard the rescuers shouting as they came closer. I could mark their progress by the bending tops of the corn plants they crushed on the way. "Over here," I yelled. "Yoo hoo! Look for the big yellow balls. Ha ha ha ha ha!"

My laughter was cut short by a new thought, which sent my mood up still higher. "Wait a minute," I said, almost afraid to let logic follow its inevitable course because I wasn't sure how I might react to something so wondrous. "Wait a freakin' minute," I said. "This dream didn't start with some stupid chase. . . it must have been earlier! Of course! When I was so tired. I fell asleep a long time ago — which means that Shirley didn't leave me! Shirley loves me! And I love her! And I didn't get fired. Why would they? I'm a great reporter! Hello? Huh? It's you guys? What are you still doing here?"

The yakuza loomed over me. I could see the concern in their faces. I blinked rapidly. Lucid dreams weren't supposed to carry on once you're truly awake. They also weren't supposed to hurt. The parts of my arms they grabbed were definitely sore. I saw through an armpit flap on the jumpsuit the purple start of a bruise.

"So you're not dream guys?" I asked pathetically.

Neither answered. They heaved together to bring me up to a standing position.

Yes, that was pain alright. It wasn't a dream. It was a nightmare. A nightmare I was living for real. "Gentlemen," I said, surrendering at last to my fate, whatever that was going to be. "Have either of you seen Aah-ru?"

There is no passion to be found in playing small — in settling for a life that is less than the one you are capable of living.

Nelson Mandela

ELEVEN

Toshi Takahashi was waiting for me inside one of those luxury trailers-on-steroids, the kind of uber-den an A-list star might relax in between takes on a film shoot. It was parked at the far end of the empty lot past Agnes's street. I wondered, would a loud scream reach her — or does metal insulate against sound? Why hadn't they taught us useful information like that in high school instead of algebra?

Takahashi was taller than I'd expected. When he got up from his leather captain's chair, I saw with a sinking feeling that we were about the same height — so much for any physical advantage. Although he wouldn't have needed it anyway with his henchmen still crowding me at the elbows. What did they think, I might try to jump him?

He was handsome, too, I had to admit. No wonder Lindy had been charmed. He had a movie star mustache that could have been modeled after Clark Gable's. He extended a hand that glittered. The ring on his middle finger carried an emerald the size of a hazelnut. A diamond-heavy Rolex dangled on his wrist. Two trinkets in, and he had already proven himself worth more than I would earn in years. At least I had him in the digit count — he too was missing half a pinkie.

"Thank you for coming, Mistah Brododsky," he said. He hit my name spot on, first try, one of the few people to do that in the past month.

"Call me Earl," I parried.

"Earl," he replied in a working version of the real thing. The bastard. He smiled in a way that lifted his trimmed mustache but didn't reach the hard look in his eyes. "And you, please, call me Toshi."

"Right. Toshi." Li'l buddy.

"I hope you will pardon my wear," he said, motioning with a tiny flourish to his glossy pajamas. The material could have been silk, unless there was something more expensive. He struck me as the type to have a whole wardrobe made from the skin of endangered animals. "I was not certain what time you would be able to arrive," he explained. "I am afraid I have just awoken."

"No problem," I answered, feeling exposed in my pink, pocket-laden, galactic suit. "You'll have to pardon my attire, too. I'm thinking of switching tailors."

His expression didn't change. Some sense of humor. Here he was kicking my ass all over the board and he couldn't even concede a pawn? He motioned with the less expensive hand for me to take the chair facing his. Naturally his chair was set higher, putting his eyes at least six inches above mine. One more move in his favor.

The bald-headed goon grunted something, then smiled, but no one responded.

Toshi cleared his throat. "Now. You don't know one thing about me, right? Nor about my company, nor even Japan. Yet you write all kind of garbage. So tell me, please, why do you make up so much information against me?"

I should have had a ready answer, but I drew a blank.

He went on before I could think of how to start. "And why do you repeat this accusation about me supposed to be leader of Japanese criminal organization?"

"A yakuza."

"Yes."

"You're not?"

"No."

"Oh. Sorry."

He said nothing for a moment — watching me, perhaps searching for a weakness, which shouldn't have taken so long, unless it was a case of too many openings to choose from.

"Just out of curiosity," I said to break the silent stalemate. "How do you explain the cut-off pinkie? Isn't that the classic sign of yakuza atonement?" I was pretty sure I had that part of Danny's primer right, although a part of me still worried that I might have been confusing the act with something I'd seen in a kung fu movie.

"Boating accident," he said.

"Oh." I pictured him on the deck of a stretch yacht, hands in the pockets of a smoking jacket while the hired crew did the actual sailing. "Just the pinkie?"

"Also concussion." He pointed to his head.

"Oh." I considered the unlikely prospect that he was telling the truth. "So you're not a criminal kingpin? An underworld boss?"

"No."

"A ranking member, maybe."

"No."

"Oh. Well. Heh heh. Maybe I don't believe you."

"You claim this. You write this in your newspaper. So — show proof."

"I don't have any."

"Then you have nothing. Reporter."

"No. I mean, well, yes. Sorry about that."

His eyes slid to the permed underling, who said nothing. When he turned back to me, he sounded genuinely disappointed.

"Earl, Earl, Earl," he said, and then confirmed it: "You disappoint me."

I looked down. Caked in mud, my bare feet poked absurdly out of the zippered cuffs of the borrowed jumpsuit. "You're not the only one," I admitted.

"Did anyone see you?" he asked.

I looked up in confusion but he was talking to his staff.

"No. Nobody see."

Why would they do this in English? Weren't they both Japanese? Unless it was for my benefit. Or harm.

"Good," Toshi said. He steepled his fingers under his chin. "Very good."

I raised my hand. "I'm pretty sure I saw Perry heading out to work just as we were getting here. You know, the garage guy? He kind of nodded, a little 'hey-what's-up?' thing. You guys sure you didn't see it? Probably just a bad angle or something. I've always had excellent peripheral vision. People even remark on it. One year the gym teacher recommended me for a study. So, it was definitely Perry, I'm almost certain. He did this short little umph motion of the head, not so much a grand 'Hello' or anything like that but all the same, a nod is as good—"

"Shut up," the bald one said, jabbing a stubby finger almost into my face. The one with the perm made a fist to feel the skin of his knuckles.

"Whoa. I thought you guys weren't gangsters," I said.

"I am not," Toshi clarified. "These gentlemen may speak for themself. But better they do not since their English is horrible. That is no matter. Instead they may use certain. . . alternative method of communication, shall we say?"

"I see," I said, but he knew that I didn't. Didn't want to, anyway.

"Yes. Various. . . technique they know to get message across, shall we say?" He held up his hand with the missing digit as if to study the manicure of the four remaining nails.

I swallowed. Boating accident my ass. "Look. You can't kill me," I said in what I hoped was a fierce voice. "You'll never get away with it. I sent a letter to my editor, okay? He knows all about you. If anything happens to me, it'll be obvious who did it. They'll come after you, they'll chase you down like a dog, you'll go to jail and never get out. And last time I checked, they weren't letting people bring their yachts into federal prison."

He laughed, perhaps more to display his teeth than to express amusement. The others joined in with even less mirth. When the boss laughs, you don't need to ask what's funny.

He smoothed down his pencil mustache and gave me the disappointed look again. "Do you realize how difficult it is in this country to prosecute for murder when police cannot find body of alleged victim?"

I swallowed again. "No?" was all I could reply.

"Does the name Jimmy Hoffa mean something to you?"

"That was you guys?"

"Earl, Earl, Earl." He rubbed his temples as if my very stupidity was making them hurt. "Calm yourself. I am not going to kill you. Why not? It is an excellent question — but for another time. For now, it would not be good for business. Not so long as you are still valuable, shall we say? To me, I mean."

The glimmer of a way out of this thing entered my mind for the first time: I might get away intact after all. I felt encouraged by the prospect, and also by the boost in self-esteem. At least someone seemed to appreciate me, even it was just a mobster in froofy pajamas.

"Now. Let us discuss what is good for business. You will write article again. But this time, you will write the truth."

"I w-w-will?" I stammered. The enormity of the thought weighed my shoulders down. Where would I even start?

"You will explain that what you have written so far is totally wrong. You will apologize. You will admit you lied, about everything, from very beginning. Starting with that which you wrote about me, and including so much nonsense about this silly tree and its miracles. It does not make miracles, it cannot answer people's wish, you will have discovered. On the contrary — it is cursed, it is, in point of fact, a bad tree — very bad. Because it cannot make your wish come true. It does opposite of that — it destroys anyone who goes too near to it. That construction worker idiot was just the start, you have discovered. All type of people are being hurt by mistaken belief in this tree. Put some terrible occurrence in there, if you wish. Maybe car crash with some believers inside all getting killed — would that be effective? Better you may say with a bus, like in Nepal — one of those big tour bus with the two deckers. But my goodness, listen to me, why am I trying to tell you how to do your job? I have seen ample evidence of your journalist style. You know what to do."

"No, I do not. I'm not going to lie, not for anyone. Especially not for you."

His mustache went way up this time, revealing two wide rows of perfect teeth. "You will add information that Filco Incorporated — after your much extensive investigation — is discovered to be one of the most kind and helpful community-oriented corporation in the country. No, not country, too small — in the world. How can this be? Because you have researched very deep into this matter. Now you know, Filco has business with many effective charity organization to help elderly, sick people, handicapped children, and so on, et cetera, et cetera. Feel free to use my name in that part. My full name. Spelled correctly, if you please."

"Look, you can go on spinning your little fantasy world all you like," I said. "I'm not going to do it."

The permed thug reached into a drawer to clatter noisily around before producing a meat cleaver. He flicked a fingernail on the edge, letting us see he was satisfied it was sharp.

"You wouldn't," I said, keeping my eyes on Toshi.

He shrugged.

The first uplifting thought I'd had since arriving at the trailer came to me with a jolt. "Hey! Even if I wanted to," I said happily. "I can't. I've been fired. I don't even work at the *City Herald* any more."

The bald one laughed out loud. The others joined him and they went on that way for some time. Whatever they took for humor in Japan did not export well at all.

"I must apologize for this," Toshi said. "I was a little pissed off. You may appreciate why. So I got you fired."

"Pshaw. You? You can't do that."

"I believe I can — because I did."

"Excuse me? We have something called the freedom of the press in this country. Just because you don't like what you read, no matter how many jewels and crap you've got crammed all over your chopped-up fingers, it does not give you the right—"

"The right?" he interrupted. "Oh yes. Your newspaper's legal representative also mentioned something about right, but not for long, once I explained simple fact. That no proof would be, or could be, available to back your crazy claim of a project to make nuclear waste dump. Nor is evidence possible of pets being harmed by radioactive waste from any Filco plant. Although, to give credit, complaint about pet behavior have gone up 145 percent. Also, most of what you wrote about me personally could be called slander and libel and subject for litigation. Expensive litigation. My reputation is worth how many millions. So? Of course they were happy to hear my offer to drop my claim — in return for discipline action about your job."

So that was it: I was the pawn. Sacrificed, just like that. Swept out of the game. The cruel nature of this hit me like a body punch, not just to me, but to my idea of how things at the paper worked. I could imagine Hanover selling me out, for anything, really, say an extra serving of fries in the cafeteria — he didn't care. But Gallantine? Not the old man. Not His Eminence. He was old school. A "comfort the afflicted and afflict the comfortable" kind of guy.

"Mister Gallantine would never agree to that," I announced.

"But he did. Legal matter means no choice, of course, but also as favor, for close personal friend, shall we say?"

I swore under my breath. It goes to show you. Exactly what it goes to show you I wasn't sure, but I knew I didn't like it. "Suck-holes," I muttered. "All of them."

"I am not familiar with this term."

"That surprises me. Anyway, as you say, I'm fired. Well — end of story."

"Ah, but you did not permit me to finish. I got over my tizzy. My snit fit. You have been hired once again."

"Wait. Mister Gallantine agreed to that too?"

"He is expecting your story in. . ." He checked the Rolex. "Less than three and one half hours."

"No. No way. You're making it all up — I'm calling bullshit. Gallantine wouldn't let himself get pushed around like that. He despises petty thugs, and anyone else who tries to puff himself up into something important by stepping on the backs of other people. He told me so himself, practically."

He was not put out by the inference. "What he likes or despises is not our issue. Mister Gallantine is businessman."

"I won't."

"And surely, in some way, so are you." He barked something at the permed goon, who took a step closer, tapping the flat part of the cleaver against his thigh.

"Begin to write," Toshi commanded.

"Okay, okay, I will. Jeez. I mean, I would. But, what a shame, I don't have—"

The bald one put a gym bag on the table before me. Inside was my computer. He flipped the cover for me.

"How did you get that?"

"Enough with chit-chat," Toshi said in a strained voice. It may have been an act, but he really did seem about to blow. He added through clenched teeth, "Begin. . . to. . . write. Now."

I started typing. Without having decided exactly what to do, I launched into the story the way Toshi wanted it. However I might try to spin it from there, I knew, it was going to be ugly. I felt dirty already. I had come here for miracles: now I was going to need one just to get out of Fraleton with all my appendages. Never mind the permanent damage this would do to my career in journalism, or my reputation as a human being. I wondered if I would ever learn how to live with myself.

Toshi swiveled in his chair to ignore me, picking up a newspaper filled with Japanese characters. The bald thug buried his bullet head into a comic book as thick as a phone directory. The other watched me, still tapping his thigh with the cleaver. After several minutes, when I had five or six paragraphs written, the bald one stood up to lean over my shoulder. I heard him trying to sound out the words.

I threw up my hands. "I will *not* tolerate these intrusions," I said.

"What is problem?" Toshi asked, spinning around.

"The problem? I'll tell you the problem. This chair is not ergonomically designed, the lighting in here is all wrong, and this buffalo keeps breathing down my neck. These conditions are intolerable. How can I be expected to work on my art?"

The three looked at each other for an instant before breaking into a laughter that struck me as unnecessarily loud.

"Art? It's fucking newspaper article," Toshi said. "Just write it."

I got on with the story. I began cranking it out in a barely controlled fury that actually seemed to work to get the word count popping. Mortal fear, it turns out, is a great antidote for writer's block. I wrote in a white heat, watching the screen fill rapidly with sentence after sentence.

Finally I silently read it all back and saw it was everything he would have wanted. For any other client, I might even have been proud. I'd included what I believed was a particularly deft vignette about two men who had arrived as jogging partners and then left on stretchers, stricken with an ailment so rare the doctors were thinking of changing its name to Fraleton's Disease.

Toshi read my copy. He frowned at the paragraph with the joggers.

"So you have that association with communicable diseases," I explained. "You get it? Who wants to come see a contagious tree?"

"It stinks," Toshi said. "Change it."

"Excuse me. It does not *stink*."

"Not the writing," he said, "I like how you put words together — but I can't let people think there is a Fraleton disease. We must sell our product here."

"Shit. Forgot about that."

I deleted the part about the disease and replaced it with two long-lost brothers, twins separated at birth, who were reunited under the tree but then got into a fight over an inheritance that left one dead with multiple stab wounds and the other in jail. Toshi smiled for real this time. Maybe it was the stabbing detail.

Filco was the most difficult part to figure in. I ended up writing that the "formerly controversial" corporation had been studied more than any other successful business in the country and had been found to be exemplary — hoping that at least some of the readers might not know what the word exemplary meant. I described a few charitable ventures Filco had funded, but without getting too worked up. My heart obviously wasn't in it. Still I kept the theme going long enough to take a second look at the character of Toshihiko Takahashi, that much-misunderstood wizard of high finance who was only now beginning to be appreciated by others beyond his admiring colleagues. It was hard to read back without wincing.

Before wrapping up I felt I had to account for my own role in the public confusion. I briefly considered pleading temporary insanity, a condition brought on by eating too many Ding Dongs sold beyond their buy-before date — they really did offer them that way in Trish's store. But I couldn't go through with it. Instead I came clean: I admitted I'd been wrong. I wrote that I'd been driven, by the media machine, by people's soaring aspirations, but mostly by my own self-interest, to exaggerate some of the facts.

"The only miracle here," I wrote to sum up, "is that I let myself go on to such lengths to make up the story, bringing shame onto my publication, my profession and myself — and for that I am truly sorry."

"Yes. That is more like it," Toshi said, nodding. "Very nice. And I apologize myself to you for what I said earlier. This *is* art."

If he meant it in the sense of the word stemming from "artificial," he was not far off. I hung my head over the keyboard without looking at it. I just wanted the whole thing to be over.

"So send," said Toshi.

"Can't," I answered, squinting under eyelids that felt like sandpaper. "Not without a phone line."

Toshi produced a polished walnut box containing a silver-coated satellite phone. It even had a jack for a modem connection. It must have been new to them too — they looked at me to figure out where to plug the cable in.

I wondered how much they knew about e-mail. Toshi certainly had enough money to hire people to push buttons for him, and the thugs didn't seem the type to have spent much time learning their way around the Internet. Perhaps this was my last-minute chance to save the day, my only way out — I could just send the story to somewhere in the Yukon.

I was wrong. When I started to feign memory loss, Toshi helped me type in the correct e-mail address for Hanover at the paper. We sat and listened as the modem dialed, connected, then zapped in the story that would save my skin for now, but bury me for good later, anywhere in the world of media.

"Done," I said. "Check and mate — you win. Now if you don't mind, I'll be on my way. I need to sleep."

Toshi didn't answer. The two goons weren't looking at me.

"They've got my story," I reasoned. "Your story. There's not much else I can do for you here. What's the point in us bugging each other?"

He finally nodded to accept the point. "So long as you understand. You screw us, we screw you, harder."

"By boating accident?"

"They happen."

"You're a persuasive guy for someone who isn't a yakuza."

"I am businessman."

"A job's a job."

"You do what you must."

"Life sucks, get a helmet."

"Thank you for stopping by," he concluded, as if we were tidying up a simple business arrangement. He opened the door, letting daylight stream into the interior.

I thought it would be a relief to get away from the danger, but once outside the trailer the dread didn't disappear. My mind said run, although my body insisted on a sullen tromp.

"Oi! Earl! Wait!" Toshi was hailing me from the doorway.

I stopped. I was still too near to make running a prospect — as if it would make a difference.

"You ever need a job in public relations?" Toshi called out happily. "You give me a call. I like your style!"

I made it back to the park in a stupor. My head drooped heavy in a hang-dog slump. The future loomed before me: terrible as I felt now, I knew it would get worse. Despite my miraculous re-hiring, the chances were obviously not good it would last. So I didn't have a job, or a girl, or a backbone — but really, why think small? I didn't have a life.

My Toshi-approved piece would, in less than three hours, go public. It would spread from the newspaper in all directions at once — to other papers, the Internet, radio, TV, probably around every construction site and office water cooler in the land. The story would likely have died soon anyway; no frenzy can last for long. This way people would get a final twist to wrap it all up — a gleeful little pull back of the curtain, revealing the entire tawdry affair, something to be atoned for only by the last interesting piece of personal theater worth watching, my own journalistic act of suicide.

Then I could begin adjusting to my new working life. I could reinvent myself. There were other jobs. Despite everything they said about the paperless office, mail delivery was still hanging on. I could operate a hot fry unit. Customer service wasn't going away anytime soon. Maybe I could even start again, slowly, in journalism — doing paste-up, say, at the *Pennysaver*. Life would go on. The general public would forget about me before my head even hit the basket.

The park crowds, of course, would vanish. The circus comes to town, the circus leaves town. I had to admit, my going down with the story had a certain ring of inevitability to it. I had captained this shipwreck so I should sink with it to the bottom. Ignominy — I wasn't sure how to pronounce it, but realized I should have learned long ago. I'd been beaten before and it wasn't all that bad. That winning streak I'd gotten onto hadn't really changed me. I knew what I was, at heart: losers understand their place. They don't expect much else, so defeat is almost comforting for the way it confirms your own expectations. But still — there was one tiny bone stuck in my craw, and it was a notion I could not shake. Filco would win.

Filco and Toshi. Scoring one for the bad guys everywhere: the creeps, the bullies, the thugs, the money-mongers, the social frauds who wore silk pajamas not necessarily because they liked silk but because they could, the way other people couldn't. So the forces of darkness and greed would cut one more notch into their belts while the rest of us, the real people, took another kick in the teeth.

And the Miracle Tree would be lost. Cut down, most likely, or even worse, plasticized. It might only be a matter of time before one of the corporate theme parks bought the rights to create a replica and turn it into the prime attraction at some Wishland. . . Where Your Dreams Come True at thirty-four dollars a pop.

All of this shouldn't have meant much to me beyond the personal career disappointment — which was enough, I knew. But I couldn't help being bugged by the rest of the story, and the more I thought about it, the more bugged I got.

Mrs. Grady, as a girl, must have looked fetching when she stood under the tree and asked only for her beau to survive the war and come back to her. And all those people like her, asking for things that might have been silly or noble or sad — but what difference did it make when it was their purest hopes put into words? Who could say their wishes weren't worthy? The Miracle Tree was the place where anyone could go to whisper them, where they could believe their private desires were a part of something bigger, and a sign, or maybe a promise, that no matter what kind of crap life threw their way, a better future was possible. Didn't we all deserve something like that?

I threaded my way through the crowd, nudging slower people aside, excusing myself over and over, trying to merge with the general flow rather than force things, hoping to pick up on the more peaceful vibes that a good part of the crowd seemed to connect with effortlessly. I wanted to blend in this time.

As I got nearer to the tree I actually thought I felt something. It was, despite the circumstances, a vague sense of well-being. I almost didn't believe it myself: I realized I should be wary of my own fragmented emotions, but just as quickly dismissed the reticence — it was enough to feel real again. I sensed myself beginning to move in synch, matching the emotional lifts and flows of the crowds around me. Some people even smiled at me. I think I smiled back.

By the time I reached the tree, I was conflicted again, this time by the audacity of my own positive response. Imagine me having the gall to feel anything but remorse at the imminent demise of the Miracle Tree. My own capacity for self-deception was apparently boundless, and yet another cause for reflection.

I stood under the tree, enveloped in its massive glory, wondering if just being that close could be enough to absorb some of its aura of strength. Definitely, I decided — and to prove it to myself, slipped under the rope and sat down beside Sun Deer. I sat like him, cross-legged, with my back to the trunk, and copied him by folding my arms across my chest. I sat as immobile as if I'd grown there on the spot and could only be moved by transplanting.

For the first time, Sun Deer seemed interested in me, at least enough to turn his head to look in my direction with a curious expression. "Little Brother," he murmured for a greeting.

"Funny you should say it like that," I said. "I actually could be, in some sense. I'm Native American, you know."

"Yes, you told me."

"No: this time I mean it."

He raised an eyelid in appraisal. But not for long — he closed it again to resume his impersonation of a statue.

"You know what else?" I said, wondering if I would ever be able to laugh at the ridiculous position I'd just put myself in, talking to this man as if I were one of his compatriots when he obviously wanted nothing to do with me. "I always got the impression that you didn't like me."

He said nothing. His eyes stayed closed.

"Or not even that," I went on, "because that would mean you cared enough to have an opinion, which you clearly don't. Which probably doesn't matter, although I still can't help feeling a little put out by the fact that somehow you disapprove of me."

"Why would I?" He said it almost without moving his lips.

The conversation was already taking more effort than I wanted to spend: I shouldn't have bothered. I wished I could have the space to myself — just plop down and sprawl out and stay that way for a little while — or for a long, long time. Let them fertilize me along with the tree. If only I could be there alone.

Instead I continued with the conversation. Past the point it should have gone, perhaps, but I was beyond caring. "You ever think of sharing some, I don't know, sense of solidarity?" I asked. "I mean, listen to you — going on about our people this and our people that. Yet when one finally does show up, you're not even interested enough to say hello. Some great leader you turned out to be. Maybe you're just a big phony."

Even as I heard myself say it, I knew it had been fueled by the bitterness of my impending failure. Obviously I'd gone too far. But Sun Deer didn't flinch. I started back-pedaling. "But hey. Don't listen to me. Takes one to know one," I said.

He remained motionless.

"Might as well be talking to the tree," I muttered.

He unfolded his arms, then stretched out his legs. He massaged his kneecaps while still staring out at the crowd. Finally he turned to me, nodded once, then said, "Racist."

I was so surprised I actually turned to look over my shoulder. But he was looking directly at me. "Say what?"

"Now you're listening."

"You didn't just say...what I thought you just said — not about me."

"There's no future in it, Little Brother."

"You're telling this to me? You didn't even hear what I said. I am Native American — for real. My own dad showed up tonight, my real dad, he told me — well, so far as he knows. But so what — it's true."

"Who you are, it's one thing. What you think, that's something else. But how you act, that's what counts. Look at you: you've been judging people since the day you got here — based on how they look."

"I have not."

"What's a racist but someone who thinks they know you before they know you? We call that prejudice. You pre-judge us. You've been doing it to everyone. Like you've been doing to me, ever since we met."

"I have not. You can't call me that. You don't know what you're talking about. I'm not what you.... I don't believe this. George is the one who calls Chinese—"

"George, he hates everybody equally — only he doesn't, because it's obviously a front. But you ever notice? He listens to people."

"He listens? So what? He gets paid to do it. I can listen, I'm listening right now, and I still don't believe—"

"Earl. Relax. You're not a bad kid, I think you might even get somewhere. You've got balls — but you're a product of your society. Doesn't mean you can't grow out of it, that's all I'm saying."

"Say what you want. It's bullshit."

He sighed. "I don't worry. Not much anyway, because it can't last. It only survives if people keep feeding it, with ignorance or hate. And I believe supplies of those are running out." He looked at me sideways. "In fact, I'm almost sure they are." He stood, wrapped his blanket around his shoulders, then walked away into the crowd. It parted for him as far as I watched him go.

I was alone behind the protective rope, but not liking it after all. I was still reeling from the accusation — if that's what it was. I wasn't sure anymore what to think, about anything. Could I have been racist? I still didn't see it, but I knew I wouldn't want to see something that unseemly in myself. Which was perhaps a start, if I were ever going to think clearly through this thing. I was sure I didn't hate anyone, at least not for their looks. But he might have had a point about the judging. Shirley used to accuse me of something similar: although she at least said I painted everyone with the same caustic brush. My answer was always the same: it wasn't my fault the human race kept letting me down.

I stood up, as if I were resolute, willing myself to be strong — mentally, morally, politically, however it came to me. I pivoted to face the tree, put my palms together and closed my eyes.

"I want," I began, speaking softly so no one would hear — then, because I didn't care whether they heard or not, I went on in a louder voice. "I want to stop lying."

It took a moment for the scope of that idea to settle into me. "Well, at least less than I used to. A lot less. And I also want you, Miracle Tree, to stay here, alive, just like now, with no plastic or fake stuff trying to make you into something you're not. And I want. . . more than anything. . . I want Shirley. I know, I understand, I accept the fact that I don't deserve her, and probably never did. Fair enough. I'm not arguing that. But I want her to come back anyway, and to agree with me to put all the weird stuff behind us so we can have at least one more clean shot at being together, to see if we really do belong to each other or not. And so I can prove to her that I really can be the man she'd want me to be — even if it is going to be a work in progress. Okay, Miracle Tree? I guess I must be over my limit by now. Well, maybe I'll catch you later, then. Right. Peace out and all that. Oh wait — one more thing, if it's not too much trouble? Maybe you could send me a sign. Something small, it doesn't matter — just so I'd know."

I let my hands drop. I looked up. The tree was brimming with life, its glossy leaves shimmering above me in sun-flecked blobs of green and light. A single leaf broke off high up in the canopy and began to fall. It flipped and spun as it drifted down through the branches. I stood in place and held out my hand: I would not move. Down the leaf fluttered, as if ordained, directly towards me, until it just missed the edge of my palm before landing on the ground between my feet.

Shirley was in the parking lot, directing traffic. Despite the dog's breakfast of cars and vans and trucks and buses already there, she appeared to be making headway. People fed on her confidence: they trusted in the prospect of some grand design only she could see. Even when it didn't make immediate sense to them, drivers listened to her and backed up, turned around, or squeezed in at odd angles according to the intricate choreography of her twisting wrists and pointing fingers. Before long she succeeded in creating a makeshift alley wide enough to allow the stream of newly arriving vehicles to form their own section along a path leading to the grass. Two obvious routes now appeared, going in and out of the site, for the first time since the parking lot jam had formed. That was my Shirley.

Several of the arrivals getting out of cars in the new section looked Indian. A few of the men wore ponytails; denim jackets and beads were popular too. Someone planted a flag with a warrior brave in profile, and from somewhere unseen a single steady drum beat began. Sun Deer's people were here at last. I considered greeting them in some kind of fraternal way, but was stuck trying to decide just how.

Shirley caught my eye and turned away — then, despite herself, she turned back. "Earl," was all she said. It was a start: she didn't sound angry. She raised an eyebrow at my pink jumpsuit, but didn't follow up with a question.

"Shirley?" I replied. It came out like a plea.

"Can't really talk now," she observed. She whisked her hands towards her own chest and then over her shoulder, directing me to a spot immediately behind her so I wouldn't get run over.

"No. Me neither," I said. "Busy busy. You know how it is." I felt my throat tighten. This was not how Shirley and I communicated. Not how we used to, anyway.

She glanced quickly back at me. I thought I detected genuine concern in her eyes, as if she still truly cared. But if so, she immediately dispatched it to its proper place with the same efficiency she was using to direct the cars.

"You'll rally," she pointed out. "You always do."

I wondered if it could get any worse. What could compare to the agony of standing so close to Shirley without holding her by the shoulders, running my fingers through her hair, saying something stupid just to watch her face as it bubbled over with laughter. Now we were talking as if we weren't the same people, the ones who had practically grown up together. Then I realized it could, and would, get worse, as soon I brought the house of cards crashing down on the town with my final story. Just when she seemed to be finding her place, too.

"I need to tell you something," I said. I took in a breath for courage, but it didn't help. I kept my mouth closed.

"When all else fails, try honesty," she called over her shoulder.

I hadn't been thinking of that. It sent my thoughts in another direction. "Okay. Who's Barry?"

She didn't turn from her traffic duties. "Nobody that concerns you."

"I mean really. You said he was a customer. What does that mean? Some executive vice something or other with a hair weave and a Porsche?"

"What are you talking about?"

"You're right, what was I thinking? It would have to be some Salvadoran dissident who spent eight years in political prison and now just wants to make up for lost time, conjugally speaking."

This time she did turn around, to say pointedly, "Barry is a friend. I'm not sleeping with him. And that's all there is to it."

"Whatever."

"I was thinking of sleeping with Lindy, though." She was back facing the cars.

I let that idea race around my brain. In normal circumstances, I might have tried to spin that one to get out of my jam. Here I just felt blank.

"She is kind of cute," was all I could come up with.

A VW camper van puttered up to Shirley's knees. The driver looked at her with a tilted head and a hopeful grin. She pointed to where he should go, and he responded with a grateful wave.

"Hey, Shirl. Guess what, I found my dad."

"After all this time? That's great," she said without enthusiasm.

"No, not that one. My real dad."

She turned back. The probing look again. Maybe I really was losing it?

"It's a long story," I explained. "But we're going to meet up again."

"That's good," she said cautiously, returning to the traffic.

"I was thinking," I said. "Next time, I could introduce you."

Wrong tactic: I saw her shoulders stiffen. She spent more time than necessary explaining something to an Audi driver. When she was done, she looked at me for just an instant before whipping her head away. She started an elaborate pantomime to convince five or six cars to form a line and snake through a narrow opening together. Once they were on the move, in unison, she turned back but spoke towards the ground at my feet.

"Listen, Earl. We can still be friends." She may as well have added, "Although it won't be easy being friends with a cur."

"Friends." I felt my head nodding for me. "Sure."

"Not like that. I mean it. Really. You know."

"Yeah. Why not? Friends. That would be. . . you know what? I'm going to go right now. For a walk."

I didn't wait for a goodbye. I ordered my legs forward, hurrying through the sea of vehicles back into the park. I didn't turn back: for all I knew, Shirley could have collapsed to her knees. She could have been watering the site with tears, holding her arms out to me in a gesture of desperate reconciliation. Except that I did know: that wasn't her style. She tackled a crisis like some people do the crossword puzzle. And even if we did prolong the discussion to sort our relationship out, what did I have? I streamed through the clusters of people as if they were not even there, not in any way that mattered.

I was brought up short by the sight of Harold holding court for a crowd of several hundred. He stood with his head bowed, waiting for the last conversations to fade into a respectful silence before beginning. "It is true, everything you have read. I was a man lost."

My termination from the paper had not lasted long enough to kill my previous story. Harold must have read it too, along with the crowd. The match was still on — for now. Just wait a couple of hours until they got to the final round, I thought: knock-outs all around. I felt awful for the way they were still engaged. It was like watching a movie which someone had already spoiled by revealing the surprise ending. They shouted encouraging comments to Harold, making him look up as if surprised to see he wasn't alone. He acknowledged me with a brief lift of the chin, not enough to break the spell.

"I was a slave," he went on. "A slave to a liquid master. I thought it was my friend. At times, truly, it was my only friend. But at what price? I am here to tell you — this friend took my job, this friend took my money, this friend took my wife and my children — and it was this, this friend. . ." he raised his head to look briefly at me again, "which drove me to crime."

The confession appeared to make him even more endearing to his listeners. Calls of sympathy and support came from all directions. Harold had gauged the appetite of the crowd for redemption: the lower he would go, the more they would love him, and yearn for his deliverance. Did he represent something in themselves they hoped might also be redeemed? I couldn't muster the gumption to think it through, even though the parallels to my own predicament were obvious. I told myself I should walk on, but had to first satisfy my curiosity over how much Harold could admit to in a single address.

"Arson," he said sadly. "I burned things. Too many things." The shouts of support rang out from various directions. "And mayhem." It was quieter for that one. "Petty forgery." Not too many eager about that crime either. "Major vagrancy. And theft. And robbery."

The shouts came back doubled. Someone began weeping noisily. "Tell the truth, brother," a man exclaimed.

"Then I found solace," Harold continued. "I was moved by the recent stories of those rewarded for their sincerely expressed wishes under the leaves of this mighty vegetation, to reform my own life. I asked for one thing only. To be freed from the demon desire for drink."

"Tell it like it is!" exclaimed a lanky woman in a sequined tracksuit. Her eyes fluttered with the first signs of evangelical ecstasy.

"And so it came to pass," Harold went on — his dramatic pauses getting more dramatic — "Verily. Since that day, not a single drop of liquor has passed between my lips."

A few people applauded, tentatively at first, until they were rapidly joined by hundreds of others. Did they realize "that day" meant yesterday?

He held up his hands to quell the adulation. "I thank you. I do. For your generosity," he said, nodding, "but it is misplaced. Your boundless spirit of loving kindness to one of your fallen own is due not to me but, you must understand, to the Miracle Tree itself. All thanks to the Miracle Tree! Say it with me now! Long live!"

"Long live!" returned an army of voices.

"The Miracle Tree!"

"The Miracle Tree!"

"Which is why, today, right here, right now, on this hallowed acre, I am pleased to announce the auspicious beginning of the new Save the Miracle Tree Preservation Fund. All donations to be used towards maintaining a permanent home for the tree, right here, where it belongs, in beautiful, bucolic Fraleton."

More applause came in, this time combined with cheers and whoops. The crowd surged forward as if Harold held the secret to eternal joy. People jostled to be the first to get money into his cupped hands.

I left, wishing I'd gone earlier. I must have been slipping badly to think I could collect a few crumbs of redemption from any scheme thought up by a guy like Harold. I lowered my head to stride away quickly but an elderly woman with binoculars around her neck caught up to me. She was joined by three or four others and then several more — all from the crew that had spotted me when I was running in my underwear. They still seemed upset.

"Mr. Earl Brododsky," the first one declared, standing directly in front of me. She made my name itself sound like an accusation.

"Ma'am," I answered. "And ladies." When would it end — was this just the beginning, of a long, dragged-out series of apologies I would be making? "I wanted to say, about earlier, when I was outside, in public, in my under. . . I mean when I was dressed, well, inappropriately." As if my present attire were any more reasonable.

"Oh hang that," one of the women said from the back.

"Like we care about your gauchies," added another.

As they pressed in on me with their earnest expressions, I thought about Sun Deer: his scathing words came back to me. I did pre-judge people. I might not have called it racist, and these ladies were all white anyway, but I'd done it again, nonetheless: I'd taken one look and sized them up as a bunch of birdwatching biddies.

"Do you realize what's happening here?" the first one asked.

"Sadly, I think I do."

"The warblers are seriously overdue for their annual migration."

"I did not know that."

"They've never been this late before."

I nodded. Maybe they had a point — I just wasn't in the mood for birds.

"It's because of the crowds, you see. They're afraid to land."

"I'm sure they'll land somewhere."

She was scandalized. "They've followed these migrating patterns for generations. The parents teach the young. Don't you see?"

"It's a real issue," I said, trying to make my face appear sympathetic. Birds, at a time like this. I checked my wrist, pretending the watch still worked, and shrugged an apology for having to hurry off. This thing about getting to know people for who they really were? It was going to take some work.

"Generations!" the woman called out to my receding back.

The deadline was eighty-four minutes away, according to the wall clock at Buffy's. It shouldn't have mattered to me, since I'd already sent in the story, but it did still mark the cutoff time for any changes.

Yet what was the point of torturing myself with the possibility? With Toshi so clearly in command, there was no hope: his threat to get me if I screwed him again was still the only offer on the table.

That's when it came to me: he was bluffing. I got excited by the prospect, and whipped myself into a lather of speculation. He had nothing, and he knew it, so he cooked up a tall tale of threatened mayhem, without actually doing a thing. And here I thought I'd been on a run of creative inspiration with my tree stories. No, I was out of my league. Look how easily I was sent packing as soon as a real contender showed up. When Toshi raised the stakes, he scared me out of the game so fast I hardly knew what we were playing. In reality? He didn't have a thing. The whole Gallantine ruse was just that — a ruse!

To prove it I called the *Herald* from Buffy's pay phone. As I waited for the connection I played it all out in my head, trying to spot the flaws in my new conceptual model, yet realizing everything filtered down to the same result: Toshi was full of it. He just talked tough — and because was a liar, his threats were worth no more than the spittle he produced when making them. His line about being pals with Gallantine should have tipped me off: our editor in chief would never bow and scrape like that, not to anyone, certainly not to a corporate goon in two hundred dollar pajamas.

"Earl!" Gallantine's voice boomed into the receiver. "I'm glad you got me in time. I hope we can forget our earlier difficulties. It was all a misunderstanding, but we're beyond that now. You with me, son?

"Yes," I said, sounding a little uncertain even to myself. "I think."

"Good. Excellent."

"Mister Gallantine, you're not really a friend of Toshi Takahashi are you?"

He paused, then tried to cover the gap with a throat-clearing display. My heart felt like it was filling up with lead.

"Friend, associate, whatever they call it these days," he said at last. His voice sounded grim. There was another pause. I already knew all

I needed, but he went on. "He's not so bad — a rather determined individual. And a remarkable people. Now, about your story."

"You've seen it?"

"No."

"There's something I should have told you earlier about the tree. About all the stories I've been doing on the tree, in fact."

"I know. Earl, I understand — and I'm pleased to hear from Mister Takahashi that it's all been worked out. Well done, my boy, sparkling job. I understand things got a bit shaky there for a spell, but you're coming through for us, and I appreciate that. A good man cleans up his own mess, Earl. That's what I always say."

"Right. And Chief?"

I imagined in the delay that followed he was holding the phone out to stare at it. Finally his voice came back. "Son?"

"Is there any chance that, when this is all over, and my mess is all cleaned up, as you say, I can still have my job?"

He chortled, but not unkindly. "Earl, my boy. Why, you're still the first one on my list for a promotion!"

"Wow. You really mean that?"

He stopped laughing. "Ask a stupid question, get a stupid answer. Your personal items will be mailed to you."

After I stumbled away from the phone, I found myself walking aimlessly, first up and down Fraleton's few streets, then around the park, then back to the tree. It seemed a good a place as any to wait for the final curtain to fall. I pulled out my laptop and flipped the lid to read my final story again. My working epitaph.

Agnes was nearby, standing alone in a patch of grass left vacant when the members of a reincarnation sect left together for a shared prayer. She stood as I'd seen her before, a tiny figure looking all the smaller next to the bulk of the tree. There was a vague hint of a smile on her lips as she lowered her head.

I watched her with a jumble of emotions. This time I couldn't resist — when she finished, and seemed about to leave, I touched her elbow. "Hello again," I said. "We didn't get much chance to talk about this last time. I'm sorry to hear about your husband passing on."

"Thank you," she answered.

"If you don't mind my asking. I couldn't help seeing you here and wondering. This isn't for the record, I'd just like to know for myself. What do you ask for? What is it you really want?"

"Oh, that." She smiled. "I thought I was through with wishes once Lawrence and I got married. We had the ceremony right here, under the tree. It was a smaller then, but of course that was fifty-three years ago. What a lovely evening it was: the whole town came out. We had a band set up right over there so we could all dance on the grass."

She pointed over my shoulder and gazed at the spot as if by force of imagination she might turn the throng into close friends gathered for a summer night's celebration of love and devotion. "I still do this from time to time, but now it's to ask for other people. I just hope they can be as happy as Lawrence and I were." She smiled again, and this time her eyes went liquid. "That's all."

Maybe there was really was something about the tree that affected people. Even if it was no more than the power of a positive idea they created together, if it worked, it worked. And if it happened often enough that a few decent folks in a forgotten town in the middle of nowhere had come to believe that good things really did happen to good people, who was I to deny it?

The sad truth weighed even more heavily on me when I saw the time on the giant screen. Agnes and the rest had seventy-two minutes of wishing left before the deadline passed and my final story ran.

For every complex problem there is an answer that is
clear, simple, and wrong.

H.L. Mencken

TWELVE

George slumped on the front steps at Grady's, looking glum, one elbow propped against his suitcase.

"You're not leaving?" I asked, almost pleading. We weren't exactly friends, but I felt better when he was around. Sun Deer was probably right: George's assumed surliness was just an act — deep down he was all right.

"The hippo is back on its feet," George explained with a sour expression. "The station manager called me this morning."

"What about the tree? It's your story as much as mine. And all these people?"

"Networks got it beat every which way to Tuesday, according to the manager. He's not a miracle kind of guy. What can I say?"

"But shouldn't you stay? To keep ahead of the competition? You can't just give up — CREP will get everything first."

"You didn't hear?" He smiled in a way I hadn't seen him look before; on anyone else, I would have called it wistful. "William met a dame. After wishing for one right on the air, the big sap — during a live feed, under the Tree, like he really meant it. And then, boom, a few hours later, she shows up. Don't ask me how, but I suppose they hit if off. So he wets the bearded one, decides he's in love, and phhht, he's outta here. They split this morning."

"William left?"

"Said they were moving to her place in Tonga. She's an island girl — looked like it too, all cinnamon-skinned and curvy. Tight bod, probably from all the surfing. Her father's the king, or some such." He shrugged and stood up, rolling his suitcase down the sidewalk.

"George, wait," I sounded desperate even to myself, "before you go — did you wish for anything?"

He spat. His unhappy expression turned miserable. "What in hell for?"

I considered giving him a heads-up on the hurricane about to blow out the story, but I let him go. He was right about the networks being all over it — just as well for him to leave now and get out clean, like William and his island honey. That way he'd be spared the sight of watching me go through my public meltdown. Even someone like George might find that dinnertime conversation somewhat awkward.

Without no better plan, I plodded up the stairs to get my luggage. Just packing my bags, I told myself, no big deal, although I couldn't avoid the thought of even that simple act being a metaphor for my life. That crappy suitcase of my father's, for instance — my faux father's. Had it all started with him? Maybe I could blame everything on my upbringing, or lack of it: if I'd been living a lie my whole life, how else could I have turned out? Whoever I was, Indian or mixed or nothing special at all, I would still be what Sun Deer said — a product of my society. But what did that mean?

I stripped off the pink jumpsuit to put on my own clothes. The first act of my rehabilitation would be to return the space suit to its owner — and if that proved impossible, at least I could leave it in the vicinity of the galactic campers with the hope that it might somehow find its way home. I carried my suitcase downstairs and was about to head into the kitchen for some tangerine juice when I heard Shirley. I stopped behind a bookcase.

She was asking Mrs. Grady about the Wobblies. They talked while measuring out peppercorns to add to the jars of beets they were canning. So that was why the whole house smelled like sugar and vinegar and spice. I wondered, not for the first time, whether I had the observational skills to be a real journalist. I started to walk quietly back up the stairs.

"Earl," Mrs. Grady said in a voice so tender I thought I might choke up. I turned to see Shirley looking stricken. She spun around to rearrange the copper pots on the opposite wall.

"Hi, um, everyone," I said.

"Why don't I just see how those onions are coming along," Mrs. Grady said. She practically ran to the basement. Shirley watched her go. It could hardly be avoided now. We were alone again, no distractions. This certainly seemed to be it, the last goodbye, the irrevocable end — or the beginning of the end. We still had the apartment to sort out, unpleasant as that might be.

"So," I said, and then paused. "Shirl. My, uh, world."

"Are you all right?" she asked. The ordeal, the many ordeals, must have taken their toll. "I mean really," she said, peering into me. I recognized the look: it was the same expression she once used on a golden retriever that had been hit by a car.

"Oh, sure, me? I'm fine," I answered, then wondered what it was about my character that led me to automatically say the opposite of what was so obviously true. "Actually, Shirley, I'm not. What happened? I mean, what happened to us?"

Her first reaction was a flinch of emotional pain, which came and went over her face like heat lightning. It was replaced by something even harder to see: now she was deeply, utterly, sad. "Not us," she said. "You." She thought it over. "Okay, not you. Me. You didn't change. Maybe I finally did. I figured out a few things I should have seen a long time ago."

"I admit," I said, a little petulantly, "I'm not perfect."

She briefly smiled. "Wow. There's the most honest thing you've said all week. Think you can build on that?" Sarcasm was not her strong point, but she had learned it pretty well over the years from me.

"Shirley, I never lied to you."

That hit her like a slap. "You lied—" She shook her head slowly at the enormity of the effort it might take to complete the sentence — or paragraph. "You lied about everything. You've been lying all along. Ever since I've known you."

"I. But. Wait. You know."

"And I'm the fool for not seeing it earlier. Love is blind all right. Well, I was a bat."

"C'mon Shirl, this isn't easy for me."

"This morning, you know what I did? I looked up some history sites, on the Internet? Something had always kind of troubled me, and now I know why — your grandfather wasn't with the original Sandinistas."

"His picture was in the paper. You saw it."

"I found the caption this time. He was *held* by them. For ransom."

It had been so long since we first met I'd forgotten how I neglected to correct Shirley's original mistake. "So? He was still with them. Wasn't he?"

Her face sagged. She was hurt.

"In a manner of speaking?" I tried.

Her mood was threatening to flood into me. I sensed it like distant tear gas, first a sniff, next a little sting in the eyes. Before long I'd be gushing.

"You lied to me," she said. "You lied to Lindy. You lied to the paper. You lied to, I don't know, how many millions of people who have been buying your bullshit about all those miracles."

"Shirl. Listen. I don't expect you, or anyone, to understand right now. I don't understand right now. But I never meant to hurt anybody. Honestly. I was just trying to do my job. To make a job out of it. You know — turn into a real reporter, like we all want."

"Earl. You never did get it. It's not about your career: it's about your life. Do you really believe you were meant to be telling people things they need to hear? Say, for example, oh, I don't know, the truth?"

She didn't expect an answer. It wouldn't have helped. The sadness had enveloped her. Her upper lip fought against it with a quiver, then gave out. She lowered her head and cried — not the quaint little puppy-murmurs of a movie actress who looks all the more beautiful with her big eyes glistening — this was shoulder-heaving, puffy-eyed, snot-flowing sobs. It was excruciating to watch.

"Here's the truth, Shirley," I said. "I love you."

But she waved the words away with a flutter of her hands and fled out the front door.

I went upstairs for a final check of my room. Grady appeared in the hallway with his hands in his back pockets, rocking on his heels. I gathered from his expression he had heard from his wife about Shirley and me. I couldn't tell whether he disapproved or was simply curious to see what a young man looks like in the last stages of total collapse.

"You're going then."

"I am."

"Back to the big city."

"I guess."

"Want some advice?"

I imagined a tirade about the proper layering technique for compost. "Not really."

"Good, because I'm not one to give it. But my wife isn't so circumspect — she says to tell you: that girl is a catch."

"Like I don't know that," I said morosely.

"We all do," he continued. "That wasn't the point. She said I have to tell you the second part: you're a catch too."

I sat on the suitcase to hold my head in my hands. "Oh, man," I said, not even sure where to start. Now I was about to let Mrs. Grady down too.

Grady looked dismayed at what he'd done. "Told you I was no good at advice. But I can listen pretty well, for what it's worth — and you look like a fella who needs to spill."

I did? I hadn't felt any urge to come clean to Grady. He had seemed pleasantly removed from all the nastiness I'd been involved in. I saw no reason to dredge him deeper into my problems, but when he extended his hand, holding a leather-bound hip flask, I was touched.

"It's from the war," he said, "I haven't used it in years. Take it."

"No, really, I couldn't. This is too much, it's an heirloom, it's—"

"I don't mean take it, take it. I mean drink. Then you give it back to me and I drink." He switched to a kindergarten teacher's exaggerated pronunciation. "We call that shar-ing."

I took a sip. It was sweet on top of my tongue followed by a mild sting in my throat — brandy. Not so bad.

He frowned at the tiny amount I'd swallowed. "Jesus Murphy, Alice, take a slug."

This time it burned my tongue and left a warm after-trail all the way down my chest.

"Yeah!" Grady said. "That's how we did it in Europe, during the big one."

I sat on my suitcase, he sat on the bed, we drank and talked. I told him the story — my story, starting with my frozen lake rescue from a mystery man who turned out to be my real father, leading to Shirley and our chance meeting in high school, taking in Lindy and her scoop, then concluding with the damning article that in another thirty-eight minutes would serve as the sad conclusion to the Miracle Tree story.

"You mean the newspaper hasn't been printed yet?"

"Most of the it has, hours ago. They hold the front page until the end in case something happens.

"Then you'd better come with me — fast. There's something you need to see."

I stood up at once. He tried to, but either the brandy or the severe bow of the bed conspired to keep him down. He struggled like a man wrestling from the inside of an invisible net before finally breaking free and standing up.

"This bed sucks!" he said.

He hurried down the stairs and out the door with me at his heels. We ran towards the park and then past it, upriver from the area where I'd lost my shoes.

I was impressed by his pace and sense of purpose. No wonder we won the war, I thought, but then he walked straight into a thicket. Maybe I should have hung on to that flask after all. I was plotting how to get him safely back home to bed when the leaves parted. Through the gap I could see a brick building no bigger than a phone booth. There were no windows, nothing to peek into — the brick was interrupted only by a rusty iron door with a faded sign that read, Fraleton Electrical Works. Danger. Absolutely No Entry.

Grady took a darting look over his shoulder and then slipped something out of his shirt pocket. He fit it into the lock. When it didn't turn, he swore and jiggled until the door opened at last with a creak that made him wince. He looked over his shoulder again, then motioned with his head for me to follow before slipping inside.

It was too dark to see a thing. I felt his bony grip on my elbow.

"Down here," he said. I heard a clunk and then the slide of metal. He had lifted a manhole cover, letting light in from below. Lining the concrete hole was a ladder with metal U-grips leading down. He was already down about twenty feet before I even started. "Hurry up," he called up in a half-shout that echoed.

When I reached him he was standing in a circular room big

enough to hold six separate doors, all closed. A single bare bulb above his head lit the room and bent his shadow over the round walls. He walked to a door marked C and knocked in a pattern that sounded like Morse code.

He looked back at me and grinned. There was no answer. He tried the knob, but it was locked. He knocked out the code again, this time louder. Still no answer. He thumped on it with his fists. "Come on, Morning, you silly bugger, get up!" he shouted.

The door opened to reveal Morning Mist, rubbing his eyes with his palms. "Hey, man," he said to me. He looked back at Grady with his eyebrows raised. "You sure about this?"

"We have a problem," Grady told him.

Morning Mist didn't look alarmed, or particularly concerned: he just yawned. "'Scuse me. I was really out there for a while. Had a good time last night, but a little too much of it, if you know what I mean." He sniffed the air, picking up our brandy breath. "And I believe you do."

He stepped aside so we could enter. The room's concrete ceiling was low enough to make Grady stoop more than usual, but it was spacious inside. Metal-covered control panels full of bulbs and switches covered two of the walls. Two metal swivel chairs spun around in unison. Facing me were Harold and Sun Deer.

They looked at each other, then at us, waiting for an explanation. Grady did it rapid-fire. "He's got a story that's going to run within the hour that changes everything. It's pro-Filco. Says the miracle stuff is bunk and it's all been a scam. Once it goes to print, the whole thing's over."

Morning scowled. "Sleeping with the enemy, bro?"

Sun Deer's expression didn't change.

"He didn't have a choice," Grady explained. "Filco has his gonads in a vice and they're starting to squeeze. They've got his paper running scared too. Toshi Takahashi called in some crony chips — he and the paper's top brass are as good as boner-buddies."

Harold stroked his chin. "Damn," was all he could say.

"It will mean our tree is kindling," Grady said. "And everything else goes down with it."

"Yes," agreed Sun Deer.

"So I figured," Grady continued, steadying a waver with a hand on the back of Sun Deer's chair, "our only option is for Earl to discover the real story."

"Ah," Morning Mist said. He was wide awake now. "And which real story would that be?"

They looked at each other. Three pairs of eyes turned to a door labeled No Entry. Each seemed to wait for someone else to speak first.

"There's almost no time," Grady pointed out.

"Little bro, you don't use a pacemaker do you?" Morning Mist asked.

When I said no, he produced a ring of keys and singled out the biggest one. "Quickly, then," he said.

The door opened into a white-washed four-foot-high tunnel that ended at another manhole cover. Beneath it was another concrete hole with metal hand rails. I followed Morning at a scrambling pace. Grady and Sun Deer hurried behind us.

We emerged into room painted olive on the lower half and cream above. The shelves were stocked with emergency rations labeled in military stencil.

An awful thought swept through my brain. "Nooo. Not wacky survivalists, too," I moaned.

Morning Mist laughed out loud.

"These were the city's air raid shelters," Grady explained.

"Oh, right," I said. "The mayor mentioned something about that."

Morning pointed to three doors. "Bet he didn't mention this." He stood before the middle door. He paused just long enough to make sure I realized I was in for a treat, then yanked it open.

It revealed a room no bigger than a closet. It may have been a closet, at one time, but now it was all but filled with a refrigerator-sized box covered in black metal. A panel of switches and lights glowed on the front. It gave off an electronic hum I could hear and feel in my chest.

Morning pointed up to the ceiling. "The Miracle Tree," he said. "We're right below it."

"And this?"

"The most powerful electromagnetic generator in the Western Hemisphere."

He turned a dial slightly to the right: the hum increased in pitch. I felt an odd tug, a bit of twinge, something near my rib cage, but nothing I could define.

He moved the dial again: the hum grew louder and higher. The pen in my shirt pocket flew out and stuck to the machine with a loud clack.

"Oops," Morning said, "forgot to tell you about that." He eased the dial back down to retrieve my pen.

"Where did you get it?"

Harold spoke up. "It's mine, or it used to be — my lab's, actually. Once we got closed down it wasn't like they were going to need it anymore, so I sort of borrowed it."

"Oh right," I said. "Ze souss and norse and meedle poles. So this is why the watches and compasses and machinery go wonky."

Harold nodded. "A parlor trick, really."

"And the chainsaw?"

"We didn't know he was going to start the job sloshed," Morning Mist said. "Redneck could have cut off his own leg."

"And the power tool short-circuit."

"No, that had nothing to do with magnets," Grady said with a mischievous grin. "Simple sabotage."

I was incredulous. "You four cooked up this whole thing from the start?"

"We five," Morning said. "Mrs. Grady said we had to try something.

It was also her idea to bring Sun Deer on board once he showed up."

Sun Deer nodded. "They're good people," he said, as if that explained everything.

I shook my head in disbelief. "You went to a lot of trouble to play a science-fair joke on everyone," I said. I felt dumb, having been caught in the same trap as all the people I had considered so gullible.

"It is *not* a scientific joke," Harold said indignantly. "You are standing in the presence of what is arguably the most significant negative ion generation experiment ever conducted in public."

"Whatever you say," I replied. I wasn't in the mood for a lecture.

Morning Mist turned earnest. "No, man, check him out. Harold's on the ball with this one. It's all about ions — the whole world is. This is a way of using stuff that's in nature already, only in a better way."

"It works," Grady said. "I can attest."

"They speak the truth," Sun Deer added. "Greater flows of energy, enhanced well-being. Did you not notice it in the park?"

"Better work performances," Grady said, starting a list on his fingers. "Increased awareness, clearer concentration." He grinned wickedly. "Enhanced libido — feel any of that going on?"

Before I could answer, Sun Deer spoke again.

"Everyone experiences the earth's flows of electromagnetic energy whether they know it or not. Call it what you like: we know it happens because we can make it happen. Now we just want to make sure it's used properly so it can benefit people elsewhere."

"But. . . I. . ." was all I could say. I had the feeling I was staring at a science test I hadn't studied for.

"Before a big storm people get antsy, they feel tense, right?" Harold said with a touch of impatience. "We know that happens because of a buildup of positive ions — that's been proven. Then lightning strikes to release the energy and restore the balance, the storm passes, and you feel refreshed, better than before. Why? All those negative ions are now in the air. Those are the ones you want. The same thing happens at the seaside, or by rivers, or waterfalls — moving water generates negative ions."

"It's our way of adjusting to electrical forces that are already there," Grady added. "And we shouldn't we be in tune? Our bodies are mini power plants. Your brain waves, what do you think they are? Electrical current. The heart pumps, but on what signals? The electrical ones it makes itself. We're walking generators."

"Humans are magnetic," Harold said. "Electricity and magnetism go together. We don't realize it but we're tied to the earth's core just like birds that use the magnetite in their brains to migrate. That's what this machine is all about. Do you have any idea what it might be worth to get this kind of stuff packaged? Who wouldn't pay a bundle to feel better all the time?" His eyes bulged at the prospect.

"But it's not about money," Morning was quick to interrupt. "It's about creating harmony. Restoring the natural balance. Peace, love, the whole groove."

"Okay, okay, you made your point," I said. "I remember reading somewhere that the first people who studied electricity used to buzz themselves on purpose because it made them feel better. But even if it does work, why sneak around? Why not just tell everyone?"

Harold looked at me. The bulging eyes went back to normal. "I've been trying to tell everyone for thirty-eight years. People don't listen. They believe what they believe, the scientific community included. We could use electricity to heal things, but we don't. Why don't we? Because we can't. Why can't we? Because modern medicine is bio-chemical. There's a drug for everything. And why is there a drug for everything?"

"Because the goddamn pharmaceutical companies want it that way," Grady answered. "But troops, listen, we don't have time for this."

"Somebody at least tell me why you went to all this trouble — for a gizmo."

"No," Morning said. "It really was about the tree. I did the first AP story, the one you saw — I knew a guy who used to string for them before he went to Thailand to become a monk, so I sent it out in his name. That was after we heard that Filco was going to buy up the park and take out the Miracle Tree. We had to do something. We knew we were against a huge corporation. Who would listen to us? Then you picked up the story and it became the next big thing in cosmic phenomena. You were good, man — better than good, more than we could have hoped for. All of a sudden we had a world of support."

He rubbed a palm over the machine, using the reverent strokes of a new car owner polishing the hood. I didn't know what to say. Everything they said proved I was a dupe. So was I supposed to feel good or bad about it now?

"We love this town," Grady said. "We love the Miracle Tree. They're kind of the same thing. We don't want to see either one get trashed."

"But Filco isn't in the nuclear waste business," I said.

Morning laughed out loud and clapped me on the back. "Didn't you think that was a good one?"

"I'm not sure 'good' is the word I would use. It was dishonest."

"You're the one to know. The stuff you've been doing? Incredible. I loved the one about the blind kid who got to play hockey again. It actually brought a tear to my eye. I meant to ask you, was that real?"

"I had the ball," I said, glumly. "I was running with it."

"We've all been impressed," Sun Deer said. He added, to nods of agreement, "And we're all indebted to you, Little Brother. Friend."

"I wish you could stay that way. But my pro-Filco story goes to the printer in, like, minutes. I have to tell you, once the spin on this thing shifts, it'll get ugly. People will be out of here like bats out of. . . somewhere. And Filco will have its way."

"That's why you have to stop them," Grady said.

The others looked at me too. Sun Deer nodded. He smiled — as if he had confidence in my ability, as if we really were on the same team.

"How?"

Harold patted me on the back. "You're the reporter," he said. "Think of something."

"Only make it quick," Grady added, pointing to the wall clock. Deadline was eighteen minutes away.

I sprinted back to Grady's. I ran so hard my side ached, but I would not stop.

Shirley was in the bedroom, packing up to go.

"Listen," I said between gasps. "I'm sorry. About us, about everything. It's my fault, I know that, and I don't blame you if you spend a lifetime being mad at me for everything I did or didn't do. All I can say is give me a chance. You see the best in people. Maybe this time you can see it in me."

She tilted her head to one side. It wasn't an outright refusal. "What?" she said quietly.

"I've got fifteen, no fourteen, minutes before the most important deadline I'll ever see — and I need you to help me. I have to write a story."

"What story?"

"The only one that can save the tree."

I blurted out as much as I could in the next forty-five seconds. She listened to the pitch, thought it over for an agonizing moment, staring at me with a calculating expression as if we'd never met.

"Do you believe in the Miracle Tree?" she asked at last.

"If that's what it takes, sure, I always—"

"No. I need to know — and you have to think before you answer. Then tell me the truth."

"I—"

"First think. Then answer. This matters, Earl. "

So I did. I saw the second hand of the desk alarm clock sweep like a summons, but I thought. I watched Shirley throughout. She eyed me as if I were a chemical concoction she'd never mixed before, one that could turn into some elixir but might also blow up.

"I made a wish," I said at last, "under the tree. You know what I wished for?" I took her hand in mine. "I wished for you."

Her hand didn't pull away.

"And then I asked for a sign. It even sent me one, or tried to." I shaped her hand into a cup to show her how it had happened. I took the leaf out of my pocket and recreated the slow drift down, followed by the miss.

"I might have gotten it, too," I said. I put her and my cupped hands together, forming a bowl so this time the leaf would fall perfectly inside. "If I'd known how to ask."

She kissed me, quickly, on the lips. "The phone," she said. "You need to call the paper. Now."

I nearly flew down the stairs to the living room, with Shirley behind me. I got Betty, and barked at her to put me through immediately to Gallantine. She didn't pause to say hello or good-bye.

Ever since I was small, I have wanted to say what I was about to say in an actual newspaper situation. "Mister Gallantine," I announced, hearing the excited quiver of my own voice. "Stop the presses!"

"But we wrapped twenty minutes ago."

"No! Noooooo. There's a change to my story. It's critical. You have to stop the presses!"

"We haven't printed here since '88, you should know that. Everything gets sent directly to the plant at Balmoral — it all goes by computer."

"Computer? Mister Gallantine: press the stop button!"

Of course he didn't want to, but I had expected that. So had Shirley: it was her idea to do what I did next. I took her directions in one ear while passing them on to him. The *Weekly Times* would receive my revised story within two minutes of his refusal, we explained, including the details of his curious relationship with Toshi Takahashi.

The silence didn't last long. He was a fast thinker: he knew when he was beat.

"You're on then, sport. I'll call in the stop — or at least the hold.

But you have to send me your story right now."

"Yes, well, my story. Thing is. . . ah, I haven't written it yet."

He let out a hiss of air like a pressure cooker emitting steam. His voice came back in a measured tone, but insistent. "Listen to me. You have exactly. . . eleven minutes and thirty-five seconds to write that article. If don't have it by then? We go with the original and no more questions asked. Ever. Deal?

"Deal!"

"By the way, Earl?"

"Harmy?"

"Anyone ever tell you that you remind them of Stoopovich?"

Lindy walked in the front door as I put down the phone. Shirley and I practically tackled her in tandem. "Help us!" we said at the same time.

"You two are intense," she said, looking at us in turn for a clue on how to react.

"We'll work out the relationship crap later," I said. "Please?"

"He says he's sorry too," Shirley added.

The three of us sat together at the laptop, me typing while they honed the sentences to make everything fit.

> FRALETON – A Letter to Our Readers from Earl Brododsky:
>
> Many of you have been following the story of the Miracle Tree in the *City Herald*. Some of the incidents may have sounded too incredible to be true. There's a reason for that, which can now be revealed.
>
> I wrote those articles.
>
> After everything that has happened here, I'm not sure how to know what's "true" any more, but I will admit this: not everything happened exactly as it was described. A little embellishment turned into a bigger exaggeration which grew into a huge lie.
>
> For that I apologize to every reader of this newspaper.
>
> I apologize as well to anyone who got caught up

in the drama my newspaper reports helped launch.
I am honestly sorry for what I did.
I was wrong.
I accept the blame.
I also apologize to Toshihiko Takahashi, the new
CEO of Filco Corporation. I wrote things about him
and his company that were not only speculative but
also unkind and at least partly untrue.

Mr. Takahashi may have been justifiably upset
with my portrayal of him as a yakuza gang leader
driven to dastardly acts by corporate greed.

Maybe he does have gangster connections— I
didn't invent the fancy pajamas or the severed pinkie.
But maybe he doesn't — some people just like silk,
and accidents do happen.

I wish now I had been more diligent in my
reporting duties instead of leaping to conclusions
which the known facts at the time could not
support.

I also wish Mr. Takahashi had not confined me
against my will and threatened me with bodily harm,
or worse, if I didn't write an article favorable to his
financial interests.

I believe the correct terms for this are kidnapping
and extortion. But I do not intend to press charges
against Mr. Takahashi, at least not for now. I would
rather extend the hand of reconciliation, which he
can shake with as many fingers as he chooses.

The way I figure it, this article makes us even. He
can't kill me now because it would be too obvious. So
that's part of the deal too. I invite him to consider my
well-being as part of a good business strategy.

As for Filco's corporate intentions for Fraleton,
I wrote that it was planning to construct a facility to
accept radioactive waste. I am no longer convinced
this is the case.

It is perhaps more likely that Filco's plans are,
and were all along, to construct a hi-tech and maybe
even "clean" genetic research facility at the site of the

Miracle Tree. This may be a good idea, depending on what you think about genes — but at that spectacular site?

I believe the unique Fraleton setting might be better devoted to the establishment of the world's foremost scientific institution researching the beneficial aspects of negative ions.

If the Filco Corporation, or anyone else with loads of money, is interested in supporting this potentially life-altering work, I can tell them who to call.

If it sounds too wacky for serious scientific work, consider the fact that a remarkable experiment along these lines is being conducted right now at the site of the Miracle Tree.

A powerful underground electromagnetic generator — the same device responsible for some of the mysterious electronic occurrences around the tree, starting with the construction crews that couldn't cut it down and all the stopped watches — has at the same time been emitting negatively-charged ions into the vicinity.

Visitors to the site experience beneficial effects remarkably similar to those felt by people in negative-ion-rich environments in nature.

These may include elation, inner calm, enhanced energy and greater libido. I can personally testify to the veracity of these claims, although, admittedly, I didn't notice any improvement in the area of inner calm. But that might have been just me.

Could negative ions, perhaps together with the power of positive thinking, explain the many "miracles" associated with the tree?

I am not qualified to answer. I will say this: the Miracle Tree has been providing Fraleton residents with a focal point upon which to express their hopes for generations, long before scientific experiments on it were ever considered. If they believe it works, and are living the enriched lives that prove it, why doubt them?

Miracles, I now believe, don't have to be stunning feats of physical wonder. They're not all thunderbolts out of a blue sky. They can be as quiet, and as intimate, as a glance between two strangers about to become lovers.

But let me continue with my apologies.

I would like to express my most heartfelt regret to a talented colleague whose work I made the terrible decision to steal.

Lindy Rondelle is a dynamic reporter who uncovered a scoop on the buyout of Filco by Mr. Takahashi — at least it was a scoop until she made the mistake of trusting me, her friend, with the information.

I took it and turned it into something else to try to save my own skin. For that I am sorry beyond my ability to express in words. I hope she will forgive me.

Lindy has a brilliant future in journalism which should only be enhanced once her valuable work on this assignment becomes more widely known. Without her help, in fact, I could not write the article you are now reading.

I would now like to address my boss, the editor in chief of this newspaper, Harmon Gallantine. It was Mr. Gallantine, when I first began this job, who gave me some simple but powerful advice: write only the truth.

It took some time, Mr. Gallantine, but here it is. Yes, I agree, it is late. I wish now I hadn't gotten off to the start I did, nor made it worse with every new article I wrote.

You would probably enjoy nothing more right now than to fire me, again, publicly. While I can't blame you, I'm afraid that won't be possible — because I quit.

I have decided to stay here in Fraleton. I am planning to open a small but comfortable bed and breakfast in a partnership deal with Grady's

Inn, the finest small-town specialty dining and accommodation resort on the continent — except that my place will have solid bedding.

Finally, after all the apologies, one big thank you.

I would like to express my eternal appreciation to a colleague, a partner and the best reason I will ever know to try to do right in this world, Shirley Alton.

I have not made it easy for Shirley these past few days. I have let her down in ways that make me cringe even to contemplate.

Nevertheless, Shirley has agreed to stay here in Fraleton to focus on community work. Together with prominent activist Sun Deer and local residents, plans are already being made for an aboriginal affairs conference center, an international women's agricultural institute and a variety of youth education programs.

I have no doubt her efforts will succeed to make the community and the world better for us all.

As for whether our efforts to stay together, and in love, will also succeed, I wish I could be as confident.

The truth is, I don't know — but I think I've got a shot.

For a while here I believed I had lost Shirley for good. Then I made a wish under the Miracle Tree. For now, at least, she says she's willing to give me a chance.

And that, I can honestly say, is all the proof I need. I hope it is also enough to solve the mystery many of you have wondered about all along.

Because the answer is yes: wishes made under the Miracle Tree do come true.

DAVID TRACEY is a journalist and environmental designer specializing in community ecology. A certified arborist, he is the Executive Director of Tree City, a non-profit organization in Vancouver "helping people and trees grow together." He is also the author of *Guerrilla Gardening: A Manualfesto*.

The cover shots were taken under a spreading Caucasian wingnut (*Pterocarya fraxinifolia*) on the corner of Comox and Chilco streets in Vancouver. According to a local resident who heard it from an elderly neighbour, in the same month the pics were taken (May 2010), the tree turned 100 years old.